PRAISE F
FROM THE CAMPAl
THEREABOUTS

"I almost died laughing. In fact, I probably should be dead."
—Richard Lewis (Recovering comedian)

"In their debut novel, Bleicher & Newton make it clear they are in the forefront of a new generation of political satirists. They are funny and they are smart. I recommend that you read their new book as soon as possible."
—Corey Brettschneider, PhD, author of *The Oath and the Office: A Guide to the Constitution for Future Presidents*

"Part satire, part romp, and wholly enjoyable. From the Campaign Trail or Thereabouts will take you into the most absurd, darkest corners of our American psyche. Bleicher and Newton are talents to watch."
—Caren Lissner, author of *Carrie Pilby*

"Reading this book made me feel exactly how Sir Alexander Fleming must've felt when he discovered penicillin: 'OMG, I've accidentally found the cure to every ailment I have. My marriage, my desire to drive across country, the lack of laughter in this library, Republicans, Russians, this gross staph infection. I think it's a staph infection. Is it? Is it cancer? Hilarious!' Read it now, and you can feel all that, too."
—Jeff Kreisler, author of the bestselling satire, *Get Rich Cheating*, winner of the Bill Hicks Spirit Award for Thought Provoking Comedy, Exec. Producer of *The Final Edition Radio Hour*, probably a cancer victim.

FROM THE CAMPAIGN TRAIL
OR THEREABOUTS

FROM THE CAMPAIGN TRAIL
OR THEREABOUTS
A NOVEL

MICHAEL BLEICHER
& ANDY NEWTON

HUMORIST BOOKS

New York

First Printing: 2019

ISBN 978-0-359-80726-0

Humorist Books is an imprint of *Weekly Humorist* owned and operated by Humorist Media LLC.

Weekly Humorist is a weekly humor publication, subscribe online at weeklyhumorist.com

110 Wall Street New York, NY 10005

weeklyhumorist.com - humoristbooks.com - humoristmedia.com

For Art Garfunkel, with gratitude for the high harmonies.

1
"You Mean the American Election?"
January 5, 2016

"Is this quail?" Harold asked in a whisper, leaning in close to examine the contents of the chafing dish in front of him.

Pattie glanced over at the tray. "Cornish game hen." She spooned some fingerling potatoes onto her plate.

"I thought they were hiring waiter service for the evening. They could have at least served quail." Harold prodded at his dish. "Or lobster tail."

Pattie looked around the room as she waited for Harold to dress his salad. "The Apfelbaums went all out for Natalie's fortieth."

"*Forty*," Harold groaned. Thin and neither tall nor short, he had crow's feet forming around his eyes, slightly thinning blond hair, and an easy indifference to his surroundings. "Only three more years. I always figured I'd own a brownstone by the time I was forty."

"That was my hope, too." Pattie fidgeted impatiently. "Come on Harold, you're not frosting a cake. Just ladle it on and go."

"Pattie, I think this is *Paul Newman* dressing!" Harold hissed contemptuously. He twirled the dressing with the ladle. "*We* could buy this!" Pattie gently took the handle out of his hands and dripped a judicious amount of vinaigrette onto her field greens. The pair took their seats around an oblong mahogany table lined with a finely-woven red cloth. Slightly worn pewter candlesticks with the letters "MA" embossed at the base sat on either side of a small glass bowl filled with tangerines and pine cones.

"Natalie, I love these candlesticks," Pattie said cheerily, leaning down the table. Apple-cheeked with wavy black hair, she had a wry smile and probing, dark brown eyes.

"Oh, thank you!" Natalie, who was dressed in a tight-fitting ensemble of black pants, blouse, and sweater, replied. "Those are my grandmother's. She brought them with her out of Germany in 1933."

"Pattie, your grandmother didn't happen to bring in anything like that, did she?" Harold asked through a mouthful of game hen. "We could have it appraised."

"Ignore him," Pattie said, attempting a laugh.

"Oh, speaking of, did anyone happen to read that article in *The New Yorker* last week on antique forgeries?" a slim man with an Aquiline nose and a crop of carefully unkempt hair asked, looking up from a wine label he was examining.

"No, I didn't, but *Pattie*! You must be so proud!" Natalie exclaimed from the head of the table.

Pattie blushed. "I didn't even know I was up for—"

"Oh, don't be modest, Pattie," Harold said, washing down his food with a sip of wine. "For crying out loud, you just won a Peabody!"

"Pulitzer." Pattie rolled her eyes and attempted a look of comic exasperation.

"Right, right, a Pulitzer." Harold dabbed his mouth with his napkin. "They are such engaging little blurbs she writes, the television summaries." He prodded the hen. Natalie coughed uncomfortably.

"Well, it was an exploration of Julia Louis-Dreyfus, the cult of celebrity, and second acts in American life, but yes, I certainly had no idea it would be this big."

"And how's your work going, Harold?" the slim man asked. "Are you still covering the metro desk?"

"Harold's covering the entire tri-state area now," Pattie interjected before Harold could swallow his mouthful of bread. "If you have a tip about a sewage crisis in New Jersey, you can tell him directly, these days."

"Actually, Harold, if you wouldn't mind, I'd love to pick your brain about that," said a short, rotund older woman sitting across the table. She wore a purple pantsuit and a hat topped with a large arrangement of flowers. A small pair of square, transition-lens glasses were perched halfway down her nose. "When I first ran for the New York State Assembly, I championed a platform to revamp the sewer systems of our towns upstate," she added proudly. "'Drain the Septic Tanks!' was our slogan," she chuckled.

"Oh, sure, perhaps later this week?" Harold asked brightly, sensing the spotlight. "I'm off the clock now."

"That was the McCornish Bill, right?" Pattie asked.

The woman's face dropped. "Well, that was a piece of very compromised legislation that was ultimately adopted after popular pressure forced them to do *some*thing."

"This hen is dry," Harold whispered to his wife. "Really, how much are lobster tails for eight? If *I* were heir to a toothpaste fortune—" Pattie nudged him under the table.

"While we're eating, can we perhaps change the subject from such matters as sewage or New Jersey?" an implausibly young-looking man with impassive hazel eyes, stubble, and a prematurely bald head interjected. "I don't know if any of you saw the *36 Hours* on the Cyclades. Anthony, did you?" he asked, nodding his head in the direction of the slim man. "You and Natalie were there two years ago, right? I couldn't believe they omitted Paros in favor of Mykonos. It's like, am I reading *Frommer's*?" The table laughed.

"Oh, Greece," Natalie said wistfully, looking over at her husband. "Can we go back?"

"When would you like to go?" Anthony asked.

"Yesterday," Natalie replied with a smile. "The Elounda Beach Hotel was heaven on Earth."

"Did they go back to the drachma?" Harold interjected. "I have to imagine, since the economic crisis there, it must be a tourist's paradise."

"Still on the Euro, actually," Anthony replied without making eye-contact.

"If you go back, you *need* to charter a craft," the rotund woman declared. "After my city council run, I spent three months sailing the wine-dark seas. It was such a healing voyage."

"Do you think they'd still take my drachmas if I brought them to one of those exchange kiosks at the airport?" Harold asked, leaning over the table to address Anthony. "I still have about fifty dollars worth saved from when my parents took me the summer after college, is the thing." Anthony looked at him blankly. Natalie pretended to laugh, then stopped quickly, realizing that no joke had been made. Harold coughed, his face reddening slightly. "That was really quite the trip," he stammered. "Of course, I guess we all remember our first time abroad. The sights, the smells. Everything was so cheap there, I sure remember that." He gave a forced laugh. "Not that it mattered," he added quickly.

Natalie turned to Pattie. "Pattie, when was the last time you were there?"

"Oh, yeah. Let me think," Pattie gazed thoughtfully across the table into a watercolor portrait of an African woman wearing a tribal headdress. "I didn't get that far on the Switzerland trip, or the...jeez," she smiled. "I guess I haven't been since I was in eighth grade. That was the first time I'd been anywhere further than Paris."

"Natalie, this is great," Harold interrupted. "Is this quail?"

"I went with my best friend—Natalie, you'll love this. Your lab partner from seventh grade chemistry, Shirley Burden, and her step-father, Mr. Rose—well, we call him Charlie now."

"Shirley!" Natalie exclaimed. "I forgot how close you two were in middle school. What was that like?"

Pattie shrugged. "It was right after the marriage, so they let each of them bring along a friend so it wouldn't be so awkward for Amanda to be there with him *and* the kids."

"Well, dear, this can be the second time someone's paid your way to Athens," Harold interrupted again. He turned to the rest of the table. "We're headed to Greece this summer, all on my editor's dime," he added.

"Uh-huh?" Anthony asked disinterestedly.

"A little-known trick of the newspaper trade," Harold said proudly, taking a tangerine out of the centerpiece bowl. "I just have to get myself assigned to cover something there, like the debt crisis, or afternoon naps, and there's two weeks in Greece, bought and paid for. And of course, as long as I'm there, who's going to notice an extra order of *moussaka* on the expense reports back in New York?" He winked at Pattie.

"Well, we didn't discuss paying for it that way," Pattie laughed tensely. "It's for our tenth anniversary. We're still in the planning stages, but I always think that's half of the fun."

"Of course," Anthony agreed. "You really should wait until the early fall to go. You've read *The Colossus of Maroussi*, I presume? Miller describes September in Greece with such poetic accuracy. You should read it now, if you haven't already. You'll be transported." Pattie nodded thoughtfully, smiling. She glanced over at Harold, who had placed the tangerine rind next to his plate and was dipping a corner of his napkin into his water glass.

"Harold, have you ever thought about covering trials?" Natalie asked. "I think that would be fascinating. Peering inside the justice system. Actually, do you know who wrote that *Times* piece on the first Freddie Gray trial, the one that starts tomorrow."

"Right," Harold said, confused. "Freddie Gray."

"Oh!" the rotund woman interrupted. "Wasn't that *horrible*? That poor boy. His whole future ahead of him. I saw his picture in the newspaper. He looked like such a fine, thoughtful young man."

"Yes, very thoughtful," Harold agreed quickly, grabbing on to this nugget of information.

"Well, he had a series of drug charges and minor crimes," Anthony corrected. "But of course, you have to account for the environment in which he grew up..."

"Right," Natalie agreed. "If you adjust for how, if he had grown up in a normal environment, there would be no criminal record and no cloud over him."

"That's what I've *always* said. When I ran for the Queens Library Volunteer Coordinator position last fall, I pressed hard for more public programs. We need to get these children off the streets and back in schools!"

"Of course, you can understand the rioting," the bald man explained, reinserting himself into the conversation. "Some protest, even unrest, is healthy. Much like how the body sweats when it's suffering from a fever, it's a way of cleansing, of breaking that societal infection." He gently reached for the bottle of wine.

"I'm right there with you," Anthony agreed. "But did they need to start looting? I mean, what political point are they making by smashing a window and running off with a plasma television?"

"And all the destruction," Pattie added, disapprovingly. "They burned that CVS. I think it only hurts their cause when people see that violence." Harold nodded vigorously.

"And that waste," the bald man concurred. "It hurts *them* more than anyone else to set a CVS on fire. It hurts their protest, it hurts indigent people in their communities that shop at CVS, and it hurts the optics."

"Right," Natalie exclaimed. "I'm all for protesting police violence, but, you know, there's a correct time and place for it. When they block traffic and shut down a city, don't they sort of *become* the aggressors?"

"There's a difference between activism and anger," Anthony declared. "You want to have your people being the ones getting attacked. You don't want them to be the ones looting and burning. You know who understood that, was Dr. Martin Luther King, Jr. He understood optics." There was a chorus of "mms."

"Of course, it is good, like you said, to see the community sticking up for itself," Natalie began.

"Yes," Pattie affirmed. "It's really beautiful." There was a pause as the table reflected.

"They have fantastic seafood in Baltimore, I recall," Harold added. "Crab. Shrimp. Probably even lobster." His right thigh began to vibrate. Harold reached into his pocket, retrieving his phone and glancing at the screen. "Jeez, I'm off the clock!" he moaned. "My editor," he explained to the table.

"You can take it in the study, if you'd like," Anthony offered.

"Oh, terrific. Probably just calling to see if I want to upgrade to business class for my flight to Athens." Harold reached for a second tangerine as he stood up. Pattie slapped his hand away.

"They're decorative, Harold," she hissed.

He shrugged and put the phone to his ear as he exited the dining room. "Hello, sir? No, no, I'm working from home tonight. Sir, I promise you, that man *is* a magician. I'm just waiting for a source to—oh? Oh, a new assignment?" Harold walked down a short, dark hallway lined with black-and-white photographs, into a wood-paneled room filled with bookcases. Several imposing masks, evidently African in origin, hung high on the walls. His heart swelled with envious appreciation.

"Something different this time, sir? Not another D-Train masturbator, I hope. No, just, the last time you said that—oh? Covering the election? Well, if I catch the LIRR, I can probably be in the—how's that, sir? You mean the American election?" Harold bumped into a bookcase jutting into the center of the room, knocking to the floor a small, phallic folk-art statuette. "No, sir, that was just the power adapter for my laptop. It fell to the floor, sir. Yes, hard at work, right. I'll sleep when the news does." Harold picked up the statuette and, noticing a fresh gash in the wood, gingerly placed it back on the shelf, rotating it around carefully.

"Sir? I thought that Joshua Martin was covering the Republican primaries. Didn't you move him from his post in Moscow just for that purpose?" Harold listened intently. "*Really*? On tape? And his stories are different now? The last one was all about what a great dancer Putin is? What a shame, sir. And right after he landed the American election, too. No, no, absolutely. My gain, sir, one hundred percent." Harold picked up a thick ballpoint pen off of the desk in the center of the room and examined it under the overhead lights for a moment before slipping it into his pants pocket. No one would notice a missing pen here, he concluded.

"You know, sir, it occurs to me that Martin's termination probably affects your coverage of Europe in general. For example, who's covering Greece now? Well, Europe is pretty small, sir. I assume Russia and Greece are practically the same beat. Anyway, Greece is in the midst of a massive debt crisis at the moment. I hear they may even go back on the drachma. Perhaps I could cover both the American election and the debt crisis. I'm sure there would be some coverage of our election on Greek TV. *Sky News*, sir. It's on all over Europe. I'm sure they would be talking about the election on a regular basis. I could plan to be in the room, or in the hotel bar, maybe, if there's a TV in the hotel bar, and sort of take notes when the election comes up on *Sky News*, and just send that right along to you." Harold examined a large, antique stapler sitting atop two volumes of Winston Churchill's *A History of the English Speaking Peoples* and made a mental note to obtain some rare books.

Pattie poked her head into the study. "Everything okay?" she whispered. "Natalie's about to serve the tiramisu."

Harold held his hand over the phone. "Ask her to wrap up my hen!" he mouthed. "I didn't finish it."

Pattie rolled her eyes and slipped back out of the room.

"Pattie! Throw a couple rolls in there, too!" Harold called after her. He took his hand off the phone. "Sorry, could you repeat that, sir? No, no, I just got distracted by an email. A confidential source just emailed me. Right, multitasking, like always. My first stop? Des Moines? Uh huh." Harold twirled the rotary dial of a large black telephone mounted to the side of a bookcase. "Sir? It occurs to me that Des Moines is not especially close to Greece. Well, I hear that the Elounda Beach Resort has satellite TV in each room. They probably get *Sky News* there. Ah. So that's a definite 'no' on the *Sky News* angle. Got it. No, Iowa sounds lovely, too. No, sure, if there's going to be a primary there. Right, sir."

Pattie returned with a small plate of tiramisu. "Natalie insisted that you not miss out," she said quietly.

Harold placed the plate on the *History of the English-Speaking Peoples*. "I heard something about cappuccino?" he whispered. "Yes, sir," he stammered, turning his attention back to his call. "So I assume I'll follow the big players on the trail. Hillary. Mitt. Ted who? Ted Cruz. So the Democrats would have the first female nominee or the first Hispanic nominee. A Republican? Oh, right—*that* Ted Cruz. No, of course I'd heard of him, sir," Harold said quickly. "Yeah, so those two. How's that? Right, and sixteen other candidates. No, of course I know that, sir. Do you think I don't read our paper? Every Sunday, like clockwork. Uh-huh, daily, sure."

"The election?" Pattie mouthed.

"Yes, sir, the chance of a lifetime. So, I'll be covering Ted and the sixteen other Republicans. And the Democrats are running just Hillary this year? Well, sir, I've been knee-deep in my beat, if you will. No, of course I know who Sanders is. Sir? Before you jump off, I was wondering if we could just play a quick game. No, a political one. I was thinking, maybe you could just rattle off the names of all of the candidates, and then I can see if you named them all. Hello? Hello?" Harold looked at his phone, pocketed it, and picked up the plate of tiramisu.

"What's this about the election?" Pattie asked.

"Bad news, Pattie," Harold said woefully through a mouthful of mascarpone. "It seems that our grand plans for Greece are out."

"What? Why?"

"Well, apparently, there's a video of some Russian honeypot pooping on the chest of one of our reporters, which has created some objectivity problems, and now I have to cover the presidential election in his stead."

"What? Harold!" Pattie exclaimed. "That's incredible!" She looked at him with fresh admiration. "See, I told you, if you just started checking your email *once* over the weekend."

"Well, yeah." Harold pursed his lips. "But it puts the kibosh on our Greece plans, since I'll be more or less on the road from now until November."

Pattie paused, considering before she spoke. "That's probably just as well for us, right?"

"Just as well?"

"Come on," Pattie smirked. "Two weeks of time alone together to reconnect? Talk about treating the symptom, not the cause. What do we even pay Dr. Rothstein for?"

"Pattie," Harold said sternly. "We had this conversation when you threw away your sock puppet."

"Harold, you can't even get through a single session without using Gary the Goat as a buffer. How were we ever going to survive two weeks alone together in a foreign country?"

"That's why this will be so much better than Greece! There won't be so much pressure, relying on each other to figure out what signs are for the bathroom. Just you, me, and the great American wilderness. Like Lewis and Clark but in a rental convertible."

"How's that, then?"

"We can expense the convertible."

"No, the part about about me."

"Well, you'll come with me."

Pattie laughed. "What about my job? The charity boards I'm on? Film Forum is about to have a retrospective on Fellini!"

"Pattie, this is what Dr. Rothstein was getting at when he gave us the dream journals and the olives. You need to feed *all* of you."

"Harold, I can't babysit you while you take a tour of America's lesser-known pig farms. This isn't like that assignment your editor sent you on out in Montauk. This is the election. I just can't leave for that long."

Harold sighed impatiently. "But that's the same excuse you gave when I wanted to go to Niagara Falls last month. You can write your little blurbs *any*where. At some point, it's now or never." Harold gave the stately desk a determined tap. "A great American road trip could be just the B-12 shot our marriage needs. New Orleans, Nashville, Chicago, San Francisco—and what about this? San Diego?"

Pattie perked up. "San Diego?"

"Oh, Pattie, you'd *love* San Diego. It's everything Greece is and more. It's warm. It's sunny. Waiters have to wash their hands before leaving the restroom."

Pattie thought. "I *have* always wanted to see San Diego."

"Oh, I hear it's lovely. I hear there are seals that come right up onto the beach. Seals! And we won't have to pay for any of it."

"Sure," Pattie said. "I've heard that before. Who ended up having to drive back to the South Huntington Pottery Barn with a personal check?"

"No, this is different. I have to go *anyway*. Who's going to know if you're staying in my hotel room? Who's going to notice a few extra entrees when I submit my meal receipts? Do you have any idea how many receipts that paper gets in one day? Nobody's going to notice an extra Cobb salad. That's practically the motto of the journalism industry, Pattie."

"I don't know. When do we leave for San Diego?"

"Well, first we have to stop at Des Moines, but I assume we can find our way to San Diego pretty early on."

"Isn't California's primary in June?"

"Is it? See, this is why I need you with me." He placed his hands on Pattie's shoulders. "Anyway, once I get on the road, I'll have plenty of latitude to make my own decisions. You don't work your way up through the sewage industry without getting a little discretion to follow a story wherever it leads, honey."

Pattie hesitated. "I don't know."

"Pattie, remember when you shared the entry in your dream journal about the dairy farm? Remember the promise?"

"Okay, okay," Pattie sighed, gently removing Harold's hands from her shoulders. "I bet San Diego would be nice in the spring."

"You'll be sunning yourself and sipping margaritas before you can even say 'trial separation.'"

*   *   *

"I can't read about him without remembering the Weismans' ALS fundraiser a few years ago," Harold smirked, looking over Pattie's shoulder at a *Newsweek* article as they settled into their plush, leather business class seats and waited for the ground crew to finish loading the plane. Expressionless passengers filed past their row, hauling oversized roller suitcases behind them, which slammed into Harold's armrest one after the other.

"Ugh," Pattie groaned. "The longer he leads in the polls, the more worried I get."

"Are you kidding? Someone like Trump won't last long. Remember at the fundraiser? He tried to motorboat the mother-daughter catering team, and then he stood up to give a toast to AIDS. The other candidates will eat him alive."

"I just think he's touched a nerve with all those poor white voters. The divisiveness is calculated. Remember his thing about the Mexican rapists?"

"He's in love with me," a woman sitting behind them announced into her phone. She anxiously ran her free hand across her tight-fitting two-piece baby-blue velour couture tracksuit. "Like, madly in love. He has a beautiful home. He treated me the way Todd treats you."

Pattie sighed. "They say Trump might win the Iowa caucus."

"Don't be ridiculous. Have a little more faith in the American electorate than that. These primaries always attract one or two yahoos and attention-grabbers, but they fizzle out when the voting starts." Harold clicked open a can of Diet Sprite. "I saw the same thing in the runoff for Queens County Waste Commissioner. Trust me."

"I said, Brad adores me the way Todd adores you. No, it's identical. He took me ring shopping already. He showed me the one he wants to get. It's only been a month. I'm freaking out," the woman behind them went on breathlessly.

Harold reached into the satchel placed between his feet, pulled out the latest issue of *The New Yorker*, and began to flip through its pages. "Oh lord, did you see he's still talking about that ridiculous border wall? Disgusting."

"It really is," Pattie concurred.

"He wants me to meet his mother and his sister," the woman continued loudly. "I'm obsessed with him. We were staying at the Doubletree overlooking freaking *Times Square*."

Harold looked over his shoulder. "How long is this going to go on?" he whispered to Pattie.

"Depends on if Brad ordered room service," Pattie replied.

"I'm freaking out. He wants me to move to New York. I met his son. His son adores me. His son adores me the way your daughter adores you. He's five. But his son's a cancer."

"Excuse me, miss?" Harold leaned over his seatback. "This really sounds like a coach problem."

"Hold on," the woman said into the phone. "Some guy is talking to me." She covered the receiver. "What?" she asked Harold.

"You know, a lot of work gets done by people sitting up in this part of the plane," Harold explained impatiently. "Hence the term 'business class.'"

The woman stared at Harold for several moments, surveying him with a mixture of confusion and disdain, before turning back to her phone. "I dunno, this bald guy was trying to talk to me. He's lucky Brad wasn't here. I don't know what to do. I've never left San Francisco. Oh.

No, okay, if you're at the restaurant. Yeah. I'll call you when I'm at my layover in Des Moines, okay? Will you pick up when I call? Okay. Bye, babe."

"Thank goodness that's over with," Harold muttered to Pattie.

"Hi, Trish?" the woman said into her phone. "Oh my God. I just spent two days with Brad in New York. I'm freaking out. He got us a room at the Doubletree overlooking freaking *Times Square*. He's in love with me."

Pattie rolled her eyes. "It gets worse and worse. Look at what he said about his Muslim ban last week." She pointed to a block of text on the glossy magazine page.

Harold tsked. "Most Americans won't support that kind of talk, Pattie. You know who supports someone like Trump? Fat people who shop at Walmart and 'don't know' about college and eat macaroni and cheese out of a box. For dinner. No bread crumbs. No Asiago. They think it's an acceptable way to live. To come home and pour cheese dust out of a box into a pot of macaroni and eat it. They do that until they die. People like us don't think that way, and you can't win an election without winning the metropolitan areas," Harold declared.

Pattie smiled. "Remember you trying to hide the box mix your mom used to make the mashed potatoes our first Thanksgiving?"

"With the parsley she puts on it, it's practically her own recipe." Harold shifted in his seat. "But a ban on Muslims? What is it, 1922?"

"Right!" Pattie agreed. "Take that nice Pakistani couple we sublet our apartment to, for example. You couldn't find a more pleasant pair."

"Definitely," Harold agreed. "I'm so glad we found them. People like us have a duty to reach out to people like them." Pattie nodded. "I wish there were a website like AirBnB, but it matches you up with people of color," Harold continued. He took a long sip of Diet Sprite and was quiet. "You don't think they'll use our candles in their rituals, though, do you?" He attempted to read Pattie's face. "It's just, it'd be a shame if they burned down all the wax, is all."

"Their what?"

"During the holy feasts," Harold whispered. "How many candles do you think those burn up?"

"I think it'll be fine." Pattie rolled her eyes.

Harold nodded, unconvinced. "Oh, huh—did you know Anthony Weiner is married to Hillary's Chief of Staff? Huma Abedin. Small world." Harold pointed to a color picture of a handsome couple exiting a limousine.

"Everyone knows that." Pattie examined a three-line review of *House of Cards* on *Newsweek*'s "Culture" page.

"Honey, I'm out on a garbage barge in New Jersey. I don't have time to find out about this little thing and that little thing."

"And yet you read *Town & Country* cover-to-cover every month," Pattie mumbled.

"Affluence meets influence, Pattie." Harold looked more closely at a spread on the following page, examining a bright photo of Huma Abedin in a tight-fitting white blouse and black pencil skirt conferring with Hillary Clinton. "Quite an attractive woman, too. Makes you wonder why he would be sneaking around on her."

"Got a crush on her?" Pattie snorted.

"Of course not! You just wonder how someone like that would be feeling. Out in the public eye. Rubbing elbows with movers and shakers. Blazing trails. But she's human, too. Delicate, vulnerable, just like the rest of us," Harold mused. "Like all great women, she's probably a Russian nesting doll of paradoxes. Look at that face. So strong, and yet so sensitive. Wow." He turned the page. "Obviously, the man has some issues."

"Well, when we catch up with the Hillary campaign, I'll just bow out of the anniversary trip, and you can go be her shoulder to cry on."

"Pattie, you seem startlingly uninterested in probing the inner workings of the human psyche."

Pattie gazed out the airplane window at a line of orange-vested workers drearily lugging suitcases onto a conveyor belt that fed into the aircraft's underbelly. "I think I already get a lifetime's worth."

2
"Joan Rivers Is Dead, Folks"
January 9, 2016

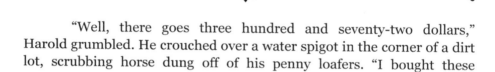

"Well, there goes three hundred and seventy-two dollars," Harold grumbled. He crouched over a water spigot in the corner of a dirt lot, scrubbing horse dung off of his penny loafers. "I bought these specifically to cover the election."

"And yet you're always stealing my pens." Pattie took a sip from a stainless steel thermos full of coffee.

Harold stood up straight and patted imaginary dirt off his pants. "Alright. Let's go find the turnip truck and talk to some of the Iowans who fell off it." Harold and Pattie set off through the entrance to the state fair. The sky hung gray above them, and chill winds whipped through their slight frames as they walked toward a large expanse of brown grass lined by rows of booths festooned with colorful paper ribbon and wooden signs featuring handmade depictions of corn and tractors. Crowds of people pushed, weaved, and meandered, while the din of competing loudspeaker systems and the smell of various types of fried food filled the air. Prodigious metal tubs, full of crackling potatoes and lumps of raw dough, sputtered molten grease at hungry passersby.

"So, we're looking for John Kasey," Harold said, fishing out a crumpled receipt from his pocket and reading a hand-scrawled note on the back.

"Kasich," Pattie corrected.

"Um, that's not what it says here, honey." Harold squinted and surveyed the crowds.

Pattie rubbed her arms together rapidly. "God, I'm cold." She unscrewed her thermos again and took a sip. "I don't know how these people do it."

"What else are they going to do here? Pray?" Harold stopped momentarily to inspect a booth where a line of older men in trucker hats were throwing darts at a mural depicting two men admiring a wedding cake, a woman of indeterminate ethnic origin wearing a little black dress, and men in white lab coats holding a telescope. "Although I must say, I'm really impressed by the Des Moines Des Luxe hotel. Four stars or not, when I heard the name, I thought it'd be a real armpit, but our room *is* warm, upscale, and airy, just like the guidebook promised," he gushed.

"Good thinking, asking for an upgrade at the front desk."

"Life's far too short to stay in a 'courtyard view' room." Harold burbled excitedly.

Pattie ignored Harold and opened the map of the state fair she had picked up at the entry gate. "It looks like the Seventh-Day Adventist Corn Maze is down this main road and to the left. That's probably where all the candidates are," she said. "We should head there."

"Sounds like a plan to me. If we find John Coccyx soon, maybe we can get back to the Des Moines Des Luxe before the sauna closes. What a beautiful hotel."

"Don't you think you should put in a full day here?"

"It was the pun in the name that made me wary at first. Stay away from puns, Pattie. That's my advice to you. If I die before you, just keep your distance from businesses with puns in their names." Pattie checked the map, not listening to her husband. "I'll be looking down from above," Harold continued, "making sure you don't wander into any restaurants called Garden of Eatin'."

"Just knowing you won't be too preoccupied with finding the five-star resorts in Heaven means so much to me," Pattie said absently, craning her neck to try to spot the entrance to the corn maze on the other side of a cotton candy stand. "It should just be around there."

"Honey, is that Mitt?" Harold gasped, pointing to a tall, salt-and-pepper-haired man with a sad smile and glasses slipping down the end of his nose, who was walking toward the couple accompanied by a phalanx of aides. "Mitt would never miss out on a chance to pander. Mitt! Mitt!"

"Sorry!" the man said as he passed by. One of his aides handed Pattie a tiny toy turtle that read "Jeb Bush, Joyful Tortoise" on the underbelly.

"That poor man," Pattie sighed.

"Honey, we're never going to find John Kennedy if we stick together here. We should each go look for him separately. Whoever finds him first calls the other one, and we meet back here."

*   *   *

Pattie wandered down the fair's main thoroughfare, pushing her way through crowds of people lined up for food stands and carnival games, looking for the entrance to the corn maze. She shivered and turned up her jacket collar. Further down the path, she saw a large white tent and a raised platform. She could vaguely hear an amplified voice bellowing through the loudspeakers lining the stage, which became more distinct as she approached the crowd.

"Ladies and gentlemen!" the nasal-sounding voice bellowed. "It's *common knowledge* in Chicago's gay community that Obama actively visited the Chicago bathhouses when he was an Illinois state senator! He was a *regular*! That's right, a regular! That's where he met Rahm Emmanuel! That's where he made the backroom deals that got him the presidency! And our *Muslim*-in-Chief thought he could keep it a secret! Now does that sound like the kind of person fit to run the country?"

"NO!" shouted the crowd in response.

"Does that sound like the sort of person we want running *America*, our great Christian nation?"

"NO!" the crowd shouted again.

Pattie squinted to see the man on stage to whom the voice belonged. He was a heavyset figure, wearing a white suit jacket he could never hope to button closed. Underneath, American flag suspenders strained to keep his pants in position. His cheeks were flushed red, and they jiggled as he shook his head with emphasis. As the crowd offered their eager rejoinders, the man would remove his wire-frame glasses and brandish them to applause.

"What kind of communities was he organizing, folks? I have a few ideas. But you know who would know? The men he had murdered. That's right! The gay blacks in Reverend Wright's church. Larry Bland and Nate Spencer. He and Rahm Emmanuel had 'em gunned down so that no one who knew the truth could speak up while he took the White House. Now, does that sound like someone we want running *our* country?"

"NO!"

"*Does* it?"

"NO!" the crowd roared again.

"Can you believe that fucking traitor?" a goateed man asked Pattie. He wore a black bandana emblazoned with what, on closer inspection, appeared to be the Ten Commandments circumscribed by a border of bullet holes.

"I just got here," Pattie said.

"Now folks, take a look at Michelle Obama. See how strong that jaw is? See how big those arms are? Folks, I don't have to spell this out for you. Michelle Obama is a man. She had a sex change. Now, who do you think knew about this? Joan Rivers, folks. And what happened to Joan Rivers? Now, I don't have to tell you that. Joan Rivers is dead, folks. Same as Larry Bland. Same as Nate Spencer."

"That son of a bitch has got some nerve on him," the goateed man continued. "I'll tell you something, it's a miracle no one's shot the Liar-in-Chief right in the fuckin' head."

"Hmm," Pattie replied.

"I think it's 'bout time we took our country *back*?" the man on stage shouted. "Now what do you say to that?"

"YEAH!!" the crowd cheered.

"Is this where John Kasich is going to speak?" Pattie asked a woman to her right. She was wearing a Confederate flag infinity scarf and a motorcycle jacket with a design of Jesus Christ riding a bald eagle.

"I hope not! That guy is a *cuck*."

"Uh huh," Pattie said.

"He's gonna lose so bad," the woman sneered. "Like a dog."

"Thanks," Pattie said, concluding that John Kasich wouldn't be appearing at this particular stage. She made her way toward the edge of the crowd, worming through people who seemed particularly disinclined to notice her or to move.

"Not to mention, I have it on the highest authority that Obama has a yeast infection!" the speaker bellowed as Pattie swiftly made her way out of earshot.

She spotted Harold back up the thoroughfare, not far from where they had initially parted ways. He was arguing with a bearded man who was clutching a goldfish in a clear plastic bag. Pattie walked over to meet her husband. "Harold, what's going on?"

Harold turned to Pattie. "I was just explaining to this gentleman that *that* goldfish rightfully belongs to me." He turned back to the man with the fish. "My balloon clearly burst *before* yours did. The carney stuck me at the end of the line where he couldn't see me clearly, even though I *insisted* on a center squirt gun."

The man with the goldfish drew a revolver from his jacket pocket.

"Right, okay, well, two sides to everything," Harold stammered, grabbing Pattie's arm and quickly walking away. "Enjoy the fish!" he called out over his shoulder.

"Harold, did you find Kasich?"

"Pattie, who do you take me for?" Harold replied. "Of course I found John Lasik. We had a very thoughtful discussion about the great pyramids of Egypt. Did you know they were used to store grain?"

"I'm not sure that's correct."

"Sure it is! Pattie, the man is a doctor."

Pattie paused. "Describe the person you spoke with?"

"Oh, you know what he looks like. African-American fellow. Loves to speak with his hands. Sounds like he's addicted to horse tranquilizers. Very pleasant."

"Honey, that was Dr. Ben Carson."

Harold thought for a moment. "The TV therapist? I don't think so."

Pattie sighed. "Do you still have that list I made you?"

"I thought we both left those with Dr. Rothstein."

"No," she said testily. "The list of the presidential candidates."

"Oh, right! I transcribed it," Harold said proudly, fishing a crumpled receipt out of his right jacket pocket.

Pattie rubbed her eyes. "Kasich has a slightly grizzled face. Blue eyes. A full head of hair. Oh, and he's white."

"Okay," Harold furrowed his brows and squinted, trying to imagine a man who fit Pattie's description. "I think I can find him now. Did you try that tent over there?"

"Yeah," Pattie said distantly. "Some people are really troubled."

"Okay." Harold consulted a map of the fairgrounds. "I'll check by the Pentecostal Pig Raising Competition, I guess." He looked up. "Christ, do you think they're trying to resurrect pigs, Pattie?"

"I think they mean pig raising like, 'bringing up the pigs'," Pattie explained. "To maturity."

"Ah," Harold said. "Like children. Well, I suspect they do a number on the pigs, too."

"I'm going to find a bite to eat. Preferably something not encased in hardened lard."

"They have cotton candy!" Harold said. "I'll meet you back here in twenty minutes. Gotta put on my reporter hat."

Pattie made her way down a side path that smelled particularly strongly of saturated fat. She passed a young girl who had spilled her popcorn. The girl was near tears. "Mackenzie Grace!" a compact, stout woman with short hair yelled. "We take you all the way to the state fair and you drop your popcorn? C'mere!" The girl remained in place. Her mother stepped toward her and whacked her daughter's behind three times. "Show you to drop your food, miss," she huffed.

Pattie spotted a food stand offering chicken cutlet sandwiches. Deciding it was her best option because the bun, at least, would not be fried, Pattie lined up.

"Oh, man, do you think he's showed up yet?" a young man in line ahead of Pattie excitedly asked his friend.

"Nah, dude, when he shows up, you'll know it. You'll hear the helicopter," replied the friend.

"Yeah, yeah," agreed the first man. He appeared to be in his early twenties. He wore an "American Militia" sweatshirt and had the letters T-O-R-N tattooed on the fingers of his left hand. Acne scars riddled his face. "I heard when he was here in August, he gave people rides in his chopper."

"Yeah, man, my cousin Brittany Ann went up in it."

"*Bro*," the man gushed.

"Dude, when she got out of the helicopter with him, she was crying."

"He must have been so inspiring."

"Seriously." The youth paused. "She went to the doctor a lot that next week."

The men ordered and stood aside to wait for their sandwiches. "Were you two talking about Mr. Trump?" asked the man working the deep frier. He was stocky with translucent blue eyes. He wore an *ushanka* made out of dark fur to protect his shaved head from the cold and spoke with a hint of an eastern European accent.

"Yeah, bro," the first young man replied. "You a Trump fan, too?"

"Very much so," the cook said without emotion.

"MAGA all the way, dude," the other young man chimed in.

"MAGA," the cook sounded out the term slowly. "Yes. Here is your food. Chicken sandwich with a side of dressed herring."

"The fuck?" the first man asked.

"This is your state fair American cuisine," the cook said.

The two men paid and accepted their food but wandered off confused. "He'll be deported once Trump wins anyway," the second young man reminded his friend.

Pattie quickly paid for and received her sandwich. She ate it next to a nearby trash can, figuring she could expedite the process. She heard someone yelling, "Pattie! Pattie!" and saw Harold running toward her, wincing as he sashayed to avoid a man in a wheelchair who was muttering about the Chinese.

"Did you find Kasich?" Pattie asked.

"No, I was trying to lose the goldfish guy. I saw him in line at the baseball toss," Harold panted. "I think I need new shoes."

"Do you want the rest of this?" Pattie offered the remaining half of her soggy chicken sandwich.

"Blech," Harold winced. "I'll have the dressed herring, though."

"So, no luck with Kasich, then?" Pattie asked again.

"No, no luck. The closest I came to a Washington insider, I'm afraid, is some pathetic, overworked intern. Marco something-or-other. The lone Hispanic hire they keep around for the Speaker's photo ops."

"Marco Rubio?"

"Something like that." Harold shoveled a forkful of herring into his mouth. "The poor guy. They must work him so hard. He was a nervous wreck just talking to me. Sweating the whole time. I felt bad for him. You want to tell a person like that, quit your job, lose the suit, and open that dance studio you've always dreamed of."

"Honey, Marco Rubio is also a presidential candidate."

"Um, no, I don't think so, darling." Harold shook his head. "This fellow looked like a teenager dressed in his father's work clothes."

"Right. The senator."

"No, no, you remember those people from college. Went straight to Washington after graduation, got an internship on the Hill. Thinks he'll rise up through the ranks. The kind of kid who reads Dinesh D'Souza for fun and says that free health care sends the wrong message to the poor. He didn't say a thing that didn't come out of the Reagan administration, except that I had nice eyes."

"That still sounds like Marco Rubio, the presidential candidate."

"Oh," Harold said. "Well, I have him going on for five pages about whether Idina Menzel is the next Bette Midler, so I guess there may be a story there, if your hunch about him being a presidential candidate is right."

*   *   *

"Excuse me, you haven't seen Casey Kasem wandering around here today, have you?" Harold moved his way through the crowd of fair-goers, his eyes peeled for a middle-aged white man. At the far edge of the fairgrounds, next to a Coors Lite truck and beer stand, he noticed a woman standing on a makeshift stage, addressing a smattering of people. At stage right stood a middle-aged, wealthy-looking white man wearing a puffy Gore-Tex jacket over an exquisitely-tailored blue suit. "That's probably John Krazinski," Harold said to himself. He pushed his way through the crowd, toward the man in the bespoke suit. The woman on the stage was arguing that America knew, in its heart of hearts, that it would love to see Carly Fiorina on stage, debating Hillary Clinton, this fall. Harold breathed into his hands as he waited for the unknown woman to introduce John Costanza.

"Are you on next?" Harold asked the man, seeing an opportunity to score his journalistic coup while the woman onstage enjoyed the sound of her amplified voice.

"Heh," the man chuckled. "I gotta be on all the time."

"Life of a presidential candidate, huh?"

"You're telling me," the man laughed. "I've always got to be somewhere, do something. Most days, I don't even get four minutes to myself in the john. Carly's pounding on the door, telling me we have to go meet with donors."

"I've heard campaign managers can be real task masters sometimes."

"Oh, I can't *stand* the campaign manager. 'Get on the bus, Frank!' 'No chewing gum in public, Frank!' 'Don't talk about the divorce, Frank!' Talk about controlling."

"Sounds like a nightmare." Harold flipped open his notepad and began scribbling furiously, his reportorial instincts kicking in.

"The worst part is when there's a debate coming up. You wouldn't believe how many times she needs to rehearse the same goddamn responses. Over, and over, and *over* again. As though anyone even listens to anything but the two soundbites CNN pulls the next day."

"Uh huh," Harold nodded, still taking notes.

"Oh, and you can't imagine the Purell that woman goes through! Ten bottles a week sometimes. Twenty when we're below the Mason-Dixon line. Every time she shakes a hand, it's, 'Frank, I need the sanitizer. Frank, I told you not to stray too far with that sanitizer!' You'd think she'd at least wait until *after* meeting a line of people to put on Purell, but she needs it after each *individual* person. It's crazy." He shook his head. "Though, I guess I'd be out of a job, otherwise." Frank laughed again, this time less convincingly.

Harold closed his notebook. "I have the name of an excellent licensed practitioner on the Upper West Side if you ever need someone to talk to," he said solemnly.

*   *   *

Across the fairgrounds, Pattie was still hungry, not having had much appetite for the chicken cutlet sandwich. Deciding to bite the bullet, she lined up at a corndog stand.

"You don't happen to have any chipotle mayo back there, do you?" A middle-aged man with a full head of gray hair leaned over the counter to inspect what condiment options might be hiding in the back. A group of aides in their twenties crowded around him. "Who puts relish on a corn dog, for Christ's sake? Kevin, run out and see if you can score me some chipotle mayo, would you?"

Pattie got out of line and approached him. "Excuse me, Governor Kasich?"

The middle-aged man turned around, his mouth full of food. "How are you doing, friend?" he asked. He turned to an aide. "Get me a napkin, already," he whispered.

"I'm Pattie Carlyle; I write for *The New Yorker*." Pattie reached out to shake his hand.

"Glad to meet you!" Kasich shook her hand. "Sorry about the relish there. Can you believe that? You wanna taste the dough and the salt. You gotta wonder what they put relish on there for."

"Yes," Pattie said. "Do you have a second to chat? I'd love to get a statement." She pulled out her notepad and flipped it open to a clean page.

"Can you believe the selection of chips? They don't have Lay's. Lay's! Your standard potato chip. Goes with everything. Brandon!" He called an aide. "Go back to the bus and get a bag of Lay's."

"Governor Kasich, now that you've been on the campaign trail these past few months, what would you say are the primary issues voters are concerned with?"

"Oh, good question." Kasich tried to tear open a mustard packet with his teeth, and it squirted all over the front of his coat. "I've had such a great time on the campaign trail, talking to voters, going to union halls, mom and pop stores, diners. Oh, the diners. There was one in New Hampshire that made their own maple syrup. Poured it all over the most delicious johnny cakes you've ever had. Piping hot. We spent three or four hours there. Every time I'd make the rounds, I'd get back to my table and there was another stack just waiting for me."

Waxes rhapsodic about the homespun virtues of small-town America, Pattie wrote.

"Another place in Chicago," Kasich continued, his eyes sparkling. "Never did find out what oil they used for the French Fries. Must've been goat fat or something because the guys behind the counter—they were from the Mideast, you understand. Couldn't stop eating them, anyway. Must've spent an extra thirty minutes in the bathroom, threw us all off schedule. A little case of the runs never hurt anyone, though," He gnawed off another bite of the corn dog.

"Yes, yes, good," Pattie said as she continued to write. "And what do you think will be your biggest challenges as you head into the Iowa caucus?"

Kasich bit into the corndog again. "Gotta make sure no one catches this. Can't end up like Rick Perry." He signaled one of his aides. "Kevin, make sure we have a complete media lockdown while I finish this corndog. Sweetie, you won't take a picture of me, will you?"

"Um, no." Pattie grimaced. "Your secret's safe with me."

"To eat one of these things, you end up looking like a D-level actress trying to make rent," Kasich explained.

"Donald Trump has been surging in the polls lately. How confident are you in your chances of beating him in the primaries?"

"Oh, Donald Trump, the man is a clown. Sure, he can draw a crowd, but he doesn't listen. See, I listen to the voters. I'm out there traveling, listening. I was in Cedar Rapids last week. Found this gorgeous steakhouse there. Man alive, you wouldn't believe the T-bone they brought out to me. Hoo boy. Thank God for heartburn medication, you know? Would've been the first candidate to die on the trail!" He licked his lips. "Except for Robert Kennedy, obviously."

"Yes, thank God!" Pattie forced out a chuckle for good measure. "Governor Kasich, I think I have all I need for now. Um, I'll be in touch if I have any follow-ups." Pattie turned to leave.

"One more thing," Kasich added, barely masking a burp. "You said you're from New York? Next time you're home, you have to go to Second Avenue Deli and get the pastrami on rye. Now, most people can't tell the difference between corned beef and pastrami. But me? I'm a pastrami man; all the way. They're both brined, is the thing, so, granted, there is a fair amount of overlap there. But it's the spices they use. And the cut of the meat. Now, the cut is key, sweetie. See, corned beef is typically a brisket. Now, pastrami can *also be a brisket*, but the cut is closer to the navel. And pastrami is smoked, while corned beef is boiled. So, really, there's no contest there."

"Great!" said Pattie, striding away at ever-greater speed. "Good luck in the campaign!" Kasich waved.

*   *   *

"Where have you been?" Pattie asked, finally reuniting with Harold at their meeting point. He was sweaty and flushed. "And why are you out of breath again? Did you see the goldfish man?"

"No, no," Harold wheezed. "I think I may have just joined the Victory Baptist Church," Harold paused to catch his breath. "The elect are surprisingly fast, Pattie."

"You owe me," Pattie teased.

"Oh? Did you buy me more dressed herring from that stand?"

"I found John Kasich for you."

"Oh," Harold said, slightly crestfallen. "You asked him questions about the campaign, right?"

Pattie rolled her eyes. "Of course I did. You might say he's kind of a wonk. Definitely a detail-oriented guy. Strong opinions."

"Great," Harold said, coughing and spitting. "I hope that's not blood." Pattie stared at him. "They don't like it when you leave, Pattie!" Harold wiped his mouth on his jacket sleeve. "Tell you what. Why don't we head back to the car? If we leave now, we can get in a good forty-five minutes of sauna time before it closes!"

3
"I Mentioned This Was at the Ritz, Right?"
January 15, 2016

The following transcript was found within a classified dossier covertly obtained from the Kremlin.

PETROV: Thank you for agreeing to meet with me, Mr. Trump. I would like to congratulate you on the campaign you have run so far. We have been quite impressed.

TRUMP: We?

PETROV: Your, shall we say, sympathizers in Russia.

TRUMP: Oh, of course, of course. You know, the people love me. There's no question about that.

PETROV: Take off your hat, sit for a while.

TRUMP: What hat?

PETROV: Never mind. Just sit.

TRUMP: You see the legs on that waitress?

PETROV: *Desyat.*

TRUMP: I should come back to this joint when I'm looking for my next wife.

PETROV: Yes, yes.

TRUMP: Ten years or a hundred thousand miles. A good rule of thumb. They get all grabbed-out after that.

PETROV: Yes. Mr. Trump, we would like to discuss your progress in the campaign ahead.

TRUMP: You've never seen winning like how we're going to win, Petrov. We're going to win New Hampshire. We're going to win California. We're going to win Iowa.

PETROV: Mr. Trump, we are sorry to report that you will not win Iowa.

TRUMP: You'll see, Petrov. You'll see. You know how many people watched the *Celebrity Apprentice*? More people than watched the Oscars.

PETROV: Mr. Trump, Russia has shown you much generosity over the last thirty years. As I am sure you remember, our country has been there to assist you in your moments of need.

TRUMP: A lot of very famous people wanted to be on my show, Petrov, and I had to turn them down.

PETROV: For too long, our countries have failed to understand each other. For nearly a century—

TRUMP: John Travolta. Wesley Snipes. River Phoenix.

PETROV: For nearly a century, we have regarded each other with hostility and competition. And for what reason? You yourself have enjoyed a very splendid and productive relationship with Russia and her people.

TRUMP: Such beautiful women in Russia. Gorgeous women. And I've been with many of them. You ever stay at the Ritz? Terrific, terrific hotel. So many beautiful women, I've met at the Ritz.

PETROV: We are aware, Mr. Trump.

TRUMP: After the election, maybe you could send over a couple women for Trump TV. We'll need anchors. They don't have to know how to read. We'll get a big name to read the news. Someone terrific. Wayne Newton. And the women, maybe they can hula hoop or something while we run a news crawl on the bottom.

PETROV: Mr. Trump, we wish to help you in this campaign.

TRUMP: Of course. Everyone wants to help me. I get so many phone calls. I get phone calls everyday, from people asking, how can we help you? But I don't take their money. I do not take their money.

PETROV: Mr. Trump, there are many ways we can assist you.

TRUMP: I actually do take the money, but you wouldn't believe how well that line plays.

PETROV: Mr. Trump, we can offer you financial support and many other types of support, as well. However, there must be some conditions.

TRUMP: Right, I know. Nobody can know about Trump TV until after the election. Here's what Roger says. We say I was robbed and I should have won, *then* we announce Trump TV. Maybe right before Thanksgiving. You know Roger, right?

PETROV: Mr. Stone and I shared a very productive afternoon on Mr. Deripaska's yacht, yes. He is, how you say, *well-connected*.

TRUMP: You're telling me, Petrov. Has he ever taken you to that club of his?

PETROV: Mr. Stone is a great friend of many, as our country has been a fast friend to you. And Mr. Trump—

TRUMP: A few too many chunkies for my taste, but some of the younger wives were pretty nice.

PETROV: Mr. Trump—

TRUMP: Too bad they had to shut down because of that ringworm outbreak.

PETROV: —Mr. Trump, there are many ways for friends to repay each other.

TRUMP: Oh, don't worry about that, Petrov. Trump TV is going to be so, so successful, we'll get that all taken care of. I am a winner, Petrov. I don't back down.

PETROV: Yes, Mr. Trump. That is a start.

TRUMP: Just tell everyone to sit tight for a few months.

PETROV: Mr. Trump, our relationship has moved beyond dollars and cents or loans and accounts.

TRUMP: Terrific. You are gonna love this TV station, Petrov. Just wait.

PETROV: Let me be clear. The Russian government holds information about your activities in Russia that would be extremely damaging to your, how do you say, "brand," if it were to become public.

TRUMP: No doubt about it, I have had some beautiful times in Russia. One time, at the Ritz, I stayed in the Presidential Suite, where Barack and Michelle spent their trip. Let me tell you. Let me tell you. I hired some—

PETROV: Mr. Trump, you hired *shlyukha*, as we say in Russia. Prostitutes.

TRUMP: Right, and they peed on me. It was tremendous.

PETROV: Now, of course, if the American media—

TRUMP: And apparently, some of them even know how to farm.

PETROV: We believe, if such a story were known by the American people, not only your electoral chances, but also your business fortunes, would suffer irreversible harm. In Russia, Mr. Trump, we call this *kompromat*.

TRUMP: You know that they were from a service, right? Top notch girls. Nines, tens. These weren't just women off the street.

PETROV: Yes. This service was a front for the FSB, you understand.

TRUMP: Okay, so, what's your point? I paid them, didn't I?

PETROV: Actually, there is still an outstanding bill for—

TRUMP: One of them got nervous and couldn't pee. I'm suing her.

PETROV: Mr. Trump, the Russian government is prepared to release—

TRUMP: I mentioned this was at the Ritz, right?

PETROV: We will release the videotape of these events, unless you agree to certain conditions.

TRUMP: Right. For one, I want a copy of the tape.

PETROV: The Russian government will work to secure your electoral victory, with the understanding that, once elected, you will approve a change in policy toward Russia and help the Kremlin to erode the American government from within through mismanagement and corruption.

TRUMP: Oh, you don't need to tell me. The people running this country are so, so corrupt. I'm a businessman, Petrov. I will make the best deals. I will call China and talk to China. I will run this country like one of my businesses. You can depend on that.

PETROV: That is precisely our hope, Mr. Trump.

TRUMP: I am a draw, Petrov. Did you see me on *Saturday Night Live*? I hosted it. They told me it was the highest-rated episode they had since the week after 9/11. I was very, very funny. A lot of people called the next day to say that I should host the show regularly.

PETROV: Mr. Trump, we will be in touch again soon. Until then, consider our offer. You can reach me through my associate, Paul Manafort.

TRUMP: Oh, you know Paul? Terrific guy. Balls like a horse's ass.

PETROV: Yes, he was instrumental in the recent elections in the Ukraine. A very hard-working individual.

TRUMP: Oh, believe me. Not as hard-working as me, of course. Not as hard-working as me. But a very, very good guy.

PETROV: The time will come when it will be appropriate for him to join your campaign team in an official capacity, but for now, we will proceed with your current staff.

TRUMP: Sure, sure. Hey, listen, did Putin get the case of breath mints I sent him? Those are from Mar-a-Lago.

PETROV: I am uncertain of that detail.

TRUMP: Tell him, next time a girl gives him the business, put one of those in her mouth first. Incredible, Petrov. Let me tell you. Just incredible.

PETROV: Yes, Mr. Trump. Thank you for your time.

TRUMP: Like someone stuck a battery jumper cable on your penis. Just incredible.

4
"I'm a Journalist in Chains!"
February 7, 2016

Pattie and Harold stepped out of Mamma Maria and into a small sidestreet, buffeted by the harsh winds of a Boston night. "Ooh, there's nothing like a New England winter, is there?" Harold asked, rubbing the sides of his arms vigorously.

"Yeah, it's charming how they stow their trash in the snow banks like that," said Pattie.

"Mm-hmm," Harold agreed. "Doesn't it just stir your blood being up here? I remember coming for Head of the Charles when I was at Columbia. You came up here all the time from Brown, right?"

"I think I came up to Boston once for a Counting Crows concert," Pattie huffed into her coat collar. "Let's go back to the hotel." The narrow cobblestone streets were lined with Italian restaurants, bakeries, and heavily bundled couples rushing in and out of the cold. The small brick buildings blended into the clear dark night. In the distance, a white church steeple rose into the stars.

"I can smell the ideas in the air, can't you? You can just feel we're in a town of learned men. People of finer tastes. Harvard. MIT."

"Tufts?"

"Yes, sure, Tufts, too, I guess."

"Let's just get back to the Fairmont," Pattie shivered. "The Des Moines Des Luxe was one thing, but are you sure this didn't raise any red flags?"

Harold and Pattie turned to cross the street and hail a cab. "I think I earned it after a month of those Iowa towns," Harold grimaced. "What a relief it is to be back in civilization. Look! Not a pig in sight!" Harold spread his arms wide to reveal the conspicuous absence of pigs, knocking his hand into a man staggering across the intersection from the opposite direction. "Oof, I'm sorry, sir. Just reveling in the beautiful night we're having."

"Why dontcha pay attention t'where ya goin', ya fuckin' cocksuckah!" the man shouted.

"I, uh," Harold stammered. The man shoved Harold back in his tracks and stumbled across the street. "Come on, honey, let's cross down the block."

"Fuckin' queer! You think you're bettah than me? I'm a fuckin' cop!" the man called out over his shoulder. Harold and Pattie rushed down the street.

"You were saying about all the learned men?" Pattie teased.

"Well, that was an aberration, honey," Harold explained. "On the whole, Boston is really quite a—"

"FAGGOT!" a man yelled out of a passing car.

"Let's catch that cab, shall we?" Pattie flagged down a faded red taxi, and they climbed in. The back seat smelled of sweat and disinfectant. "Where to?" the driver asked. "The Fairmont Copley Plaza," Pattie told him. They lurched forward, the cab jimmying and bouncing roughly over the uneven streets.

"My stomach," Pattie groaned. "If you can't expense my dinner, I think I'm about to return it, anyway.

"This is why it's so good that we rented the Porsche, even though we have to wait overnight for it," Harold explained. "It'll feel like a taut dancer." Pattie said nothing.

"So where you guys from?" the driver asked. He was a heavyset man, wearing a sweatsuit, and reeked of cigars.

"New York," Pattie replied.

"New York! Great town. My buddy Johnny lives in New York. Terrific guy. Hooks me up with Percocet whenever he's back in the city."

"What did he just say?" Pattie asked quietly.

"Well, you know how expensive health care is," Harold whispered.

"Yeah, Johnny's a pal alright," the cabbie went on. "Helped me out of a bind once or twice back in the day. Great guy, Johnny."

"Right," Harold said, feigning a laugh.

"Johnny and I grew up together. Same block. South End. Different neighborhood then. Lotsa spades came in. Johnny and I stuck together, though."

Harold and Pattie were silent, and the car shimmied and rattled, churning their stomachs.

"Shit. Missed the fuckin' turn," the driver grunted. They were quiet. The breaks whined as they pulled to a stop light. The driver coughed into his hands and rubbed them together. "You know, for it to be first degree murder, they have to prove you had intent," he offered.

Harold and Pattie glanced at each other. "This is why we need the Porsche!" Harold hissed.

"I always had good friends. You gotta have good friends," the driver continued.

"Right," Harold agreed.

"Back in the '70s, me and Johnny would be out at the club every night chasing tang. You could always count on Johnny to score. Slick-ass motherfucker. He had black wavy hair, and he'd grease it back. Back in those days, you didn't need to take a dame back to the Fairmont, like you're doin' here. You could just pop a tent on the bank of the Charles. 'Hey honey, I got a tent!' All you need to get some puss."

"Harold," Pattie whispered, "I want to get out of here."

"Ha ha, right!" Harold said. "It's better not to trouble him," he explained to Pattie.

"Yeah, my friends always looked out for me. Catch me when my temper got away from me. Boy, did I used to have a temper. I don't any more. But I did. Killed a kid once."

"Uh huh," Harold said slowly. The cab jumped over an expansion joint as the driver pushed it up the deserted turnpike. Far in the distance, a large yellow-and-red Shell sign cast a glow over the frozen river.

"It was at this bar, fucked out of my mind on poppers. Kid made me real mad. *Real mad.* So, you know, I shoved him. Not hard, just, you know, a good push, 'cause he made me real mad. But I'm a big guy, so he fell right back into the bar, cracked his head. Luckily I had buddies on the force. They told me right away, boy. They told me, the kid's dead, you gotta get out of town. Great buddies."

"Right," Harold said.

"But, hey, the story's got a happy ending," the driver offered, apparently noticing the apprehension in Harold's voice or the expressions on his and Pattie's faces in the rearview mirror. "Turns out his heart just stopped on the operating table in the hospital. But they got it going again. So he didn't really die. But it was a bad situation for a while there. I thought I killed him. But I don't do that no more. I got two daughters. I love 'em. My wife doesn't let me see 'em, but they're great girls. I take good care of 'em."

"Right," Harold said.

"Here y'are. Fairmont. Nice hotel." Pattie bolted out of the car, slammed the door, and walked briskly through the gleaming revolving doors of a Beaux-Arts stone building that stretched across the city block. Harold sat silently in the idling car, checking each of his pockets while the driver admired the hotel's radiant forecourt. "Listen, you guys have a great time in Boston for me, alright? An' if you need anything, a ride to the airport, a couple Oxys, here's my card. Just gimme a call. I'll hook you up," the driver offered.

"Oh, sure. Thanks so much," Harold said carefully, quickly taking the man's card.

"Yeah, I can get you Oxys, no problem," the cab driver boasted. "I got a solid hookup. My buddy out in Dorchester."

"Right. You know, we're going to New Hampshire tomorrow, so we don't have a lot of time for that," Harold said nervously.

"Man, if you two're looking to party to*night*, I can hook you up right now."

"No, I wouldn't want you to go to any trouble. We're actually probably going to spend the rest of the evening inside, as it happens. Early day tomorrow, you know." He reached for the door handle.

"That's the *perfect* time for Oxys. It's no trouble." The driver opened his glove compartment and rummaged around. He produced a gallon-sized Zip-loc bag filled with pill bottles and thrust them into Harold's reluctant hands. "I'm helping you out," he declared.

"Um, thanks," Harold said. "I do tend to get sore throats in the winter, so, you know."

"Man, you just crush one of these, cook it, and boom." The driver popped his lips.

"Well, that's very generous. Thanks," Harold mumbled.

"Five hundred twenty-three bucks," the driver demanded.

"What?"

"Buddy, I don't set the fares. Twenty-three bucks from the North End into town? You ain't gonna pay less than that."

"And the five hundred?"

"You think I'm running a charity here?" the driver spat. "Oxys ain't cheap. You ain't getting some Mexican street tar cut with aspirin here."

"Uh-huh," Harold said nervously. "Do you take cards?"

"Yeah, I'm on Square."

Harold paused for a moment, then helplessly handed the driver his card. "I get miles on that one," he said as the driver swiped it.

"Awright, buddy! Boy, are you gonna have fun tonight." The driver rolled down his window and lit a cigar.

"Thanks. Uh, have a good night." Harold stepped out of the cab, placing the Zip-loc bag inside his overcoat, and the driver pulled away, the cab sputtering and groaning down the block. *"Motherfucker!"* Harold heard the driver yell at an oncoming car.

Pattie was waiting for Harold inside. String quartet echoed faintly throughout the airy lobby. Harold paused to admire the vaulted ceilings and glimmering chandeliers. The light reflecting off the shiny, cream marble walls and floors made the long room sparkle, and well-dressed couples with refined, ageless Dutch faces seemed to glide past him. He felt at peace. "What are you holding in your jacket?" Pattie asked.

Harold's eyes widened. He looked around. "I had to buy some Oxys to get out of the cab." Harold held up the Zip-loc bag by the corner as if it were a dead animal. An older woman with a mink stole glanced at him.

"Harold, those are illegal!" Pattie hissed.

"You saw that goon. He had me captive! I don't know. It all happened so fast. I'm going to throw them out as soon as I find a safe place to leave them, obviously." He tucked the baggie back into his overcoat. "I got miles."

"You're impossible. I want you to get rid of those right now."

"Pattie, I can't just leave hundreds of Oxys in the *Fairmont*. Once we get up to New Hampshire, I'll leave them by the side of the road, or something."

"Sure, better to leave them in their natural habitat." Pattie turned and started for the bank of gold elevators.

*   *   *

"Are you not talking because you're angry?" Harold asked pleadingly as he followed Pattie through a set of automatic doors, passing underneath a mounted purple-and-red sign reading "Mall of New Hampshire." He pulled their suitcases behind him, dripping wet and leaving trails of grayish water in their wake, and paused to adjust a carpetbag visibly stuffed to the gills and awkwardly draped across his slight chest.

"Well, that's just terrific," Pattie grumbled, typing frantically on her phone. "I missed my deadline, and now my editor's going with the freelancer's review of that derivative New Museum exhibit instead."

"Pattie, how was I supposed to know it would start snowing? *You* try driving a sports car in the snow."

Pattie sighed heavily. "Right."

Harold shook his head, smiling distantly. "It felt incredible before the crash, though. You could really feel the road."

"I still think you should've left a note."

"No, they could trace it back to the paper, and God knows what would happen. Besides, did you see the car we skidded into? Cloth seats." Harold shook his head witheringly as he paused to adjust the strap on the carpet bag. "If anything, I did that man a favor."

Pattie ignored Harold, striding across the mall's forecourt to a large plastic map of the main floor positioned underneath a bank of escalators. Three levels teeming with illuminated brand names and shoppers wearing puffy winter jackets rose above them. Skylights filtered the gray light outside into the forecourt, giving her the feeling of being neither entirely connected to nor detached from the rest of the world.

"We sure made good time once we got in that tow truck," Harold offered, glancing at his watch. "I've got an extra half-hour."

"Just as long as it all worked out for you," Pattie said acidly.

"Oh, come on, Pattie. Try to make the best of it. Hey, weren't you saying when we were stranded in front of that Cash for Gold place that you wished you had a better scarf? Look where you are now! It's kismet."

"That's one word for it."

"Here, why don't you go look for a scarf, while I'm watching this little rally. Save the receipt." Harold winked.

Pattie chewed the inside of her cheek contemplatively. "And a sweater."

"A sweater, sure! A nice cableknit, perhaps. Go hogwild."

Pattie studied the map again. "Okay. Just text me when the rally's over."

"Will do," Harold grinned. "Heck, you know, I've got some time to kill. Maybe I'll buy myself a new belt. One of those big, thick ones, like the other reporters have." Harold motioned with his hands to demonstrate the thickness of other reporters' belts.

"I think your belts are fine," Pattie shrugged.

"No, mine are too thin and reedy. I need to look the part. This is the *election*, not an unlicensed Papa Smurf rubbing up against tourists outside the M&M store."

"Suit yourself. It's your money."

"Right," Harold winked again. "Oh, hey, they have a Brooks Brothers," he said to himself, studying the map. "Pattie?" he called as she set off toward a large illuminated Macy's sign at the opposite end of the pavilion. "Try to keep the sweater under thirty-five, okay?"

*   *   *

Proudly wearing a brand-new thick leather belt, Harold wandered the third floor of the Mall of New Hampshire, looking for some indication that a politician was in the vicinity. He paused outside of a Sunglass Hut to get his bearings and examine in the polished glass windows the wayward wisps of blond hair that constituted his old hairline when he noticed a group of fresh-faced, well-dressed people assembling a microphone stand and talking to an older, salt-and-pepper-haired man in a loose-fitting suit. The older man had glasses that had fallen halfway down his nose and an apologetic smile, as though his mother were reprimanding him for sticking his hands in a tub of ice cream. He looked vaguely familiar.

Harold was approached by a blond youth in cowboy boots. "Are you going to stay for the Governor's speech?"

"Which one?" Harold asked. "Hang on, I have a list." Harold fumbled in his coat pockets. The cowboy-booted youth walked back over to the guilty-looking man. "Is it Michael Dukakis? No, hold on. Is it Al Smith? Is it Charles Curtis?"

"Hey, Guess-Who guy?" another youth said, this one wearing a cowboy hat. "Are you with the press?"

"How did you know? It's the belt, right?" Harold asked.

"You look unhappy," the aide shrugged. "Anyway, Jeb Bush is giving a speech now. You want to cover it?"

"Where?"

"Here."

"*Where* 'here'?"

"*Right* here." The cowboy-hatted youth pointed. "That's Jeb."

"The man doing his own sound check?"

"Uh huh. He's going to talk about his plan to revitalize the economy and the middle class."

"You mean, the man who just spilled Orange Julius on his shirt?"

"Just, stand over there." The youth ushered Harold over to a roped-off area with a handwritten sign that read "Press." Harold noticed that he was the only person there.

Jeb approached the mic hesitantly and tapped on it a few times. "Is this thing working alright? Just, give me a big thumbs up if you can hear me."

Harold gave a thumbs up from the deserted press box.

"Hi folks. I'm so sorry to bother you like this. I'm—sorry, coming through? No, go right ahead. Sorry. Go ahead." Jeb paused to let a family make their way into the Sunglass Hut. "Sorry about that, everyone. So, as I was saying, I hate to interrupt your day shopping, but I'm running for president. I just—well, I just wanted to say a few words here. Sorry. Yeah, no, go right on through. Yeah. Lots of sunglasses back there."

"There you are!" Pattie said. Harold turned around to see his wife striding toward him.

"Can't come in, dear; this is the press pen."

"They didn't have any good scarves," Pattie whispered. "Is that Jeb Bush?"

"They didn't have any scarves?"

"They were all too bright."

Harold nodded. "What about the sweater?"

Pattie shrugged. "This far north, it's all last year's fashions."

"Folks," Jeb continued, speaking to a middle-aged couple who had stopped on their way to try on Ray-Bans, "I just wanted to say, I love America. I think America is a land of hope, but also of promise. Of wishes, but also of dreams. I want to help America ask its questions and find its solutions. Sorry, no, go right through." The family continued toward Macy's. "Sorry to bother you. This is an inconvenient spot. I only have a few more minutes, and then they told me they need to start setting up for a middle school dance troupe. So, if you can just bear with me for another moment, and then I'll be out of your hair."

"He looks like he tried to have intercourse with a pig, but someone walked in before he had got up the nerve," Harold whispered to Pattie.

"A pig?" Pattie asked.

"They always go for pigs, dear."

"Why?"

"I'm not sure. Maybe because their flesh is so similar to humans'."

"Uh huh."

"What are you doing?" Harold asked.

"Just taking notes for Dr. Rothstein."

"If you let me—give me the opportunity to, to lead, that's my plan," Jeb continued. "To guide, and to envision. And to be patient. My mom told me to be patient when I was little. Oh, did she make me feel bad, sometimes. She wouldn't even need to say anything. She'd just sort of look at me and cut me down with this glare that made me feel so sorry to even be alive. I felt so bad for disappointing her, I just wanted to curl up and hide. A turtle is patient, but he also has a shell he can curl up into when he needs to hide. Boy, did I wish I were a turtle." He looked up, seemingly surprised there were still people around. "I want to help the mothers of America."

At that moment, Jeb's voice was drowned out by a blaring horn section and a heavy, swinging backbeat. "But, anyway, God bless—I said, GOD BLESS—Gosh, what's going on here?" Jeb turned to a fair-haired aide standing next to the podium. "Chicago cover band, sir," the aide replied. "They're directly below us. Apparently they perform every Wednesday at four."

"Ohh," Jeb sighed. "Well, I guess I was pretty much done, anyway."

*   *   *

"This feels like a boat, Pattie," Harold complained as he sped through a corner on I-91 in a rented red Mustang. "I'm not locked into the road. In the Porsche, the steering was telling me about the undulations in the road! The *undulations*! That's what makes driving a joy." He tore up the highway, perhaps too quickly for the icy roads. "I mean, honestly, what self-respecting car rental establishment doesn't have a Porsche or two available for customers with more discerning tastes?"

"This is a sports car, too, Harold."

"A *Mustang*. American muscle cars. It's not about how fast a car is; it's about whether it *dances*. Americans think everything is about pounding, pounding, pounding. The Porsche is like a Frenchman. The Porsche *romances* the road."

"Dear Lord."

"I was speaking figuratively," Harold explained. "It's all about finesse, darling. Something the Europeans know more about, I have to say."

"Shh," Pattie instructed, squinting at her tablet. "I'm trying to edit *your* interview with Jeb Bush."

"I didn't—oh, you mean, when he tripped over your suitcase after?"

Pattie nodded. "Once you take out all of the apologies, you're just left with a Freudian anecdote about a toy boat he had in Kennebunkport."

Harold shuddered. "It's a wonder the man ever took a bath again."

"Seeing as I don't have my own article to worry about now, I could type up your notes from his speech at the mall, too, when we get back to the hotel after Hillary's primary rally." Pattie cleared her throat. "God, I hope she wins tonight." She glanced out of the car's side window. "New Hampshire is certainly dreary."

"All this snow will just help us to appreciate San Diego even more," Harold explained. "When we get to California, it'll be like those videos of deaf babies getting hearing aids installed."

"Shouldn't you slow down?" Pattie asked, placing her hand against the car's ceiling to steady herself. "The roads seem pretty slippery."

"I'm afraid I don't have much of a choice in this behemoth," Harold protested. "The accelerator is like a cinder block. You just slam it down. So American. It's pornographic in its lack of subtlety. *Unh. Unh.* Boring. You know, I bet the Hillary rally will—*LOOK OUT!*" Harold slammed the brakes as the car hit a patch of black ice. Too late to prevent a crash, the Mustang spun out of control and into the median strip, stopped only by the five-foot snowbank that flanked the road.

Harold and Pattie sat in stunned silence, listening as the motor quietly sputtered and died. "Shit," Harold said.

*   *   *

"I distinctly recall ordering a Mustang with satellite radio," Harold grumbled as he pushed different buttons on the dash. Pattie was silent. "Is this a Portuguese music channel?" He hit the scan button again. "But they wrote the *rules*, friends," a man intoned. "The rules for the moral universe. Now, Ted Cruz is a man of faith, and a man of principle. Who will lead us to the sunlit fields, friends? God led His people out of Egypt, but it took—" Harold changed stations. "Bernie Sanders drawing record crowds to—" He turned off the radio.

"You know, I keep hearing about Sanders," Harold said. "Would we agree with him?"

"He reminds me of my Uncle Lenny. Remember, the guy who took all the sterno cans at our wedding?" Pattie continued reviewing her notes from the Jeb Bush interview.

"I hope the hotel is nice." Harold ventured.

"I hear there's a Hillary rally you're supposed to be at, first."

"It's called compartmentalizing, Pattie. When I'm doing a story, I'm like a laser. A very *efficient* laser. When I'm taking 'Harold' time, I think about—you know," Harold waved his hands through the air, "whether the facial scrub I'm using has a proper exfoliating agent. Compartmentalizing." He tapped his fingers on his skull.

"I'm going to see if I can flag down a passing car." Pattie opened her door. "At the very least, maybe I can find someone to murder me and bury me in the woods." Pattie tentatively waded into the snowbank and trudged her way closer to the side of the Interstate. She squinted into the distance, trying to flag down a neighborly New Hampshirite from the vague shapes of oncoming traffic. After several unsuccessful attempts at waving down someone neighborly, however, Pattie noticed an SUV cruising down the highway, topped with a siren and bearing the New Hampshire State Troopers insignia. Pattie continued waving her arms until the cruiser slowly pulled up next to the rented Mustang. Two burly, red-faced men were inside. One, who wore sunglasses, stepped out.

"Can we help you, ma'am?" the sunglasses-wearing officer asked.

"Yes—yes, thank you for stopping! My husband has us trapped in a snowbank over—over there in that Mustang," Pattie stammered, relieved and shivering from standing outside.

"Hank!" the trooper called to his partner. "C'mere. I think we got a domestic."

"A domestic?" Pattie asked incredulously.

"The guy trapped her in a snowbank, she says."

"You okay, ma'am?" the other officer asked, getting out of the car and placing his hand on the gun in his holster.

"I'm fine. It's just—my husband rented this Mustang, and I *told* him it was too icy to be—"

"We see this all the time," the first officer said. "They all seem to drive these muscle cars. Lemme guess, you spoke up—maybe with a little more lip than a husband would appreciate—he pulled off the road, took the tire iron out of the glove compartment? Twenty miles to the next town. What a mess."

"Actually, it has run-flat tires!" Harold called out from the car.

"Whassat, buddy?" Hank asked.

"There wouldn't be a tire iron," Harold explained, opening the car door into the snow and stepping out, "because the car has run-flat tires. The tire deflates slowly while you—"

"Hey, buster, who told you to get out of the car? Whyn't you put your hands on the hood where I can see 'em?"

Harold froze in his tracks. "My hands on the what?"

"On the hood!"

"Okay, okay." Harold slowly backed through the snow to the front of the vehicle, placed his hands on the hood, then nervously stood up again. "By the way, officer, my rental agreement's in the glove box still."

"Keep your hands on the hood, Harold," Pattie hissed. Harold obliged.

"Alright," Hank said, taking a step toward Harold. "This woman says you've been threatening her."

"Officer, I'm afraid this is just a misunderstanding. I'm a journalist from New York. I went to Columbia."

Hank grunted. "Can I see your license and registration?"

"Of course, of course," Harold said. "Can I move my hands? I'm just going to put my left hand in my back pocket to get out the license, and then I'll have it right back in view for you. Or—tell you what—Pattie, could you just reach into my back pocket there and get the officer my—"

"You can get it yourself," Hank said.

"Wonderful, wonderful. You know, we went to the Christmas gala for the New York City Patrolmen's Benevolent Association. Here you go, officer," Harold said, slowly pulling a small cream plastic card from his wallet and handing it to Hank. Hank squinted at the photo, frowning. He held it closer to his eyes, then raised it above his face, tilting his head and studying it intently. Then Hank looked back at Harold, surveying his upper forehead.

"I, um, had a different haircut then," Harold mumbled.

The officer smacked his lips. "What's your address?"

"308 West 87th Street, Apartment 4C," Harold said slowly. The officer squinted at Harold's license. "E.B. White used to live there, as a matter of fact."

The officer nodded and handed Harold back his license. "Now, because this is a domestic, we're going to have to take a look through the car."

"I can assure you, it's not a domestic, but yes, by all means," Harold said. "Search the whole thing."

"*Harold...*" Pattie whispered, raising her eyebrows meaningfully.

"They can sense fear, Pattie," Harold whispered. "We have nothing to hide."

"Rich, go ahead and search the car," Hank called to his partner. The other officer set out toward the Mustang, his boots crushing the snow underfoot.

"Ma'am, you don't have to talk to your husband anymore," Hank winked at Pattie. "Matter of fact, why don't you wait in the cruiser? Get your pretty little face out of the cold. Go ahead and sit shotgun." Pattie glared icily at him.

Rich opened the Mustang's doors and bent into the car, looking on and under the seats, checking the glove compartment, and opening the center console.

"Hank!" Rich called out. "Bring them over here and take a look at this."

"What is it?" Hank asked. Rich held up a Ziploc bag filled with orange-brown pill bottles.

"Looks like someone's got himself enough Oxys for a few months here," Rich said.

"Huh now," Hank said, turning back to Harold. "Those yours?"

"Wh—What?" Harold's eyes widened. "I think that's my wife's birth control medication."

"*Birth control*? You got a couple hundred OxyContin pills in your car. You steal these off the Manchester High JV football team or something?"

"Oxy*Con*tin?" Harold pronounced the word slowly, as if it sounded foreign to his ear.

"Don't play dumb, buddy," Hank warned. "These pills will fetch you five hundred dollars on the black market. Easy."

"And that's not even including cab fare," Harold muttered under his breath.

Pattie stepped forward reluctantly. "No, officer, I can explain. It's all a big misunderstanding. We were in Boston—"

"And I left my bag unattended at the airport for *two minutes* while I went to the men's room" Harold interjected. "Some layabout must have unloaded these on me. I would have said something, if I had seen it, because obviously—"

"Honey, you don't have to protect him anymore," Hank told Pattie, ignoring her husband. "I knew you were trouble as soon as I saw your poor, sweet wife standing out on the highway," he snarled, turning back to Harold. "All these pills? That's possession with intent to sell. That's serious charges, bucko."

"Officer, this can all be explained very easily. You see, my husband is an idiot," Pattie began.

"I *told* you, you don't have to protect him anymore," Hank said. "Your pretty apple cheeks look darn cold out here. Whyn't you get in the car and wait while we take care of your husband here?" He smiled.

"We're gonna have to bring you and this bag of pills down to the station house," Rich said, walking back to the group while cradling the bag in his left arm.

"You find anything else?" Hank asked.

"Just a lot of little tubes of hand cream," Rich shrugged. "Say 'Fairmont' on them."

"Pattie, make sure they give us a receipt for all that hand cream," Harold cut in.

"Harold, shut up," Pattie pleaded.

"Rich, radio the precinct. I'll get the cuffs," Hank instructed. "Would you mind just waiting there for a moment, sir?" he asked Harold.

"Pattie!" Harold whispered. "You should be filming this!" Pattie stared blankly at Harold.

"This could go viral, Pattie! Well, maybe not viral, but just think, if they start beating me—"

"Hands forward please, sir," Hank requested. "Just let me know if these pinch too tight." He snapped a set of gleaming metal handcuffs onto Harold's slender wrists, checked to ensure they were secured, and trudged back to the police cruiser, where Rich stood speaking into a walkie-talkie.

"Did you hear that? 'Tight?' It's going to start any second," Harold whispered excitedly. "Like what we were talking about with Anthony and Natalie. Like Freddie Gray, Pattie!"

Pattie rubbed her hands together and shivered, ignoring her husband.

"Honey, get out your phone! I'm a journalist in chains! Get this, honey!"

Hank returned and led Harold to the SUV. Pattie followed the pair, burrowing her hands in her jacket pockets. Harold craned his head back to catch her eyes.

"Get out your phone and frame in tight on my face for this part," Harold implored under his breath. "This is abuse!" he shouted.

"Watch your head, sir." Hank helped Harold into the back seat.

"I guess that's it for the Hillary rally," Pattie sighed as she climbed into the front.

"Don't worry, honey," Harold said, leaning forward and grinning through the wire mesh barrier separating them. "I'll be out tomorrow, and then pretty soon...San Diego!"

*   *   *

"Officer!" Harold called. "Is any sort of a breakfast service provided? Perhaps a poached egg, or a basic omelette station, or even a simple platter of lox?" He sat on the edge of his bunk, attempting to make as little contact as possible between the jail-provided linen and his Italian trousers. The prison was surprisingly bright. Yellow lights glared down. The walls and floor were a grimy brown. Harold sat alone in a holding cell containing only a bench with a mattress and, for some reason, a pail. A small window in the cell across the hall let in a sliver of the cloudy morning. An overweight security guard occasionally paced the corridor, but otherwise, it had been silent all night.

A burly, swarthy officer slowly approached Harold's cell from down the hall. Harold turned to face him. "I suppose it's not of much concern to you, but that mattress was deplorable. It was like sleeping on a straw tick. Go down, Moses, to the Sleep Train."

"Sir, your card's been declined," the officer stated.

Harold snapped to his feet. "Declined? That's a joint account!" He wrinkled his brow. "There should be a $7,000 line of credit on there."

"I dunno, it didn't go through," the officer replied, uninterested.

"Well, run it again," Harold offered.

"I tried running it three times, sir."

"Okay," Harold thought aloud. "There should be a United MileagePlus Visa in my wallet, too. Run that one, I guess."

"Okay," the officer said, emotionless.

"Actually," Harold brightened, "definitely run it. I may get double miles for this."

"Fine," the officer replied over his shoulder as he walked away.

"Maybe run it twice!" Harold called. "More miles! And bring the receipt!" He smoothed out his trousers and ran his hands through his hair. As Harold heard the hallway door click closed behind the officer, he noticed a grubby pair of hands folded, resting on the jail bars of the cell next to him.

"Eh, what you in for?" whispered the voice belonging to the hands.

Harold remained silent, hoping the man was addressing someone else.

"Did you hear me?" the gravelly voice repeated. "I asked, what're you in for?"

"Who, me?" Harold asked. He coughed a couple times and attempted to speak in a deeper, rougher tone. "Oh, some serious business. Serious business. They, uh, busted me trafficking Oxys across state lines."

"Oh?"

"You bet," Harold assented, slapping his thigh. "And, uh, wife beating."

"Oh."

"Yeah, I'm a savage, man," Harold continued. "Almost killed a kid once."

"Huh."

Feeling encouraged that his story was holding water, Harold decided to further engage his fellow convict. "How about you? What're you in for?"

"Voter fraud."

*   *   *

The swarthy officer returned with Harold's watch, belt, wallet, and credit cards. "You're free to go," he said, gruffly.

"The card went through, did it?"

"No need," the officer said. "We ran some tests on those pills you were picked up with. They're Tylenol. No bail, you're free to go."

"So I didn't get double miles?" Harold asked, slightly crestfallen. "I was here all night!"

"Nope. You were just carrying around a bag of Tylenol. Whoever sold those to you must've taken you for a real sucker."

"A sucker?" Harold asked as the guard unlocked the cell door. "I'll have you know," he huffed, "that when I was at Columbia, a guy on my floor freshman year *sold* marijuana." He fastened his belt and straightened his shirt sleeves. "So there's not very much I haven't seen."

"Right," the officer agreed flatly.

"He made everyone call him Big Dog," Harold said defensively. The officer turned and headed back toward the door, leaving Harold standing alone in the hall. "So, can someone from the station give me a ride to the Hilton, or do I have to call a cab?"

*   *   *

"You tried to expense bail?"

"Pattie, I was arrested in the line of duty!" Harold called from the shower. "If I can expense a Segway tour of Staten Island, then surely—" Harold trailed off as he began to gargle. He stepped out of the bathroom into the main room of his suite at the Hilton Nashua, a palette of tans and creams that looked identical to each previous room the couple had shared on their trip. The bedroom had a large window that looked over an empty parking lot and, beyond that, into the parking lot of an office park. The sun had faintly broken through the clouds, making the day brighter, but not more cheerful. Harold put on a clean shirt. "I hope they refill our body wash when they make up the room," he griped. "It took the whole bottle just to wash the smell of prison off me."

"Shh," Pattie said, turning on the TV She flipped through the channels, looking for coverage of the rally they had missed the night before. "Look at what those women are wearing!" she exclaimed, switching back to a Spanish-language channel she had initially passed.

"It looks like they've got sticky cups over their breasts instead of bras," Harold mused. "Is that a Mexican cultural thing?"

"I think it's more of a strapless dress thing."

"I thought maybe it had something to do with the *quinceañera*," Harold explained. "You know, becoming a woman." He watched in silence for a few seconds, brooding. "I can't believe that cabbie scammed me."

Pattie glanced at him. "You're just lucky he took you for an easy mark, that's all I can say."

"An easy mark? Pattie, I lived down the hall from a bona fide drug dealer at Columbia!"

"Listen to what you just said, Harold."

"He *sold* marijuana. He made us call him Big Dog."

"Of the Long Island Big Dogs?" Pattie smirked.

"Connecticut, actually. His real name was Tucker Dash, but he made people call him Big Dog when he was, you know, actively dealing." Harold slapped aftershave on his cheeks. "It was complicated."

"Look at how much Bernie won by. I can't believe it!" Pattie exclaimed.

"Sanders won?" Harold asked. "I guess I should write that down. The boss is probably going to want to hear about it."

Pattie looked at him askance. "I'll turn up the volume." An older man with glasses and a rim of frayed, curly hair was seated uncomfortably before an electric-blue backdrop on MSNBC.

"Oh, look, they're interviewing him now! Louder, Pattie. I'm going to take dictation."

"Dictation?"

"I'll tell my editor I got an interview with Bernie Sanders. He's not watching TV right now; he's in meetings all day."

"That's Art Garfunkel talking, not Bernie Sanders."

"From Simon and Garfunkel? The tall one? What's he doing there?"

"It looks like he's a celebrity surrogate for Bernie," Pattie shrugged.

"Why do Democrats always grab the nearest celebrity to stump for them?" Harold asked. "Do they really think that's who the American electorate is going to relate to? I mean, it's blatant pandering." Harold sat down on the bed. "Unless it's Alec Baldwin. What a treasure." On the TV, Art Garfunkel squinted at the host, an animated, short-haired woman. "Well, I can still take notes. Do they have stationary in the room?"

"Here," Pattie handed him a notepad.

"And a pen?"

"Honestly, Harold."

"Pattie, I was recently liberated. Cut me some slack."

"Yesterday, the people of New Hampshire told Washington that they're ready to see true, progressive reform in this country," Art Garfunkel, significantly balder than on album covers, asserted on the screen. "In fact, it reminds me of when Paul and I first hit it big in '65 with the 'Sound of Silence' record. People told us then they were hungry for substance in their pop music."

"He has a nice speaking voice," Harold commented. "Very gentle."

"No, yeah, Paul wrote that one," Garfunkel sighed. "No, I tended to contribute in other ways. The high harmonies, for example. Lots of the high harmonies."

"Honey, did he do anything after Simon and Garfunkel?" Pattie asked. "I don't feel like I've seen him anywhere."

"I like that Bernie is very upset by the gap between the rich and the poor," Garfunkel explained. "I think that's central. When Bernie says, Hillary gave a speech, she got $275,000 for that speech. You got to give a very good speech to earn that money."

"Did they sing 'Monday Monday'?" Harold asked. "That would be a good headline. 'Art Garfunkel, famous singer of 'Monday, Monday,' attacked Hillary Clinton's paid speeches."

"No, dear," Pattie said absently, turning up the volume.

"Well, where the harmony should come in, for one thing," Garfunkel replied, testily, from the flat screen TV "Should it come in right at the first measure, or should it come in at the second measure? What color should the harmonies have? What shape?"

"How do the harmonies feel when they caress your cheek?" Pattie grumbled, getting up to make some coffee from the miniature in-room machine.

"Right, shape. These are the sort of nuances that only someone with a certain artistic third eye can divine, you see. But, as I was saying, Bernie's winking at this 'we know the power of whoever backed Hillary, and she's beholden to them,' and that's how America works until somebody says, 'not with me.'"

"This is good stuff," Harold said, hunched over the nightstand, scribbling down Garfunkel's words on the tiny pages of his notepad. "Can you check the desk to see if there's any more paper?"

"Why don't you just use your laptop?"

Harold opened his mouth to speak, then paused and thought. "This is the way I was trained," he said evasively. "It's hard to explain to someone who isn't a journalist."

"I'm not sure who Paul's voting for, no," Garfunkel continued. "No, I don't speak to Paul that much, actually. He's not as politically involved as I am. See, I tended to have fairly heady discussions about politics back in my days at Columbia, whereas—no, Paul went to Queens College. No, the one in Queens. Right."

"Oh, a fellow Columbia man!" Harold exclaimed.

"Maybe you could use that connection," Pattie offered. "Reach out to him for an interview."

"Pattie, do you have any idea how many people I'd have to call? This isn't my whole life."

"Yes, it would be exciting if Paul made an endorsement. No, I don't think it would lead to a reunion. Paul doesn't typically do these sorts of appearances," Garfunkel explained. "Well, maybe we don't all need to be recording *Graceland*."

"Do you think he donates? We should check the newsletter," Harold mused.

"'Diamonds on the Soles of her Shoes?' Sorry, I can't say I'm familiar with the individual songs on *Graceland*," Garfunkel said evasively.

"Oh, I love that song!" Pattie said. "You forget how many great songs Paul wrote."

"Well, let me just say, this is only the beginning for Bernie and his revolution. I like Bernie. I like his fight. I like his dignity and his stance. Yeah, right, like 'The Boxer.' No, that was Paul, too."

"I wonder who Karen Carpenter would've voted for," Harold wondered aloud.

"Thank you for having me on, Mika." Garfunkel nodded. "Yes, and if I see Paul. Right."

"Well, that takes care of today's work," Harold said as he mimed dusting off his hands.

"Harold, that was five minutes," Pattie said, opening her laptop to check her editor's changes to an article about the death of the three-camera sitcom.

"I want to get down to the Jacuzzi before the post-lunch influx of preteens," Harold explained. "My *splenius cervicis* is knotted up something awful."

"Maybe you should send your boss a report first." An unread message drew Pattie's eyes back to her screen. "Just, given the primary last night and everything."

"You know, definitionally, I don't think you could even call this room a suite. A real suite has a Jacuzzi tub in the bathroom. But I guess for New Hampshire, it's just an achievement that the bathroom is indoors."

"I think you just found your lede."

"My back hurts from sleeping on that pitiful excuse for a mattress," Harold protested. "You know, when we get back to New York, remind me to get involved in prison reform. That was horrendous."

5
"I Hear We'll Pass Redwood Trees!"
February 28, 2016

"Just think, Pattie! Us, gazing through the glass roof at the stars shimmering in a winter's night," Harold enthused. "This'll be glorious." The couple edged their way down the aisle of the California Zephyr's lower level, headed for the observation deck. There were not many luxury transcontinental railroads left, Harold had reasoned, so it made sense to look for voters uncomfortable with the present on a relic of the past, if those voters must be looked for at all. That the train made its last stop in Emeryville, just a ten hour drive down the California coast from San Diego, was purely an incidental benefit.

"There's just something romantic about traveling by rail," Harold mused as he and Pattie reached a narrow set of maroon-carpeted stairs leading up to the observation deck.

Pattie wrinkled her nose. "Do you smell that?"

Harold shook his head. "I feel just like Cary Grant. The dapper gray suits. Sipping gimlets in the bar car with Eva Marie Saint."

"I feel like a fucking geriatric," Pattie muttered as she reached the top of the steps. The observation deck was crowded with wrinkled, white-haired men and women sitting in boxy, plastic blue swivel chairs, looking out of large windows at an unchanging expanse of frozen brown fields. "Is that Omaha?" a woman asked her husband loudly, pointing at nothing in particular.

"Oh." Harold stopped, deflated, at the top of the stairs.

"Not exactly James Mason and Martin Landau."

"Well, the transcontinental meeting of Bingo Night aside, I'm sure the scenery will pick up once we get out of the Midwest." Harold assured her. They started down the aisle of the car. "I guess these are the famous fields of amber." He bent over to peer out the window. "Or, that is, the fields of mud."

"Stunning." Pattie sighed. "It doesn't look like there are two seats together anywhere up here."

"Pattie, most people never get a chance to see mud like this."

Harold picked an open seat at the far end of the car. Pattie looked around helplessly and meandered down the aisle until she found an empty seat next to an older man clutching a well-worn wooden cane. The man turned to her and smiled.

"Pretty, isn't it?" he asked Pattie in a raspy voice. He was barrel-chested with broad, meaty shoulders hunched by age. Pattie noticed the tops of his hands were tough and leathery, showing signs of old, long-faded scars.

"I told Ethel that we would travel from New York out to San Francisco by train after V-E Day," the man explained. "But she fell pregnant, see. Before we even bought the tickets. Guess I had been overseas too long. So, we meant to go for our fifth wedding anniversary. But I was getting into the stamp business at that time, see? And with two kids at home by then. So, now we're going."

"Uh huh," Pattie nodded. "Stamps?"

"Rubber stamps," the man said proudly. "'100%.' 'Nice Job!' 'From the Law Offices of Waldo Zuckerman and Associates.' That sort of thing. Ended up owning my own factory!"

"Wow," Pattie said, unable to match the man's enthusiasm. The train click-clacked steadily below the halting conversation.

"Problem is now, I have to get up every hour to go to the bathroom," the man confided, lowering his voice.

"Right," Pattie agreed.

"Every hour. I sit down. I get comfortable. *Ding*. I gotta get up, walk down the whole car, down the stairs—which isn't easy, with my legs—go into the little bathroom. Lock the door. The damn train jostles me around so much, and I only packed so many pairs of pants, you know? Then I walk back up the stairs. Hope no one took my seat. Sit back down. *Ding*. The whole way from Chicago, it's been."

"That must be frustrating," Pattie ventured.

"Well, it's better than sitting in Akron and watching *Wheel of Fortune*," the man countered. "At least you get a little culture here."

"Right," Pattie said.

"The high point for *Wheel* was the late eighties, maybe the early nineties," the man explained. "That Vanna White. Woo boy. Darling gal. You'd just tune in every night to see what outfit she had on. Those sequins. Loved those sequins."

"Uh huh. I think my husband is calling me." Pattie stood up.

"Uh huh?" the man asked. "Pleasure to meet you." Pattie nodded as she strode toward the end of the car, where Harold was chatting with an elderly woman.

"And you say he never won the color television set?" Harold enunciated loudly, for the woman's benefit. She was dressed in a white loose-knit sweater, dotted with ambiguous stains, bright blue pants, and wide-soled New Balance tennis shoes.

"Never." The woman shook her head, her face set in a permanent grimace. "Fifty-two years. Every May, we'd go to the company picnic. Alvin Watkins won it twice. Twice! Of course, his daughter ended up going to Swarthmore, so you know, they were a sharp family. Charles was so narrow. Stared straight ahead. Had blinders on, like a mule."

"Oh, thank God," Harold muttered as he looked up to see Pattie. "I mean, thank God he finally bought you that Pontiac, at least."

"Oh, you had to give Charles such a hard time to get him to do *anything*," the woman complained. "I had to keep after him all morning and all evening. 'The Studebaker is going to cost more to fix than if we just bought a new car.' What an impossible person."

"Yes," Harold agreed. "Impossible."

"Every year, he would say, 'Beatrice, maybe if I have a good year in this old insurance game, we'll take the train out west.' Well, I don't have to tell you, it was *never* a good year. I don't know what he *did* at the office all day."

"Horrible," Harold said.

"But then," Beatrice said, brightening, "they discovered the cancer too late for anything but palliative care. And here I am." She inhaled slowly and serenely. "Oh, there's so much to see. I hear we'll pass redwood trees."

"And I hear they're as tall as skyscrapers," Pattie chimed in, egging on Beatrice. Harold looked up at Pattie mournfully.

The woman wheeled around and surveyed Pattie. "Oh, is this your wife?"

"I sure am," Pattie confirmed.

"You're a good match for each other. You're both about the same height. That's good. You want the woman to be shorter than her husband. Or at least not taller. Not like me and Charles. You know, Charles used to say he was five feet, nine inches," the woman complained. "But he was five-*eight*."

"Ah," said Pattie. "What a liar!"

"I hear the national average for men is five-seven, actually," Harold said, somewhat defensively.

"And Charles had this mole he wouldn't remove," Beatrice continued. "I kept telling him, 'You need to get that mole removed.' And, of course, being Charles, he never did. And then on our second date—"

Harold stood up. "I'm afraid I need to go get something to drink," he explained abruptly. "It was a delight to chat, and I hope we see each other again before California."

"Oh," Beatrice paused, confused. "Well, alright. Be sure to find me later."

Harold and Pattie returned down the length of the observation car, back toward the stairs.

"You cut that woman off pretty rudely, don't you think?"

"It had to be done," Harold said resolutely. "The longer I spoke to her, the more I found myself envying Charles."

*   *   *

The bar car likewise did not quite match Harold's visions of train travel. Linoleum, not marble, lined the floors. The bar itself, far from being done in wood and brass, seemed to be made out of beige vinyl and polyurethane, and rather than being dimly lit, standard-issue Amtrak bulbs made the car an unmysterious, clinical yellow. The entire room appeared is if it were designed to be hosed down on a regular basis. A haggard woman wearing a black straw hat and fake pearls sat hunched over a 24-ounce can of Miller High Life in a booth in the back corner of the car.

"Finally, a place that serves both alcoholic beverages and methadone," Pattie said.

"Pattie, once we get to San Diego, we'll be sipping margaritas on a rooftop, gazing at a gorgeous Pacific sunset," Harold reassured her, squeezing her hand. "Although this is certainly different than in the movies." They sat down on plastic stools with cracked seats.

"Señorita!" Harold called to the bartender. A slight Indian woman looked up from her Sudoku puzzle.

"Two gin gimlets, if you please," he asked cheerfully. "Like Cary Grant," he explained to Pattie.

"We have Miller High Life," the bartender said simply.

"Hmm," Harold thought aloud. "No cocktails to speak of, then? We're sort of having a bit of a celebration."

"We have Budweiser Lime-a-Rita."

"What on *earth* is that?" Pattie whispered to her husband.

"Something that state school graduates drink out of cans," Harold whispered back.

"It's part margarita, part beer," the bartender explained. "Budweiser is the official margarita partner for Amtrak in 2016," she added rotely.

"Well, shoot, Pattie, we're on vacation. Go with the devil you don't know. Two Lime-a-Ritas."

"I guess it's kind of half a cocktail," Pattie reasoned. "Half cocktail, half fermented bathwater."

The bartender dropped two small, clear plastic cups in front of Harold and Pattie, opened two cans of Lime-A-Rita, and poured them for the couple.

"Excuse me, but do you happen to have any glassware that I wouldn't normally use to rinse and spit with?" Harold asked. The bartender looked at him. Seconds passed. "I see," Harold smiled uncomfortably. "No, this works. Disposable." He and Pattie slowly and silently drank their Lime-A-Ritas.

"I taste the lime," Pattie offered. "And hints of disinfectant." Harold said nothing. The smile on his face slowly withered.

The woman in the back corner booth suddenly snapped up straight in her seat, coughing to dislodge a wad of phlegm. "Men make fantastic liars," she muttered nervously to the car. "If you like curvaceous women, you should support them." Harold and Pattie looked around. The bartender continued her Sudoku, and the woman leaned against the window and sighed.

"I thought the views would be better," Harold admitted. "Maybe when we get out to Big Sky Country."

"This train doesn't go anywhere near Montana," Pattie reminded him. Harold reached into his jacket's inner pocket, pulled out the *California Zephyr* map he had taken in Chicago, and studied it.

"Well, I guess we can see the sky anywhere," he shrugged. "It's only a few more days." He and Pattie continued to drink slowly in silence. "It would be nice to get out and stretch in the fresh air, though, wouldn't it?"

"By the way," Pattie continued. "I had to transfer some money out of savings to pay for the train tickets."

"You didn't use the credit card?" Harold asked. "Pattie, think of the miles we could've earned."

"We've reached our limit on that card, Harold," Pattie said. "On all three cards, actually."

"And I didn't even get miles at the police station," Harold groaned.

"Apparently renting and crashing two sports cars adds up," Pattie sniffed.

"They really undersold the insurance," Harold complained. Pattie looked askance. Harold sighed loudly. "These Lime-a-Ritas are not very good."

They sat in silence. The train rattled down the tracks. The sun was setting, and traces of pink permeated the cloud cover. Pattie watched the telephone wires out the window as they traced parabolic slopes, punctuated by slender dark poles.

As the couple were about to finish their drinks, or at least decide that they could bear no more of them, the bar car's sliding doors opened, and the man Pattie had spoken to earlier walked in with an older, expansive woman, whom Pattie assumed to be his wife.

"Oh, hi, again, little lady." The man lumbered over to the bar and sat down two seats from Pattie, his wife sitting beside him. Harold leaned forward to get a good look at the newcomers.

"Honey!" the man called to the bartender. "Two Miller High Lifes!"

"Jesus, they *drink* those," Harold whispered to Pattie.

"You know, I don't think I got your name earlier," the man said to Pattie. "I'm Al, Al Deevers. This is my wife, Ethel."

"Pattie," Pattie said, extending her hand. "This is my husband, Harold."

"Mmf," Harold said, swallowing. "Sorry, I had a mouthful of this Lime-a-Rita. Harold." Al Deevers stared judgmentally at him.

"That's a fancy drink for a fancy boy," Al chuckled. "Nice clothes." Harold glared at him.

"Are you from Chicago?" Ethel asked.

"No, New York," Pattie replied. "And Al said you're from Akron?"

"Yes, just outside Akron," Ethel said. "Streetsboro, Ohio."

"You may have heard of it," Al wheezed, leaning toward Harold, "from the famous goiter prevention iodized salt experiments." Ethel beamed.

"Makes me a bit embarrassed to just be from New York," Harold chuckled.

"Well there, Harold from New York, what is it you do for a living?" Al asked crustily.

"I'm a journalist," Harold smiled.

"A journalist!" Ethel exclaimed. "Do you write for the *Enquirer*? I just can't believe what that Kenny Rogers did to his mistress. His songs are so *catchy*." She shook her head sadly, then immediately perked back up. "Anyway, journalism—how glamorous."

"Glamorous," Al snorted, taking a sip from his Miller High Life. "That's certainly one word for it."

"Well," Harold began, eyeing Al, "it *can* be glamorous, but don't let Hollywood fool you. It's a lot of hard work. Not a job for anyone afraid of late nights at the office, battling the tyranny of the blank page." Pattie choked on her Lime-a-Rita. Harold glanced at her and straightened in his seat. "And Al, what did you do?"

"I was telling Pattie here about my days in the stamp business," Al said proudly. "Got my start in 1946 as a salesman, see, and eventually got enough contacts and saved up enough money to go into business for myself. Bought a controlling interest in a factory. Summer of '74. We had a big order of 'Nice Job!' stamps. Rush job. Back to school sales, see. What a madhouse. Can't say I don't miss it, though." He tapped his cane against the countertop. "A real way for a man to earn a dollar, *building* something," he declared, looking at Harold.

"Sort of the Gustave Eiffel of rubber stamps," Harold smirked. "Where would our nation be without the great classroom accessories industry?"

"Harold," Pattie warned.

"Bought myself a few Cadillacs that way," Al said testily. "And it wasn't always easy. When the recession hit, the factory closed. The Chinese introduced a line of animal puns that became very popular. And they made them so cheap! 'Toad-ally fantastic.' We couldn't compete with that."

Harold leaned closer to Pattie. "Sadly freeing up more time for such undesirable activities as counting past a hundred and using polysyllabic words," he whispered, not quite softly enough.

"And did all that book learning ever teach you how to swing a baseball bat or use a saw?" Al asked. His eyes took on a steely glare.

"Al, *please*," Ethel demanded.

"I was always more focused on higher pursuits." Harold shrugged.

Al lifted himself up from his plastic stool and peered down at Harold. "*Higher* pursuits? Listen, mister, there's nothing low about providing for your missus and the kids with an honest day's work. Maybe in New York City, all of you reporters are too busy drinking *Lime-A-Ritas* and trying out different ways to go to bed together, but where I come from, a man is a man if he brings home the bacon for his old lady at the end of the day."

"Hey, I can provide for my wife just fine, thank you very much."

"Well," Pattie interjected.

"Well, granted, it's more of a two-income household, with, you know—in a metropolitan area—it helps if your wife has something of a nest egg—"

"So you're a freeloader? Your wife could walk tomorrow, and where would you be? All dressed up in your fancy shirt with nowhere to drink your coconut margaritas?"

"Actually, this is more of a lime-flavored beer product that—"

"Tell you what," Al said, slapping the bar counter. "We'll see who's the man around here. We'll see who's the better husband, "

"Ah, we're going to have a listening contest?" Harold smiled.

"We're going to arm-wrestle, son," Al challenged.

"*We-ll!*" Harold laughed nervously. "It's a battle of upper body strength you seek, is it? I should warn you, I was coxswain on the Columbia crew team. Yes, sir, pushing those oars."

"The coxswain doesn't row," Al challenged. "He just sits there and calls things out."

"Well, I had to go to most of the dry-land workouts, nevertheless," Harold protested. "Not the gym days, sure, and Wednesday evenings, the literary magazine reviewed poetry submissions, but I did my fair share of lunges."

"This is gonna be a walloping," Al chuckled.

"Is it?" Harold asked defensively. "How would you like to make this competition of ours a little more interesting?"

"You gonna take off your shirt and do a little dance you learned in New York?"

"I'm going to bet you. Fifty dollars."

"Harold, our savings," Pattie said impatiently.

"Twenty dollars!" Harold corrected.

"You're on," Al agreed. "Gonna buy me a few Miller High-Lifes with my winnings."

"Or I could just stick a cup out of the window and collect run-off from the train's air conditioners," Harold offered.

"Alright, put 'er up," Al challenged. He carefully hoisted himself up with his cane, teetered down the length of the bar, and placed his elbow on the bar counter, extending his hand. Harold rose, rolled up his shirtsleeves, breathed on his hands, rubbed them together, and made a "*huh!*" sound. He walked down the bar and sat down, resolutely, across from Al, cracking the plastic stool. Then he stood back up and began stretching his arms. The bartender turned her newspaper over and began filling in the crossword.

"Really, I can't believe these two," Ethel hissed to Pattie.

"Yeah," Pattie agreed, watching Harold swing his arms around like a baseball player preparing for an at-bat. "They're morons."

"Oh, don't talk to me about fools," Ethel laughed. "You know, there's a woman in my book club who never reads the book. Not a single time! She comes for the conversation and the pastries. And she thinks we don't notice that she never has anything to say!"

"We have the exact same woman in my book club in New York," Pattie laughed. "Only in her case, she comes for the white wine!"

"The only time she talks, it's to say she agrees with what someone else already said. Like clockwork. One week, I should leave the pastries at home. I bet you she won't be back again after that."

"Probably not!" Pattie and Ethel chuckled. "You know, it's funny how some things are just universal," Pattie mused.

"It sure is," Ethel agreed. "The whole reason I did the book club in the first place is to try to educate myself a little."

"Of course!"

"I like to get a little culture wherever I can," Ethel continued. "You know, I got pregnant right after Al got back from the war. In those days, women in my town didn't have any use for college. We had a little window during the war, actually. But once all the men came back—well, I don't have to tell you. You're lucky you grew up when you did."

"Oh, the book club is a great idea," Pattie enthused. "It's important to get out and keep learning. I try to go to a museum, or to a reading or a play, as often as I can. It keeps me feeling human."

"Oh, I know exactly what you mean!" Ethel gushed. "Last month, the girls and I took a day trip to Cleveland and ended up seeing the Rock & Roll Hall of Fame. Now, I didn't really understand all of that when it was happening, but oh, the costumes! You wouldn't believe how tiny some of those singers were."

"I bet," Pattie laughed.

"And I try to stay active in my town," Ethel added. "You can learn so much just by getting together with your neighbors and sharing ideas."

"I know what you mean."

"Why, just last week at my meeting, our neighbor, Dale, was explaining how there was thermite found in the debris at Ground Zero. You know, 9/11? On some of the news footage you can see something burning very hot, like thermite. Now, kerosene doesn't burn like that. That's what Al says, and Al knows a thing or two about kerosene."

Pattie paused. "I'm sorry?"

"If someone were going to heat ten floors evenly enough to collapse straight down on themselves, it'd take more than just some big slosh of fuel all over the place," Ethel tutted. "I'm not saying the Twin Towers wouldn't have fallen, mind you. I'm only saying they wouldn't have fallen the way they did, and certainly not to complete destruction."

Pattie stared at her new companion.

"Now," Ethel continued brightly, "the next thing is, a building collapse of this type would have had its metal and material examined for years. All the emails Dale forwards me point this out. This steel was hauled out and re-purposed as quickly as possible. That looks a bit queer, doesn't it? Especially when the government provided no proof that the hijackers were ever aboard the aircraft, never identified any of the aircraft, *and* refused to release their computer models to the public?"

"Uh huh," Pattie said blankly.

"Do they have nuts here? I like something to snack on," Ethel asked.

"I think I saw a couple, yeah."

At the other end of the bar, Harold finally sat back down on the bar stool and grabbed Al's hand. Al immediately pushed Harold's arm backward onto the counter. Harold yelped.

"Twenty dollars, Mister Media Man," Al smirked, extending his other hand.

"Bad day for arm-wrestling," Harold complained, reluctantly reaching for his wallet. "My carpal tunnel was acting up. That was the problem."

"Sure, fella. The money."

"There was never any problem with my upper body strength at Columbia," Harold explained as he counted out one-dollar-bills.

"Now, you just sat in the boat and yelled," Al said, getting impatient.

"Yes, but it takes a great deal of fortitude to be so compelling," Harold countered. "Next time we ride the *California Zephyr*, I'll challenge you to a shouting contest. Then we'll see." Harold reluctantly handed Al the money.

Pattie excused herself from her conversation with Ethel and walked over to tend to Harold, who was furtively massaging his bicep.

"Did the alternate coxswain workout regimen inadequately prepare you for this?" she asked.

"*Alternate* coxswain?" Al laughed. "I'm impressed you lasted as long as you did!"

"Yes, well, the main coxswain contracted mono when he came back from studying abroad junior year, so I filled in quite a bit."

"Pleasure doing business with you." Al tipped his cane at the couple. "Ethel, darling, you about ready to go?"

"Oh, do we have to?" Ethel, who appeared to have been talking to the bartender, pleaded.

"Let's get back to the observation car. I think we may be coming up on Nebraska soon." Al helped Ethel off of the bar stool, and the pair slowly inched their way up the steps toward the observation car, both seeming to balance their weight on Al's cane.

Pattie stared at the floor, her mouth slightly open in thought. "So in the last half-hour, we spent forty dollars on arm-wrestling and Lime-a-Ritas."

"What's more valuable, Pattie, money or my pride?"

"I don't know. How much do divorce lawyers usually cost?"

"So we lost $20. We'll make it up in California!"

"How on earth do you figure that?"

"We'll be driving down the 101, remember? Surely, we'll stop in Solvang on our way down to San Diego. It's a kitschy little Danish village. It's in all the guidebooks."

"And of course, Solvang pays people to stop there."

"No, silly, they'll have free parking. If we stop there for lunch, that's twenty dollars on parking saved right there. See? It all comes out in the wash."

"Free parking," Pattie challenged.

"It's Danish; everything will be free. If we had a baby in Solvang, we could even get free babysitting while we're there, too. You know, a little time for *mor og far* to explore the windmill replicas."

"Maybe they'll offer some socialized mental health services, as well."

"Of course," Harold said cheerily, not listening. "And after Solvang...San Diego! We'll see the famous San Diego seals, sunning themselves on the white sand beaches." They sat in the bar car watching the unchanging plains while the last hints of daylight dwindled. Harold's phone rang.

"Hello? Oh, hello, sir." Harold put his hand over the receiver and turned to Pattie, "Shh, it's my editor!" Pattie, who hadn't said anything in several minutes, began to protest, but Harold raised his eyebrows and clenched his teeth. Pattie shrugged and quietly shifted over a seat, peering over at the bartender, who was still working on her crossword puzzle. Harold put the phone back to his ear. "Yes, sir, I'm just on the trail in Ohio, the swing state. Yes, sir, famous Ohio, home to the stamp factories of America."

"Gene Kelly," Pattie suggested to the bartender, who looked up, smiled politely, and did not write the actor's name into 32-across.

"It's a real cross-section of America here, sir," Harold continued with false brightness. "I'm talking to the Rust Belt voters who have been left behind by the twenty-first century. And the twentieth, not to put too fine a point on it."

"Weiner Dog," Pattie said, pointing to 8-down on the puzzle. The bartender nodded silently and filled in the answer.

"Yes, well, the mood I'm getting here is, uh, 'getting left behind.' You know. Other states sort of getting out ahead of Ohio. Hitting their growth spurts first, as it were. Making out with the girl states in the back corners of the dance while Ohio is sort of standing by the punch bowl, telling jokes. No, sir, that's a joke. A humorous extended metaphor to explain—okay, well, it'll be clearer in tonight's dispatch. No, of course there'll be a dispatch tonight. Just like every other night. Really? You've only gotten two or three dispatches this whole time? Huh. That's very odd, sir."

"Asteroid belts," Pattie whispered, grinning.

"How's that? Oh, no, sir, I've been staying in Ohio for a good three or four days now. Yes, at the Holiday Inn Cincinnati. Well, you know, I don't like to waste too much company money, sir. Huh. An expense report for two Amtrak tickets? Well, sir, between you and me, the Ohioans are not very bright. Perhaps they just mislabeled the receipt."

"Summertime Blues." The bartender shooed Pattie away.

"Dinner charges for two, sir? Every night? Well, restaurants aren't what they used to be, either. I had some crab cakes in Boston that you'd think were all filler. 'Jumbo Lump' is supposed to—no, well, I eat a lot, sir. No, yes, two entrees and two glasses of wine every night. Yes. Obviously, I have a problem, sir. No, actually, the flatbread was an appetizer, sir. Yes, just a little something after a long day in the Mall of America. So the expense reports are itemized like that, are they? Interesting. No, no, just curious."

"Creole," Pattie said, craning her neck to get a better view of the paper.

"And the paper won't accept that charge, either, then? No, sir. It's only that it would've been nice to hash out these rules beforehand, is all. Uh huh. Well, how about the paper pays for half the suite at the Des Moines Des Luxe, and I pick up all the room service? What about room service and the charges for the sauna? No, the in-room guest handbook did *not* make it clear that the sauna was available only for a fee. Oh, it *is* outrageous sir. These guests are paying good money. No, in fact, sir, if you wouldn't mind making those same points to the manager. Well, regardless of who pays for it, it's a moral issue."

"Decimal." The bartender gave Pattie a thumbs up.

"Sir? If I could actually make one addition to the latest expense report. Yes, I need to add a twenty dollar cash payment. Well, sir, I've been taking the pulse of America on the train—I mean, in Cincinnati— but one of the people I spoke to was a bit of a gambler, a tough customer. Well, sometimes a reporter has to get his hands dirty, I don't have to tell you. I think we both remember the dry-cleaning bills I was reimbursed for after the D Train story."

"Medusa." Pattie tried to pull the paper closer to her, but the bartender moved further down the bar.

"Ah yes, the Garfunkel interview! Yes, sir. That one was a real get. Well, you know, he's a surrogate for Sanders these days. As soon as I found out he's a fellow Columbia alumnus, I pulled a few strings to get in touch with him and make that interview happen. Anything for the story, sir. How's that? Well, word on the beat is that Sanders has been making a surprising push. Oh, you've heard? Well, um, especially in California. Yes. I hear he's going to make quite the surge in California. I was thinking I would stay out west through the California primary, so I could really catch the action in the key California battlegrounds, like San Francisco and Solvang and San Diego. You know, the tipping points. Solvang, sir. It's a Danish village. Oh, it's a paradise of social engineering, sir."

"Queen of *mean*," Pattie said slowly, enunciating the words for clarification. The bartender nodded, realizing her earlier mistake.

"Alabama, sir? But that's so far from California. Oh, I see. Yes. And you're certain my expertise wouldn't be better served in a more contentious primary, like California's? Well, I guess we're looking at different polls, sir. Sorry? You hope the Alabama story will be written to a higher standard? Higher than what? Well, *you* try getting John Kasich to talk about something other than cured meats. No, no, that's making fun of John Kasich, sir. Yes, no, I'm sure if someone could, it would be you. Of course, sir. No, Alabama it is. Well, I think I can be there in about six or seven days, sir. Oh. No, no, tomorrow is fine. Right, what else would I be doing, exactly. And who have you arranged for me to meet with? A circular man named 'Bull' or 'Stag'? Professor Gates. Right. No, I am writing it down now, sir. Oh good, we'll be talking about race? One of my specialties, sir. In undergrad, I took a number of classes on—ah, of course, an editors' meeting. Right. Bye for now, sir." Harold put down his phone.

"Esau," Pattie said to the bartender.

"The *Times* crossword doesn't usually go with Japanese names very often, does it?" Pattie and the bartender glared at Harold.

"That's a Biblical name," Pattie corrected him.

"Ah, of course, Esau, son of Sam. I'm more familiar with the King James translation, is all."

6
"Just a Little Alabama Humor"
March 1, 2016

"Well, no, no actual rowing, per se. But you've got to have good rhythm. And you must be able to project. Not to mention, you wake up very, very early. It's a specialized role." A chime rang as Harold pushed open a grease-smeared glass door to a Waffle House tucked into the corner of a desolate strip mall. A fleshy woman behind the counter looked up at the pair from the register and half-heartedly waved her hand, gesturing to the numerous vacant booths lining the walls. She wore a black apron and an off-gray polo shirt, her long bangs tucked under a matching visor, fanning her hair out against her forehead.

"And you thought we needed a reservation," Pattie scoffed as the two slid into one of the red vinyl booths.

"What a stroke of luck!" Harold beamed.

"The stupid California Zephyr says they're not responsible for lost items," Pattie groaned, glancing at her email. "I'm never going to get that suitcase back."

"On the bright side, the bag I *did* take had all of those Harry Truman figurines." Harold picked up the plastic menu that was laid out in front of him on the table. "That's two years' worth of Christmases taken care of right there."

"I hope you have room on your desk."

"Buck up, honey! We're about to experience real, down-home Southern cooking. Bacon grease and shortnin' and grits! Like something out of a blues song."

"Harold, I keep a certain *item* in my makeup bag that's hard to acquire south of the Mason-Dixon line."

Harold snorted. "What? A dictionary?" Pattie said nothing and picked up her menu. Harold studied her. "Aren't you glad we decided to drive here instead of fly?"

"Sure, *decided*," Pattie sighed.

"There's nothing quite like being out on the open road." A faraway look entered Harold's eyes. "Wheels on the pavement, eyes on the horizon, America just around the bend. Following Steinbeck's tracks, Kerouac's open highways."

"I remember that scene in *On the Road* where Dean pays 'premium pricing' to rent a Chevy Silverado." Pattie glanced at the shiny red pickup truck parked outside, visible through the large front windows.

"They can take away my airline tickets, but they can't take away my pride." Harold looked at the menu while Pattie scanned the white, linoleum-tiled walls, largely devoid of pictures. In a corner near their booth was a small ad for "America's Waffle House" featuring a rotund, maternal-looking African-American woman with jet-black skin, large red lips, and shiny white teeth, holding a bowl filled with waffle mix. Along the bottom of the plastic frame, in small, jagged letters, someone had etched "HILLARY HAS A HAIRY ONE."

Pattie looked back down at her menu. "I'll just get the grilled chicken salad," she announced.

"Hmm," Harold grimaced. "I was thinking we'd stick with something 'Scattered, Smothered, and Covered.' Lord knows how thoroughly they clean the vegetables here. You could have a Montezuma's revenge sort of situation. Or Stonewall Jackson's, I guess."

"I'm not sure that's what these people mean when they say the South will rise again." Pattie flipped her menu over and studied the all-day breakfast offerings. "Anyway, who said we're going to get the same thing?"

Harold looked up. "Oh, no, we can only order one meal between us for a few days."

Pattie stared at him. "Have I ever told you how proud I am to be your wife?"

A round, bright-red woman meandered toward their table. "You folks ready to order?"

"Are the eggs good today?"

The waitress shrugged. "If you like eggs."

"Terrific!" Harold tapped the corner of his plastic menu against the tabletop. "Cheese-in-eggs it is, then."

"And for me a grilled chick—" Pattie started.

"No, that's enough," Harold interrupted, placing his hand over Pattie's. "Remember Appomattox, dear."

The waitress flipped her notepad shut and walked back behind the counter. Pattie scowled at Harold. She picked up her menu and resumed studying it, blocking her face from view.

"You'll be thanking me in a few hours when there isn't a hole in your colon the size of the Louisiana Purchase."

The chime on the front door rang again. Harold peered over his shoulder to see a bloated man wearing a Norfolk-Virginia Beach sweatshirt and cargo jeans and his shorter, but similarly proportioned wife, amble into the diner. The wife exchanged a familiar wave with the stout woman behind the counter as they took the booth bordering Harold and Pattie's. A doughy boy with a red, tired face and a plain white T-shirt draped down to his knees slammed open the door and ran to the booth to join his parents, followed closely by a young girl wearing a sequin halter top and a miniskirt.

"Auburn's finest," Pattie murmured.

"Can you imagine not only paying money to go to Norfolk-Virginia Beach, but being so proud of the fact that you buy a sweatshirt to advertise it?" Harold whispered. Pattie snickered.

"So Ashley and Craig are getting married on Saturday morning, now, 'stead of Sunday," the woman said. "Four months in and she isn't showing yet, but you can't blame them for wanting to do it as soon as they can."

"Poor bastard," the man chuckled. "With that *mother*-in-law. He's gonna have to wait on her hand and foot." His wife laughed.

"Another triumph for abstinence-only sex education," Pattie whispered.

"Honestly, I'm surprised these people figure out what goes where," Harold said, holding up the menu to hide his mouth.

"I'm gonna get the mac and cheese with a side of fries," the girl announced.

"Amber, you will *never* get a man if you keep eating mac and cheese every meal," the mother chided. The little girl slumped in her seat. "Anyway, with how fast those two have to throw together that wedding, I'll be surprised if they even have flowers in the vases," the wife continued. "Give that to me," she snapped at her son, prying a black plastic hunting slingshot from his hands.

"And let me just say, Jeanelle is not happy," the woman continued. "Of course, she naturally assumed she'd be the first to marry, being older and all. Which anybody would've thought, since her whole body isn't already sagging all the way down to South America the way Ashley's is. But you never can tell."

The woman spat a wad of gum into her hand and crushed it against the underside of the Formica tabletop. "I saw Jeanelle just yesterday on her shift at Big Ed's Beach Towel Wholesale," she added. "Which, by the way, Amber, I bought you a towel with Princess Elsa on it. Now *there's* a girl with a good figure."

"I don't know what Jeanelle does to these men she spits out," the man shook his head. "Can you believe, Royce taking up with that black woman who dances by the airport, over her?"

"It's an embarrassment, is what it is," the woman said reprovingly. "Not that there's anything wrong with the woman being a black."

"'Course not," the man agreed. "But that doesn't mean, if you have a bloodline, and you worked hard over generations to keep it a certain way—well, it's not so easy to understand why you'd want to...introduce *that* blood, see. After all these generations."

"Bloodlines." Pattie shook her head. "Oh, brother."

"It's like the Hapsburgs with half as many teeth and double the hemophilia."

"Actually." Pattie fished a notepad out of her back pocket. "Why don't you interview them about Super Tuesday?"

"What? Here?"

Pattie cocked her head. "What did you do on the trash barges all day?"

Harold thought. "There are some really beautiful views of the financial district on a clear day."

"The thing about Ted Cruz is, you just want to punch him right in that weak jaw of his," the man at the next table declared. His son snickered as he methodically whittled a notch into the table with a pocket knife.

"See?" Pattie slid her notebook across the table to Harold. "The circumstances couldn't be better. Your paper loves stories about racists in diners."

Harold winced and flipped open the notepad.

"He looks like such a little weasel. Like a shifty little salesman," the woman agreed, as her husband slapped the pocket knife out of their son's hand.

"There's something I just don't like about the way he talks," the man continued, bending down to pick up the fallen knife. "He's always smiling at you."

"Are you going to take notes?" Pattie implored.

"I'm not married to this job, honey," Harold scoffed. "Let's just enjoy the moment for a change."

"And have you seen Cruz's wife? She looks like a hag, too," the woman chuckled. She opened a packet of Splenda and stirred it into her ice water.

"Oh, I saw her on TV. She makes Ashley and Jeanelle look like those girls you see on the infomercials after midnight, speakin' of," the man laughed. He paused. "But he is pro-life."

The waitress brought Harold and Pattie their food. After the couple had forced down as much as they would dare of the fried eggs, soggy and uniformly drenched in a neon yellow cheese approximation, they got up from the booth to pay at the register, meeting the family at the counter. The little girl was surveying her reflection in the revolving pie display case. Harold and the other woman moved forward to pay at the same time.

"Excuse me," Harold said.

"Oh, don't worry, honey," the woman said, handing the cashier her receipt for the meal. "Thanks, Darlene. It was great as ever."

"No, *excuse me*," Harold insisted. "I was here first."

The woman harumphed. "I don't think so."

"I very much recall seeing you sitting down at the table when I got up to go pay," Harold explained. "*Then* you got up and followed me."

"Well, the way I figure, it's not about who got *up* first; it's who got *here* first," the woman said testily. "And that's *me*, pal."

"You couldn't possibly have gotten here first when I clearly have the hypotenusal route to the register. Just take a look at where our two booths are in relation to where we are now."

"Listen, mister," the woman said, slamming the black plastic Waffle House check tray down on the register counter. "Why don't you take the *heypotenusal* route to the train station and get a one-way ticket on the Go Fuck Yourself Express?" She took out her wallet, paid the cashier and strode to her husband, who was waiting in a blue pickup truck outside. She waved toward her children as she climbed into the truck. The boy was kicking a small candy machine nearby, while the little girl picked flowers among shards of glass scattered around the base of a stripped sapling.

"Pattie?" Harold asked. "Do you have a twenty?"

*   *   *

"Thou shalt not covet thy neighbor's wife," Pattie read off a billboard as the Chevy bounced and jostled past farmland down Route 147. Every half mile, the couple had passed a billboard displaying, in sequential order, one of the Ten Commandments.

"Hey, just one more to go!" Harold pointed. "And only 16 miles to the Superior Nut Company, by my calculations."

They passed another billboard advertising Madame Jenna Tell's XXX Adult Superstore and Shower Rental.

"Truly among God's people now," Pattie said.

"The battle for the American soul, writ large in advertising," Harold observed. "Someone should come down here and write a book about all this."

They bounced down the road. Pattie shifted in her seat. "I hate to say this," she began, "but I think we need to pull over at the next stop we see. I had too much water at the Waffle House."

"What was going on there, Pattie? The busboy must've refilled your glass twelve times."

Pattie shrugged. "He seemed so nice. This poor African-American guy. I didn't want to insult him."

"I'm not sure when we'll see another stop, is the problem."

"Hold on, I'll look it up on my phone." Pattie pulled out her phone to search for the closest place. "When you Google 'truck stop', the top three search results are, 'Are truck stops safe for women?'"

"I imagine that question sort of answers itself," Harold said. "Madame Jenna's is the next exit, if you need to go that badly, or you don't have a hankerin' for nuts."

Pattie sighed. "Well, I can't hold it all the way to the Nut Company." She clenched her jaw. "So to Madame Jenna's we go."

"Alright," Harold said. "But, quickly, because I'm meeting Professor—what was his name? The fellow at Auburn. The interview." Harold tried to recollect the man's name. "It's something like Beauregard

Lee Calhoun or Jefferson Davis Carter IV. Whoever it is, he'll spend the twenty minutes waxing nostalgic for democracy's halcyon days of poll taxes and police dogs."

"Honestly, Harold, this is what I was talking about when you had to go to the opthamologist after that run-in on the D Train. You have to do a little *research* before an assignment. You can't just fly by the seat of your pants as though your whole career is the Friday morning discussion section for Modern English Poetry, and you're the only person who's not hungover."

"There are macro people and micro people," Harold shrugged. "A macro person is thinking: *the election*. A micro person is thinking of all the states that are voting on Super Tuesday, like Alabama, and Massachusetts, and..." Harold trailed off. The engine hummed. "Gosh, there sure are a lot of empty fields in this state."

*   *   *

Harold parked their Chevy in front of Madame Jenna Tell's XXX Adult Superstore and Shower Rental. Massive semi-trucks flanked them on either side, hauling Acco brand paper clips and Gerber baby food, respectively. He and Pattie climbed down and stretched. For the first time in days, the sun was shining brightly, and the trace humidity that far south provided a welcome respite from the chapped lips and dry, cracked hands that they had become accustomed to further north.

"It looks like the bathrooms may be over there," Pattie said, gesturing to a small brick edifice about thirty yards away from the main store. "Be sure to note the time for the police report later." She headed in the direction of the restrooms.

Harold stood outside, squinting through the Superstore's double glass doors to make out the details of the neon signs and faded posters from the sun's glare. He considered taking notes while he waited but remembered that he had left his notepad with the New Hampshire state troopers. Perhaps, he thought, it might be necessary to obtain a new one before his interview. It was good to have something to hold during those exchanges. It made the interviewee feel like the whole thing was more professional. Concerned that this outpost would be the last opportunity to purchase a notepad—and, on further reflection, a pen, as backup—Harold pushed open the double doors, careful to avoid the unsettling smudges on the glass, and entered.

He recognized the smell from previous assignments. The walls of the store, colored in deep purples and rich maroons, were decorated with the establishment's more eye-catching merchandise: rubber recreations of genitalia, strappy lingerie, and revealing costumes suitable for infantilizing the opposite sex. Tall metal bookshelves were arranged into rows in the center of the store, showcasing Blu-Rays with such titles as *Look Who's Coming at Dinner*, *Uncle Ron's Mobile Tampon Emporium*, and *Korean Ass-Eaters VIII*. In the far corner of the shop, near a painstakingly-arranged display of battery-powered paraphernalia, were two plastic booths and a small Subway sandwich franchise. Two bearded men in flannel shirts sat in one of the booths, eating meatball subs and discussing alternative routes from Gainesville to Biloxi.

Harold wandered toward the Subway counter, stopping to inspect a mannequin wearing a white nurse's outfit. He felt the material of the skirt between his fingers, shook his head in disapproval, and continued on. He had noted that, with the exception of a forty-dollar specimen that could perform many additional, unnecessary functions, there were no pens for sale in the Superstore. Looking about despairingly, he noticed a pad of make-your-own sandwich ordering slips at the unattended Subway counter and a small golf pencil beside it, glanced around, and pocketed both. It was a minor recompense for being unable to enjoy the free parking in Solvang.

*   *   *

Pattie stood over a dismal metal sink, vigorously washing her hands. Behind her, a group of women called to each other over a chorus of hissing showers. "Fuck!" a woman shouted, as one of the showers abruptly stopped. "Any of you gals got a quarter?"

"Yeah, kicking it over to you, honey." The first woman thanked her.

"Was wondering where you were keepin' those quarters," another woman joked.

"We all got the same storage facilities here!" the second woman yelled. The others hooted.

"You can't take that for granted these days," another woman chimed in, "what with all these sickos being allowed into the bathrooms."

"Oh, I know. It's just awful," the first woman responded.

"It's perverted, is what it is. And they want to just piss anywhere."

Pattie stood in the doorway, revolted yet curious as to where the conversation would go next.

"This whole country's going to hell in a handbasket."

Pattie heard one of the showers turn off. "Alright, I'm gonna go into Madame Jenna's real fast to check out the strap-ons."

"Oh, hang on, honey, I'll go with you. You know, when I was driving through Missouri last month, I picked up one of those Z-680s. Bucked my hubby like a pinball machine. He just loved it."

*　　*　　*

"So, what did you do while I was in there?" Pattie asked as they bounced their way toward the Holiday Inn, Auburn. "Buy yourself some nipple clamps?"

"Pattie, please," Harold said uncomfortably. "You know I have unusually ticklish nipples."

"But you went inside, didn't you?" Pattie teased.

"I needed a notebook," Harold said quickly.

"I don't think you can interview politicians while taking notes in something shaped like a vulva."

"No, no, it's a regular pad of paper. Great price, too. So, do you want me to leave you at the hotel before the interview?"

"Sure," Pattie agreed. "I've had enough for one day. I'll probably go down to the bar and watch the Super Tuesday returns come in."

"Oh, right," Harold said. "I keep forgetting that's today."

*　　*　　*

Harold knocked on the door to Suite 606 in the Political Science building at Auburn University and walked in. An older woman with short hair and glasses slouched open-mouthed over a computer at a small stained oak desk. It took her several seconds to notice that Harold had entered.

"Can I help you?" she asked slowly, blinking up at him.

"Yes, I have an appointment with—oh, what's the name? Reginald Jackson Hatch, I think?"

The secretary stared blankly. "Are you the reporter that's coming today?"

"Yes," Harold said. "I'm with the—"

"Professor Gates has been waiting for you," she said kindly. She pressed a button on the telephone. "Mr. Carlyle is ready."

"Oh, splendid," Harold said, pulling the Subway ordering pad and golf pencil out of his jacket pocket. A heavy wooden door opened, and a husky, middle-aged African-American man with a bushy mustache emerged.

"Harold Carlyle?" the man asked.

Harold looked around. "Yes?" he asked, quizzically.

"Theodore Gates," the man said brightly. A look of confusion flashed across Harold's face. He leaned over the desk to look at the secretary's appointment book. "Harold *Carlyle*?" he whispered to the secretary. She nodded slowly.

"Pleasure to meet you," Professor Gates said, extending his hand. Harold shook it vigorously, his eyes widened with excitement. "Come into my office, and we can chat."

"Theodore Gates?" Harold asked.

"Yes?"

"No, just—right. Great, actually."

Professor Gates led Harold into his office. Large, dusty tomes lined rows of shelves, and the floor was littered with small piles of books and papers.

"So is this your office?" Harold marvelled. "How suitably imposing, yet…humane." He lowered himself into a plush, leather-backed chair in front of Professor Gates' desk. "I like it." He smiled broadly at Professor Gates, who mumbled thanks. "Mahogany?" Harold asked, rapping his knuckles on the expansive desk. "Very nice. Empowering." Professor Gates nodded in acknowledgement as he took a seat, closed two windows on the computer monitor, and spun around to face Harold.

"Okay," Professor Gates said. "So, what do you want to talk about?"

"Oh, gosh, whatever you want to talk about, really. I'm the student, here," Harold offered apologetically. Professor Gates stared back at him. "Sorry, one second." Harold flipped over the pad of build-your-own-sandwich order forms he had stolen from the Subway stand and wrote "Professor Gates - <u>Professor</u>."

"So, obviously, there's voting today," Harold began. Professor Gates slowly reclined in his plush chair. Harold gazed at him admiringly. "Have you done much work in critical race theory?" he asked chummily. "That was probably my favorite area of study, as an undergrad at Columbia."

"I think I may have taken a class or two in grad school. It's been so long," Professor Gates answered. "I only have a limited time to speak, so."

"Right, sorry, I didn't mean to *colonize* your ti—" Harold underlined the word "professor" again on his notepad. "You'll have to forgive me if I'm a little scatterbrained," Harold explained. "I was up late watching a documentary about Eldridge Cleaver's time in Algeria."

"No problem," Professor Gates waved his hand dismissively.

Harold nodded. "It made me think, you know, we really should have a universal basic income in this country."

"It's certainly an interesting idea." Professor Gates tapped his pen against the desk. "So, the election?"

"Right, right, the election. Sorry, I know how valuable your time must be. Especially—I imagine they're always on your back about—well, not *literally*—just expecting—" Harold surreptitiously attempted to fan his face with his free hand. Professor Gates stared at him. "Sorry, I'm just searching for the perfect word. Like, you know what I really admire? How Obama never talks too quickly, because he's so thoughtful about choosing his words. It inspires me to be a more precise thinker."

Professor Gates leaned his head back against his plush leather chair and reached for a thick, hardbound volume with *The Politics of Individualism* embossed on its spine in gold letters, opened it to a bookmarked page two-thirds of the way in, and began to read.

*   *   *

"Excuse me." Pattie leaned over the counter to get the bartender's attention. "Could I get another, when you have a chance?" The bartender nodded quickly and turned back around to face the cash register. Pattie surveyed the other patrons in the dim light of the bar at the Holiday Inn as the news coverage of the election broke for commercials. Two middle aged men, ostensibly in town on business from their attire, sat at the far end of the bar with an empty stool between them as a buffer. They commented loudly on the basketball game playing on a smaller second television, neither addressing the other. At the center of the row, an older, graying man, whom the bartender addressed by name, carefully stacked the cash necessary to buy his next drink, fussing over the edges of the dollar bills to ensure that they were aligned. Closer to Pattie, a married couple wearing matching striped polo shirts were drinking piña coladas. They both held their phones, their faces lit up by the screens' blue light. Numerous tourist guides lay unopened on the bar in front of them.

As Pattie wondered what sort of people vacationed in central Alabama, the wife rose from her chair. "I'm gonna hit the head, darling." Without looking up from his phone, the husband slapped his wife on the behind six times in quick succession. The wife left the bar without acknowledgement.

The TV, returning from a commercial break, was flashing exit polls from Super Tuesday states, accompanied by colored maps of rectangular, red states. Pattie discovered, with surprise, that Donald Trump was outperforming Nate Silver's predictions. She sighed and checked her phone to see if her editor had sent back notes on her piece about the forgotten legacy of *The Bob Newhart Show*. All the men at the bar cheered, and Pattie looked up to see Trump's face above a solidly red map of Alabama.

"Trump!" The man in the polo shirt let out a high pitched whistle. "Taking the country back!" He pounded on the bar with his right hand. Pattie glanced at him quickly and looked back at her phone, navigating to *Five-Thirty-Eight*.

"Oh, I knew he would come out on top," the bartender grinned. "Donny's a winner!"

"He's the only one who tells the truth. That's why," the man explained. "He's going all the way to the White House."

"The White House," the bartender reflected. "Then things'll really turn around."

"Yes, sir!"

"Well, this calls for a celebration," the bartender announced with satisfaction. "Next round's on the house, fellas!" The bar cheered. Pattie smiled without looking up from her phone.

"Isn't this terrific?" the man next to her asked. He had pretzel crumbs in his goatee. At first, Pattie didn't realize that he was addressing her.

"Oh, um, sure," she responded half-heartedly.

"Trump, he understands us working people," the man continued. He slammed back the rest of his piña colada. "Once he gets into the White House, he's gonna give all those D.C. crooks the kick in the keister they've had coming." He slapped the bar counter to prove his point.

"Uh huh." Pattie put down her phone and turned her gaze to the television, tapping her fingers nervously on the counter.

"Here are your drinks!" the bartender placed fresh glasses in front of Pattie and the man next to her.

"Thanks," Pattie murmured.

"You a Trump supporter?" the man asked, his eyes still on Pattie.

Patte sighed. "I think he set himself up to be very successful today," she said emotionlessly.

"Don't sound too enthused about it to me," the man said suspiciously.

"I haven't been paying too much attention to the election, what with work," Pattie lied.

"Too much attention? We got immigrants running all over the border! Obama's bussing them in and giving them free drivers' licenses so they can vote for the Democrats! And you're not paying attention?" He glared at her. "You a Hillary supporter?"

"Ted Cruz," Pattie lied again, eager for the conversation to finish.

"Ted Cruz? That Jew-y looking guy?"

"I think he's Hispanic," Pattie said, wondering why on earth she was bothering to clarify Ted Cruz's ethnic origins.

"Even worse!" the man laughed. "But you can't fool me with that nose, or that dog of a wife."

Pattie turned her attention back to her phone.

"Say, you look pretty Jewish yourself. That why you're such a Cruz fan?"

Pattie was silent.

"Yeah, that hair, and those little eyes? You gotta be at least a quarter Jewish. Melissa!" the man called to his wife, who was returning from the bathroom. "Doesn't this woman look Jewish?"

"Oh yeah! You look like that band teacher I had at Wilson High! Mrs.—what was her name, Rick?"

"One of those Jew names. They're all the same. Goldberg or something, I guess." The man laughed again. "*This*-berg, *That*-berg."

"It certainly gets very confusing when the international banking cabal holds its annual summit meeting," Pattie smiled, standing up, putting down a ten dollar bill, and leaving the bar.

"Kike!" the woman called out.

*   *   *

"So it's like—I don't know if you saw the Charlie Rose program on hip-hop," Harold offered, "—probably the most vital of contemporary art forms, in my opinion."

"I didn't catch that," Professor Gates muttered, underlining a sentence in his book.

Harold coughed. "Um, I'd like to ask you about the mood on campus."

"Oh?" Professor Gates glanced at Harold without putting down his book. "A real question. Good, yes."

"As a leader and a public intellectual, do you detect any sense of—I mean, you don't have to look very far for examples of the kinds of things that—Martin Luther King, you know. Or Malcolm X, or Medgar Evers." Harold flushed. "The way a human being can become a lightning rod or an avatar for a social phenomenon, or a type of hope." He looked up from his notepad. "You know?"

Professor Gates exhaled. "Not sure what you mean, Derek," he smiled politely. "To tell you the truth, I thought we were going to discuss demographic changes."

"I understand, sir," Harold said solemnly. He put down his pencil and leaned forward. "*I'm not one of them*," he added, lowering his voice conspiratorially. "You can talk to me off the record, if you just need to get it off your chest. I understand. This year has been—it's been traumatizing for *me*, and I'm—" Harold tilted his head down— "so I can only imagine—"

"Thanks for your time," Professor Gates said abruptly, standing up. "I've got to get home."

"Do you want me to walk you to your car?" Harold asked earnestly.

Professor Gates took a tweed jacket off the coathook on the office door. "I'm fine. Thanks, Derek."

"Theodore," Harold stood up as Professor Gates swiftly exited his office, shutting the door while Harold gathered his coat and messenger bag. Harold opened the door and followed. "Thank you *so* much for your time and for your contributions. Not only to academia, but as a role model." There was a catch in Harold's throat. "Your bravery inspires me. When I accepted this assignment, I expected to see some ugly sides to this country and some people with hate or fear in their hearts. But, Professor Gates—" Harold rushed to follow Professor Gates toward an elevator at the end of a musty hall. "I am honored, and touched, that I got to meet an American hero today." He reached into his pocket and pulled a business card from his wallet. "Please, take my card. If you ever need anything—if you ever need an ally—please never hesitate to give me a call."

*   *   *

Harold walked back to the rental truck, hopeful that Professor Gates didn't see his car and get any wrong ideas. As he climbed into the driver's seat, he pulled out his phone.

"Pattie?"

"Harold, you are not going to believe what just happened to me. You were absolutely right about this place. Bunch of backward rednecks."

"Pattie, don't be so dismissive. There is so much richness and diversity here, if you dig beneath the surface. Pattie, I just met the most amazing black man."

"Professor Gates?"

"*YES!*" Harold exclaimed. "How did you know he was black? It was the most life-affirming surprise."

"I looked him up."

"He's not just an African-American. He's an *African American.*" Harold waited for his wife to appreciate the distinction. "You'd have to meet him to understand."

"Harold, this couple in the bar started spewing anti-Semitic invective at me."

"Pattie, I'm going to share some of the wisdom I saw today. Model yourself after Theodore Gates. Learn to rise above all of that and achieve your true potential. He's let years of racism roll off his back. It's beautiful. He doesn't let it stop him from anything he wants to achieve."

"Are you on your way back now?"

"Just leaving." Harold started the engine and shifted the vehicle into drive. "Would you mind logging into my email? I need to file something about the interview by five."

"I don't have any idea what you talked about in the interview."

"Well, a lot of it was too painful for him to really put into words."

"Weren't you supposed to talk to him about demographic changes in Super Tuesday voting?"

"Right." Harold's face fell. He pulled the truck off of the campus road and onto a state highway. "Well, just say, 'Professor Gates, a busy African-American scholar, confirmed that demographic changes played a significant role in the voting. Vote totals from many states have begun rolling in.' And then if you could just name the states, dear."

Pattie sighed.

"Well, embellish as you see fit."

"Maybe you want to mention how this string of Trump victories suggests that the rising wave of nationalism and far-right extremism sweeping Europe may be coming to American shores?"

"Does it? Well, it's just a prediction, so no harm in throwing that in. I'll be there soon; I'm near a field. Get it? Just a little Alabama humor."

7
"Mention It Was the Ritz"
March 3, 2016

The following transcript was found within a classified dossier covertly obtained from the Kremlin.

PETROV: I am pleased that we could meet here in the...München Weinerhaus to discuss matters.

TRUMP: Well, I thought you'd enjoy a bit of your homeland, you know.

PETROV: Sure. Mr. Trump, I would like to congratulate you on your success so far in the primaries. It has been most impressive.

TRUMP: Well, I'm an impressive person. That goes without saying. People are impressed by me. Very impressed.

PETROV: Of course. We are very pleased that you have selected—

TRUMP: *All* of me, I might add. Each part of me is very impressive.

PETROV: —Michael Flynn to join your—

TRUMP: Have you seen Rubio? Small guy. Probably only had sex with two, three women, and that's including his wife. Very, very *un*impressive guy.

PETROV: Yes. As we were saying—

TRUMP: Once, I stuck a spoon up a waitress' skirt. Nothing happened to me. I'm a star, Petrov. I do what I want.

PETROV: Our agents have made contact with General Flynn, and he appears to be most amenable to the arrangement we have made. While he may not share our ideological leanings, per se, he certainly has that most distinctive of American tastes.

TRUMP: Sausage?

PETROV: He accepted the cash payments.

TRUMP: Oh, yeah, of course he did. You know, Marla Maples said I had the best cock she's ever seen. Her words, Petrov. Just quoting her. Her words.

PETROV: We must reiterate, Mr. Trump, that it is imperative that General Flynn keep a low profile in the coming months.

TRUMP: I wouldn't worry about that, Petrov. I'm extremely charismatic. You put me on the screen, no one's paying attention to Flynn. Did you get *The Apprentice* in Russia? Fantastic show. I dominated every episode.

PETROV: Yes, we are certain that as long as you continue your demonstrations of...charisma, you will dominate public attention through the rest of the election. The Kremlin is anxious, however, that General Flynn's financial history with Russia not be exposed before the election.

TRUMP: Why? Who'd blame him for being a good businessman? We need more people like that in government. I'm a businessman, and I've done tremendous business in Russia.

PETROV: It might spark suspicion of Russian influence in your campaign.

TRUMP: What influence? This is what campaigns do.

PETROV: That is our experience, yes.

TRUMP: Do you remember when I sold Trump Wine? A very good wine, by the way. No one ever told me if Putin liked the case I sent over.

PETROV: Yes, the Kremlin appreciates your generosity. But it is imperative that you and the other members of your campaign—how do you say it in America? *Throw off the scent.*

TRUMP: Speaking of scents, this sauerkraut smells disgusting. I don't know how you guys eat this stuff.

PETROV: Mr. Trump, we note, with some satisfaction, that you are beginning to break away from the pack in the Republican polls.

TRUMP: Is that a surprise? I'll go down the list. Rubio, probably five inches. Cruz, probably four inches. Carson—well, he's black, but he just dropped out.

PETROV: You easily trounced Governor Bush, who was initially assumed to win the nomination.

TRUMP: So low-energy. I came up with that. "Low-energy Jeb." People loved that. I would say it at the rallies, and they loved it. "Low-energy Jeb."

PETROV: And Mr. Christie, too, seemed to have a rather paltry showing.

TRUMP: Fat guy. I never even had to come up with a nickname for him. I would have called him "Fat Chris" or "Fat Christie."

PETROV: Our projections have you holding your lead through the primaries, assuming no major changes to the current state of affairs.

TRUMP: His first name and his last name are almost the same, too. I could have said something about that. "Who is this guy? He has the same names." I could have said that.

PETROV: With that in mind, we urge you to avoid making any further...obscene comments in public forums. Now that you are the frontrunner, the Kremlin believes that you need to appeal to a broader base. You must begin to appear, as your media would say, presidential.

TRUMP: Of course, of course. I can be so presidential, believe me. Just like that, and I will become the most presidential person you have ever seen. Nobody is more presidential than me, Petrov. Nobody.

PETROV: Excellent.

TRUMP: I just need to go into that debate tonight and set the record straight about my penis.

PETROV: Mr. Trump, we would strongly urge you not to take such an action.

TRUMP: I guarantee you, Petrov, there's no problem. I sat next to Mary Steenburgen at a party. I guarantee, no problem. She can tell you.

PETROV: Mr. Trump, we believe tonight's debate would be the perfect venue for you to turn this new page we discussed. We've prepared a folder for you—

TRUMP: Are these more photos from the Ritz? Thank God someone thought to film that.

PETROV: This is a collection of, how you say, "talking points" about issues important to Russia and America, for the betterment of the relationship between our two countries.

TRUMP: You know, the Obamas stayed at that hotel. That was in their suite. Right in their bed, you know?

PETROV: For starters, when you are asked a question about foreign policy—

TRUMP: It was real thoughtful of you guys to leave eyedrops in the room. It burns when they miss, let me tell you.

PETROV: —It would be good to read this list of Russia's key objectives in the Ukraine and Baltic states.

TRUMP: I'm the best reader, Petrov. I read all the time. Except, I'm so busy. So busy. People need me for everything. Sign this, go speak here, be on this TV show. Everyone wants a piece of me, you know? And then I have to go to bed with the old ball-and-chain, *bonka-bonka*.

PETROV: We have also prepared a statement for you to memorize regarding your relationship with President Putin.

TRUMP: Let me stop you right there, Petrov. No one wants to hear me memorize things. It's not me. Americans like it when I tell the truth. Like when I called Carly Fiorina a dog. They loved that. My poll numbers went up.

PETROV: Mr. Trump, Russia is prepared to release the video you spoke of to the American media if you do not comply with our requests. As we discussed, this would irreparably damage your business interests across the globe.

TRUMP: Listen, no one got upset when I did it in Monte Carlo! What's the big deal about Moscow?

PETROV: Mr. Trump, this would become public knowledge.

TRUMP: Mention it was the Ritz.

PETROV: Mr. Trump, let me present this differently—

TRUMP: Very nice hotel, the Ritz. So many in-room movies. Things you don't even get in America.

PETROV: You see, we have—

TRUMP: What did you call them? Cossacks? Those guys could fuck, huh?

PETROV: Mr. Trump, your telephone calls to Ivanka were also monitored by Russian intelligence while you were at the hotel.

TRUMP: And the statement about Putin is at the top of the first page, then?

PETROV: Yes.

TRUMP: Terrific, terrific. I'll give it a good once-over, Petrov. Don't worry.

PETROV: That is good to hear, Mr. Trump. We have very high hopes for the future of our relationship.

TRUMP: Tremendous, tremendous relationship. I'm a big admirer of the Russian people, Petrov. Those peasant gals you used to put on your Commie posters? Such tremendous knockers.

PETROV: To the point of our future collaboration, we have an operation in the planning stages, as we explained to Michael Flynn, to obtain information from the Democratic email servers. Once we release it through our asset in London's Ecuadorian Embassy, we anticipate that your media will, how you say, "pick up on it," distracting the public and further tarnishing Secretary Clinton's reputation.

TRUMP: You know who you should set them on? Megyn Kelly. She absolutely has it out for me. I can't understand it, Petrov. I can't understand it.

PETROV: I believe you will be very pleased with the information on Secretary Clinton that our services are able to produce.

TRUMP: Are you going to finish your *Strudel*?

PETROV: Please take it as a gift.

TRUMP: Mmf. You ever just want to slop one of these all over a peasant gal's hoo-has? Times like these, I miss hosting *The Apprentice*.

8
"We Were Going to the Art Museum"
April 21, 2016

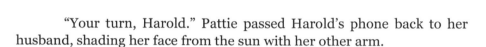

"Your turn, Harold." Pattie passed Harold's phone back to her husband, shading her face from the sun with her other arm.

Harold inspected the word Pattie had just submitted in their mobile Scrabble game. "'Gets'? That's the best you can do?"

"Who's winning?" Pattie asked tartly, sipping an Arnold Palmer.

Harold squinted up at the sun, which was reflecting off the almost-white cement around a lima bean-shaped pool at the Grand Teepee Apalachee Inn at Tallahassee. "I think it's moved again," he said, pointing up at the sky. He and Pattie stood up and moved their chaise lounges a few inches to the left, the metal bottoms scraping the concrete. Pattie lay back down on her chair, slinging her arm back over her eyes. The U-shaped motel surrounded the pool deck on three sides. The open side was blocked by a white metal gate separating the pool from the motel's parking lot, where an aged Chevrolet with faded brown paint sat in the sun.

Harold fanned the collar of his cabana shirt, soaked through with sweat in the Florida humidity, as he pondered his next word. He decided on "baklava" and handed his phone back to Pattie, who quickly typed in her entry and returned it to him.

"'Just'? Pattie, you have an English degree, for God's sake."

"It's a triple word score," Pattie shrugged. She dabbed beads of sweat off her forehead with a towel and eyed the small pool indecisively, its water the color of mouthwash. After travelling to Florida in mid-March to cover its primary, Harold had discovered that there were several weeks before what he deemed to be the next relevant elections. He decided that extending his stay in Tallahassee from two nights to one month would raise fewer red flags with his paper's travel agent than a pair of one-way tickets to California, and despite Pattie's skepticism that proximity to Billie's Swamp Safari was, in fact, comparable to San Diego's beaches, the couple had remained there for the better part of four weeks. From there, he had been filing updates on the days when his motel's dial-up connection was not otherwise monopolized by the divorced man staying next door.

"You know," Harold said, fanning himself and tugging at his collar, "Riley's probably fixed the air conditioning by now, if you're ready to head up to the room."

"You've got a call," Pattie said, handing Harold his violently buzzing phone.

Harold looked at the caller ID. "Oh, it's my editor," he grimaced. "He's probably calling about Philadelphia. Should I let it go to voicemail?"

"I'll pack my bags."

*   *   *

"Look at the flowers, Pattie," Harold admired. The pair strolled up the Ben Franklin Parkway. Clouds were breaking, and the sun was beginning to light up what had begun as a dismal morning. The world seemed to relax with the assurance that spring had finally arrived. Trees with pink bulbs, incipient blossoms, and the year's first green buds stretched out on either side of the wide thoroughfare that led to sloping lawns and a huge neo-classical building. Pattie consulted a map she had picked up at The Rittenhouse Hotel's concierge desk, deciphering a crowded town square filled with cartoon illustrations of historical sites.

"You know," Pattie ventured, "the museum's open tomorrow. Maybe we should just go to the Trump rally, like your editor said. I mean, it's right here."

"If I wanted some mouth-breather to ram his body mass into me in order to make a point about Muslims, I would've stayed for the afternoon feeding at Voodoo Rita's Tallahassee Alligator Extravaganza, honey." Harold pointed down the road. "To the art."

"But you brought your press pass and everything."

"Pattie, you're the one who showed me that video. They pushed that woman right down." Harold shuddered. "Michelle Fields."

"Don't worry, they only assault women reporters."

As they neared the sprawling neoclassical marble edifice, a mass of people came into focus. The crowds formed a vague, snaking line, which appeared to wind around the back of the museum and deeper into the park. A row of double-parked police cars blocked traffic from the arteries that conjoined in a large oval roundabout.

"Those are the museum steps over there," Pattie said, standing on her tiptoes to see past the throng of people. "Jesus, what a crowd."

The predominantly Caucasian masses stood ten to fifteen people across, many sporting red hats and garish varieties of American flag clothing. One man wore a white jumpsuit with bricks traced across it in black Sharpie. On the front it read, "TRUMP WILL BUILD THE WALL" in red letters. In the middle of the pack, a middle-aged couple sat in camping furniture, holding hands and smiling at the others milling about them. At their feet, an assortment of buttons and signs was displayed for sale, featuring such slogans as "Finally Someone With Some Balls," "Planned Parenthood Lies To You," and "Trump Digs Coal."

Three policemen on dark brown horses patrolled the sides of the gathering, cordoning them off from a smaller group of young people chanting and holding large poster boards with the phrase "Trump = Nazi" carefully stenciled in rounded, glittery blue letters. The group only had one megaphone between them, which they took turns using. The current speaker appeared to have diverged from his discourse on Trump to note that society didn't sufficiently honor Berta Cáceres.

"Do you see the way to the museum?" Harold asked, shouting over the din of the crowd.

"Maybe if we find where the line ends, we can go around."

"Well, let's ask someone." Harold approached a gaggle of young men standing in a semicircle on the edge of the crowd. "Excuse me, is this the line?"

"You can just cut in with us, bro," one of them replied. He had closely cropped blond hair, steel gray eyes, and an athletic build, which was prominently displayed by a tank top bearing the University of Pennsylvania's crest.

"Oh," Harold stammered. He adjusted his Brooks Brothers shirt reflexively and quickly slipped the press pass hanging around his neck into his breast pocket. "I don't want to cause any trouble with the rest of you." He shifted his weight back and forth. "You know, every man for himself in this country, right?"

"Go right ahead." He slapped Harold on the back, and Harold stumbled further into the circle.

"Uh, terrific, thanks!" Harold mustered, finding his balance. "Pattie, come on," Harold motioned to Pattie, who stepped forward reluctantly.

"Where're your flags?" another young man asked. This one had an unusually narrow face, as though the midwife who delivered him had overused the forceps. He sat atop a red ice chest, legs spread wide apart, cradling a can of beer. A few stray hairs were cultivated on a face that seemed developmentally unready to grow a full beard.

"We were going to the art museum," Pattie said, testily.

"And then you saw all this going on? That's dope," the man atop the ice chest enthused.

"Absolutely," Harold agreed. "What year are you at Penn?" he asked, nodding toward the first man's tank top. "I went to Columbia," he offered by way of explanation.

"We're all seniors," the tank-top wearing man replied. "Except fucking Ethan!" The other men laughed. One of them slapped a tall, overweight individual on the back. He had thick, curly red hair and appeared to be already under the influence. "Fuck you, Chris," Ethan mumbled.

"I take it you're all the sporting type," Harold said.

"Yeah, how'd you know?" Chris, the tank-topped man, asked.

"You're all wearing basketball shorts," Pattie muttered.

"Birds of a feather, I guess," Harold said, shifting his voice to an unusually deep register. "I was waking up at five am and out on the Hudson when I was in undergrad."

"Ah, no shit?" Chris slugged Harold on the shoulder. "You want a beer, man? Bean, get this guy a cold one!" The man atop the cooler, ostensibly Bean, lifted the lid beneath him and tossed a dripping can in Harold's direction. Harold braced for the catch, cupping his hands. The can bounced off the tips of his fingers as he made a futile attempt to juggle the beer before it fell onto the grass.

"I usually catch those!" Harold attempted a laugh, shaking his hand, which smarted from where the can had made contact. The students said nothing. Harold cracked open the can disconsolately.

"Great meeting you," Pattie interjected. "We actually have a full day ahead of us, so we don't have time to toss the disc around and chase tang."

"Oh, ye—" Harold began, when Ethan slapped him on the shoulder.

"Man, you can't leave now," Ethan said through a belch. Harold's eyes widened. "You just opened that beer!"

"Ah, right!" Harold laughed nervously. "That's a no-no, Pattie!" He straightened his shirt and took an expressive swig out of the perspiring can. "So, what sport do you guys play?"

"Lax," Bean said proudly. "'Cept for Chris, now, 'cause the dumbass got himself suspended."

Chris shook his head. "Dude, she was blacked out. There's no way she could even *remember* what happened."

"You weren't even fucking careful."

"I can't help it if some psycho bitch can't handle her Malibu. The Board's just trying to get all the donors off their back. Going on a fucking witch hunt."

"Gay as fuck," Bean spat. "Persecution."

"It's fucking ridiculous that they'd suspend me for five whole games. I mean, just 'cause of some Asian chick?"

"The whole system is out for guys like us," Bean agreed. "Everybody else gets special treatment."

Ethan belched. One of the other students slapped him on the butt and grinned.

Harold sipped his beer quietly, eyeing Pattie. Pattie, standing as far away from the group as she could, mouthed the word "*Leave*" to her husband. He nodded quickly, then shrugged.

"You know, they won't even hire white guys now?" Chris asked. "They barely even let them into colleges. It's so fucking hard to get into Penn if you're white. It's like, the hardest way to get in." The others in the circle nodded in agreement.

"My buddy Blake said there were four black guys in his starting class at Goldman," added the student who had slapped Ethan's rear. "You just know three of them can barely fucking read. Then the fourth one's probably one of those random dudes who's good as shit at everything."

"Total affirmative action bullshit." Bean crushed his empty beer can and tossed it into the grass.

"When do you think they'll start letting people in?" Chris asked.

"They're probably getting it ready with flags and shit," the nameless student offered. "I heard Bruce Springsteen is gonna play."

"*Sick*," Chris approved. "Everyone's so fucking psyched we finally have a real man running for president."

"Is this your first Trump rally, bro?" Bean asked Harold.

"No, we covered the one at the beer hall in Detroit," Pattie said. Ethan stared at her breasts.

"'Covered?'" asked Chris. "You guys press or something?"

"Er, yes," Harold said hurriedly, placing his half-full beer can in the grass and preparing to make a run for it.

"Fucking media," Bean muttered.

"Well, we may be journalists, but we assure you, today we are here strictly for *pleasure*," Harold insisted.

"Really?"

"Oh yes, we're ardent Trump fans, just like the lot of you." Harold looked over to Pattie, signaling her to go along with the charade. "You know, to hell with Syria. American Exceptionalism worked for us once, am I right, fellas?"

"Sure did!" Chris slugged Harold on the arm, proudly.

"Manifest destiny!" Harold yelled, rubbing his arm. The group fell silent. Chris opened another beer.

"Is that the name of a ship or something?" Ethan asked.

*   *   *

Inside the rally grounds, Harold and Pattie were corralled into the small press pit at the foot of the stage, having displayed Harold's press pass at the entrance to avoid what he deemed "assured violence" in the general seating. At the front of the pit, two cameramen from CNN were running sound checks on their equipment. A third man in a suit, apparently the news producer, spoke loudly into his phone as he paced around the camera setup. "Yeah, yeah, so just run the rally with the headline, 'Trump Rally in PA.' Uh huh. No, no commentators. No, just the whole thing. Right, straight until *Erin Burnett On Top. Out Front*, whatever. We used that headline in Pittsburgh? Okay, then, how about 'Trump Speaks to Crowd in PA?' Yeah, with the ticker on the bottom. Uh huh. Sure, just a ticker of things Trump said earlier today is fine." The producer hung up the phone and looked up at the empty stage, popping a stick of gum into his mouth.

"Don't you think that's tantamount to free advertising?" Pattie asked.

The producer looked over at Pattie, not having previously registered her presence nearby. "No, trust me, we charge even more for ads when we run these rallies," the man assured her.

"My mistake." Pattie turned around and wandered the confines of the press pit, marked off from the rest of rally crowd by a tiny yellow ribbon tied around a row of white plastic stakes.

Harold, meanwhile, stood by the right of the stage, trying to figure out how to record the rally using his phone's Voice Memo app. "Hello? Hello? Testing, testing. Grapefruit." An overweight man in his thirties wearing a Guns'n'Roses T-shirt approached him. "Need some help?" he asked.

Harold looked up from his phone. "Oh, that would be wonderful. Thank you. Wanna make sure everything comes through loud and clear, you know? Like I'm interviewing the man."

"He *is* the man," the other reporter smiled. "But only *Breitbart* gets the sit-downs."

"*Brietbart*, huh?" Harold asked, wondering where he had heard the name before. "Wasn't he on *Face the Nation* a couple Sundays ago?"

"He's gotta throw some crumbs to the Hymies every once in awhile," the reporter explained while, for some reason, going through Harold's email inbox. "But the cucks in the MSM don't tell the truth, so after a while, they're not going to get shit."

"Oh, sure, the cucks," Harold said blankly. "I think I can figure it out from here, thank you," he added, attempting to snatch back his phone.

"I'm not done," the reporter snapped. "Yeah," he continued, navigating through the security check-in on Harold's Twitter account. "The Goldies push their agenda every time. *Every time.* Have you seen this bullshit about Michelle Fields?"

Harold froze. "Seems like kind of a gray area to me," he said carefully.

"Bullshit," the reporter grunted, not looking up from the phone. "She wasn't assaulted. That whole thing is made up."

"Ah, okay." Harold politely reached forward.

"The skypes planted that story to make Trump look bad," the man grumbled, jerking the phone away from Harold without looking up from its screen. "They're scared shitless of Trump."

"Sorry," Harold said timidly, gesturing for his phone. "It's just, I'm due for an app refresh."

"Nobody pushed her. That bitch just fell over. It's crowded in those rooms."

"It normally updates overnight, see, but I didn't get a chance to charge my phone."

"I mean, did you see what she was wearing? A tight black skirt?" The man swiped out of Harold's "encryption" settings and returned the phone. "She knew what she was doing."

"Did you get the voice memos working?"

The man turned to walk away. "Yeah, you're all set," he called over his shoulder. "Cuck."

"Say hi to Rudolf Hess for me," Harold muttered. He spotted Pattie on the other end of the press pit, chatting with a slight young man in a wrinkled blue suit, and he crossed the pen to meet them.

"Even if Trump's campaign somehow manages not to flame out before the end of the primaries, there's no chance he has the messaging strategy and the mastery of Big Data to give him a chance against the Clinton campaign," the young man lectured. He spoke in a high-pitched voice that bordered on prepubescent. His long, tapered fingers came together to form a miniature temple, which he pointed at Pattie as he spoke.

"Look, no one wants a Hillary presidency more than me, but I worry her message has just become part of the wallpaper," Pattie sighed.

"Hillary's policies are a fresh take on tested values," the young man countered, running his hand along the contours of his aggressively sculpted, slicked-back brown hair. The press badge slung around his neck identified him as a reporter from the *Washington Post*. "Think of Fabio Trabocchi at Fiola Ristorante. His primary colors are old Italian standbys, but with that added modern flair." He straightened his glasses. "If you've heard of Fiola Ristorante. In Georgetown."

"Uh huh." Pattie nodded. "I just think, you know, cliched as it sounds, we in the press spend too much time listening to each other. I mean, look around at this crowd."

"*These* people?" the man laughed. "These people won't even know how to find the voting booth."

"I'm just saying, more and more, I'm afraid Trump could win the whole thing."

The young man quietly considered Pattie's statement for a moment, nodding slightly, and then suddenly burst into hysterical laughter, doubling over and hyperventilating into his hands. "*A real chance*," the young reporter gasped. Pattie shook her head with disgust and walked away.

"I thought that gentleman made some really cogent arguments," Harold offered, following behind Pattie. "Think of Hillary's health care plan like spaghetti bolognese. Now—"

"Oh, shut up."

Harold and Pattie settled into the middle of the pack of journalists as the sound of countless generators whirring to life overwhelmed the crowd's din. Behind them, people cheered "Trump!" and "Make America Great Again!" Pattie gasped as she saw a woman swing an American flag backpack at a protestor in a *saari*.

"Ladies and Gentleman," a man's voice announced over the public-address system. "Please welcome television personality and star of the hit 1982 film *Zapped!*, Scott Baio!"

"Chachi in *Happy Days*," Pattie explained to a puzzled, but applauding, Harold.

"I *know*," Harold said defensively.

Scott Baio ascended the stairs to the stage and jogged to the center podium, waving at the roaring crowd. He wore a striped button-down shirt and suspenders, in homage to his title role in *Charles in Charge*. As the rally-goers continued to cheer, he tugged at his suspenders and grinned. The crowd's applause grew. He leaned in to speak as the audience quieted. "Thank you for that warm welcome, everyone. From the bottom of my heart. And thank you, Mr. Trump, for asking me here tonight. Now, are you all excited to hear Mr. Trump speak?"

The rally crowd erupted into raucous applause, some reinitiating their earlier chanting.

"And maybe, before then, I'll sing a little bit." Scott Baio flashed a toothy grin at the audience, then began, in a breathy baritone, "*What was in that ki-iisss? I've never felt like this.*" He surveyed the crowd, beaming expectantly. "*Just tell me what your secret is,*" he continued, waiting for the audience to join in.

Harold held his phone high up above his head. Pattie glared at him. "Just trying to get a clear recording," Harold explained. "Could be worth something."

"My fellow Americans," Baio continued, disappointed, "I'm *proud* to be an American. America: The greatest country God ever created." The crowd whooped in agreement. "But it doesn't mean getting free stuff. It means sacrificing. Winning. Losing. Failing. Succeeding. And sometimes doing the things you don't want to do—including hard work—in order to get where you want to be. That's what it means to be an American." Near Harold and Pattie, the *Breitbart* reporter whistled in approval.

"The Democrats want to change that. They want being an American to mean how many checks you get from the government. How much responsibility you can shift onto other people. How much violence in the streets hardworking, *real* Americans are willing to put up with. And the Silent Majority is about *sick* of this crap!" The crowd roared.

"Now, how many of you used to watch *Happy Days* on Nick At Nite? Or on ABC? Hands together, here. How many watched *Happy Days?* A lot of you. How many wish things could be the way they were in those days? Safe neighborhoods? Everybody had a good job, right? How many people feel that that's slipping away?"

Pattie took out her notepad and flipped to a fresh page. Harold exited out of the recording on his phone to Google whether Tom Bosley was still alive.

"By the way, did you know that the ratings actually went *up* after Chachi joined the show? Hands together, hands together. Who knew the ratings went up after Chachi showed up?"

"Is that right?" Harold asked Pattie incredulously.

"Let me tell you something. I've seen a lot of America in my thirty years in this business, telling your stories. And until Donald Trump ran for President, I didn't see *anything* that brought America together like we did all those years ago. Not since *Happy Days*, folks. Hands together!"

"Did you know Ralph Malph and Richie weren't in the finale?" Harold asked, staring at his phone.

Pattie continued to take notes. "Yeah, everyone knows that," she said absently.

"Why didn't they go to the wedding?" Harold was concerned.

"Something about the army. Shh."

"They were in the army? Pattie! Look at this! Richie grew a mustache?"

"I tell you, Philadelphia, this Tuesday, you will enter that ballot box with a clear choice in front of you. You can either go with the establishment elites, corrupt career politicians who are only in this for themselves and their CEO friends. Or you can go for Donald Trump, a man doing this from the goodness of his heart, who genuinely wants to help. A man who knows how to get things done. A man who says what he means, and means what he says." The crowd roared. The *Breitbart* reporter appeared to be crying. "I can't tell you how much of an honor it is to stand up here and talk about a man that I trust with the lives of my family and the health of our country."

"'Health of our country,'" Harold repeated, looking over Pattie's shoulder as she wrote.

"And now, ladies and gentlemen, please rise and remove your hats for 'The Star-Spangled Banner'." Baio tapped the microphone, placed his hands behind his back, and raised his head. "*Ohh say, can you see, by the dawn's early—*"

"Ladies and Gentlemen," a much louder man's voice boomed over the public-address system. "*The next president of the United States!*" Scott Baio stopped singing and looked around. The sound system began playing the Rolling Stones' "You Can't Always Get What You Want" as a rotund man with a shaved head and Eastern European features escorted Baio off the stage. Abruptly, the Stones' song was cut off and, after a few seconds, replaced by Neil Young's "Rockin' in the Free World," which in turn was truncated without warning and, after another pause, replaced by Bruce Springsteen's "Born in the USA," which, too, stopped playing after only a few bars, and after an accidental shriek of microphone feedback over the public-address amplifiers, the announcer informed the crowd that a royalty-free recording of "America the Beautiful" would now be broadcast as Donald Trump prepared to address his supporters.

The crowd's cheers grew deafening — their stomping feet shaking the earth beneath Harold and Pattie — as a surprisingly corpulent man, flushed-faced and topped by what appeared to be someone else's very unhealthy golden hair, took the stage to a synth-laden, New Age jazz rendition of "America the Beautiful." He seemed less to revel in the adulation than to survey it angrily, measuring the crowd's size and volume and weighing it against some unsettled score.

Pattie gazed up at the figure on the stage with a mixture of fascination and revulsion. Standing before thousands who agreed with his every word, he nevertheless spoke as if attempting to persuade—or at least wear down—some immovable opponent unimpressed with any of it, the crowds, the buildings, the models, the full head of hair. He appeared to preternaturally sense and direct the crowd's energy, his pugilistic sentences bobbing and weaving as he whipped their anger, resentment, and undiscerning bloodlust into a frenzy. After an applause line, he would pause and point into the ether of supporters, shrug as if to say, "that's the way it is," and assess the crowd's response, seeming to search for more in them than they could give.

The man's feverish poetry burned within Pattie's head, placing her in a temporary fugue state. She would not have been able to recall a word the speaker had said, had Harold not been recording the entire speech on his phone:

Well, either you're closing your eyes
To a situation you do not wish to acknowledge
Or you are not aware of the caliber of disaster
Indicated by the presence of illegal immigrants in *your* community.
Well, ya got trouble, my friend.
Right here, I say, trouble right here in Philadelphia!
Now, sure I love Hispanics,
Very proud to say it,
I'm always very proud to say it.
I've done so much for 'em and hired 'em to paint Trump Tower *golden*.
Let them cook at my restaurants,
And build hotels, and do turn-downs.
But do you think that China lets
A mil-yion *muchachos* cross the border
To come and wander their streets
Taking jobs Orientals oughta do?
Well, just as I say,
It takes judgment, brains, and maturity to make
Great deals, really, very great deals—

I say that any boob
Can sneak on over without a wall there, folks,
And I call that dumb!
The first big step on the road
To the depths of total chaos.
I say, first, a bad *hombre* in a pickup,
Then gangs on every corner!
And the next thing ya know,
Your daughter's dating some guy who's here without papers

And listenin' to some big out-of-town drug lord,
Here to talk about cocaine smugglin'.
Not a roll of cough drops, no, but bags of heroin in the back of a van
Coming on over our border in broad daylight,
Right into Houston—make your blood boil?
Well, now, I should say!

Now, friends, lemme tell you what I mean.
Ya got China, Ja-pan, Iran, Russia,
Countries that know the difference
Between a winner and a bum!
With a capital "B,"
And that rhymes with "C," and that stands for China!
And all year long,
All those coal jobs're gonna be fritterin' away,
I say, all those jobs'll be fritterin'!
Fritterin' away to Mexico; look at Ford, folks,
Moving factories out, then the jobs go, too.

Never mind taxes gettin' higher,
Or the roads or the airports, or policemen gettin' shot.
Never mind getting money from Germany
For seventy years, with our boys over there
Without a "thank you" in return, and that's trouble;
Yes, you got lots and lots of trouble.
I'm thinkin' of the deal with Iran,
Bowing to Japan, free trade with China, and ISIS sneaking in here too,
Ya got trouble!

Folks!
Right here in Pennsylvania!
Trouble with a capital "T"
And that rhymes with "C,"
And that stands for China.

Now, I know all you folks are the right kind of people.
I'm gonna be perfectly frank.
Would ya like to know
What kinda awful chaos goes on

With these dudes hangin' around your streets?
They'll be looting your houses, guys with no education,
Shooting folks in drive-bys like cold-blooded fiends!
And *braggin'* all about how they're gonna cover up a gang-rape with a riot
One fine night. They leave the projects, headin' for the subway,
Turning Philly to a *war zone*!
And *hip-hop*, shameless music
That'll grab your son,
Your daughter,
With the arms of a jungle animal instinct.
Mass-steria!
Friends, the city streets are the devil's playground!
Trouble!

> *Crowd:*
> Oh, we got trouble

Right in the Inner City!

> *Crowd:*
> Right in the Inner City!

With a capital "T"
And that rhymes with "C"
And that stands for China!

> *Crowd:*
> That stands for China!

We've surely got trouble!

> *Crowd:*
> We've surely got trouble!

Right here in Pennsylvania!

> *Crowd:*
> Right here!

Gotta figure out a way
To keep the young ones in their choice of school.

Crowd:
Our children's children gonna have
Trouble, trouble, trouble, trouble, trouble...

Mothers of Philadelphia,
Heed that warning before it's too late.
Watch for the tell-tale signs of corruption:
The moment Obama calls a lobbyist on the phone,
Does he give away a piece of the healthcare bill
To his Harvard golf buddy?
Is there a mystery about his college grades?
A check from Iran hidden in the West Wing?
Is he starting to memorize sayings
From Islam and the Koran?
Are certain *words* creeping into his conversation?
Words like...
Like "Apologize?"

Crowd:
TROUBLE

A-ha!
And "Gender-Neutral Bathrooms?"

Crowd:
TROUBLE!

Well, if so my friends,
Ya got trouble!

Crowd:
Oh, we got trouble

Right here in Philly!

> *Crowd*:
> Right here in Philly!

With a capital "T"
And that rhymes with "C"
And that stands for China.

> *Crowd*:
> That stands for China!

We've surely got trouble!

> *Crowd*:
> We've surely got trouble!

Right here in Philly!

> *Crowd*:
> Right here!

Remember the *Maine*,
Plymouth Rock
And the Golden Rule!

> *Crowd*:
> Our children's children gonna have
> Trouble, trouble...

Oho, we got trouble.
We're in terrible, terrible trouble.
Our unfair press and our libel laws are the devil's tool.

> *Crowd*:
> Devil's tool!

Oh yes we got trouble, trouble, trouble!

> *Crowd*:
> Oh yes,

MICHAEL BLEICHER & ANDY NEWTON

We've got trouble here
We've got big, big trouble

With a "T"!

Crowd:
With a capital "T"

Gotta rhyme it with "C".

Crowd:
That rhymes with "C"

And it stands for China!

Crowd:
That stands for China!

Remember, my friends, listen to me because I pass this way but once!

*   *   *

"That's why I never bought into religion," Pattie said as they rode in a taxi back to their hotel. "Too many group activities." She collected her hair in her hands and attempted to wring it out like a towel.

"Right," Harold agreed distractedly, playing back portions of the rally speeches on his phone. "Maybe if priests knew how to work a room better." He noticed that he was locked out of his email and reset the password. "All in all, though, that wasn't *as* bad as I thought it would be." Pattie looked at him in disbelief. "We saw that *Happy Days* guy. I didn't have to do any punching."

"We met a rapist, and someone poured a beer on my head."

"He thought you were Middle-Eastern, dear," Harold explained. He regarded her closely for a moment. "It's something about your eyes, I think."

"I'll keep that in mind." Pattie took the notepad out of her pocket and began elaborating on the notes she had taken earlier, scribbling in the margins of the page.

Harold watched her. "Are you mad at me now?"

"No," Pattie said in a manner that did not fully put the question to rest.

"How about this? Travel agent be damned! Let's go back to the hotel, you can wash all the domestic beer out of your hair, and then tomorrow...San Diego!"

9
"They Have Crudités Here"
April 23, 2016

"That's probably it over there," Harold said, gesturing across the street, "the place that looks like a gas station parking lot, only with more prostitutes."

"You don't know those are—oh. Oh. No, okay. Let's cross further down the block."

Luggage in tow, Harold and Pattie hurried across the busy street to the Philadelphia Bus Terminal. "I just need to stop in at that CVS and buy some sunblock," Harold explained. "After all, that California sun is going to be mighty strong in...San Diego!"

Pattie rolled her eyes. "By the time this bus gets to San Diego, it'll be time to come back to Philadelphia to cover the primary vote."

"What, they don't have CNN in California?" Harold grinned. "They've got everything in California. We'll get off the bus, and we'll see the beach! Seals sunning themselves!"

"I'll find our bus and save us a couple seats," Pattie said, apparently less excited to see the beach.

"Great! Here, take my bag," Harold said, handing Pattie a duffel emblazoned with the Columbia University crest.

"Harold, Bus 1809! Remember!"

Harold smiled and waved a confirmation as he hurried down the sidewalk to the CVS on the corner, making a wide arch by an opening to an alleyway to avoid a homeless man and his dog camped under a blue tarp. Pattie entered the bus terminal's lot and soon found a single-story Greyhound bus double-parked in the middle of the forecourt matching the number on her ticket. She placed her and Harold's suitcases in the bus's undercarriage and climbed aboard. Breathing through her mouth as she entered, she set her overnight bag above a pair of matted-carpet gray seats in the second row and sat down.

Pattie gazed listlessly out the tinted, smudged window as the other passengers filed past her row looking for open seats. What had begun earlier that morning as a light mist had become a drizzle, streaking the glass in acute slants. On the curb, a pierced and tattooed couple kissed messily under the terminal's gray, concrete overhang. It was unclear whether they were waiting for a bus, had disembarked from one, or had simply decided to come to the terminal for a change of scenery.

Pattie checked her watch and looked around anxiously, seeing that the seats around her were rapidly filling. Behind her, three handsome teenagers had spread themselves and their backpacks across a row of seats and were chatting loudly in Italian. An elderly Asian man with urine stains down the front of his khakis shuffled up the bus stairs, clutching a *Playboy* still in its plastic wrapper. Noticing her staring, the man flashed Pattie a crooked grin as he passed, his head shaking slightly with a tremor. Pattie smiled politely in return, then quickly pretended to look for something in her jacket pockets.

*   *   *

Disappointed that it did not carry the Soléo Organics All-Natural Sunscreen that his usual apothecary offered, Harold emerged from the CVS dejectedly holding a bottle of Coppertone and headed back up the block toward the bus terminal. "Bus 1809?" he murmured to himself. Previously unaware that buses were assigned numerical designations, Harold entered the forecourt, slowly circling each parked bus in search of any displayed numbers.

Pattie spotted him from her window seat. The driver had wedged himself behind the wheel of the Greyhound and was warming up the engine. Pattie frantically knocked on the glass and waved, trying to attract Harold's attention. Harold, however, was distracted by a white bus with an American flag design across each side and a handwritten sign in the front window reading "1809 for America!" Although this was actually an invocation of Abraham Lincoln's birth year by the Republican National Committee, Harold, still marveling at the heretofore-unknown mysteries of bus travel, assumed it was headed to San Diego and climbed aboard.

Inside, he was surprised to find that the usual rows of seats had been removed; instead, long, soft leather benches lined either side of the cabin. Dark red carpet ran down the center of the aisle, with tables of snacks, liquor, and M&Ms set out. A high-definition TV screen, broadcasting *Fox and Friends*, was mounted in the rear. Relieved he had booked a luxury bus, Harold looked around for Pattie, noting with slight confusion, albeit mixed with a sense of mild reassurance, that the other passengers seemed exclusively to be Caucasian men who were obviously familiar with personal hygiene. A surprising number of TRUMP 2016 signs were stacked under the center table. A large, red-faced man wearing an Oxford shirt, crisp jeans, bomber jacket, and neatly polished cowboy boots approached Harold.

"Carter Page?" he asked.

"Sorry?" Harold replied, confused.

"Glad to hear Manafort brought you with him. I've only heard good things. I would've been in the Seychelles last week, but I had a gallstone."

"Uh huh," Harold said nervously.

"Not that any of us were in the Seychelles last week," the man winked.

"Is this the—" Harold began to ask.

"Well, listen," the man continued, pulling a cigarette out of his inner jacket pocket and lighting up, "you just sit over there, and we won't say anything, and you won't hear anything. And help yourself to the refreshments. I dare say you've got a taste for vodka at this point." He winked again. Harold attempted to speak, but the man slapped him on the back, turned, and helped himself to the bowl of M&Ms. Harold heard the bus door hiss closed behind him.

He hurriedly pulled out his phone and sent Pattie an email headed, "where are you???" The bus suddenly lurched forward, causing Harold to stumble. A young man with slicked-back hair wearing a blue suit helped Harold onto one of the leather benches. "Hi there, Mr. Page," he said. "Can I get you something to drink?"

"Um, do you have water?" Harold asked.

"Sparkling or still?"

Harold had longed to hear those words since his journey around the country began. "Sparkling," he said. The answer came from deep within his heart.

"Coming right up," the youth grinned. "Taylor Pinkus," he added. "Aide for Senator Sessions."

"Is that right?" Harold replied, taking a glass of Pellegrino from him.

"We met last week in the Seychelles," Taylor Pinkus reminded Harold. "Of course, you were busy and probably don't remember."

"No, no, I remember," Harold said absently. He didn't want to hurt the young man's feelings.

"Rest assured that I forwarded the Senator the *communique* from Mr. Mercer through the secure server, as per Mr. Gorka's instructions."

"Oh, good," Harold nodded, sipping his Pellegrino. "Yeah, we're really happy with the secure server. You can never be too sure, you know." Taylor beamed. "Could I have some more ice?"

Taylor leapt up and returned in seconds with a shiny ice bucket dripping beads of condensation. He grasped the small metal tongs in anticipation. "One cube or two?" Harold considered. "Two," he declared. The phone in his pocket buzzed. He glanced at the screen to see a reply from his wife. "I'm on the bus. Where on earth are *you*?" Pattie wrote.

"May I get you anything else, Mr. Page?"

Harold looked up. "Not at the moment," he smiled, putting the phone back in his pocket. "If I do, I'll be sure to get you."

*   *   *

"What the hell, Harold?" Pattie grumbled under her breath as she read her husband's latest reply: "Got on wrong bus. They have crudités here!" The Greyhound driver jockeyed for the right of way among the downtown traffic as the bus inched out of the city. Pattie shook her head, returning her phone to her coat pocket after adding to a draft of the "I-statements" she planned to recite at their next phone session with Dr. Rothstein.

Across the aisle, a woman noticed Pattie's frustration. She leaned across the empty aisle seat next to her. "Is all well?" she asked. Pattie looked over, surprised by the interjection. The woman appeared to be of Middle Eastern descent and spoke with a slight accent. She wore a maroon sweater and khaki capri pants. "Yeah, I'm fine," Pattie sighed, smiling.

"It is just that you look like Rachel when Ross came to her office with a picnic."

Pattie chuckled. "Yeah," she looked at the woman askance, taken aback by the reference. "Yeah, I guess I do feel a little like Rachel. Although I think the least my husband could have done was send a barbershop quartet over to let me know he got on the wrong bus."

"He got on the wrong bus?" the woman asked, incredulous. "What a meathead."

"I guess it doesn't matter as long as he gets to California," Pattie sighed. "He's so excited, you'd think he were singing 'California, Here I Come' in the Pontiac with the Ricardos and the Mertzes."

The woman's eyes lit up. "So you are going to California?"

Pattie chuckled again. "That was the plan, but somehow, I doubt it."

"Well, if there is anything I learned from *I Love Lucy*, it is that even the best laid plans can end with somebody locked in a freezer."

"We should all be so lucky."

"You know your television!"

"Well, for me, it's a passion and a paycheck," Pattie smiled, "but you're pretty well-versed yourself!"

"Oh, I have always *loved* American television. Ever since I was a little girl in Kabul. I would sit in the den and watch the old shows that came in over the satellite dish my father assembled on our roof. When the school closed, I would spend my afternoons with the television, waiting for my father and brothers to come home from their work. Occasionally, I would wish to go outside and play with my friends, but father told me that the television was my friend now. So, I would sit, and I would watch the *Dick Van Dyke Show*, and I would wait for them to come home. Then one day, I remember, I was watching the episode where Rob thinks the hospital gave him the wrong baby, when I heard many, many screams in the courtyard outside. My neighbor came to get me then, and she told me my father and brothers were now in many pieces and would not be coming home. I remember, because she interrupted the final scene, where the other parents come over and Rob finds out they are black. It was soon after that I came to this country."

Pattie shifted in her seat. "That's a classic scene."

*   *   *

Harold reclined in the surprisingly supple black leather seats. "Did I see that there was a *charcuterie* plate?" he asked Taylor Pinkus.

"Yes, sir," Taylor affirmed, leaping up and striding to the back of the bus, where he spoke to a bald man holding a plate of cured meats. The bald man shook his head reluctantly. Taylor nodded in Harold's direction. The bald man gestured toward Harold, as well, a skeptical look on his face. Taylor whispered something in the bald man's ear, who raised his eyebrows in surprise. Relenting, he handed Taylor the plate. Taylor sauntered back to Harold. "Compliments of Mayor Giuliani, Mr. Page," he said, handing Harold a selection of cured meats.

"Would you mind fetching me a clean plate?" Harold asked.

"Of course, sir."

"And I believe something was said about a fresh baguette?"

"I'm afraid Gov. Christie already made his way through that, sir."

"Sad," Harold shook his head.

"Mr. Giuliani also indicated that his contacts in the New York Field Office are available for a meeting on the twenty-eighth," Taylor added.

"Right, the Field Office, sure," Harold replied, his mouth full of prosciutto. "Tell him I'll have to pencil it in for now."

"Certainly, sir."

"So, there's no bread at all?" Harold persisted. "No pumpernickel? No rye?"

"Unfortunately, Mr. Manafort re-routed some of the food budget to cover the cost of the data team's ostrich jackets, sir."

"I'll have to speak with him," Harold said resolutely, folding a piece of salami into quarters. Taylor nodded deeply.

"All right, folks!" the red-faced man in the bomber jacket called out. "If everyone could quiet down, we got a presentation for you before we get to Pittsburgh and pick up Jared Kushner." The men murmured amongst themselves as they settled into seats around the largest table in the back of the bus. An exceptionally corpulent individual, wearing a suit that Harold adjudged to have been purchased from a wholesale outlet store, picked a bunch of grapes off of the table and began eating them noisily. "This here's Johnson," the red-faced man continued once everyone had seated. He slapped the back of a man who was seated next to him. "He's gonna talk to us about our strategy in the general. Johnson, take 'er away."

Johnson cleared his throat, shuffling some papers in front him. He had a punctilious air, with thin wireframe glasses and a haircut that obviously had not been updated since the early nineteen-nineties. He took a legal pad out of a handsome leather satchel and cleared his throat again.

"Gentlemen," Johnson began, "We've spent the last four years analyzing the data from the 2012 presidential election and developing a roadmap from the trends it shows us to virtually guarantee that 2016 turns out differently." There were a few murmurs of assent.

Harold placed a half-eaten slice of capocollo onto his plate and reached into his jacket's inner pocket for his phone. He opened his voice memos and, checking to make sure that no one was looking, hit "record." Pleased with his reportorial instincts, Harold turned to Taylor, who was watching Johnson with rapt attention, to inquire whether there were any way to get a cappuccino.

"We can break down our learnings into six key takeaways," Johnson continued. "As the electorate becomes more diverse, younger, and further removed from the culture wars of the Baby Boomer years, our party will have to evolve along with it. This means drastically changing, not only our public perception, but also our policy platform— in a conspicuous, substantial way. First, voters are telling us that we need to enact meaningful immigration reform. Our data shows that we risk alienating Latino voters with some of our more hard-line immigration rhetoric. Now, it goes without saying, this is an increasingly impactful segment of the country."

The men were silent; some nodded, while others looked skeptical or whispered to one another. The corpulent man finished the grapes and summoned Taylor Pinkus. Taylor nodded, walked to the back of the bus, rummaged through some drawers mounted to the back wall, and returned with a bag of Goldfish snacks, which the man accepted happily, his eyes twinkling.

"This speaks to our second and much broader point: we must begin listening to minority voters. Nixon's political legacy of law and order served us well for decades, but America was about 80% white in 1972. Today, that number is 63%, and our projections show that that will decrease further to 60% by 2020. Now, some whites vote Democrat, but almost *no* blacks or Latinos vote Republican."

Harold, losing interest, gazed out the window. The bus passed a dilapidated building with a sign reading, "VIRTEOUS CHINA

PLUMBING FIXTURES." He was disappointed, but unsurprised, to discover that Pennsylvania appeared to be covered with the same detritus of abandoned factories and neglected junkyards he had seen from New Hampshire to Auburn. San Diego would be different.

"Third," Johnson announced, raising his voice slightly to hold the group's attention, "gay marriage is here to stay. The American people appear to be accepting the idea of homosexuality at an increasingly nonlinear clip. In 2001, 57% of Americans opposed gay marriage. Today, 56% *support* gay marriage. We have to run on a 2016 platform, not a 2000 platform, and that means softening our stance on gay marriage and our rhetoric on homosexuality." Johnson turned the page on his legal pad. "Now, are there any questions before I move on to the next three points?"

The table was silent. The corpulent man, his head tilted back as he dropped Goldfish crackers into his open mouth, swiveled around to survey the expressions of the others around him. The red-faced man leaned one elbow on the table. "Anyone got any thoughts?" he asked.

A man in the corner raised his hand. "Why don't we just prevent minorities from voting?"

"That sounds more my speed," the red-faced man declared. "Johnson, you're fired."

*   *   *

"Wait, you are *that* Pattie Carlyle?" the woman asked.

Pattie couldn't help but flash a toothy grin. "Yes."

"I love your writing! I bought the online subscription, and I read your pieces as soon as they publish! You are so insightful. I loved your article about *The Bob Newhart Show* the other week. 'Hi Bob!'"

"Well, thanks, Noor," Pattie smiled again. "That's really nice to hear. Truly."

"So do the networks send you television shows before they come out?"

"They do, yes. We call them screeners," Pattie explained. "In the biz." She chuckled at herself, unaccustomed to meeting a fan.

"Oh, that would be thrilling! How did you become a critic of television?"

"Oh, it was fifteen years ago, when you could still make money doing any of this work. The market's completely changed now."

"But there is so much more television to write about these days!"

"We *are* in the Golden Age of TV," Pattie agreed. "Though, if I have to watch another series featuring a melancholic white man with a drinking problem, I think I'm going to blow my brains out."

Noor looked aghast. "Oh no," she murmured, shaking her head from side to side. "This outcome would not be good at all."

"Oh, um," Pattie stammered, correcting, "most shows are doing an ensemble thing these days, anyway." She forced a laugh. Her phone buzzed, and she quickly reached for it. Harold had replied to her earlier email inquiring where he was, writing, "Pennsylvania, I imagine? It's nothing but industrial waste sites and Arby's." "We're on our way to Pittsburgh," Pattie typed. "See if your bus stops there and I can meet you."

"Sorry," Pattie apologized. "We're trying to meet up in Pittsburgh."

"Pittsburgh!" Noor exclaimed. "I am getting off in Pittsburgh."

"Is that where you live?" Pattie asked politely.

"The aunt of my mother lives in Pittsburgh," Noor replied. "She has a nice home. Someone painted a swastika on her garage door recently. She has premium cable. She gets HBO! I watch all of the shows you write about, like *Veep*. You enjoy *Veep*, I believe?"

"A modern classic, I think," Pattie opined.

"Yes. Oh, I am so excited to see my *eimmat eazima*," Noor smiled.

Pattie's phone buzzed again. "Yes to Pittsburgh! We're picking up that Kushner boy there. Was he the older or the younger brother? The kid who hid behind the potted plant and let Trump grab his wife at that Clinton Foundation fundraiser last year." Pattie typed back, "They're *both* the younger Kushner."

"It looks like my husband will be able to meet me in Pittsburgh after all," Pattie said to Noor.

"That is wonderful news! Does he know where the bus is arriving? I am sure my *eimmat eazima* can drive you to a motel."

"Oh, what a generous offer!"

"As long as you do not come over to the house. She is embarrassed about the swastika."

"I completely understand," Pattie said sympathetically

"My uncle tried to paint over it, but he bought the wrong shade of blue, and it does not match the rest of the garage."

"Ah," Pattie nodded. "I had that problem when we redid the den."

*   *   *

"We'd like to bring up Brian for the next presentation," the red-faced man continued. He took a handkerchief out of his pocket and mopped a few beads of sweat off his forehead. "Brian is the founder of The Chieftain Group. They've successfully managed media and communications strategy and advertising for congressional and gubernatorial campaigns since 2006. I want you all to listen to what he has to say. This guy's a real hotshot. Rhodes Scholar. Harvard Business grad. Hates Jews. Brian, you got the floor."

"Thanks, Roland," a bald, blue-eyed man in a blazer and jeans said, stepping up to take Roland's place at the front of the bus. "We have some tested approaches to dealing with the enemy, here at The Chieftain Group. I think we can all agree that these days, more than anything else, a candidate is worried about 'gotcha' questions and media traps."

Harold emailed Pattie. "Goebbels' intern is speaking. Will be at Westin Pittsburgh in about a half hour to pick up the boy who would be king. Apparently they have Westins in Pittsburgh."

"We all know Mr. Trump is prone to certain flights of whimsy when it comes to Twitter. That's one of the reasons why his followers tend to hail his every word. It's an asset. But the media likes to twist those statements, as we know. The worst thing Mr. Trump can do, in this case, is *apologize*. Some of you may be familiar with the Winston Churchill quote, 'Never surrender!' Trump must double-down on his statements when the media dare to question."

The corpulent man scrunched his nose, looked around, quietly stood up, and slowly made his way to the back of the bus, where with great effort he knelt down and began to rummage through a black mini-fridge.

"Through sheer insistence, eventually he will have even the most stalwart skeptics questioning the facts. And then he will succeed, through the force of his resolve. A triumph of the will."

"How far away are you?" Harold wrote Pattie. "They're out of cured meats here, and I'm ready to leave."

"I cannot stress enough the importance of hitting the ground running once we officially move into the general election," Brian bellowed. "The Hillary campaign is chock-full of veteran political operatives, and we need to spring a lightning-fast attack if we want a fighting chance. Hillary's lead in the polls includes voters who should be in our camp. We need to cut into Hillary's lead early on so that we have the living space we need as we build a Republican empire that will last a thousand election cycles."

The bald man Taylor had identified as Mayor Giuliani walked over to the corpulent man, who was eating a thick slice of *Sachertorte* with his hands. Mayor Giuliani whisked the plate out from under the corpulent man's chocolate-encrusted stubby fingers. The corpulent man made a lunge for the cake, but Giuliani bopped him on the head with a closed fist and walked off, retrieved a knife from the cheese plate, and plopped down on a couch in the back of the bus, where he savored the rest of the *Sachertorte* with deep, sensual delight. The corpulent man remained where he sat, licking his fingers sullenly.

"The media tries to divide us at every turn," Brian continued, his voice rising to a fever pitch. "It is a cabal peddling stories that aren't true, spinning facts to suit their agenda. You and I know that in the process, they're stabbing ordinary Americans, who trust them, in the back. To prevail, we must divide and conquer. The lying press won't quit until they've rammed their globalist agenda down the throats of every honest American. And for that reason, we need to be just as aggressive as our enemy. Now, what does the final solution to this crisis look like? It's a world without CNN, without ABC, without the New York *Times*. But until we can be cleansed of this international media conspiracy, we must continue forward; always forward." The crowd applauded. Roland's eyes were damp. He stood up to shake Brian's hand; they embraced.

Taylor approached Harold, bearing a small, steaming cup. "Your cappuccino, sir." Harold nodded and gestured for Taylor to place it on the table before him. "And I heard Roland indicate that there was a *clafoutis* being held in reserve?"

*   *   *

"Most people think the show became too broad after season four, but I am a fan nevertheless. I cannot help it."

"Well, sure, you can't beat the chemistry of that ensemble. And 'The One Where Everyone Finds Out' is as good as anything they did before Chandler and Monica got together."

"Indeed," Noor agreed. "I love the dancing of Phoebe!" Pattie shaded her eyes against the afternoon sun as the two waited in the forecourt of the Pittsburgh Westin, an unremarkable, tan-concrete-and-blue-glass tower claustrophobically hemmed in by other tan concrete structures. The morning's overcast skies had cleared over the course of their ride across the state, leaving Pattie to perspire in the thick, humid air that had replaced them.

"According to Harold, their bus should be pulling in soon." Pattie looked at her phone again. "Though, he doesn't seem to have the best sense of where he is, exactly. 'Off the highway now. Just passed a place that turns rocks into smaller rocks.'"

"Is that a job?" Noor asked.

About to fake her way through an explanation of stone quarries, Pattie was relieved to spot a large bus, festooned with American flags, pull past them up the hotel's front drive. "That must be them."

Inside, Harold attempted to wave discreetly out the heavily tinted window to Pattie as the bus slowed toward the far end of the forecourt. Brian, who had taken the adjacent seat, glared suspiciously. "Jews," Harold explained, nodding out of the window.

"You're supposed to hold your hand straight-out, friend."

"Oh, that's right," Harold laughed nervously. "My mistake."

"Alright, everyone," Roland said, rising again to speak. "The prince regent is climbing aboard soon. Remember what Don McGahn warned us about in Baltimore."

"Cuck," a gloomy-looking, liver-spotted man muttered. He sloshed around the contents of a dark blue thermos and slugged it back.

The bus' front and rear doors hissed open. Harold looked around. The men were forming a group by the front door to welcome Donald Trump's son-in-law, with Mayor Giuliani and Brian jostling to be at the head of the pack. Harold slinked to the back entrance and made his way down the stairs.

Jared climbed the stairs of the front entrance, wearing a dapper blue suit and carrying a leather satchel on his shoulder. "There he is," Roland gushed. "How's the big guy today?"

"Me?" Jared asked, looking around quickly. He tugged on the cuffs of his shirtsleeves. "Fine." He looked down and tightened his grip on the strap of his satchel.

"We have a special guest for you today," Roland grinned. "Carter Page, who's been helping us so much these last few weeks."

"Donald said I only had to speak to Kislyak today, and that was it," Jared said petulantly. "I didn't know I had to talk to anyone on the bus."

"Oh, *no, no*," Roland anxiously clarified. "You don't have to talk to him. He just wants to shake your hand and tell you personally how much he's doing for our cause."

Jared sighed. "Okay."

"Rudolph!" Roland snapped. Mayor Giuliani edged forward. "Where's Carter Page?" Giuliani looked around in confusion.

"What does he look like?" the mayor asked.

"I think he's blond," Roland answered.

"I heard he was bald," another man called out.

"Someone told me he has big bug eyes," the gloomy-looking man grunted.

"I've been personally assisting Mr. Page," Taylor Pinkus chimed in. "He's sitting right over—huh."

"Where'd he go?" Giuliani asked.

A smile of comprehension slowly spread across Roland's face. "Sly devil. He must've slipped off to grab Kislyak in the bar before Eric and Don Junior get here."

"Yes sir," Taylor agreed. "I told him that Senator Sessions received the *communique* that—"

"Your job was to watch him," Roland snapped. "Sit down." Taylor sat down.

"May I sit, too?" Jared asked.

Outside, Harold jogged back down the drive to meet Pattie, who was patiently listening to an animated Middle Eastern woman.

"'What is the show about?'" the woman asked. "'The show,'" she continued, changing her voice, "'is about *nothing*.' 'Well, it is not about nothing.'"

"Hi, honey," Harold cut in. He gave Pattie a peck on the cheek.

"No, it's about *nothing!*"

"Who's this?"

"This is Noor. She knows all of *Seinfeld*'s fourth season by heart."

"D-A-L-R-I-M-P-E-L?" Noor asked.

"Harold," Harold said. "So is that Farsi?"

"Arabic," Noor said cheerfully.

"How melodious!" Harold exclaimed, smiling warmly. "And you're going to San Diego?"

"I am coming to stay at my great aunt's house, here in Pittsburgh."

"Oh, that's great. Are you staying with her for the feast?"

"Feast?"

Harold nodded in what he felt was an inclusive manner. "*Rashomon.*"

"Ramadan?"

"Such a beautiful experience," Harold affirmed. "That's the one with all the candles, right?"

"I am afraid that my aunt does not allow open flames in the house anymore."

"Alright," Pattie interjected, "Noor's great-aunt is just parked around the corner. She was kind enough to offer to drive us to a motel. Your bag is in her trunk."

"Really? Us?" Harold asked. "*But your shoulders are showing*," he whispered to Pattie.

"Come, come!" Noor called. Harold strode toward a decrepit Honda Accord from the early 1980s that was idling across the street. "No, silly man!" Noor laughed. "Over there!" She pointed to a sleek, forest-green BMW parked around the corner.

"Oh!" Harold exclaimed as he slid into the back seat and heard the satisfying tank-like thunk of the doors. "This still *smells* nice! What year is it? 1993?"

"2009," Noor's great-aunt replied cheerfully.

Harold leaned over to Pattie, "Say what you will about their facial hair habits, but Muslims have excellent taste in automobiles. It's a status symbol thing, don't you think? To prove they belong? Sad what this country is coming to."

Noor's great-aunt started the ignition. The Monkees' "I'm a Believer" blasted over the sound system.

"Is this the Harmon-Kardon audio system?" Harold asked.

"Yes, of course," Noor's great-aunt replied pleasantly. They glided down the road.

"One doesn't feel any road imperfections," Harold marvelled. "If you're not doing anything this week, for a small fee, would you be interested in going to San Diego?" he asked Noor's aunt.

10
"That Came From *My* Account?"
May 10, 2016

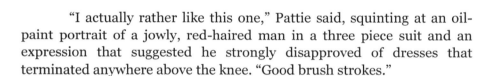

"I actually rather like this one," Pattie said, squinting at an oil-paint portrait of a jowly, red-haired man in a three piece suit and an expression that suggested he strongly disapproved of dresses that terminated anywhere above the knee. "Good brush strokes."

"My art history professor at Columbia called those 'power strokes,'" Harold observed. The pair inched down the line to the next piece, a clay bust of the man from the previous painting.

"You know," Pattie ventured, "I'm starting to think that the Sheldon Memorial Art Gallery consists exclusively of likenesses of Sheldon." She took a pamphlet from a plastic holder mounted on the wall near her.

"Well, it's right there in the name, isn't it, dear?"

"Right." Pattie leaned in to examine the tiles of a glass mosaic depicting a much younger Sheldon, clad in football regalia, scoring a touchdown. "I just figured they weren't quite so literal with the 'memorial' theme."

"In Lincoln, Nebraska, you take whatever art you can get," Harold smiled. "Look at the ripples of his jowl there, Pattie."

Pattie glanced at her watch. "You know, the polls have been open for a couple hours..." she hinted.

"Honey, I'm *in* Lincoln. That's as much work as they're going to get out of me." Harold consulted the gallery map. "It looks like there's a life-size statue of Sheldon in the next room. Supposedly, it's made entirely out of metal from his canning business."

"I'm just saying, you're finally in your editor's good graces with that story about the Republican bus. Why spoil a good thing just to see some portraits of a dead man and go to The Germans from Russia Museum?"

"That museum is actually closed on Tuesdays. I checked."

"All the more reason to get down to a polling booth and interview some honest, wholesome American voters."

"I think we have a read on America," Harold said confidently. "Something about manufacturing, making sure that babies are born to fifteen-year-olds who don't want them, and AR-15's, right? See, the day's work is done, and we still have time to see Sheldon's stamp collection."

Pattie sighed. "I'm a little burned out on Sheldon. I'm going to sit down over there."

"That's an installation, Pattie! Sheldon's favorite sitting bench!"

Pattie paused before the bench, an unpainted wooden board propped up on two matching stands. "Sheldon enjoyed a good sit," Pattie read aloud. She looked back at Harold. "Man is a universe unto himself," she sighed.

The phone in Pattie's pocket suddenly began to emit a persistent series of chimes. A stout woman wearing a red blazer shouted "No phones!" from her post in the corner of the long room.

"Sorry!" Harold called. "Pattie, really," he scolded under his breath. "The signs in the foyer were quite clear."

"Harold!" Pattie whispered. "Look at this!" She thrust her phone under Harold's nose. Her screen was stacked with notifications from Twitter. "dont mess with our boy trump or youll be 1st in line for the camp," one read. "skype ((((globalist)))," read another.

Harold looked aghast. "Oh my god." He put his hand over his mouth. "Is Skype the one where you send money to people?"

"No it's the video—I don't think that's what they mean."

"*Voices down!*" the guard shouted.

"Pattie, we have to go outside if we're going to talk," Harold cautioned. "This is a memorial to a man who lived a full life."

* * *

Outside, the pair stood under the shade of a sapling to shield their eyes from the harsh glare of the midday sun. Pattie furiously scrolled through her Twitter mentions, reading slur after slur. "What's going on?" she demanded. "Why is this happening? I'm not even Jewish!"

"Yes you are, one-quarter" Harold corrected. "Your grandmother. Your bubba."

"*Bubbe.*" Pattie had little patience. "How would these virginal, cave-dwelling failures of natural selection have ever figured that out?"

"The Internet, I guess," Harold shrugged. "The Germans from Russia Museum has an online ancestor list, for example."

"Listen to this! 'i wanna shove my dick up ur fat nose because i probably couldnt find ur pussy under those jewfro pubes.'"

"That's a remarkable amount of thought he's put into it."

"Oh my god, Harold," Pattie slapped her husband's arm. "Look at this one!"

Harold read the latest tweet that had been directed to Pattie's account. "u & ur cuck huzbnd spread anymore trump lies thru the MSM & we come 4 u. crystallnacht part 2."

"Trump lies?" Harold was puzzled.

"Harold, he must mean that article you wrote! What you heard on the RNC bus!"

"No, no, I already got a letter from Stephen Miller about being on that bus," Harold reminded her.

"Well, I'm guessing this troglodytic sack of flop sweat wasn't copied on it. 'lincolns a gr8 place 2 get raped, kike bitch.' How do they know we're in Lincoln?"

"Did you download the Sheldon Memorial Art Gallery App? It has geo-tracking. See? That way you can share which room you're in."

"Dammit, Harold. For all we know, one of these mouth-breathers could be stalking us."

"Pattie, they have so many bigger fish to fry if they're after someone Jewish. Did you know Wolf Blitzer is Jewish? Ted Koppel? Jewish. Barbara Walters? Also Jewish. The media is filled with Jews, Pattie."

"We need to go back to the motel. *Now.*"

"Well, alright, but the National Museum of Roller Skating closes at four."

"Our marriage may not be operating much longer than that."

*   *   *

"I'm surprised they found so many photos of you," Harold mused. "When I search your name, a bunch of entries for some hypnotist in Australia come up."

"This is a picture of me half-inside of an oven," Pattie said in shock.

"See how stupid they are, Pattie? That's a home oven. The Nazis didn't use those. There's no way any neo-Nazi dumb enough to make that mistake would be able to get to Lincoln, Nebraska." Harold and Pattie sat together on the edge of an unsettlingly spongy bed topped with a slightly stained white comforter that had seen better decades. Each hunched over their respective laptop, they frantically navigated between their email inboxes and various social media accounts.

"This is a picture of my face photoshopped onto someone's naked body."

"Jennifer Lawrence's," Harold explained. "Those are circulating."

"ShawshankSammy00001 says he's going to shove the Sunday paper up your bald ass."

Harold blanched. "Jesus, Pattie, the Sunday has the Style section!"

"At least the Sunday Review tends to bend left." Pattie continued to scroll through her Twitter feed. "Oh, shit. *Bubbe!*" Harold leaned over on the bed and saw a picture of Pattie's grandmother photoshopped onto the emaciated body of a concentration camp prisoner. Next to her, Donald Trump, dressed in a tan Nazi uniform, held a luger to her head.

Harold's phone rang.

"It's my editor, honey. Don't worry; he'll know what to do." Harold got up from the bed, putting the phone to his ear, while Pattie continued to scan the litany of incoming messages bombarding her computer. "Hello, sir? Sir? Sorr—Sir, before you say anything, I can assure you, I've been canvassing the polling centers since six a.m. this morning. Right, I—sir? *What*? Who's a cuck? No, sir! We don't even leave the bathroom door open if one of us is in there, sir."

"Someone called me a liberal snowflake!" Pattie shouted at her laptop screen. "A snowflake? But *he's* the one tweeting at *me*!"

"Stop my inflammatory tweets, sir? I'm sorry, I just didn't think *Midnight In Paris* was up to the standard of Woody Allen's earlier—oh. What? That came from *my* account?" Harold put his free hand over the receiver. "*Pattie!*" he hissed. "Have I been tweeting inflammatory things?"

Pattie looked up.

"My editor says my Twitter account has been spewing racial slurs and conspiracy theories all morning," Harold whispered urgently.

"You didn't rewatch *JFK* after I went to bed last night, did you?"

"*Pattie*, this is seri—No, of course I didn't tweet that, sir. Calm down. My account must have been hacked, sir. No, I barely use the Internet on my phone. No, sir, I'm *married*, remember? I'd have no need to—malware? Well—sure, you can't discount the malware, sir. Exactly, right there in the name. Bad ware. Right. So there's no telling what it would tweet."

"'Weak Jewess?' Is he tweeting from the 1920s?"

"I can assure you, I did *not* write any such things about the Chinese. They've made so many contributions to America, sir. Dams, education, noodles—the list goes on and on. No, just three off the top of my head."

"MAGA-Carta_7 says he'd throw me one." Pattie shook her head. "Generous."

"No, sir, of course I'll tweet out an apology and a retraction. No, I don't know *anything* about the sexual appetites of Syrian women. I didn't even study abroad my junior year, sir. Right, so my life stayed the same. To be honest, I don't even know if they have 'kitchen tables' *per se* in Syria, much less if that's—right, no, the apology. Yes, I'll get to that soon. Well, speaking of Twitter, I'm in the midst of a related family crisis, as a matter of fact. My wife has been assaulted by an army of anti-Semitic trolls on Twitter today, sir. Yes, sir. Vicious invective, sir. As a matter of fact, it has to do with that rather incisive piece of reporting I did last week. Well, she's here righ—" Pattie waved her arms "—right on the other line, calling from New York. On the phone. I put her on hold. Well, work is my first priority, sir. But yes, she is in a bad state, what with all the harassment."

"Pyotor_dimitriov12999 tells me, 'Kindly get yourself fucked!'" Pattie sniffed. "I guess perhaps I'd better get in touch with MAGA-Carta after all."

"No, sir, it really is awful. Pictures of her being put into a home oven. They've even found out about her Jewish grandmother and dragged *her* into this, if you can believe it. Yes, her poor bubba. *Bubbe*. Why, what did I say?"

Pattie lifted her computer off the bed and tilted it to the side. "Oh, I get it. Maybe next time, try making the star of David with a program other than Microsoft Paint, *Sean*."

"Yes, it really is a nightmare. Pull me off the trail for a couple of weeks? Actually, sir, that would be incredibly helpful. As you can imagine, both my wife and her grandmother are very distraught, and I really ought to be there for the both of them. Well, sure, back to New York is one option, but her bubba lives in San Diego, and it would be best if I made sure she was holding up."

"Harold," Pattie hissed, "what are you doing? You know my *Bubbe's* been dead for eight years."

Harold placed his hand over the phone's receiver. "Do you want to go to San Diego or not?" He brought the phone back to his mouth. "I mean, I'd hate to take time off. I live for the road, sir. You know that. But in these difficult times, if there were some way to combine work and duty—perhaps a special report from San Diego. You know, I've been hearing a lot about Hispanics, and—I see. Sure, there's plenty I can do for my wife from New York. Right, where my wife is. Yes, maybe *Bubbe* can fly out to spend some time with us. Good idea, sir. Yes, we can take her out for Chinese food. Bubba loves Chinese sir, sort of tying into my earlier point. You know, there's the place on Broadway and—oh, of course, sir, if the lox is just sitting out. No, don't worry; I'll delete all of the Tweets. Ah, no, that was one of mine. No, I was just marvelling at the women's track team's ability to—as you wish, sir."

Harold tossed the phone onto the bed as he sat back down next to his wife, who was fuming. He leaned over and studied the image expanded on her laptop screen. "I know that's supposed to be a caricature, but that's the spitting image of my eighth grade music teacher, Mr. Katzenstein."

"Harold, I can't believe you!" Patti erupted. "After everything I've been through today, you try to use my dead *Bubbe* as a ruse to get to San Diego?"

Harold shrugged. "You know, when life gives you lemons..."

"We're both pushing forty! How is your editor supposed to believe that *Bubbe* is still alive?"

"Oh, old Jews are built like Volvos, Pattie. She could still be running."

11
"They Had Weapons of War, Pattie!"
July 18, 2016

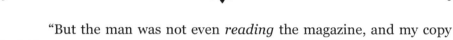

"But the man was not even *reading* the magazine, and my copy had the second page of 'Three Perfect Days in Taipei' torn out," Harold protested, as the couple wheeled their suitcases through the automatic doors of the Best Western Cleveland.

"Right," Pattie sighed. "I'm only suggesting that next time you avoid getting into a screaming match with a complete stranger."

"The operative word there is 'stranger,'" Harold countered. "How was I supposed to know he was an air marshall? Like I told him, they should really make those guys wear uniforms." Harold peered up at the lobby's low ceiling and sighed. Cork tiles formed a grid overhead. He noted that a fair number of them were stained from some prior leak. Two small benches with tired-looking brown sofa cushions flanked either side of the tan-walled lobby, above which hung anodyne watercolors of what Harold supposed was the Cleveland skyline.

"Checking in?" a perky woman in a dark blue blazer asked from behind the modest front desk.

"Carlyle, Harold and Pattie—"

"With a 'C'? Just a moment." The woman's long red manicured nails made sharp, staccato tapping noises across the keyboard. Harold gazed back out of the hotel's electric sliding glass doors, watching planes from the nearby airport take off with a noticeable sense of longing. Pattie gave him a half-hearted pat of encouragement.

"We have you on a high floor, sir!" the woman announced. She put one key into the machine and tapped on the keyboard. "Room 218."

"I thought you said you had us on a hi—right. Room 218. I can already picture it," Harold groaned to Pattie. "Not only does my editor send me back out on the road after my wife has been *traumatized*, he books me in a room where you can't even see over the hedges out the window."

"No wonder print is dying," Pattie muttered.

"We have a complimentary coffee machine in the lobby, and there's a bowl of oranges right here at the front desk from six to ten am," the woman advised them. "Although you should come down before about eight if you want an orange, because that's when Mrs. Halverston usually gets up, and she loves oranges."

"Thanks for the tip," Pattie smiled, picking up her satchel.

"Do you two plan to do any sightseeing while you're in town?"

"Not if we can help it," Harold muttered under his breath.

Pattie nudged him in the ribs. "My husband will probably be taken up with work, but I would love to learn more about the sights."

"Right," Harold grumbled. "Is the river scheduled to catch fire this week?"

The woman considered, then reached underneath the desk and produced a placemat-sized map printed on thin paper. "This has all of Cleveland's top attractions," she said brightly, laying out the map on the desk in front of them. Harold and Pattie leaned over to study it.

"There's two dots," Pattie said, confused.

"Yes! This is the hotel," the woman said, pointing a long red nail to a box in the lower left corner with a bright yellow star next to a gray area marked "Airport." "And this is the Rock and Roll Hall of Fame."

"Ah," Pattie nodded. "And these restaurants," she added, pointing to a string of colorful advertisements at the bottom of the map, all showing cuts of meat. "Can we find these downtown?"

"Huh," the woman paused. "You know, none of our guests have ever asked that before." She smiled, scrunching her nose. "They would have to pay extra to get a star on the map itself."

"Another honest business crushed under the thumb of Cleveland's tyrannical board of tourism." Harold shook his head.

"Well, Big Ray's Steak and Grain House looks good," Pattie offered.

"You know, I don't even know if any of these are still in business," the woman said, studying the map. "But if you just try typing them into Google, I'm sure you could find out."

"Thanks," Pattie smiled, folding the map and moving toward the elevator.

"The Rock and Roll Hall of Fame has a cafeteria," the woman called out from behind the front desk. "It's open till five pm." She waved to the couple as the elevator doors inched shut.

*   *   *

"Oh look, a crack in the ceiling," Harold pointed out as he unzipped his suitcase. "That must be where the last guest hanged himself."

"I presume the paper puts Maureen Dowd up at the Four Seasons whenever she's in Cleveland."

Harold scoffed. "Like Maureen Dowd would ever even step foot in this metropolitan equivalent of a fanny pack."

"I don't think this is really that bad," Pattie urged, distractedly typing replies to the emails she had received during the flight.

"Pattie, the paint is *peeling off of the wood* in this room," Harold pressed, pointing to wood trim with chipped white paint that wrapped around the circumference of the brown-wallpapered, musty room. "*If* it's wood. And! *And!* Looking at the bigger picture, don't even get me started on the pitiable notion that a thin strip of wood trim and wallpaper from the Ford Administration in any way entitles a hotel to award itself the moniker 'Best.'"

"Okay, Harold."

Harold judgmentally examined the locked mini-bar. "'Best' Western. It's like Napoleon crowning himself emperor. You can't just award it to yourself."

"Well, you can stay here and continue your inspection of the furniture and glassware," Pattie said, shutting her laptop. "I'm going down the hall to get some ice."

"Ice? Pattie, are you insane? Do you know what sort of parasites are bound to be lingering in the ice machines here?"

"Harold, it's Cleveland, not Mexico. I'm sure it'll be fine," Pattie said, pocketing her phone and taking the ice bucket.

"I bet you won't take such a cavalier tone once the parasites have penetrated your blood-brain barrier."

Pattie waved off Harold's protests as she closed the hotel room door behind her. Searching for the ice room, Pattie walked toward the end of the hall. The voices of two men gradually grew more pronounced as she approached a small, brightly-lit alcove humming with the sound of machinery.

"First you guys ditch me in Philadelphia, and now you have me holed up in this flea trap," a bald man complained. He had a frog-like face and eyes that looked surprisingly like Harold's.

"Donald needs you to keep a low profile," the other man explained, sounding as though he had made the point already. He looked strangely familiar to Pattie. Despite wearing heavy mascara, a white feather boa, and what appeared to be dark stockings, she felt that she had seen the long, beaver face and leathery tanned skin somewhere before. His lisp, too, was unforgettable, yet hard to place.

"So I have to take a hundred-dollar Uber ride to the Westin Pittsburgh? Jesus Christ, Rudy. I'm the guy who's making this work for the rest of us. *And* I'm still waiting for Jared to Venmo me that hundred, by the way."

"We need to check our egos at the door, Page. There's an end-game here that's bigger than you or me. You can never, ever forget that. When I walked into the mayor's office on September 12, 2001, I wasn't thinking about 'I' or 'me.' I wasn't thinking, 'Has my assistant replaced the empty bottle of Coco in my bottom desk drawer?' or, 'Do I get to be on the big bus to Pittsburgh?'"

"So I take it you're more than happy to be relegated to the back of beyond? Really, an *airport* hotel? It's an insult."

"Carter, I'm the behind the scenes guy. You don't get New York on its feet by being out in the limelight. Besides, who puts you up at the Ritz every time he sends you to Moscow?"

"Tell Donald I'm not staying in that suite again until the hotel replaces the mattress."

"It's a developing economy, Carter. You just flip it over. Now, listen, pal. You got a date with destiny, so you better get your ice and head over to the convention center."

"What about you?" Carter Page asked, scooping ice into his bucket.

"No, I'm good here," Rudy said, fluffing his boa.

Carter Page stuck the filled ice bucket under his arm, and the pair turned and strode back up the hall, passing Pattie without batting a fake eyelash.

*　　　*　　　*

"Harold, you are not going to believe what I just saw in the hallway," Pattie began as she pushed open the door to the hotel room.

"Pattie? Pattie, thank God!" Harold called from the bathroom.

Pattie rushed to the bathroom door. "Harold, what's wrong? Did you fall?"

"No, I'm stuck!" Harold called.

"Stuck?" Pattie tried the handle.

"I wanted to wash the plane off me before going to the convention. The steam from the shower must have warped the door shut."

"Warped the door? I—" Pattie tried the handle again.

"Pattie, call housekeeping!"

"Maybe if I just jiggle it. The door can't have warped shut, Harold." Pattie rattled the handle.

"Jiggling it doesn't work! The wood has expanded, like those people whose brains get too big for their skulls!" Pattie made a face. "Don't make that face! I know what I'm talking about," Harold insisted from behind the door.

"Okay, I'll call housekeeping," Pattie agreed. She went over to the phone on the nightstand and dialed the front desk extension.

"Front desk," the chipper woman from downstairs announced on the other end. "What can I do to make your stay more enjoyable today?"

"Hi, we're in room 218, and my husband seems to have gotten stuck in the bathroom," Pattie explained. "The door won't open."

"Oh?" the woman asked, confused. "Have you tried jiggling the handle?"

"Yes," Pattie sighed. "It doesn't work. Could you please send someone up to get him out?"

"Yes, of course. We'll send our engineer up right away to help."

"Great, thank you so much."

"Have a spectacular day."

"She's sending someone up," Pattie called. She walked back to the bathroom door and continued rattling the handle. "Want me to turn on the news or something?" Pattie asked through the door.

Twenty minutes later, a knock came at the door. Pattie opened it to find a scrawny young man wearing a dark green jumpsuit. He had long, greasy brown hair and smelled vaguely of marijuana. "You called about your TV?" the man asked nonchalantly. He had a vacant look in his eyes.

"No, the bathroom door is stuck." Pattie pointed to the door behind her.

"Did you tell him about the warped wood?" Harold called.

The engineer stepped into the room and looked at the door for several seconds. "Did you try jiggling the handle?" he asked.

"Yes, many times." Pattie nodded.

The engineer tried the handle, to no avail. He looked up at Pattie. "So, what do you want me to do?"

"Letting me out would be a good start!" Harold yelled.

"Uh huh," the engineer said, slowly. He looked at Pattie. "So he's stuck in there?"

"Maybe you could dismantle the lock?" Pattie suggested.

The engineer picked a piece of dried mucus off the tip of his nose. "Hmm, yeah, maybe that could work."

"So, can you do that?"

The engineer paused. "I would need tools."

"Right," Pattie agreed.

"Yes, tools," Harold said. "Sent up Cleveland's best, did they?"

"Do you have a screwdriver?" Pattie asked.

The engineer stifled a yawn. "I think I saw one downstairs, yeah. You want me to get it?"

"Yes," Pattie said sternly. "That would be good."

"Alright," the engineer said, apparently irritated that he would be required to do additional work on this project.

"We're never going to see him again, are we?" Harold asked, as the engineer let the door shut behind him.

"Here, I'll tell you what's on TV," Pattie said, finding the remote. She scanned through the channels. "Lucy's up on Cornell Wilde's balcony, and she's trying to find a way to get down. She's tying a rope ladder to a potted plant."

Forty-five minutes later, a knock came at the door again. "Oh, great!" Pattie exclaimed, getting up from the bed. "Don't worry Harold, we'll have you out in no time!"

"It's a tad late for 'no time', but thanks, regardless."

Pattie answered the door. The engineer stood in the threshold, holding a screwdriver. "Here," he said, handing it to her. He turned and walked back toward the elevators as Pattie stood, somewhat dumbfounded, in the room's entryway.

"Wait," she called out. "I forgot to tip you!"

* * *

"I would have tried to break through the door, but it was surprisingly sturdy," Harold explained as he and Pattie exited a cab at the last corner open to traffic near the Quicken Loans Arena. "Back in my alternate coxswain days, of course, it would have been another story."

"Too bad about the bathroom door, otherwise I think we probably could've made the cafeteria at the Rock and Roll Hall of Fame before it closed," Pattie said somewhat wistfully. "I was in the mood for a decent meal."

"We'll have plenty of decent meals in San Diego," Harold replied cheerfully.

"Oh, there's a hot dog stand," Pattie said, pointing to a small metal cart at the edge of the crowd covered with a blue and yellow umbrella. "I guess that's better than nothing."

"An *outside* hot dog?" Harold was aghast. "You must be joking. Why don't we just wait to see what they have inside?"

"The food vendors inside will probably make us say grace before they hand us our meals. This is fine. Let's save some money and just get on line here."

"I haven't even had a salad yet," Harold moped. He and Pattie got in line behind a trim, distinguished-looking man with pepper-gray hair and sharp, angular features and his companion, a short, older, balding man in a baggy suit whose pale blue eyes seemed to radiate mistrust of the Hispanic family in line ahead of them.

"Filth," the bald man drawled contemptuously. The distinguished man looked at him sidelong, as if to say, "Not here."

"Is Cleveland one of those sanctuary cities now?" the bald man continued. "Seems to be the *en vogue* thing to do now. But just wait till all these cities are swallowed up in all this human garbage. Packin' ten people to a *shack*, takin' *citizens'* jobs, and neckin' right in line for the cars ride at Disney World."

The distinguished-looking man cleared his throat and quickly raised his eyebrows.

"I told Donald, you need to talk to the Mercer boy, Bannon. Fellow who runs *Breit*-something. I don't recall the name, but, you know, he's one of the only folks out there who sees the situation for what it is."

The distinguished looking man mumbled something unintelligible.

"Not like all these other so-called Republicans I know," the short man continued. "Most of them were too chickenshit to even show up this week. Can you believe that? I saw John McCain in the steam room Friday. He told me his niece had a bridal shower to go to, so he had to watch her cats. Gimme a cotton-pickin' break." The man snorted and shifted his weight to one side, grimacing. "Criminy. I got this bunion on my left foot that won't go away," he added. "Do you know a guy?"

"Miller," the distinguished man nodded. "Navy guy. Took care of my cyst."

"Would you mind giving me his information?" the short man asked, grimacing again. "Damn thing's the size of a pickaninny."

"Absolutely."

"Anyway, that's why *I'm* here. We have one more chance to make America what it used to be before this…*monkey* started letting everybody in that wants to come in, and filling up the courts with women who would've been the cleaning ladies twenty years ago. And if we've got to get ourselves into the mud, well, that's politics, Mike." He exhaled.

Mike, the distinguished man, looked absently around the crowd. "I was mainly hoping for a book deal."

The Hispanic family having received their food, the two men stepped up to the front of the line. "Yes. What are you two gentlemen desiring to eat?" the hot dog vendor asked in a heavy eastern European accent. He was a stocky man with translucent blue eyes and a head shaved completely bald.

"A hot dog in the bun," Mike said carefully. "Extra sesame seeds."

The vendor's eyes twinkled. "Of course, Mischa."

"And I also would like a hot dog in a bun," Mike's companion added, winking. "But could I have onions on mine?"

The vendor looked troubled. "No sesame seeds, Dzheffri? You are certain?"

"Oh, right, right," Mike's companion said quickly. "Seeds, yes."

"So, for you, it is also hot dog in the bun—"

"Yes, yes, hot dog in the bun with—listen, do you have the fucking flash drive or don't you?"

The vendor nodded and leaned over the stand's shiny metal counter. "The *bear*," he whispered, "is in the eagle's anus."

"Fantastic, son," Mike's companion replied, glancing around.

The vendor began preparing their orders. Mike leaned forward. "Kids doing alright?"

"Yes, they do very well. Thank you. Nikolai, he is studying computer science." He handed Mike a hot dog in a bun without sesame seeds. "Sonya, she is manager of the Ritz now."

"Not a great place to stay on asparagus night," Mike winked. "Ketchup in the usual place?"

"The ketchup is in the usual place, yes," the vendor said solemnly, handing the shorter man his hot dog. The two walked toward the rear of the Quicken Loans Arena without putting any ketchup on their hot dogs. "I love it when you can taste the pig guts," the short man said approvingly to Mike as they walked away.

Harold and Pattie approached the vendor. "One hot dog, please?" Pattie asked slowly, eyeing the pair who had just left.

"Yes, very good," the vendor answered. "Would you care for a side of borscht with that?"

"Huh, borscht?" Pattie furrowed her brow. "No, no borscht."

"Oh, wait, not so fast, Pattie," Harold interjected. "Borscht actually sounds lovely, thank you."

"Yes, right away." The vendor smiled. "Salutations, Mr. Page," he said to Harold as he began preparing their food. Pattie looked over at Harold, trying to signal his attention, but Harold was distracted by a dark-haired woman he spotted in the crowd.

"Huma?"

"Sorry?" Pattie asked.

"Pattie, I think that's Huma Abedin over there, standing by that Jefferson Davis impersonator."

"What on earth would she be doing here?"

"Scoping out the competition!" Harold squinted. "Huh. Her breasts are surprisingly large for a person of her height."

"That's not Huma Abedin," Pattie said, irritated. "I saw her at the Met two years ago. Huma Abedin is probably 5'10."

"Really?" Harold was mildly crestfallen. "Look at her lips again. Those are her lips."

"Harold, don't be ridiculous."

"Your hot dog, miss," the vendor interrupted, thrusting a paper plate with a tinfoil-wrapped hot dog balanced atop a heaping portion of borscht. "And, Mr. Page, I believe you will find the borscht this evening to be particularly appetizing."

"Page?" Harold asked, confused.

The vendor paused, examining Harold's features. "*Glaza takiye zhe!*" he muttered. "Sorry, an error," he apologized. "I thought you were another person." He quickly dunked his fingers into the steaming paper bowl of borscht, pulled out a small gray flash drive and stuck it in a pocket on his apron front. Pattie opened her mouth to speak. "It's Russian herb," the vendor explained. "Too bitter for American palate."

"Thanks!" Harold smiled. The couple wandered away from the stand as Harold gingerly took the container of borscht off Pattie's plate, calculating how to eat it without utensils or a chair. "That was considerate," he said. Pattie looked perturbed.

"Harold, didn't you think that was strange?"

Harold smacked his lips nonchalantly. "Borscht is a staple," he shrugged.

"*Harold*. That was Mike Flynn ahead of us on line back there. And that short, ornery one? I'm almost certain that was Jeff Sessions, the senator from Alabama."

"Mike who?" Harold asked through a mouthful of borscht. "Chachi?"

"That general Obama fired two years ago." Pattie corrected. Harold stared at her blankly. "Honestly, Harold, *you're* the reporter."

"Pattie, unless Obama fired him on the D Train, I had my hands full two years ago," Harold said testily, wiping his mouth with the back of his hand. "So to speak. Anyway, so what? It's the Republican Convention. Are you *that* starstruck? Honestly, you're acting just like when Lucy gets stuck on Cornel Wilde's balcony."

"Excuse *me*, Mr. Abedin. Of course it makes sense that they're at the convention. But weren't you listening to the conversation they were having with that Russian hot dog vendor? All those code phrases?" She paused, thinking. "That guy at the ice machine stayed at the Ritz in Moscow."

"What guy at the ice machine? Don't be absurd, Pattie. That vendor was a perfectly fine gentleman. Probably an immigrant. Part of the American dream of entrepreneurship." Harold swallowed. "Why, one day, he might open up the first restaurant in Cleveland."

"Harold, he stuck a computer part in your food."

"I think the parasites from the ice machine are already boring holes in your brain."

Finishing their impromptu dinner in silence, Harold and Pattie pushed further into the dense, bustling crowd of people, toward the arena's front entrance. Vendors had set up makeshift stands out of card tables, selling buttons and T-shirts with off-color designs and slogans, some of which Pattie recognized from the rally they had attended in Philadelphia. A line of police officers formed a barricade around a group of protesters, led by a man and a woman who each held a megaphone and had clearly not coordinated their use, shouting calls and responses to mismatched chants. Behind the couple, a shirtless, muscular African-American man was rapping about the Virgin Mary. Off to the side, a small cluster of middle-aged white men stood stone-faced, clutching large automatic rifles to their chests.

"Are those plainclothes cops over there?" Harold asked, pointing. "They aren't doing a particularly good job of blending in."

"I think they're demonstrators for Ohio's open-carry law," Pattie explained. "I read about them in the paper this morning. Apparently, it's not enough that they can bring their guns into any fast-food spaghetti-and-chili bucket in the state. They also need to be allowed to bring them into spaces where they can be the next Lee Harvey Oswald without the CIA training."

"It certainly gets your attention," Harold said, distractedly looking around like a zebra who has heard lions in the underbrush.

"It's ludicrous." Pattie shook her head.

"Damn right about that!" A slender, pale young man in a long, dark coat appeared behind Pattie and Harold. "What a bunch of sad losers."

"My thoughts exactly." Pattie smiled at the young man. "They're obviously compensating for some kind of shortcoming."

"You're tellin' me!" the man snorted. "If you've got a big one, you don't walk around holding it. You just keep it in the tent, waiting for the right moment for it to do its thing."

"Um, right," Pattie replied, slowly.

"The real issue is *concealed carry*," he said, grinning.

"Concealed carry?" Harold asked.

"Yeah, that's what I'm here protesting. Me and Lucille here." The young man patted a small lump protruding from under his coat, situated just below his armpit.

"How does anyone know you're protesting if the gun is concealed?"

The man's smile vanished. He thought. "Are you a liberal?" he asked.

"No, I'm a re—" Harold considered. "I'm a real gun-lover with a big one of my own," he said, less convincingly than he'd hoped. He patted the side of his hip, where he thought a gun might be holstered.

"Alright!" the young man said, raising a fist to the sky. Harold awkwardly attempted to bump fists, but the man put his hand back into his trench coat pocket. "See you in the nosebleeds!" he said, wandering off.

"What's in the nosebleeds?" Harold asked Pattie.

She shook her head. "The Ritalin will wear off before he gets up there."

Harold stopped near the entrance to the arena. A mass of people wearing straw hats and red, white, and blue clothing congealed near the main doors, vaguely funnelling into two lines.

"Do you think there's a designated entrance for the press?" Harold asked, frowning.

"Probably an abattoir." Pattie motioned toward a large plastic map of the arena mounted near the edge of the pavilion. They walked over and began studying the legend, trying to make sense of its elaborate color-code system.

"Hi, brother," a kind-looking, avuncular man said warmly. He looked like a stout relative of Harold, with the same blue eyes and thinning blond hair. "Can I help you find what you're looking for?"

"Oh, yes," Harold replied, noticing the man. "We were just trying to figure out if there is an alternate entrance to the arena."

"There is, indeed, my friend."

"Terrific." Harold grinned. "Would you mind pointing us in the right direction?"

"I'll do you one better. Why don't I show you myself?"

"We wouldn't want to be a bother" Pattie said warily.

"What bother? I was headed that way myself!" the man bellowed. "I know this place like the back of my hand. Follow me." Harold and Pattie looked at each other skeptically, but neither said a word. Pattie raised her eyebrows and shrugged, and with that, they uncertainly followed the man past the main entrance and around the corner of the arena.

"Whereabouts are you two from?" the man asked over his shoulder.

"Nevada," Harold said quickly. Pattie looked at him. "Be safe!" he mouthed to her. "Lots of really good guns there," he added, to their new guide. "Rifles, pistols, bayonets."

"I love Nevada!" the man exclaimed. "You two ever make it over to Laughlin?"

"All the time." Harold nodded. "We love it there. It's like a second home, really."

"Whenever it gets too high-falutin' in Reno," Pattie said under her breath.

"There's this one casino in Laughlin—oh, what's the name of that place?" The man thought for a moment. "It's made up to look like a riverboat. In any case, they got one of the best two-dollar steak and eggs I've ever tried. Really something else."

"Oh, yeah, I think I know the place you're referring to." Harold said evasively. "Proud Mary's?"

"That might have been it!" the man said, pausing before an unmarked door on the side of the arena. He studied a set of air ducts mounted to the wall next to it for a few moments before moving on. "Real good people there. The kind of people you'd want to find wherever you go."

"That's for sure," Harold agreed. "The right people." Pattie sighed.

"So, are you two married?" the man asked. He carefully eyed Pattie over his shoulder, seeming to study her features.

"Oh, yes, of course," Harold said. "I think it's disgraceful that more people aren't."

"Any kids?"

"None yet," Harold apologized. "Though not for lack of trying!"

The man guffawed. "You should have several, believe me. It's your patriotic duty. It's people like you who can re-purify the nation."

"Right, the nation," Harold began. He cleared his throat. "Because, what with immigration." The man nodded deeply. Pattie elbowed Harold in the ribs.

"Do you think it's much further?" Pattie asked. She glanced back up the road they had turned down. Metal barricades on the far end of the block prevented any traffic from passing, and the din of the crowd in front of the complex had grown faint. Beyond them, faceless, newly-constructed empty office buildings and parking garages rose six stories above a recently-paved grey street. Even near sundown, the heat enveloped them. Pattie grimaced with each step, her blouse stuck to her back.

"It's a big building," the man said without turning around. "Makes a great spot for a gathering, I can tell you that."

"Oh, I would imagine so," Harold concurred.

"Yep, something really spectacular," the man continued distantly. "A mass of people coming together, you know? Perfect spot." They rounded another corner, arriving at the rear of the complex. "You can get in there, second one from the left," the man said, indicating a nondescript door set in the long, gray cement back wall of the building. "They usually leave it unlocked." A wide road stretched perpendicularly away from them, crowded with more gleaming, and seemingly unused, examples of urban renewal. Pattie noticed a lone white van parked half a block away, its motor idling.

"Let's get out of here," she whispered to Harold, tugging at his sleeve. His Oxford shirt was matted with sweat stains.

"Pattie, the entrance is right there."

The man turned to face Harold and Pattie. He inspected Harold from head to toe, arms akimbo, and smiled. "I don't believe I ever got your name. I'm David." He offered Harold a beefy palm.

"Harold," Harold said, shaking the man's hand with two short, affirmative pumps. "And this is my wife, Pa—"

"Betsy," Pattie interjected, shaking David's hand, as well. She looked at Harold and shrugged.

"Betsy," David said suspiciously, studying Pattie's nose. "Didn't figure you as such, Betsy. Pleasure."

"Do you work at the arena?" Harold asked helpfully.

"Brother," David said solemnly, ignoring Harold's question. "I like you. Can I tell you that?"

"Why, sure," Harold responded. "Who doesn't want to be liked?"

"We're kindred spirits, you and I. I have a sense for these things."

"Oh, well, color me flattered."

"I could tell from our conversation that you, too, are concerned—gravely concerned—about the future of our race."

"About the wh—oh, sure," Harold said nervously. "Yes, the race. Our race. Yes."

"We—*we* understand why immigration is a threat, you see? Letting in weaker blood, darker blood—for the sole purpose of muddying our pristine blood—our white, European heritage." He glanced around. "Here, my brothers have seen us!" David waved at the van down the block. The van flashed its headlights on and off three times, and the side door slid open. Seven men jostled each other, each trying to exit first.

"I'm at the head of the line, right?" a beefy, bearded man dressed head-to-toe in camouflage and kevlar asked a still-wider, similarly attired man with a shaved head. He raised his hand. "Heil!"

"Heil! I thought we were going alphabetical."

"The treasurer goes first," the bearded man snapped, slapping the other man with his open hand. "Heil!"

"Heil!" The bald man stuck his arm out in salute, poking the bearded man in the eye.

"You numbskull." The bearded man slapped him again.

"Oh, wonderful!" Harold smiled slowly, a look of panic creeping into his Saxon blue eyes. "His brothers have seen us, Betsy!" Pattie surreptitiously slipped the phone out of her pocket, and pre-dialed 911.

"We're meeting some other like-minded, concerned citizens at the Marriott in fifteen—" the man checked his watch, "—thirteen minutes. You should join us. I think you'd find it to be a sort of homeland, if you will."

"You know, I would love to, but unfortunately, I really have to get to the convention," Harold demurred. "Plus, all I've eaten this evening is a cup of borscht, so I really need to find a food stand—"

"Nonsense, brother. *We* are the freedom fighters who will make America great." The man smiled significantly. "And Carl brought a bunch of snacks."

"Greetings, brother," the bearded man said, approaching David and raising his right arm into the air. Pattie noticed the man was carrying a large assault rifle slung over his shoulder.

"Harold, this is John," David said, returning the gesture. "He's our treasurer, and he also designs the uniforms."

"Pleasure to meet you." Harold began to raise his arm in a halfhearted salute, but Pattie slapped his hand down. "Tennis elbow," he explained lamely, grabbing his shoulder.

"Oh, and this is his wife, Betsy," David added with a slight grimace.

John cocked his head back and examined Pattie. "Betsy?" he sniffed. "Some nice curly hair you got there."

"Thanks," Pattie said slowly. "It's usually straighter. Just trying something new."

"I was just inviting Harold and Betsy to our meeting tonight," David said. "I think Harold, especially, would get a lot of out it," he added.

"Harold understands the threat to our race?" John asked.

"Does he ever," David said solemnly. "Harold, you should really reconsider. I think you'd appreciate the camaraderie our group offers."

"Just like the Elks." Harold attempted a smile. David, John, and Pattie all looked at him. "Unfortunately, we really have to get to the convention."

"You don't want to come?" John asked, absently running his hand up and down his rifle. "There'll be plenty of time for the convention afterward. Say, we'll even drive you back!"

"No, no," Harold assured them. "I would love to come if I could, but—"

"You're no longer among enemies," John said gently. He slung his arm around Harold's shoulders and pulled him in close in an embrace, the muzzle of his rifle jabbing Harold in his side. "Listen, I was nervous, too, the first time I came out to a meeting. Worried it's a sting. It's not, trust me. The Jew media wants to sow doubt among our ranks. Make us not trust each other. But we can't let them win. We're stronger together."

Harold sighed, glancing down at the gun that was pressed against his kidney. "I guess we can come for the first half."

*   *   *

"*We have to get out of here immediately*," Pattie implored in a low voice, leaning over the arm of her soft vinyl swivel chair. She and Harold sat next to each other at a long, maple table in a windowless room on the second floor of the Cleveland Marriott. At the head of the table, David was shuffling papers; his companions were pulling manilla folders out of identical brown canvas satchels. Before each of their places at the table was a neatly-stapled handout with a colorful table on it. In the corner, a young man with severe acne and cropped red hair was forlornly arranging a pitcher of water and a row of soda cans on a small refreshments table.

"They have weapons of war, dear. I don't believe we have much of a choice in the matter," Harold whispered urgently.

John leaned over and plucked a Jolly Rancher out of a small bowl in the center of the table, noisily unwrapping it. "Watermelon," he said approvingly, smacking his lips.

David looked up from the papers on the table in front of him and surveyed the room. "I'd like to call this meeting to order," he announced, tapping on the table with a small gavel. "Does anyone move to approve the minutes from our last meeting on June 11th?"

"Approved," murmured John.

"Seconded," a pale man with glasses grunted.

"The motion is granted," David said, tapping his gavel with a swift, precise stroke. "We have one item of ongoing business to attend to. John?"

John stood up. "As treasurer, of course, I have to assess fines for all noncomplying members," he began, putting on a pair of reading glasses and looking down at a yellow legal pad. "As we all know, it's a $60 penalty for failing to wear your armband to any meeting, speech, rally, picket, gun show, or picnic. I see four members who didn't wear their armbands today."

Four men at the table quietly slunk down in their chairs, slyly covering their arms with their hands. One man reached for his wallet and pretended to count his cash. He snapped his fingers and feigned a look of disappointment.

"Without belaboring the matter any further, I simply want to reiterate that these rules are in place for a reason. We are a cohesive, organized unit, and all of us wearing our *complete*, regulation uniforms is a central part of that. The offending parties may pay the fine at their earliest convenience, but no later than before next month's meeting on August 12. Thank you." John sat down. "Oh, and on a personal note, as the one who designed these uniforms, I feel obligated to add that without the armbands, the whole ensemble just doesn't pop."

David tapped the table again with his gavel. "Thank you, John. And folks, I know we don't trust the banks, but unfortunately, we can no longer take cash payments. Next, we have some items from last month that need a status update. Carl, I believe you had something exciting you were working on last time."

A mousy blond man who looked like an accountant inexplicably covered in kevlar products stood up. "I have some exciting news about our partnerships, if you all turn to page three of the monthly status chart," he announced. The other men dutifully flipped the pages of their handouts. Harold noticed the man next to him underlining the name "Carl Craigson" and writing "partnerships" next to it.

"Can I look on your paper?" Harold whispered. "I didn't get a packet."

"Of course, brother," the man said gently. "We're right here." He pointed to Carl's name.

"First, our partnership with 4chan is still in the talk phases, but we've been blue-skying a lot of different ways to plus-up the content and find some synergies between their halo offerings and our brand," Carl explained. "They're still a little gun-shy about opening the kimono when it comes to numbers, but I think if we keep our eyes on the low-hanging fruit, we're both going to be able to push our oars and leverage our core competencies on Twitter and the *Huffington Post* comments section to hit this one out of the park."

"Hmm, good," David murmured.

"Also, we're still waiting on someone to reach out to what's-his-face at Breitbart. Steve-something. He's asking us to ideate some value-adds that would enable us to tell our story in a way that leverages some of our learnings from the Michelle Obama death threats campaign in '09. Anyone want to be team leader on that one?"

The room remained silent for a moment. Finally, a scrawny man at the end of the table meekly raised his hand, shrugging.

"Okay, Tyler, I'm empowering you to take ownership of that. Let's circle the wagons by COB a week from Thursday." Carl sat down.

"Do you want to be copied on the emails?" Tyler asked, frantically scribbling down what Carl had just said.

"Only on level-sets," Carl said, checking his Blackberry. "If anything else important comes up, just ping me, and we'll interface offline."

"Okay, great," David said after waiting to make sure the conversation was finished. "Next on the agenda, we have online operations and enforcement. Richard, can you give us an update on everything that's going on there?"

"Sure," an older man sitting across from Harold said with a slight groan. He clutched the muzzle of his rifle, using it to slowly hoist himself out of his chair. "All the Internet stuff is going pretty good. Um, we haven't heard back from the lawyer for the cartoonist who draws that Pepe the Frog character the kids seem to like. Tom, here, says that unless we receive another cease and desist letter, we can keep using it in all our Photoshops and whatnot." Richard motioned to a moustached, bespectacled man who was sipping coffee out of a Charleston College of the Law Thermos. The man looked up and nodded absently. "And Tyler tells me that our vendetta against that Jewess writer is still going strong."

"Which one was that?" David asked.

"Oh, you know, that mouthy kike who writes for *The New Yorker*."

Pattie shifted in her seat. Across the table, John leaned in close, studying her nose. "What did you say your maiden name was?" he asked softly.

"John, I believe Richard has the floor," David said sternly.

"Davi—Sir. Sir, I don't think this woman is—"

David sharply rapped his gavel. "You're speaking out of order!" He tapped the table again. "I don't need to remind you that there is a financial penalty for a second offense." John leaned back into his seat, scowling at Pattie. David looked back up at Richard.

"Oh, that's it for me," Richard said, sitting back down.

"Okay, terrific. Next, I'd like to discuss our annual Labor Day barbecue and white power rally. As you're all aware, we had to disband the party planning committee after the FBI started tapping their calls, but we were able to reserve space at the Little Cedar Point Picnic Area under Chet's wife's name."

Carl leaned in. "And can we reserve grill space, or—"

"We can reserve grill space," David continued, ignoring the interruption. "Now, I know we've gone back and forth on the music selection for the event. With this group, it's a wonder we can agree on anything. Except who's the master race, that is."

The men around the table chuckled.

"Anyway, to stem any further kerfluffles, I'm going to go ahead and handle the playlist myself." A couple of the younger members at the table emitted audible groans. "Now, now, that's enough of that. Don't worry. I'll be sure to choose something that's both rollicking and true to our white values and European heritage. Something wholesome and pure."

"Like Elvis?" Richard asked.

"Yes, exactly. Elvis would be perfect."

"Actually," Pattie whispered to Harold, "Elvis' music is so deeply rooted in the bla—"

"Pattie, shh!" Harold hissed. "There's a financial penalty for speaking out of order."

"We also need to start thinking about putting together our Obama effigy for the night rally." Two men in the corner high-fived. Others cheered. "Does anyone want to volunteer to bring in the tan fabric for Obama's suit?"

The room fell silent.

"Fellas, we can't ask Richard's poor wife to pick up the supplies again. She's already being so kind to sew the tiny pants for us." Around the table, some of the men pretended to take notes, while others simply avoided making eye contact with David. "Fine, I'll buy the fabric myself, I guess. Thanks, everyone." He tapped his gavel petulantly. "Let's break for a brief recess before we move on to new business, shall we?"

David tapped his gavel on the table again, and the men began to rise from their chairs, Richard tightly gripping his rifle as he strained to pull himself up.

"We have chocolate donuts at the meetings held on odd-numbered months," the man next to Harold said as they made their way toward the refreshments table. "I don't believe we've met. Chet." He offered his hand.

"Harold," Harold replied, shaking the man's hand. "This is Pa—"

"Betsy," Pattie said, quickly shaking Chet's hand.

"You all are new here," Chet said. "Well, you joined at a good time. We have some exciting things happening."

"Right," Harold said. "The picnic."

"Oh, more than that, brother," Chet said, gingerly putting two chocolate donuts on his small paper plate. "We have a surprise planned."

"Oh? Whose birthday is it?"

"No, no, a surprise for the Republican Convention." Chet glanced quickly over his shoulder to where David was conversing with Richard. "I'm not supposed to say. But America won't be able to turn away, if you catch my drift."

"Oh," Harold said nervously. "That sounds great."

"You might say it'll be pitch-perfect."

Pattie and Harold exchanged glances.

"You know," Harold said, looking at his watch, "I think I saw a black meter maid outside." He grabbed Pattie's wrist and pulled her quickly toward the door. "We'll be right back."

"We're starting again in a couple minutes!" Chet called. Harold gave him a thumbs-up. Chet watched the doors close behind the couple, then looked back at the plate of donuts. "More for me, then."

*   *   *

Harold continued to yank on Pattie's wrist as they hurried through the sliding doors of the Marriott, onto the sidewalk.

"Harold, okay!" Pattie yelled when they reached the street, shaking off his grip.

Harold frantically glanced up and down the street. "Have they not invented cabs in Ohio yet?"

"Let's just keep walking. I'll call an Uber."

"We need to leave town," Harold said, out of breath. "Preferably before the blitzkrieg starts."

"Oh for God's sake, Harold. Did you see them? Their big surprise is probably special lederhosen."

"They had weapons of war, Pattie! God knows what they're going to do! A bunch of white nationalists planning a surprise? And they know who we are now! They're going to come after us when they find out we left."

"Abdullah is coming for us in a Toyota Camry," Pattie said, glancing at her phone. "The *Uber driver*," she sighed, seeing Harold's face. "Anyway, you have nothing to worry about. They're probably planning a Kickstarter to send Dylan Roof some jellybeans in prison right now."

"Better safe than sorry," Harold reasoned, pacing back and forth. "Let's grab our stuff at the hotel and hightail it out of here."

A Toyota Camry pulled up in front of the pair, and they entered the car. They sat in silence for several minutes. Pattie proudly read her article on whether three-camera sitcoms would ever make a comeback, which had received its final round of edits the night before and was the featured piece on the Arts landing page that day. Harold rolled down the window, attempting to calm himself with deep breaths. The thick, humid night air blew against their faces. He turned to Pattie. "You know what I take issue with? They're at the Marriott, and yet the most my paper can do for me is the Best Western." Pattie looked at him for several seconds, then turned back to her article. "I'm not saying I want to join their group, mind you, but maybe I should've chosen a different major."

Pattie shook her head. "I could have told you that a long time ago, Harold."

*   *   *

Harold dejectedly poked the mound of spaghetti noodles sitting in front of him, causing the thin brown meat sauce pooled on top of it to spill over the sides and puddle on his plate. "Did you know a Greek man invented this?" he asked, grabbing a handful of napkins out of the plastic dispenser atop the small, sticky table. "No wonder there's a debt crisis. From democracy to Skyline Chili. Says it all right there, really."

Pattie aggressively jabbed her fork in the center of her spaghetti mound, twirling the noodles around her utensil.

"You know, because Skyline Chili isn't very appetizing," Harold explained.

Pattie's eyes remained on her plate. Harold sank down in the vinyl booth to try to intercept her field of vision.

"Are you angry at the food, or at me?" Harold asked meekly.

Pattie slowly scooped a forkful of food and brought it to her mouth. She began chewing, not looking up from her plate.

"Alright, so I took you to a Neo-Nazi meeting. Are you going to ignore me until we get to San Diego just because of that? How many times do I have to apologize?"

Pattie continued to chew.

"You know, if anything, you should be thanking me. How many television reviewers can say they've been to a bona fide white nationalist gathering? Why, most people never even leave their hometowns. And here we are, traversing the country, mixing it up with racial purists.

Truly acquainting ourselves with this vast, complex land we call America." Harold forced down a mouthful of food. "A land of contradictions," he added, patting his chest.

Pattie swallowed her food, carefully reached for her glass, and took a long, meditative sip of water.

"Remember, Pattie, Dr. Rothstein said the silent treatment is a form of emotional abuse."

Pattie rolled her eyes, reached into her purse, and removed her cell phone.

"Remember, he gave us that advice column from the *Washington Post*? We adapted it into the Noh play?"

"Drop it, Harold," Pattie said, slamming her phone onto the table. "Do you really think I'm mad you took me to a Neo-Nazi meeting? This is America. White supremacy and predatory capitalism are two of our founding values."

"You're mad we had to leave Cleveland, aren't you? Trust me, Pattie, you'll be happy you're still alive after they launch their 'surprise.'"

"Oh, for God's sake, Harold. I'm tired of being your Girl Friday on this. I spent the first half of the year traipsing back and forth across the cash-for-gold shops and strip-mall alligator farms of America with you, out of some misguided faith that you'd actually get us to San Diego; I *finally* get back to New York after *your* reporting made me the target for the Joseph Goebbels Fan Club; you turn around and start *pleading* with me to go out to Cleveland for the Republican Convention, and no sooner do we get *there* then you make another utterly impulsive, reactive decision—to a disaster *you* created with those Nazis—and take us to Akron, Ohio. Not listening to a word *I* said," she fumed. "I told you I at least wanted to stay and see the godawful convention that we *actually came here to see*." Pattie speared a loose noodle.

"It sounds like the person you're really angry with is yourself," Harold said gently, placing his hand over his heart.

"It's never your fault, is it, Harold? You can't just *listen* to me!" Pattie put her phone back in her purse, snapped the clasp shut, and rose. "I'll see you back at the motel. Thank God that room has two beds." Pattie stormed out of the restaurant.

Harold considered his food sullenly. "Probably a good idea. This stuff is bound to run right through you. Miss?" He mimed signing a check to the waitress, a frail, elderly woman who shuffled over and placed a receipt on the table. Harold studied the paper and dejectedly pulled out a credit card when his phone began to ring. "Oh, what is it now?" He dug his cell phone out his pocket and groaned, seeing his editor's number.

"Hello, sir? What's cracking? I'm just sitting in the concession area of the Quicken Loans Arena. I believe I just saw John McCain, actually, so if I could call you back in a minu—sir?" Harold held the phone away from his ear. The editor's voice squawked audibly through his phone's speaker. "Sir? Sir, what's the matter? Is it Hillary, sir? Was there another scandal?" His editor's voice continued reverberating in an uninterrupted flow. Harold looked up helplessly at the elderly waitress, who was listlessly bussing his table. "Yes, sir," Harold shouted into the phone. "No, of course I know there's supposed to be a report every night. I've just been slammed here, sir. But I'll have a lengthy report on the convention for you tonight. Yes, that's what I've been working on this whole time." He held his hand over the phone's receiver. "Excuse me," he said to the waitress. "Can you just pretend to be Ivanka Trump for thirty seconds?"

The waitress looked at him apprehensively. "What?"

"I'm in a bit of hot water here." Harold nodded toward his right hand, which was muffling his editor's stream of invective. "Just say 'ya,' or something. 'Nyet.' Either one." The waitress turned and walked away with a stack of dirty dishes. Harold put the phone back to his ear.

"Ri—right. Yes, sir. Of course, sir. Uh huh, the delegates, sure. Already two steps ahead of you there. Right. No, of course we have to think about Ted Cruz. What do you suppose I've been thinking about this whole time? Well, you'll see tonight, when I send you my report. Oh, it'll be lengthy, sir. You can probably run it as the main feature in the Sunday magazine, if you want to wait a couple—right, tonight. No, of course. I'll talk to you soon, sir. I have to chase after Melania. I tell you, if she weren't Trump's daughter—" Harold looked at the phone, which finally went silent.

He leaned back in the greasy vinyl seat and surveyed the dismal, sparsely patronized restaurant. He looked out the large front windows into a shopping center parking lot across the street. The sky was dark gray, with distended clouds hanging low and stifling overhead. All day, it had felt as though a thunderstorm were coming to clean the air, but none had arrived. In the corner above the counter, a mounted television set showed two besuited white men talking over each other. At the bottom of the screen, a banner read, "Speaker Ryan to Introduce Pence Next."

"Excuse me, miss?" Harold called across the restaurant. The woman behind the counter looked up from the register, her finger lodged in her nostril. "Could you turn it up? I think I got a scoop here."

The waitress eyed him skeptically. "A scoop? You with the media?"

Harold sighed. "Yes."

"Why'n't you in Cleveland with everybody else?"

"I'm covering the townsfolk in Akron's reaction to the convention," Harold lied quickly. "Could you please turn up the volume?"

"You already ate and paid," the waitress observed.

"We barely ate any of this, so you can just use it again the next time someone comes in. The volume, my good woman."

"I think you better leave now," the waitress said, folding her arms.

"I just want to hear Speaker Ryan—"

"Find another store," the waitress ordered, pointing to the door. Harold exhaled deeply, stood up, and headed toward the door, which closed behind him with the jingling of bells. The sky suddenly boomed, and the dark clouds let forth oceans of rain. Harold walked toward the main road and back to the Akron Inn pelted by the furious downpour, his new Brooks-Brothers shirt quickly soaking through and clinging to his wiry frame.

"Well, this has been a shit day," he muttered.

*   *   *

Pattie sat up in one of the two double beds in their hotel room, her fingers gliding over the keys of her laptop. Harold burst through the front door, his clothes dark and dripping wet. "Do you have the remote?" he asked frantically.

"Harold, please, I'm in the middle of something here."

"Pattie, I'll see you and hear you later. My job may be on the line."

"This TV has a power-on button," Pattie said quietly. "You can press it to turn the set on. That's something I learned, writing my 'little blurbs.'"

Harold leaped toward the television set and pressed each of a string of buttons. "Oof, zapped myself." He shook out his hand, still slick with rain, as the set flickered on. "I don't want the in-room movie options!" Pattie pressed a button on the changer and a washed-out image of Paul Ryan's face appeared on the screen, inches from Harold's. Harold yelped and involuntarily recoiled.

"And so Galt nibbles on Taggart's earlobe. She feels his hot breath against her cheek, and it gives her gooseflesh. And Taggart whispers—Oh, they're giving me the signal. Well, you can read the rest of the story on my congressional website. Ladies and gentlemen, the next Vice President of the United States, Governor Mike Pence!" The arena on the screen erupted in applause. Searchlights flashed across the crowd, zooming in on a short woman wearing a cowboy hat who was dancing in the aisle. A tanned man with military-regulation cropped white hair and a self-satisfied smile strode out onto the stage, followed closely by a squat woman in a purple blazer with a sheath of black hair framing a Gothic face. The man raised his arm and waved at the crowd as he approached the lectern at the center of the stage.

"Mr. Chairman, delegates, friends, and my fellow Americans, thank you from the bottom of my heart. I am deeply humbled by your confidence. And on behalf of my family, here and gone, I accept your nomination to run and serve as Vice President of the United States of America." The crowd erupted into applause. Mike Pence nodded and waved, squinting into the bright lights of the arena.

"And let me thank Speaker Ryan for that gracious welcome. Paul, you're a true friend and a great American leader. But Paul knows me well, and he knows that the introduction I prefer is a little bit shorter: I'm a Christian, a conservative, and a Republican, in that order."

"Pattie, do you want a breath mint?" Harold asked, proffering a small blue mint wrapped in plastic from his pocket. "I took some from the dining car on the *California Zephyr*." Pattie glared. "I was saving this one for when I really needed a breath mint, but I want you to have it."

"I grew up on the front row of the American dream. My grandfather immigrated to this country. I was raised in a small town in southern Indiana, in a big family with a cornfield in the backyard. Although we weren't really a political family, the heroes of my youth were President John F. Kennedy and the Reverend Dr. Martin Luther King Jr."

The crowd cheered again. "I guess Michelle Obama originally gave this speech, too," Pattie muttered, her eyes fixed on her laptop screen.

"But it's such a joy for me to tell you that my mother is here. She's a wonderful lady. Truly an inspiration. Would please you join me in welcoming the light of my life, my wife, Karen." Brief applause swelled from the audience. The Gothic-looking woman in the purple blazer stepped forward, waved, and stepped back. "I couldn't do anything without Mother," Mike Pence continued glowingly.

"Pattie, tell you what," Harold said, walking over to the cabinets beneath the television set. "Let's pop open the minibar and have a snack. On me, honey. Or we could crack open this jar of pecans." Pattie sighed and turned up the volume on the TV.

"And it's such a joy for me to tell you that my *mother* is also here. Would you please join me in welcoming the light of my life, my mom, Nancy. " The camera cut to an older woman in a black dress with a fresh permanent, horn-rimmed glasses, and a proud smile. "She's a wonderful lady. Truly an inspiration."

Harold popped a pecan in his mouth, chewing loudly. "Here, Pattie. Open your mouth, and I'll throw one in." Pattie shook her head slowly. "Okay, I'll throw one in my mouth." Harold opened his mouth and threw a pecan in the air, missing by several inches.

"Of course, it's not always easy having two such amazing, generous women in my life. Mother is always there with words of support, a warm cup of milk, or a pat on the head when I need it. The other day, I was at home downstairs, tidying up our altar, and I stubbed my toe on our crucifix. It's to scale. Oak."

"Oak. That's a fine wood." Harold threw another pecan in the air, craning his head but failing to catch it.

"Boy, was I sore! But Mother heard the commotion and came hurrying down in a jiffy with a fried banana sandwich and a kiss just for me."

"Pattie, you sure you don't want a pecan? The jar's almost done," Harold winked. "Of course, I guess most of it is on the floor, if you change your mind later."

"But that's what families do. Families take care of each other. They are the cornerstone of our shining democracy. I am so humbled to be here at the request of a good man, my friend. I've seen this good man up close, his utter lack of pretense, his respect for the people who work for him and his devotion to his family."

"Who's he referring to now?" Harold asked. He took a handful of blue mints out of his overnight bag and began stuffing them into the empty jar of pecans.

"Now, if you know anything about Hoosiers, you know we love to suit up and compete. We play to win. That's why I joined this campaign in a heartbeat. You have nominated a man for president who never quits. A fighter. A winner. A strong man, a terrific negotiator. A man who has a lot of good words. And a pair of the most tremendous, strong hands I've ever seen." Pence looked confused. "He's the least racist person you know. To say nothing of—" Pence leaned forward and squinted at the camera, speaking the words slowly, "his beautiful da...daughter, Ivanka. I mean, let me tell you, she is so beautiful. Perhaps, if she weren't my daughter, I would be dating her."

"I thought it would be easier just to watch the convention on TV, but to be honest, I'm having a tough time following this," Harold said. "I should really take down some notes so I can keep this all straight." He checked his overnight bag, sighed, and searched the nightstand separating his and Pattie's beds. "How is there no paper here?"

"And it's Donald's dedication to his family that I respect most about him. For too long, the American family has been under siege by the Democratic Party. They put forward candidates like Hillary Clinton, who don't respect the sanctity of marriage, who want to redefine what family is, what being a man or a woman is. Hillary Clinton and Barack Obama want an America where men can marry men and women marry women. My fellow Americans, Donald Trump and I are here to tell you that a man has *no business* marrying a man, no matter how piercing his eyes may be," Mike Pence bellowed into the arena, which erupted in applause.

"Pattie, do you have a mascara pencil?" Harold asked, returning from the bathroom with a handful of toilet paper. Pattie looked at him quizzically. "Got to take some notes," he explained, sitting down on the edge of his bed.

"You know, in so many ways the Democratic Party has abandoned those it used to protect. Maybe they've become too entrenched in power, so comfortable at times that they lose patience with the normal legislative process. It's so much simpler to impose their values by executive order or court action. And make no mistake about it, Hillary Clinton has some big ideas along those lines, too."

The crowd whooped and hollered, chanting "Lock her up!" Mike Pence chuckled. "She wants socialized healthcare, my friends! That's not American values; that's *coastal* values. Why, in the Pence house, we pay for conversion therapy out of our *own* pocket."

"Is healthcare one word or two?" Harold asked, scribbling on the toilet paper. "Of all the times to be stuck with single-ply."

"I want to fight to bring this country back on the right course and champion the sort of morals I was raised with, all those years ago, by that cornfield in southern Indiana. I recall when I was a child, watching *Mother* proudly work over a hot stove for hours. I remember I could see the individual beads of sweat glisten as they made tiny trails down her neck, ending below the collar of her blouse. She would ask me to stand behind her and rub her shoulders as she waited for my father to come home. And then she'd turn and embrace me and ask, 'Who's *Mother*'s big boy?' And I was. I was *Mother*'s big boy."

"I think I'm just going to stop at 'hot stove,'" Harold sighed, dejectedly crumpling the ripped paper.

"My fellow Americans, I believe we have come to another rendezvous with destiny. And I have faith, faith in the boundless capacity of the American people and faith that God can still heal our land. We have but one choice, and that man is ready, this team is ready, our party is ready. And when we elect Donald Trump the forty-fifth president of the United States, together we will make America great again! Thank you, and God bless you, and God bless the United States of America!" Mike Pence waved to the crowd and turned to the woman in the purple blazer, who patted him on the head and took a plastic Hot Wheels car out of her purse, which he pocketed eagerly.

Pattie turned down the volume on the television as the coverage transitioned back to CNN's anchors. An African-American man with tiny glasses began speaking.

"Pattie, I'm sorry," Harold said. "Here's your mascara pencil back." Pattie looked at Harold for a few seconds, accepted the pencil, and shut her laptop.

"Thanks," she said.

"Look," Harold began, sitting down on Pattie's bed. "Let me make this up to you. Why don't we go to Nantucket for a few days? The Democratic Convention won't even be important until the last night, anyway. I can report on it from CNN and no one will know the difference."

Pattie sighed. "Harold, you—" she paused, and breathed. "*The car cannot be its own mechanic,*" she recited calmly. "*Santíh, santíh, santíh.*" Harold beamed. "It's your career. If you want to go to Nantucket, I'll go, too."

"Great," Harold said, jumping up. "I heard about a wonderful bed and breakfast just off the main street from Ben Schweitzman. They stayed there when the Sconset house was being re-roofed."

"I think what you just saw was Mike Pence giving a strong affirmation of American values and Donald Trump's character," an unnaturally thin young woman with bleached blond hair was saying over the African-American man.

"I'm sorry, Kayleigh, but we need to cut away from this breaking news inside the convention to cover some breaking news outside the convention." The cameras cut to a group of men in lederhosen assembling in the pavilion in front of the arena. One of them took a pitch pipe out of his shirt pocket and blew a C note. "One-two-three; one-two-three," he mouthed to the men behind him, and they began to sing. "*Edelweiss, edelweiss, every morning you greet me...*"

"Look!" Harold pointed. "That's Richard!"

"Who?"

"See that man propping himself up with his rifle?"

"Oh my God." Pattie crawled up to the front of the bed so she could get a closer look at the screen. "Well, I was right about the lederhosen."

"*Blossom of snow, may you bloom and grow, bloom and grow forever,*" the men continued.

"You know, this song was written for the musical." Pattie looked at Harold. "I guess it'd be too much for them to find an actual Nazi song, and not a show tune written by two Jewish men."

"I'd imagine the gentile version lacks the requisite sense of rhythm. Did you see the crowd clapping on the on-beat right before Mike Pence started to speak?"

"*Ededlweiss, edelweiss, bless my homeland forever.*"

"The tenors are a bit flat," Harold groused.

"So much for the master race."

12
"My Great-Grandfather Served Under Cecil Rhodes"
July 25, 2016

"There's something so primally, viscerally fulfilling about being out on the open sea. Don't you wish you could freeze this moment?" Harold asked, leaning over the ferry boat's white railing. The wind blew the wisps of hair left along his hairline up into the bright clear sky. Pattie snapped a photo of the island's edge as it grew larger on the horizon, gray dockhouses shrouded by thick green trees in full bloom reflecting into a harbor of shimmering blues. A seagull hovering above them kept pace with the craft. "And that nautical air is just invigorating." He took in a deep breath, releasing it with affected relish. "Nothing better after a week in Ohio, where the air just sits there. Much like Ohioans."

Pattie's cheeks rose into the wide, dark oval lenses of her glasses. "Look at all that open space. We should rent bicycles and explore tomorrow morning. I think there's a trail that goes all the way around Nantucket."

"Ah, yeah, if we have time, we could definitely do that," Harold said evasively. "Look, we're docking!"

The dock attendant lassoed the ferry to the side of an old, sea-worn structure, and Harold and Pattie filed down the boat's ramp, onto dry land.

"Bring the cahts out fah the luggage and stahp sitting on yah ass!" the dock attendant called out to an African-American man wheeling a cart toward the gangway.

"Great to be in New England again," Pattie muttered. They rolled their suitcases over the bumpy cobblestone landing toward a covered row of gray thatched-wood souvenir shops, out of the fierce sunlight.

Pattie consulted a map of the island displayed in one of the store windows. "It looks like our hotel is only a couple of blocks away," she told Harold, who was distracted by a revolving postcard display. "Let's just walk."

"Sure," Harold agreed. "More money for lobster tails." He tried to stuff a postcard back into its metal slot but upended the display. "Oof." He knelt down and reluctantly began to collect the bevy of scattered cards.

"Ready?" Pattie asked, looking down at the postcards scattered across the damp cobblestones.

Harold looked up. "Yeah, I don't like any of these." He grabbed his suitcase handle and followed Pattie toward the main road. Taxicabs clustered around a loading station where the road met the cobblestones and snaked back up the block. Families and older couples in pastel-colored clothes and boat shoes pushed and weaved their way past Harold and Pattie toward what seemed to be the front of the taxi line, while others purposefully headed to another loading station, further off, where a flock of German luxury cars had been patiently waiting for their owners' return.

A teenage boy wearing a light blue polo shirt and white shorts that stopped above the knee lagged behind his mother, stalling in front of Harold and Pattie.

"I don't see why I have to double with Rose again this summer."

"The Burroughs are a fine family. You'll double with Rose, or Papa may not let you use the Mercedes this year," his mother scolded. "Just be polite and mind her weak backhand." The teenager shook his head woefully as he followed his mother toward the line of cars.

Off to the side, Harold noticed a short man in a tank top, with long black hair, sunglasses, and a beard standing in front of three dark green Mini Cooper convertibles. He held a cardboard sign with the words "RENT A MINI - ISLAND DREAM" scrawled in red Magic Marker.

"Pattie, look!" Harold exclaimed, pointing toward the man's sign.

"One of the more esteemed members of Nantucket's Chamber of Commerce, I presume."

"Oh, come on. What would be better for our island getaway than a convertible? The wind blowing in our hair as we whip around the coast?"

"Nantucket is pretty small, Harold," Pattie reasoned. "Why don't we rent a couple bikes instead?"

"Um, I don't know if bikes are the best option, Pattie." Harold wheeled his suitcase closer to the cars, looking wistfully at them.

"Not when you could be driving in one of these!" the man with the cardboard sign called from nearby.

"Yeah, let's hear what Dick Dale has to say," Pattie muttered, walking over to Harold.

"Nantucket is an island of beauty, sun, great luxury, and easy living," the man began, shaking long strands of hair out of his eyes. "All the long-timers have an island car. It's kind of a status symbol here."

Harold furrowed his brow. "But this is just a Mini."

"Man, don't shortchange the Mini. When you're behind the wheel of this bad boy, you'll be able to *feel* the road," the man said. Harold looked excitedly at Pattie. "You might think you came to Nantucket to stroll around and see the lighthouse, but you haven't experienced this jewel in Nature's crown unless you've explored her in one of these."

"Okay, thanks," Pattie began. "We know where to find you if we decide to rent a car."

"Man, you think I'm just going to *be* here? I only have three cars to rent. You two are in the right place at the right time. Ten minutes later, I'd be sipping margaritas up at the American Legion. Pure serendipity."

Harold pulled Pattie aside. "Pattie, it's *serendipity*. I think we need to do this. Remember what Dr. Rothstein said about the fierce urgency of now?"

"Harold, for all we know, he stole these cars, and he's flipping them at the dock before he heads out on the last ferry."

"How would he get three stolen cars down here in broad daylight? Nonsense. The man is clearly an enthusiast."

"Hey, guys?" the man interjected, waving his cell phone. "I got a call here from one of my regulars. Says she's hot to rent all three. So you need to let me know pronto if you've reached a decision on the vehicle."

Harold looked at Pattie pleadingly. Pattie glanced over at the surf gently crashing into shore, then shrugged. "Hell, we're on vacation."

The man slapped Harold on the back. "That's what I like to hear."

"Can we just rent it for today and tomorrow?" Pattie asked.

"Sure. I'm just gonna need a thousand dollar deposit from you, plus..." the man wrinkled his brow in deep thought "...five hundred a day, and then we'll go over the features of the vehicle."

"Two thousand dollars?" Harold asked, taken aback.

"One thousand's only a deposit," the man reassured him.

"I'm afraid I don't have that much in cash," Harold began, taking out his wallet.

"Credit card is fine. I'm on Square."

Pattie started to leave, but Harold gently placed his hand on her shoulder. "Honey, he's on Square."

"Why is it so much?" Pattie asked.

"To cover any damage," the man said quickly. "It's a convertible. The top goes up and down. So, more parts."

"For two days?" Pattie challenged.

"Pattie, please. The man knows about cars."

*   *   *

"And the warm cookies are served in the breakfast nook at 8 p.m. every evening," an officious man wearing pastel orange pants and a seersucker blazer noted with a smile as he gingerly shut the door to Harold and Pattie's room with a discreet click. A breeze whistled through the lace curtains of a half-open window into the white, airy room, which was anchored by an opulent king bed covered in nautical bedclothes. Harold looked lovingly out the window at the valet pulling the Mini away from the inn's entrance and into the private driveway behind the well-manicured front garden. "I'm so glad we rented the convertible. That was fun coming up here."

Pattie glanced over at him. "Your bald spot is already the color of a persimmon."

"I don't have a bald spot," Harold said quickly.

"Right," Pattie apologized.

"All men have that, Pattie."

"Right."

"I'm serious. All men have a little area at the top of the head like that."

"Right, all men who are balding."

"I'm not balding." Harold pulled a rumpled pair of khakis out of his bag, slapped them a few times in a futile attempt to force out the wrinkles, and leaned them over a wooden suit rack thoughtfully nestled in a corner of the room.

"I have some aloe in my tote bag, if you need it."

"Save it for a bald man, Pattie." Harold pulled the TV remote out of a nightstand drawer.

"You're not already turning on the TV, are you? We've been here for all of half an hour."

"Just for a minute. I need to check the wires, as we like to say in the industry." He clicked through the in-room TV guide, landing on MSNBC, where a woman and a man resembling a store mannequin were sitting in front of a series of images of pantsuits.

"So, whereas Hillary in 2008 had a darker, more austere aesthetic, Hillary today is striving to be much bolder with these oranges and reds," the woman explained. "She's really evolved as a candidate, as you can see."

"Fascinating report, Mika. We'll just have to see whether it's enough for her to win this November."

"Definitely, Joe. And to our viewers at home, don't forget to vote in our Twitter poll and tell us what color *you* think Hillary should wear on Thursday night. But now, we go to singing legend and Hillary surrogate Art Garfunkel."

"Actor and singing legend," Art Garfunkel corrected.

"Honey, look!" Harold pointed at the screen. "He's back!"

"No, an actor, too. Well, *Carnal Knowledge*, for one."

"I thought he was representing Bernie Sanders," Pattie said.

"Honey, do you have a pen?" Harold asked, reaching for the hotel stationery.

"Well, in fact, the Sanders campaign, of which I'm *proud* to say I was a part, has had a considerable impact on the Democratic Party. Because of the momentum Bernie built in the past months, we have the most progressive party platform in decades. Similar to how the countercultural songs Paul and I made together in the Sixties radicalized the top 40. Yeah, Paul and I. Both of us, uh huh."

"My editor's going to be pleased as punch when I tell him that I snagged a second interview," Harold said excitedly as he scribbled notes. "The old Columbia alumni network coming through again."

"Well, Joe, I'm honored to endorse Hillary. I think, as a leader, she really hits those high notes, if you will. Ha ha. Well, no, we can't discount the views of the protesters outside the convention center, either. Both the establishment and anti-establishment voices need to be heard in this election, just as two voices really made those Simon and Garfunkel recordings special. It's all, as they say, in the blend."

"Do you think if I leave my shoes out tonight, the hotel will shine them?" Harold asked, chewing on the end of his pen.

"Yeah, I think you just need to fill out the slip on the nightstand," Pattie said distantly, her attention focused on her iPad.

"No, of course I stand by my support for Bernie earlier this year, Mika. Does the artist have one conception for a work of art in mind at the beginning of the creative process? Yes. Does that conception evolve as the possible becomes the practical? Yes. When we set out to record 'Mrs. Robinson,' for example—yeah, Paul wrote that one. Well, you might say Bernie's campaign was us, as a nation, brainstorming. Kicking around the ideas, like Paul and I used to do. No, my ideas, too. And, you know, Bernie's campaign was us asking, what can America look like? And Hillary is the—right, like the song. *All come to look for America*, ha ha. Yeah, I get it. No, that was Paul, too. No, I don't think Paul does these talk programs that often. Yes, that would be exciting."

"Lobster in an omelet?" Harold exclaimed, reading a small room service menu. "Color me intrigued."

"You know, I don't know how to get a hold of Paul. No, we don't actually talk that much these days. Right, no, we're not 'sharing a park bench quietly,' ha ha. Right, like the song. Yes, yes, I get it. No, that was Paul, too."

"I'm impressed that Mika Brzezinski knows so many Simon and Garfunkel lyrics."

"Honey, they're icons," Harold said, still examining the menu. "Lobster tails! Pattie, they have lobster tails!"

"Thanks, Joe; thanks, Mika. Yes, and if I see Paul. Well, I'd be happy to come on again and talk about Hillary's vision for America."

Harold switched off the TV. "I think that's enough for one day. Any more would just confuse the narrative."

"Horace Greeley would be proud."

*   *   *

"I will have the lobster tail, please." Harold seemed to savor the words as he pronounced them.

"The mussels for me, thanks." Pattie handed her menu to the waitress, gazing past Harold to the blue vista that stretched out before them. Small sailboats bobbed at the rotting dock nearby, the tide lapping gently against the salt-worn wood. The sun leaned slowly into the horizon, savoring the calm it created as its last hour suffused the blue sky with golds and violets that seemed to further insulate the island from everywhere else in the world. A falcon perched in his nest atop a lone streetlamp halfway up the pier, greedily surveying his white-peaked ocean. A breeze had picked up, lifting the marine air from the shore past the glass barricades set up around the outdoor patio where she and Harold waited for their drinks, mixing with the pleasant, comfortable warmth of the outdoor heater Harold had insisted they sit next to.

"Miss? *Miss*?" a sunburned man whose red-leather skin was stretched tightly across his outsize body demanded as the waitress re-emerged with Harold's and Pattie's glasses of white wine. The waitress slowly turned. "There's a lot of lemon in this vinaigrette."

"Uh-huh," the waitress agreed.

"A vinaigrette *can* have flavors besides vinegar and olive oil, obviously, but the lemon here is overpowering those two foundational ingredients in a way I'm not sure I'm comfortable with. Has the chef signed off on this?"

"The chef prepared the entire menu," the waitress recited.

"When you go back there, would you mind telling the chef that the lemon here is doing a lot of the work that the balsamic should be doing? I think he needs to be aware of this."

"I certainly will. Thank you, sir."

"Very good."

The waitress delivered Harold and Pattie's wine and then returned into the restaurant.

"I wouldn't normally say anything, but there is such a thing as subtlety, you know?" the man said to his wife, a slender, long-legged woman with dark red hair and the slightest of frown-lines.

"Of course, dear," the woman agreed, taking a sip from her martini. "You have to be direct with these people. It's just like with the gardener, the one at home. I have to tell him every week, 'Fausto, the hedges have to reach *three feet*, no more, no less.'"

"This is an awful selection of bread," the man groused. "French loaf does *not* go with contemporary American. And then they put out a dish of olive oil?"

"Can you *believe* these people?" Harold whispered. "What pretentious boors!"

Pattie smiled. "Listening to talk like that is exhausting, isn't it?" she asked.

The waitress returned with two covered plates and set them before Harold and Pattie. Harold smiled with delight as the waitress unenthusiastically removed the metal cover from his dish. "It's like an unveiling," he whispered reverently to Pattie.

Pattie looked down at the flaccid lobster tail sitting on Harold's plate, half-fallen out of its shell. "Looks delicious!" She rolled her eyes.

Harold eagerly cut into the tail, chomped down a bite, and made a face. "I mean," he gasped, chewing slowly and forcing himself to swallow, "I think on the island, they like to serve the lobster dry, so that you can taste the flavor." He reached for his water. "That's the difference between a restaurant like this and some *frou-frou* place in Manhattan. They let the sea breathe here."

"God!" the sunburned man exclaimed from his table. "Have you seen the *Wall Street Journal*?" the man presented his phone to his wife, who glanced at the screen with seemingly little interest. "Outrageous," she commented unenthusiastically.

"Those rent-boys in Washington just won't stop until they've redistributed every dime we make. Unbelievable. Every one of these people is beholden out the ass to special interests." The man angrily began dialing a number on his phone. "Where does what's-his-name stand on this? Our boy in the House? Chris Smith?"

His wife absently broke off a small piece of bread and began dabbing it in the plate of olive oil. "Don't eat the bread, honey; it's crappy bread," her husband scolded while waiting for his call to go through. "I'm just going to give a quick call to his nephew and ask him to relay our *dis-sat-is-fac-tion* to the congressman. That should light a fire under the ass of that do-nothing mattress salesman." He gulped the last of his gin and tonic. "Hello? This is—oh, for shit's sake." He hung up the phone in disgust. "Got the machine. What's the point of having his home number, then?"

"Oh," his wife said.

"You don't want your couscous?" Harold was troubled.

"Try it. It tastes awful. Like someone dumped a cup of melted butter over it."

Harold gamely scooped up a forkful. He shuddered as he chewed. "Interesting mouthfeel." He looked to his right, where a middle-aged Asian man and his daughter had both been slowly eating lobster rolls. The daughter was, finally, finishing hers, while her father carefully placed the uneaten half of his at the far end of his plate. He deliberately ate two French Fries, sat back in his chair, and stared calmly out at the view.

"Pattie," Harold whispered. "Do you think this man is going to finish his lobster roll?"

"What?"

Harold nodded toward the half-finished lobster roll on the man's plate. "It's just sitting there."

"Maybe he's taking a break."

"But he *cut* the lobster roll in *half* before he started eating."

"Okay."

"That suggests a premeditated plan to *only* eat half of the lobster roll."

"Maybe he's going to bring the other half back for later."

"Lobster doesn't keep. You have to eat it right away. And, believe me, anyone with the foresight to preemptively divide their lobster roll in two would know that. This guy is a planner."

"So, you want to ask him if you can have it."

"How often do you get to eat lobster like this? It's not like he would just have to give it to me. I saw a ten in your wallet."

"*Absolutely not.*"

"It should be criminal to throw away a quarter-pound of perfectly good lobster like that. Do you have any idea what his ancestors would say if they found out about this? This is waste, Pattie."

"I'm sorry; I can't let you ask a stranger for half his lobster roll."

"Remember the song Dr. Rothstein taught us? *You belong to you; I belong to me / And that's the way it'll always be.*"

"Let's get the check." Pattie signaled to the waitress, who walked over.

"Did you want to see a dessert menu?"

"Just the check, please," Pattie smiled.

The waitress reached into her right pocket and handed Pattie a black plastic book. "Thanks for dining with us," she said emotionlessly.

"Pardon me, is that man over there in your section?" Harold asked, nodding in the direction of the man to his right.

"Him?"

"Did he say anything about wanting a doggie bag?"

The waitress looked confused. "No," she said, considering. "I'm not sure if we're allowed to tell the other customers that, but no."

"Did he evince any intent at all to finish his lobster roll, now or at some future time?" The waitress shook her head no.

"*Harold.*" Pattie kneed him under the table.

"Okay," Harold reached for Pattie's purse on the ground between them and pulled out a ten-dollar bill from its hidden pocket. He leaned toward the waitress conspiratorially. "Would you mind giving that man this and asking him if he'd be interested in parting ways with the uneaten half of his lobster roll in exchange?"

The waitress looked at Harold blankly for a few seconds, then accepted the bill and turned, walking past the man and back inside the restaurant. Harold looked after her in disbelief.

"So we're set with the tip, then?" Pattie asked after the waitress had walked away.

"If she thinks she's getting a tip after that..." Harold trailed off.

"...Yes?"

"No, just," Harold shrugged, standing up. "I think twelve percent would have been more appropriate."

*   *   *

Pattie stopped to smell a red and yellow daylily lining the stone path of the hotel's back garden. "Beautiful," she said softly.

"It really is," Harold agreed from a few paces away, admiring the rolling geometric quadrants surrounding a small pond, lined with colorful flowers and neatly manicured knee-high hedgerows. A young couple had spread out on a blanket in the middle of the lawn and were unpacking breads and jams from a small wicker basket. He took a deep breath, the air still damp and chill with the start of a new day.

"How about we walk down to the main street and rent some bikes?" Pattie asked. "We can bike around the cove up to that little breakfast place I saw in *36 Hours.*"

Harold opened his mouth to speak as a groundskeeper noisily buzzed past on a riding lawnmower, muttering to himself. "Sure, we could do that," Harold said finally.

"You don't want to?"

"No, that's fine, we can do that."

"You don't want to."

Harold sighed. "No, I mean, we can, I'm just thinking," the groundskeeper looped back around past Harold and Pattie, causing Harold to raise his voice, "we already spent all that money on the Mini."

"This will come out of my little savings account, okay?" Pattie insisted as the couple ventured from the path onto the green lawn. "I want to rent bikes while we're here. What's with you? You've been awfully odd about the whole idea ever since we got off the boat."

Harold pursed his lips and thought. "Well, it's just—a lot of bad things can happen when you ride a bike."

"Oh, they have bike paths that wind around the whole island. You don't have to worry about cars."

"Not that. Things that can only happen—" the groundskeeper rumbled, scowling, directly between Harold and Pattie, forcing them to jump apart—"TO A MAN!"

Pattie nodded. "Well, they have special seats to avoid that," she said as the groundskeeper pressed on, not following any apparent path.

Harold visibly relaxed. "They do?" He thought. "I guess we could go down to the shop and see what they have in stock."

"It'll be fine," Pattie assured. "It's 2016. We still haven't elected a woman president, but we've made sure that men can bicycle and fornicate in the same day."

"Alright."

The groundskeeper continued to mow further down the grassy slope, then suddenly veered to the left, darting toward the young couple feeding each other slices of bread. The pair leaped to their feet in a panic and dodged out of the lawnmower's path as the groundskeeper shook his head, his eyes fixed on the ground in front of him.

*   *   *

"I just love all these cute little shops," Pattie commented, peering into the front window of a candy store. Her eyes followed the swiftly moving metal arms of a large contraption displayed inside as they pulled apart and refolded a sizeable blob of pink taffy. "How about we look around a couple places before we take the bikes back?"

"That works for me," Harold groaned behind her, wheeling a candy-apple-red bicycle. He walked with a wide gait, as if he'd just climbed off of a horse.

"Oh, here!" Pattie pointed to a small storefront with a fresh white façade. "Let's stop inside that antique shop." She leaned her bike against the window and gently pushed the door open. A bell chimed softly. The inside reminded Pattie of the Apfelbaums' study, but with more sunlight. Tall wooden bookcases covered in small artifacts fought for real estate with aged-looking bronze frames proudly displaying watercolors of ships. The couches and small tables were arranged so close together that they seemed to create a labyrinth. Pattie stooped to examine a mid-century coffee table.

"Look," she whispered excitedly to Harold. "Doesn't that look like the table Lucy buys in the redecorating episode?"

"Which one?" Harold sighed, rubbing his upper thigh. "The one where she wins the furniture, or the second one, where she buys a bunch of new pieces on sale and hides them at the Mertzes'?"

"The second one."

Harold frowned. "Maybe a little, but Lucy's was lower and longer." He walked around the table, studying a tufted velvet sofa housed in an ornate, carved wooden frame. "Excuse me, miss?" Harold raised his hand to flag the attention of a beautiful woman in the back of the store wearing a salmon-colored sundress and sorting a set of ceramic teapots featuring scenes from plantation life. "Would you mind if I tested out this Victorian sofa, or do you have a strict, 'you sit on it, you buy it' policy?"

"Have at it!" she called back gleefully.

Harold reclined luxuriantly in the plush cushions. "They should rent bikes with seats made out of *this*. I'm sure Prince Albert never urinated blood just because he rode his bike out to a coffee shop." He stroked the fabric. "Of course, as I understand it, if he had, he wouldn't have been able to stop, and that would have been the end of that."

"Were you looking at any particular piece?" the woman asked, setting down the teapots and gliding over to the couch.

"Oh, we're just browsing," Pattie replied, "but you have a really lovely shop. Quite a collection of pieces!"

"Thank you," the proprietor smiled with deliberate humility. "Something in my soul just responds to the mixture of aesthetics, and history, and commerce in running a little shop like this."

"Sure." Pattie smiled politely. "Have you been here long?"

"Well, I originally got the idea when I took a year off from law school to hike the Scottish highlands." She waited for a reaction. "I guess

I was torn between the desire to help others and the need to honor my spirit," she added, tossing her head back as a stray lock of strawberry blonde hair fell in place. "I went back to get the degree, but my heart never came with me." She sighed wistfully.

"I get that," Harold agreed. He attempted to cross his legs, winced, and resumed sitting spread-legged on the Victorian sofa. "I went backpacking in Maine after my sophomore year."

"Uh huh," the woman said absently. "After I left the law, I spent the first few years painting," the woman continued, gesturing to some of the watercolors hanging in the imposing frames on the wall behind her. In the middle of a row of identical seascapes, Pattie noticed a splotchy self-portrait of the proprietor standing on a pink-sand beach in a red bikini, her arm around a tall, tanned man. "But then one morning, a feeling of *ennui* came over me." She looked to Pattie. "I bought a last-minute ticket to the north shore of Oahu for the weekend, for some ocean recharge," she giggled. "When I got there, I was walking along the local shops when I found—well, when a small craft store found *me*. So as soon as I was on-island again, Daddy and I talked about business over dinner for the first time, and not long after, I opened up Elizabethan Treasures." She smiled coquettishly. "My name is Elizabeth."

"Ah," Pattie said. "So how much is this lamp?"

Elizabeth studied the lamp. "A thousand dollars."

"Thanks." Pattie placed the lamp back down on the desk.

"I have some less-expensive items in the crawl space downstairs, if your budget is slightly—"

"Oh no," Harold interjected. "Our budget is sort of, well, *you know*. Not to be *gauche*, but let's just say that's a bit less than we were hoping to spend." Pattie shot him a glare.

"Excellent!" Elizabeth beamed. "In that case, let me fetch some of my more prized items from the back. There's one in particular from the Dark Continent that I think you'll especially enjoy. Not to spoil any surprises, but it still contains most of its original human teeth."

"Delightful!" Harold gushed.

"I'll be right back." Elizabeth retreated into the back of the shop.

"I didn't realize we were up to our *shrunken head* anniversary."

"You have to play the part, Pattie." Harold leaned forward in his seat, checking to make sure Elizabeth was out of sight, then began furtively massaging his upper thighs. "We're going to have to get those herbs from Dr. Rothstein after all," he whispered. He suddenly gripped his right thigh. "Jesus, the pain is throbbing now!"

"Oh, take a Tylenol, and shut up."

"This is serious! I have a throbbing pain in—oh. My phone is ringing." Harold relaxed. "Hello? Sir? How's it going? Oh, things are fine here. It's been a relaxing couple days, minus a couple bicycle-related mishaps, but—I'm sorry? The Democratic Conventi—oh, righ—" Harold gave Pattie a panicked look. Pattie shook her head. "Sir? Sir? No, it's just that I'm having trouble making you out. Can you hear me? Oh, good. No, it's very loud here. On the convention floor, yes. Reporting on the Democratic Convention here in Chicago, sir. In Philadelphia, right, sir." Pattie rolled her eyes.

Elizabeth returned holding a dark mahogany box. "My great-grandfather served under Cecil Rhodes," she explained to Pattie, "so we've been lucky enough to pass this down. Would you like to inspect it? I have the letter of authenticity back in my office."

"I was hoping more for a vase, actually."

"Protests? Um, yes, there are quite a few protesters here, sir," Harold continued, raising his voice. "Well, you know, both the establishment and anti-establishment voices need to be heard in this election, just like those two voices really made those Simon and Garfunkel recordings special. It's all in the blend, as they say."

"Actually, if you're interested in our African collection, I have a vase that Cecil gave Neville Pickering for his twenty-fourth birthday."

"And you keep that here in the store?"

"Superdelegates, sir? Well, funnily enough, that just came up, here on the convention floor. They. They just came up. Right, all of them. Well—hold that thought, sir. I have a bulletin. Um, ten more delegates for Sanders. Yes, it's getting rollicking here. Oh, Sanders has had a considerable presence at this convention. Can you hear the chanting, sir? 'San-ders! San-ders!' Oh, well, that's a shame. Uh huh, that's what they're chanting."

"I'm afraid we can't sell the frame without the original artwork," Elizabeth was explaining.

Pattie leaned in close to inspect the painting, a collage of amorphous gray blobs circumscribing a bright blue triangle. "Well, it is lovely."

Elizabeth nodded. "It's the sea."

"No, sir, I most certainly did send you a report on the—what was it you said? Sorry, just with the chanting—right, on the Wikileaks hack. Yes, sir. The Wikileaks emails. Yeah, and the DNC emails, too. On the Wikileaks. Respectfully, sir, perhaps you're the one who's confused. I know when I first started to learn this technical jargon—"

"And is this a Louis XIV?" Pattie asked, indicating an ornately decorated armoire in a corner of the store.

"Oh, actually, that belonged to my mother."

"Sure, I can resend it when we get off the phone. Although, you know, I don't know if I get wifi here, sir. But I can dash back to the hotel, and send it, and then dash back here. So, it'll be about a half hour before you get it. Um, as long as I'm resending it, sir, was there anything you wanted me to emphasize in the report? Uh huh. Right, sure, a statement from the Clinton camp. No, I think I put one of those in there, sir. Well, you'll see, it's a big, meaty one. I meant anything a little more inside baseball, sir. Like, if there's a specific definition you'd like me to use regarding what exactly the Wikileaks is, or maybe about what happened with the Wikileaks. Maybe if you want to talk through your thinking before I—sure, okay, if they're about to sing 'Happy Birthday.'" Harold put his phone back in his pocket. "Shit," he muttered under his breath.

"Everything alright, honey?" Pattie called from the other end of the store. Elizabeth had displayed an array of bullwhips for her to examine.

"Oh, yes, yes, of course," Harold said quickly, rising to his feet, his face pained with the effort. "I'm afraid we need to get going, actually, if you're done perusing. I owe the Clintons a call."

Elizabeth's eyes widened. "Do you know Bill and Hillary?"

"Our careers have danced around each other's for the last ten years or so," Harold rocked on his heels. "What with this being the big week, I need to give them a good word." He straightened his shirt and slowly hobbled toward the door, clutching his right thigh.

Pattie stared blankly at her husband, then turned to Elizabeth. "You have a lovely store."

"Why, thank you." Elizabeth reached into a small pocket on her dress and produced a card. "Please call me if you decide you *are* interested in the straw tick."

*   *   *

Harold placed his duffel bag atop the bed and began rummaging through its contents, tossing numerous multicolored ascots over his shoulders as he searched. Pattie sat in the wicker chair in the corner of their hotel room. Her eyes followed the bright silk neckerchiefs as they sailed gently to the floor.

"Were you planning to interview Oscar Wilde on this trip?"

Harold looked up from his bag. "Huh? Pattie, can you do me a favor and look through my valise?"

"For what exactly?" Pattie rose from her chair and retrieved Harold's shoulder bag from the dresser.

"A phone number. Or a list of phone numbers. My editor gave me a sheet before we left for Iowa. Some official-looking document. I think it had the paper's masthead on it. Or a picture of a donkey. It's definitely red, white, and blue." Harold pulled a seersucker suit and a yellow Oxford shirt out of his bag. "It may have been embossed."

"I found a folder," Pattie said, producing a red, white, and blue folder from Harold's bag. "Looks plenty official to me."

"Eureka!" Harold leapt across the room, grabbing the folder from Pattie. "Was my press pass in there, too, by any chance?"

Pattie looked at him quizzically. "Yeah, I think I saw it next to your White House Correspondent badge."

"I used it at the RNC," Harold said defensively.

"To get us into the neo-Nazi meeting, or to pay for the Skyline Chili?"

"Here it is!" Harold said triumphantly, pulling out a small laminated card attached to a lanyard from the bag's side pocket. "I'd better put it on my nightstand so that I don't forget."

"Good thinking."

"Oh, look at all the pens I've got in here!" Harold bent over, pawing through the bottom of the bag. "Wow, what a windfall."

"And I was worried about not maxing out our 401(k)s."

"Pattie, remember how I was always asking to borrow your pens? No more!"

"That's wonderful. Did you find the phone number you were looking for?"

"Oh, right. In all the excitement over the pens, I almost forgot." Harold opened the paperboard folder. "Yep, got it. Hey, there are a lot of useful numbers in here. Jeb Bush's Communications Director. Ted Cruz.

John Kasich. Jeez. This would've really come in handy a few months ago."

"Great."

"You know, maybe I'll get in touch with John Kasich's people when I get a free day, just to flesh out that interview if I write a book on this election afterward."

"You could call it *Game Change*. Oh, shoot, that's already taken."

"Is it? Good idea, though. Could you hand me my phone?" Pattie grabbed Harold's phone off the bed, gave it to her husband, and sat down.

"Great. Honey, you're about to see some quality muckraking," Harold declared. He looked around helplessly. "Could you hand me some paper?" Pattie reluctantly rose to hand Harold a small pad of paper with lighthouse illustrations on it. "Thanks. I need something to scrape the mud on after I rake it."

"My pulse is quickening."

Harold dialed. "Is this Jennifer Palmieri? Sorry? Oh. Well, I have a sheet of embossed paper here with this phone number next to her name. Sure, okay, off the record, is this Jennifer? Great. This is Harold Carlyle. I'm a reporter with—how did you know that?" He scratched the back of his head. "I'm the only one on your roster who hasn't called?" Harold looked at Pattie incredulously. "Really? Well, I like to keep my ear closer to the ground in my reporting, I guess you could say."

Pattie picked up a large hardbound guide to Nantucket sitting on the dressing table and began thumbing through the glossy pages, pausing over an ad for Elizabethan Treasures.

"Sorry? No, I wasn't calling about the new slogan, actually. 'Americans Together?' Okay. Actually, I was hoping to get a statement on the Wikileaks. No, sure, if there's room in the article, I'll mention the slogan. Yeah, no, of course. About the Wikileaks, though. Um, in your own words, could you describe to me what they are exactly?"

"Huh, they have a cheese tasting course on Friday," Pattie whispered. Harold vigorously nodded his head in assent.

"How's that? You can't talk right now? You have to wash your hair before the convention?" Harold bit his lip. "Listen, is there someone else at the campaign I can speak to? Huma Abedin, perhaps? She just ordered some lo-mein, huh? Okay. Well, can you let her know that—I see."

"Oh, we could charter a fishing boat. You didn't happen to pack any dramamine, did you?"

"Is there anyone else in the office I could talk to? No one else is in the office? But I hear voices in the background. You're watching *The Andy Griffith Show*? That's just Don Knotts I'm hearing? Yes, he is a riot. No, I've seen the show, yeah. So, you don't have a statement about the Wikileaks. Okay, well, I'll just have to write 'no comment.'"

"Ask them what channel *The Andy Griffith Show* is on."

"Jennifer? My wife was wondering what channel the *Andy Griff*—sorry? The Chinese food just arrived. No, sure, nothing's worse than cold chow fun. No, absolutely. Yes, 'Americans Together.' Right, and it'd be great if you could just let Huma know that—okay, well, if her headache goes away. Thanks."

Harold hung up the phone and quietly watched Pattie read for a moment, before turning back to the bed to repack his bags. "So I think there's a ferry in forty-five minutes. That'll give us plenty of time to return the Mini."

Pattie looked up from her book. "How's that, now?"

"I can book a flight to Philly for us from the road," Harold explained, stuffing a handful of ascots in between brown and navy blue pairs of boat shoes. From Boston, it's probably one of those commuter planes the size of a tuna can."

"Harold, what are talking about?"

"My editor needs us back at the convention. I thought it was obvious after I took his call."

"*Us?*"

"Sure," Harold shrugged, pocketing a set of hotel postcards resting on the dresser. "If we catch a flight by late afternoon, we can probably get to the convention hall before tonight's speeches are over." He walked into the bathroom.

Pattie slammed the travel guide shut and tossed it onto the bed. "I'm not coming."

"What?" Harold emerged from the bathroom, his arms full of complimentary bath products. "You're my sidekick!"

"Try again, Harold"

"Well, not my *sidekick*. But, you know. The person who helps me. My fixer. Okay, not that, either. You're my *mon petit ami*." He looked at Pattie. "My little friend."

"Harold!" Pattie pounded her fist down on a pillow. "Did you even *read* the book Dr. Rothstein gave us?"

"No," Harold said testily. "Unlike *some* of us, I was actually working on the lyrics to my song." He opened the closet door and gathered two pairs of plastic-wrapped cotton slippers.

"This is our *vacation*, Harold. You *brought* us here to make up for the fiasco we had in Cleveland, which was *also* your fault. This was supposed to be four carefree days of swimming and sunbathing. All I've done so far is overpay for lobster and see my last hope of having children chafe away."

"And I *told* you, I'm going to get some herbs as soon as we get back to the mainland." Harold leaned back into the closet. "The coathangers are locked onto the rack. God, talk about paranoid."

"Look, we've already paid for the room here. Why don't I stay, and I'll just see you back in New York after the convention."

"You can't do that! This is our vacation!"

"Right, and *I* plan to enjoy it." Pattie defiantly removed a blouse from her satchel and placed it in a drawer.

Harold scooped up the paper coasters stacked next to the ice bucket. "I wish you'd think about *us*."

"But you only think about *me* when it's easy!"

"Okay, now you're just blatantly quoting my song." Harold picked up the hardbound guide Pattie had been reading and attempted to cram it into his suitcase, sighed, and reluctantly returned it to Pattie's nightstand. "You know, if you came to Philly, you'd get to see Hillary's speech."

Pattie looked at Harold skeptically.

"First woman presidential nominee, and you'd be right there on the convention floor. I can get you in." Harold zipped up his bag. "Well, maybe not the floor, but definitely the rafters. Close enough to feel the history being made."

"I can just watch the speech on MSNBC."

"There's nothing like the energy of the room, though. The bright lights. The roar of the crowd. And the balloons, Pattie! Think of all the balloons dropping. What a spectacular sight that'll be to behold." Harold surveyed the room. "Well, I guess I'm all packed. Last chance to come with me and see Hillary Clinton."

Pattie glared. "We're going to have to talk about this more." Harold nodded his head obsequiously. "But if you're getting access to the convention—" she grimaced, "I'll go."

"Great! We can talk after the convention. Let's just put a pin in this 'till after Hillary becomes the first major-party female nominee. Don't forget your blouse, in the drawer, there."

*   *   *

"He was right in this roundabout," Harold insisted, squinting through the windshield into the glaring afternoon sun.

"Well, he's not here now." Pattie unbuckled her seat belt. "I'll go get our tickets. Meet me at the kiosk."

"No, don't go!" Harold pleaded. "I need your help carrying the bags. My thighs are still sore."

Pattie sighed, scanning the roundabout. "He wasn't exactly Hertz or Avis. It's not guaranteed that he'd be in the same spot today."

"I'm pretty sure he said he'd be here." Harold glanced at the clock in the Mini's center console. "We don't have a lot of time."

"Should we check the American Legion?"

"Here, let's ask these policemen coming over. They probably think we're lost."

Two policemen wearing white polo shirts and black shorts approached either side of the Mini convertible. One of them, with a gentle, sunburnt face and lively blue eyes, tapped politely on Harold's window. "Excuse me, sir," he asked politely. "This your car?"

"No, we're just renting it. In fact, we're actually looking for the man we rented it from. Do you happen to know the guy who's usually here? He's on Square."

"This car's stolen," the officer on Harold's side said matter-of-factly, pulling a pad of paper and a pen out of his shorts pocket. "Now, can I get you—"

"Pattie, it's a sting!" Harold grabbed Pattie's left hand, which she quickly shook free.

"—Your name and driver license?"

"Of course, of course." Harold nervously reached for his wallet and handed over his license. "Harold Carlyle. I went to Columbia." He surveyed the roundabout. "This car is stolen?"

"You 'rented' a car from Dennis," the other officer explained. "He's a legend on the island. Steals things from the locals and sells them to tourists."

"Sort of a capitalist Robin Hood," Pattie nodded.

"Well, I guess if you're going to get scammed, it's better to get scammed by the best," Harold reasoned.

"He snuck onto the Kerry estate last summer and stole Theresa's prize-winning yellow roses," the first officer continued. "Sold them to a couple from Nebraska. Nice people."

"Don't beat yourselves up," the other officer said. "Jack Welch bought three pounds of imitation crab from him last summer."

"Sure, Jack Welch," Harold agreed, making a mental note to search that name. "So, um, can we just leave this with you, then?"

"Unfortunately, we have to bring you in and ask you a few questions first, just for thoroughness' sake."

Harold pursed his lips. "Even though it was a mistake? We have a ferry to catch."

"We need to get to the Democratic National Convention by this evening," Pattie explained.

"Oh," the first officer shrugged. "If you have a boat to catch."

"Just leave the key in the ignition," the other officer instructed.

"Okay, great." Harold popped the trunk and got out of the car to retrieve the bags.

"Also," the first officer ventured, "if you folks would like a little memento to remember your stay, we have some lovely watercolors for sale in the trunk of our cruiser."

"The boys back at the station made them."

"Oh, well, that does sound enticing, but we really need to run and catch that ferry," Pattie apologized, getting out of the car.

"Okay, yeah, sure thing," the first officer replied, crestfallen. "Just write to the Nantucket Police Station if you change your mind when you get back home."

"And be sure to take the survey on our homepage and let us know how we're doing!" the other officer added, waving.

"Thanks, will do!" Harold called as the pair walked briskly away toward the ferry launch.

*   *   *

"I can't believe he charged an *extra* thousand dollars to my card!" Harold repeated, reading his bank statement from his phone.

"What did you expect? The man's a con artist."

"He told me it was a security deposit! I returned the car safely, didn't I?"

"To the police, yes."

Harold considered. His face softened. "That's true. He didn't get it back. And the second thousand is the rental fee. And we *did* have the experience."

"We sure did."

"You can't put a price on experiences, Pattie, because you don't know when you're going to die. It's not like anyone counts up how much money is left on your credit card balance when it's all over."

Pattie sighed. "Harold, I told you he was no good."

"Right, no, in retrospect, that was remarkably prescient."

Pattie stared out her bus window at the tall, wide, gray buildings passing by. Streetlamps cast dim halos of yellow light onto the sidewalk. Between the shoulders of the concrete slabs, traces of a pink sunset sifted through a blanket of dark clouds dissipating after a summer shower.

"Buses are awful," Harold whispered. "Mobile trough urinals." Pattie said nothing.

The bus whined as it ground to a halt opposite an expansive parking lot. Harold and Pattie disembarked, their suitcases in tow, and crossed a set of metro tracks toward a monolithic gray stadium rising in the distance. Eighteen-wheel trucks rumbled across the highway overpass behind them.

"Are you sure we're not back in Cleveland?" Pattie asked. "Same Bauhaus-on-a-budget aesthetic, but with a whiff of 'maybe we'll get stabbed tonight' in the air."

"You'd think this complex would bring a bit more development to the neighborhood." Harold looked to Pattie, waiting for her reply. "Especially with the crowds they must get for the Seventy-Sixers games." They walked on in silence. "Or, I guess, the Sixers." Pattie ignored him, checking her phone. "As they're known in the common parlance." Pattie put her phone back in her purse. "Are we fighting?"

"No," Pattie said tensely.

"Oh, good, I was worried we were fighting." The din of raised voices grew as the pair neared the convention center's entrance. Harold shifted his duffel bag from his left shoulder to his right, pulling his suitcase behind him. "Alright. Let's go see some history being made!"

The couple continued past a metal barricade set up in the middle of the broad sidewalk. The wide road was closed to traffic. To their right, a shirtless man wearing a bandana balanced on a pair of roller blades as he clumsily strummed an out-of-tune electric guitar; to their left, behind the barricades, the space between the Wells Fargo Center's imposing walls and the metal rails was flooded with throngs of people shouting alternatively in protest and revelry. A man wearing a jacket festooned with images of marijuana leaves was moving rhythmically atop a stepladder. Next to him, another man standing on a crate was trying to engage passersby in a call-and-response about the Keystone Pipeline and Cornel West. Harold wondered if the two were linked by design, or purely by serendipity.

"It's hard to tell whether it's a party or a riot, isn't it?" Pattie asked, shouting over the noise of the crowd.

"I can hear America singing, Pattie."

"People always ask me how Kenzie got to be such a good dancer," a woman announced, waving a life-sized cardboard cutout of Jenny McCarthy in Pattie's face. "I never let a doctor get anywhere near her! Her physical coordination is leaps and bounds beyond all of the vaccinated girls."

Pattie raised her eyebrows as she watched the crowd swallow up the woman. "Let's just get inside before Bill's speech. It's at nine."

"I *know* it's at nine. You only mentioned it every ten minutes since we got on the ferry."

"I want to make sure we see it. It looks like the entrance is around this corner, past the mother-son embrace happening at eleven o'clock."

"The moth—oh, Christ, that's clearly his mother, isn't it?"

"Pretend you're not looking."

"Can I interest you in a pin?" An older woman with wavy gray hair tied back in a messy bun thrust a round metal pin into Harold's hand. She was carrying a burlap sack.

Harold stared at his hand, dumbfounded. "Is this like in Italy, where I have to pay for it now, or the Gypsies will get me?"

The woman laughed. "Of course not. Also, the proper term is *Roma.*"

"So it's free?"

"No, this isn't a Communist country, silly. Though, it *could* be." The woman tapped the face of the pin in Harold's hand, indicating its slogan, "Marx-Engels 2016."

Harold stared at the pin again. "I'm sorry, I don't want this."

"That's fine." The woman took back the pin and pulled a t-shirt out of the burlap sack. "Can I interest you in a Black Lives Matter T-shirt? It's a hundred percent cotton."

"Do the proceeds go to Black Lives Matter?" Pattie asked.

"It's a way to support the cause," the woman said evasively. "They don't exactly have a mailing address."

"I'm sorry, I'm not really comfortable buying something if it doesn't go toward supporting the cause directly."

"Well, who ironed on the slogan? It damn well wasn't Black Lives Matter," the woman said, snatching the T-shirt away. "Cunt." She stuffed the shirt into her sack and stormed off.

Harold and Pattie looked at each other, trying to suppress giggles. "Let's go in before we're accosted by any more granola-capitalist upstarts," Pattie mumbled.

"Yeah, that's enough of the public for today," Harold agreed as they joined the line to enter the convention center, which was moving surprisingly quickly.

"Tickets?" a burly Italian-American security guard asked them when they reached the doors.

"Oh, I'm a reporter," Harold explained. "I have a press pass. One second." Harold thrust his hands into his pants pockets, searching for his pass. His eyes widened. He quickly unzipped the duffel, rifling through unworn striped pastel linens. "I know it's here somewhere," he looked up. "Pattie, do you have it in your purse?"

"You never gave it to me."

"Okay, okay." Harold knelt down and unzipped his suitcase, which burst open with a dense mass of silk ascots, wrapped bars of soap, small bottles of shampoo and conditioner, a plethora of pens, and a bathrobe with a lighthouse embroidered over the breast. "It's not here, either. I *know* we had it in Nantucket! Remember? I set it down on the nightstand when I—" Harold froze. "*The nightstand*! It's still in Nantucket!"

Pattie groaned. "You took everything out of that hotel room that wasn't bolted down. How could you forget the press pass?"

"I was off the clock, Pattie." Harold had pulled a seersucker blazer out of his suitcase and was frantically checking its pockets.

"You didn't even *wear* that!"

"Folks, if you don't have tickets or a press pass, I'm afraid I can't let you in." The guard turned to block the doorway.

"Wait, wait." Harold paused, wiping sweat off his forehead. "Here's my driver license, and—one sec—I'm going to pull up my work email."

"Sorry, no can do," the guard shrugged.

"No, wait," Harold said hurriedly, "You wouldn't be familiar with New York City's infamous D-train masturbator, would you?"

"I'm getting the police." The guard pulled out his walkie-talkie. "I have a sixty-two at Gate C," he spoke into it.

"No, no!" Harold thrust his phone toward the guard. "See that story? I'm the reporter who broke it! Harold Carlyle. That's my byline! That was my eye he threatened to—well, you'd have to read the story."

"Harold, just pick up your ascots, and let's go." Pattie had moved just out of line, her arms crossed at her chest.

Deflated, Harold knelt down and stuffed the silk kerchiefs back into his bag. He looked up at Pattie as he zipped the case closed. "Those are cute shorts." Pattie shook her head no. Harold pulled up the suitcase handle and dejectedly wove his way back toward the crowd, Pattie following with an expression of grim disappointment.

"You know, if we make our way to a bar, we can probably still catch Bill's speech." Harold checked his watch. "Unless they're showing a Phillies game."

"Better yet, why don't you just send your boss a link to CBS's website?"

"No, you remember what happened after the New Hampshire primary."

Pattie moaned. "*Harold.*"

"Are you mad?" Harold looked at her inquisitively.

"Harold! That's—that's *it*. That's *enough*. You can go to the bar, or you can stay here, or you can take the metro into downtown and go shopping for a new pair of penny loafers at Brooks Brothers. I've had it." Pattie stopped in the middle of the crowd, crossing her arms and biting her lip with guarded fury.

"Look, honey, I'm disappointed, too, but these little setbacks are something we need to deal with as a team. It can't just be that you do you and I do me."

"You're actually accusing me of just 'doing me'? After everything I've done for you this year? With never a thank-you? *I* do *me*?" Pattie shouted. "Harold, you are the most thoughtless person I've ever met!" Passerby were staring. A homeless man playing "Born in the USA" on the flute stopped to listen. "We left Nantucket for *you*. We're here because of *you*. And now I don't get to see what I *came with you to see* because of *you*. So just do whatever you need to file the goddamn story, and I'll see you back at the hotel later." Pattie stormed off.

"Thoughtless?" Harold called after her. "Who expensed the Plan B medication to his work account in Tallahassee?"

*   *   *

Harold leaned over the counter to flag the bartender's attention. "Excuse me, can you tell me what French wines you have?"

"We got a selection of wines from the Laurel Highlands." The bartender polished a glass, his eyes never leaving the floor. He was a short, hairy man with a dark unibrow, arms as big as life rafts, and a concave chest. His curly black hair was greasy and matted, as if he hadn't showered in days.

"Is that Scotland?"

"About forty minutes outside Pittsburgh."

"Ah. Well, do you have any whites?"

"Just them two WOPs in the corner there." The bartender laughed at himself. Down at the end of the bar, an orange-colored, middle-aged man in a tight black T-shirt festooned with what appeared to be velvet skulls leaned in to his companion, a preternaturally tan woman with long, purple nails and an ample bosom, and nibbled her neck. They quickly began to kiss noisily, then stood up, she standing against the bar as he ground his pelvis against her. "A 2015," the bartender added, checking the label of a bottle behind the counter.

"Interesting." Harold pondered. "Was 2015 a good year for the Laurel Highlands? In any respect?"

The bartender shrugged. "Do I look like a historian?"

"Actually, I had a professor of medieval studies at Columbia who impregnated a Barnard gi—" Harold broke off, noting that the bartender's sense of camaraderie was not piqued by this chestnut. "A glass of the white, please."

"You got it."

The bar's door squeaked open and a skinny young man wearing a gray T-shirt and dark jeans walked into the dimly lit, wood-paneled main room, carrying an iPad under his arm. He spotted the couple, who had graduated to wild thrusts deeply indebted to the gyrations of hormonal birds, and chose the stool next to Harold.

Harold nodded politely at the newcomer and sipped his wine.

"Are you with the press?" the young man asked.

"How'd you know?" Harold replied.

"You look really unhappy," the young man shrugged.

"Yeah, well." Harold took another sip of wine.

"I've heard the job demands a lot of you."

"If you let it," Harold said pridefully. "Are you here for the convention, as well?"

"Yeah, they seemed to think I would be useful here. I was just going to stay home and live-tweet the whole thing, but Donna asked me to come at the last minute." He cracked his knuckles. "Brazile," he added.

"Yup," Harold replied, unsure if the man had said something impressive. He took another reluctant sip of his wine. The young man ordered a gin and tonic, which he sipped uncomfortably, apparently waiting for Harold to speak.

"Six hundred impressions. Not bad," he said, finally, pretending to be distracted by something on his tablet.

Harold glanced at him. "Do you do art for the campaign?"

"Social media. I'm one of Hillary's ninjas."

Harold nodded.

"Yeah, we're gonna drag this campaign into the twenty-first century, even if we have to do it kicking and screaming. They're still doing door-to-doors, handing out fliers. I keep telling them, it's all about data analytics now. I mean, why waste your time traveling around some fucking state like Wisconsin when you can just send out a Snap at the perfect time and have all of America watching?"

Harold nodded. "So, you do Twitter."

"Check this," the man leaned in. "We have ten guys in Williamsburg who are writing tweets around the clock for Hillary. Inspirational tweets. Comebacks. One-liners. Retweets. Total engagement, right? Talking over the heads of the media and getting straight to millennials on their home turf. Like, check this out." The man thrust his iPad in front of Harold. "Trump announced Mike Pence, right? So then we tweeted this: 'If you had any doubts about Trump sticking with his dangerous plan for America, say hello to his VP pick.' Scathing. And then we had a little infographic about Mike Pence. Boom. 'Five things you should know about Mike Pence'."

"Yeah," he agreed, "I like how you've highlighted some of the words in red."

"You want each piece of content to just grab their eyes so they can't look away."

"Like a beautiful woman in the supermarket."

"That's how we're going to reach these Bernie supporters. Targeted viral marketing. Our analytics tell us that the average Bernie voter is a white male between the ages of eighteen and thirty-five," the man explained, "Of course, that's not counting old Jews and publishers of socialist newspapers, but they don't engage with social media."

"You could tweet an infographic at them," Harold suggested. "With bullet points. Ten ways Hillary is like Bernie, maybe."

"Yeah!" the man said, impressed. He began typing a note on his phone. "Tweet Infographic - 'Ways Hillary is like Bernie.'"

"I get all these emails from John Podesta. Is that you?"

The bartender, wiping down a glass, glanced up at a flickering television set mounted in the corner, which vaguely projected a fuzzy image of a gaunt, white-haired man in a blue suit speaking behind a perfectly-arched microphone. The bartender snatched a remote control from behind the counter and turned up the volume. "If you're a young African American disillusioned and afraid, we saw in Baltimore how great our police officers can be, helping us build a future where nobody is afraid to walk outside, including the people that wear blue to protect our future," Bill Clinton intoned from the television screen mounted behind the bar, pointing into the packed hall teeming with red, white, and blue regalia.

"Now this one is tricky," the man commented to Harold, his eyes on his phone, "because Hillary is so committed to black lives, but she's also a strong advocate for blue lives, and sometimes those groups don't engage with the same content." He picked up his phone. "Let me see what data my boys in Williamsburg have. See if we can target both demos. Maybe there's something from Will Smith I can retweet."

Harold pushed aside his glass of wine. "Excuse me," he asked the bartender, "could I borrow a pen and a napkin?"

"You want another napkin? Buy another drink."

Harold slouched on his stool. "I'm sure the CNN website will have the transcript up in an hour."

"Folks, Hillary believes that *all* lives matter. I don't know how you would characterize the gang leaders who got 13-year-old kids hopped on crack and sent them out on the street to murder other African-American children," Bill continued, his face reddening as he shook his finger at the crowd. "Maybe you thought they were good citizens. She didn't."

The young man inhaled sharply. "I'm going to have to retweet one of the emergency infographics," he muttered. "Where's that picture of Hillary and Beyoncé?"

"You've got murderers defending murderers in the streets. You've got agitators defending the people who kill the lives they say matter. Hillary has a record on civil rights stretching back to the *Nixon* administration. And folks, believe me. As a woman—she knows what it's like." The crowd cheered. "She knows what it's like!"

The man chewed the inside of his cheek. "Do you think Bill pulled it out at the end there?"

"Wouldn't be the first time," the bartender said, removing Harold's glass and wiping down the counter with a gray dishrag.

13
"The American People Are Full of Surprises"
August 2, 2016

The following transcript was found within a classified dossier covertly obtained from the Kremlin.

PETROV: Thank you for meeting with me again, Mr. Trump.

TRUMP: No problem, Petrov. But can we make it quick? I'm gonna meet Ted Nugent in half an hour.

PETROV: We have a list of things to address, and when I am satisfied we are finished, we will be done.

TRUMP: A terrific entertainer, Ted Nugent. Great, great person.

PETROV: I very much enjoyed all of the speeches at your Republican National Convention.

TRUMP: Did you see Michelle Obama's speech at the Democrat Convention? Slavery. All she talked about was slavery.

PETROV: Yes. This is why the American people have responded to your campaign, Mr. Trump.

TRUMP: Frankly, if the slaves built the White House, they could have done a better job.

PETROV: Yes.

TRUMP: I've put up a lot of tall buildings, okay? I know what I'm talking about.

PETROV: Yes. I enjoyed your speech far more, Mr. Trump. And I also thought Mike Pence was quite eloquent.

TRUMP: Pence. He's a bit of a showboat, if you ask me. Too eager for the spotlight.

PETROV: Mr. Trump, we are confident, based on our psychological profile, that Mr. Pence is a submissive individual.

TRUMP: I don't know about submissive, but he's much shorter than me. It looks great on camera. I saw those pictures they took, and I thought, Trump is so much taller. People want to see that, Petrov. They want a leader.

PETROV: We can assure you, Mr. Pence will make a loyal running partner, Mr. Trump. Without getting into specifics, let us say he enjoys following orders. Whether or not a strapping black man is tightening on the leash.

TRUMP: You mean Marcus?

PETROV: Ah, you know about Marcus.

TRUMP: Through my son-in-law. They go sailing together in New York Harbor.

PETROV: In total, I would say that the convention was a successful event. I had an opportunity to meet with our mutual friends. The transition of goods was completed.

TRUMP: I thought they weren't going to bring the models to the hotel.

PETROV: The *hand-off*, Mr. Trump.

TRUMP: Yeah, you can do whatever you want with them. That's the point.

PETROV: Ambassador Kislyak also sends his regards. He was greatly impressed with your son-in-law and Senator Sessions. He learned quite a lot about the ethnic composition of your vast country.

TRUMP: Tiny Jeff. What a guy.

PETROV: Yes, Senator Sessions taught him many new terms. It has been a hard time at the Embassy to get him to stop saying "thug." He loves the word.

TRUMP: You should hear Jeff when I have Don Lemon on in the jet.

PETROV: Oleg Deripaska explained that it refers only to African-Americans, but he is using it on everyone.

TRUMP: That's how Jeff uses it, too.

PETROV: Ambassador Kislyak found your Speaker Ryan, as you call him, less interesting.

TRUMP: You won't hear any argument from me there, Petrov.

PETROV: He made the Ambassador feel his biceps four times before the conversation could proceed to a discussion of finances.

TRUMP: Ryan—he isn't so strong. First time I met him, I nearly ripped his arm out of his socket. True story.

PETROV: I would like to discuss strategies moving into the general election, if you have some more time.

TRUMP: Oh, you don't need to worry about winning that, Petrov. I have that covered. Did you see how well I did in the primary campaign? I had a nickname for everyone. People loved it. I had "Low-Energy Je—"

PETROV: Yes, Mr. Trump. I remember from our last meeting.

TRUMP: *Time* magazine wrote a story about me, and they didn't mention the nicknames. Horrible magazine, Petrov. I don't know if you get it in Russia. Nobody reads it in America. Horrible. I don't even subscribe to it.

PETROV: I have taken the liberty of putting together a report on the status of the many cyber-espionage and disinformation programs we have been implementing. The work of our great friend, Mr. Assange, has far exceeded our expectations.

TRUMP: Good, good. I'll send this over to Sean later. Do you ever catch his show, Petrov?

PETROV: Given the sensitive nature of the information contained in the file, this is for your eyes only.

TRUMP: Have someone give it to Jared, then. He reads things for me.

PETROV: The Kremlin has administered similar tactics to these in the Ukraine with very promising results. We are quite optimistic concerning the months ahead.

TRUMP: Terrific, terrific. I really can't thank you enough for all the help, Petrov.

PETROV: Yes. While we are on the topic, in the future, when you wish to ask the Kremlin to hack Secretary Clinton's computer system, please contact us directly.

TRUMP: So you did get the message. Why haven't we seen any of the missing emails yet?

PETROV: They are being held in reserve for when they are most needed in the coming months.

TRUMP: Good thinking. You know, she'll probably try to rig the election. We have to stay on guard. So, so corrupt. Have you heard about that deal? With the uranium?

PETROV: Yes, that story is one of the campaigns we initiated.

TRUMP: Oh, did you break that? You're the only ones telling the truth, Petrov. The American media protects Hillary so much. It's sick. She sold out her country for millions. Millions!

PETROV: Mr. Trump, that was *dezinformatsiya*.

TRUMP: The American people will never elect a traitor, Petrov. They will never, ever do it.

PETROV: The American people are full of surprises.

TRUMP: I don't know about that. You should hear some of the idiot questions I get asked. "Can you bring coal jobs back?" "How are you going to lower prescription drug costs?" "Can you get your hand off my thigh?" Total retards.

PETROV: Do you recall our discussion, at our last meeting, about becoming more presidential as the campaign progresses?

TRUMP: Absolutely. Did you notice the creases in these pants? You gotta tell Dimitry and Oleg about Hope, Petrov.

PETROV: Mr. Trump, we continue to be concerned about some of your more impromptu behavior on Twitter. For example, we strongly urge you to refrain from attacking the Khan family. Their performance at the Democratic National Convention received much sympathy from your people.

TRUMP: Nobody's even proven their son is dead, Petrov.

PETROV: Regardless, internal polling—

TRUMP: Do you think the women have to leave on the veil when you schwang 'em?

PETROV: —negative impact on—

TRUMP: Not that I'd blame the guy. I mean, did you get a look at his wife? I'd have her wear two veils.

PETROV: Certainly, Mr. Trump. We would also like to suggest—

TRUMP: My daughter, Ivanka, dressed up as a gypsy for Halloween when she was about eleven, twelve. Such a special age. Do they get *I Dream of Jeannie* in Russia?

PETROV: I believe the correct term in English is *Roma*.

TRUMP: You know, I was thinking, after this election is over and done with, I'm going to start a new hotel chain.

PETROV: I expect you will be quite busy with the tasks of the presidency.

TRUMP: But not classy hotels, like what I'm known for. I want to make hotels for the people coming out to my rallies. Real shitholes.

PETROV: That is an excellent idea, Mr. Trump. You will only have one chance to monetize the momentum from your first election.

TRUMP: Jared told me to call the chain "America," but that doesn't have "Trump" in it. People love the "Trump" name, Petrov. They see it, and they recognize quality. Like "Stouffer's."

PETROV: Indeed. It is wise to start making plans for after the election. In fact, the Kremlin has prepared a list of potential—

TRUMP: By the way, did Putin like the case of Trump Water? He never sent me a card.

PETROV: Yes. Putin gave the case of your water to a very thirsty journalist in St. Petersburg.

TRUMP: Great. It's the best water, Petrov. Better than Evian. People don't believe that at first. I tell them, "Better than Evian." The best water.

PETROV: Mr. Trump, we will want to take another meeting before the election, of course. But for now, we urge you to read over the file yourself, and to keep in mind the guidance we offer.

TRUMP: I'll look at it tonight. I read very, very quickly, Petrov. People can't believe it. Hope said it just the other day, as a matter of fact. I was reading an article about my campaign, and she looked up from the floor and said, "I can't believe it." *Reader's Digest*. That one's boring. *National Enquirer*. They had a tremendous story about Hillary in there; did you see it? She had a blood transfusion from a Jewish banker. The media isn't reporting on it. So, so rigged.

PETROV: Yes. Thank you for your time, as always, Mr. Trump.

TRUMP: Of course, of course. Anytime. Can you walk out with me? I think Melania's outside, and I need a buffer.

14
"A Part of History"
August 28, 2016

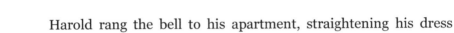

Harold rang the bell to his apartment, straightening his dress shirt as footsteps approached on the other side of the door.

"Yes?" a man asked politely, opening the door. He was short, plump, and bald, with large, inquisitive brown eyes and a bushy, black mustache. "Something else you forgot to pick up?" The man arched his dark, bristly eyebrows.

"Forgot to pick up? Oh, um." Harold rocked back on his heels. "Well, yes, actually. The wife and I were just headed uptown to a bris—to a, to a family ceremony, of sorts—very traditional—and we realized that we've been without our bedroom rug."

The man nodded testily. "Your Craigslist posting said this sublet was for a furnished apartment."

"Well, yes. Yes, I know."

"Two weeks ago, it was the candles. Then the candlesticks. Then the watercolor in the bathroom. Then the matchbooks in the odds and ends drawer. Then the odds and ends drawer."

"The matchbook was from Sardi's. My mother gave it to us."

"Then the photo album."

"Oh, ah, when we said 'furnished,' we were thinking of just the furniture-type things," Harold apologized. "I mean, we don't have a picture of your wife in the AirBnB we're renting, right, Abbas?" Harold attempted a laugh, hoping he had pronounced the man's name correctly.

"My wife?" Abbas asked, perplexed.

"Oh! Or your wiv—plural—you know. However you manage it."

Abbas looked at Harold askance. "You said you want the rug?"

"Only if it's okay with you. I don't want to intrude."

"Please," Abbas sighed, opening the door wider for Harold to enter.

"Oh, Pattie loves this end table," Harold smiled. He picked up a lamp, placed it on the floor, and ran his hand along the small wooden table that had been supporting it. "There's really nothing like the comfort of home, is there? Surrounded by all your familiar possessions."

"Yes." Abbas continued to stand by the door, his arms crossed at his chest.

"So, the quarters aren't too cramped for all of you?"

"Jahan Katoon and I are very comfortable."

"Right, of course," Harold nodded, rearranging the coasters on the coffee table. "So, does Katoon sleep on the sofa, or do you all pile up in the bedroom?"

"It is just two people," Abbas corrected.

"Right, Jahan, Katoon."

"Would you like a tote bag to carry out your rug, Mr. Carlyle?"

"Oh, yes, sure, that would be great. We keep them above the fridge. Though, I guess you would probably know that already, wouldn't you, Abbas?" Harold added, sounding out the syllables of his sublettor's name with great care.

Abbas crossed the living room, into the kitchen, and reached above the fridge to retrieve one of the numerous tote bags packed together in an even larger reusable grocery bag.

"You know, I was reading the 'Modern Romance' about polygamy that ran last weekend—" Harold began, trailing off as Abbas handed him a canvas bag. "Actually, if you can find our WNYC bag up there, Pattie's been dying to get that back, as well."

"As you wish," Abbas grumbled, crossing back to the refrigerator, with Harold behind him. He reached up and produced a red tote.

"Wonderful. And then, if I may venture into the bedroom?" Harold placed the totes on the endtable, which he had carried with him into the kitchen.

Abbas nodded in assent. "Come," he motioned, walking several steps ahead of Harold.

"Splendid, splendid. So they go out unaccompanied during the day?"

Abbas emerged from the bedroom carrying a small, thick, ornately patterned rug.

"Thank you so much, Âbba*s*," Harold gushed, tucking the rug under his arm. "We hate to bother you, but this is something of a family heirloom. It's Per—well, it's, it's from very far away."

"Understood." Abbas nodded again. "I don't want to make you late for your event."

"Oh, no trouble at all. It's not very important. Kind of a bon voyage, of sorts."

"In any case." Abbas guided Harold the four steps it took to cross from the bedroom's threshold and living room back to the apartment's front door. "I hope you have all of your things now."

"I hope so, too, *Abbás*" Harold said, slinging the tote bags over his shoulder as he lifted up the endtable. "You know, though, I was actually thinking, if we find that we're still missing a few things, in that AirBnB of ours," he began, pausing to adjust the bag's strap. Abbas looked at him quizzically. "I was thinking, you know, that you might agree to, um—" Abbas stared at Harold blankly. "Well, I'll just give you a call, you know, in advance, if I find that we're missing any more things, and I'll pop over, as I did just now, and pick them up."

Abbas nodded.

Harold took inventory of the objects in his arms. "So, we've got the bag, the rug, the endtable, and the ship in the bottle."

"The ship in the bottle?"

"On top of the china cabinet. My wife is incredibly attached to the ship in the bottle."

*   *   *

Pattie stood back up from the red brick wall she had been leaning against as she heard the front door of the apartment building clank open, Harold pushing against it with his back as his arms strained with the weight of Carlyle heirlooms.

"How generous of you to leave him the breakfast table," Pattie scoffed.

"Pattie, can you imagine how rude that would've been?" He stumbled down the last couple steps of the stoop, recovering his footing on the sidewalk.

"I'll hail a cab so we can take this stuff back to the apartment."

"Oh, first we have to stop at Magellan's to get another ship in a bottle."

"Is that thing finally gone?"

"Pattie, you love the ship in the bottle!"

Pattie laughed. "Frankly, I can't stand the sight of anything that reminds me of your Uncle Grover."

"It's probably a good thing that I broke that Myrtle Beach ashtray on the way down, too, then."

"Did you ask Abbas about moving out early this time?" Pattie asked, picking up the endtable as a cab slowed to the curb. "Seeing as we still don't have anywhere to live after the AirBnB runs out?"

"That's not how you pronounce his name, sweetie." Harold slowly crouched down to gather stray coasters that had fallen onto the sidewalk. "And, no, I couldn't be so insensitive."

"The city's not exactly oversaturated with affordable, short-term rentals. The only AirBnBs I could find available were all the way out in the ungentrified part of Brooklyn."

"What do you think we should do?" Harold asked.

"Well, there's probably a room waiting for *you* already in West Virginia."

"Oh, so *you* want me to go on the road, too?" Harold asked defensively.

"I'm just saying, my parents will let me stay with them if they know that nobody will be calling an appraiser as soon as they leave for the symphony."

"Look, I'm already hearing it from my editor. I get it. *Everyone* wants me to 'break a story.'" Harold placed a coat rack on the floor of the cab, then slid into the frayed dark blue seat. He cranked down his window, and a warm breeze flooded the backseat. "Manual windows," he mused. "When I was a kid and came into the city with Gram and Gran, the cabs still had tailfins. That's kind of crazy, when you think about it."

Pattie nodded.

"You didn't like Gram and Gran, either, did you?"

"They called Tiger Woods' wife 'a waste of a woman,' Harold."

"Because he cheated on her! Because he cheated on her."

Pattie told the driver their destination, and the cab took off down the street, narrowly missing a line of Hasidic Jews in the crosswalk.

"Pattie!" Harold nudged her, nodding in their direction.

Pattie shook her head. "You're like when someone sees a deer."

"Where do you suppose they're off to?" Harold turned in his seat and watched them as the cab sped away.

"Maybe they found a freshwater stream."

"I grew up with plenty of deer in my neighborhood." Harold pulled his head back in from out the window. "Not many Hasids." A faint chime emitted from Harold's pants, and he reached into his pocket to retrieve his phone. "Oh, the travel app sent an update on airfare for San Diego."

"Really? On Skyscanner?"

"Oh, no, I should check that, too. No, this was Roamify." Harold's phone buzzed again. "Oh, and Oyster." He scrolled through the notifications on his lock screen. "Something coming in from Wanderful, too. Looks like this is the weekend for San Diego."

"You know, I heard about an app that aggregates alerts from all the other apps."

"I should get that app." Harold scrolled through the long list of travel options displayed on his screen. "None of the ticket prices quite meet our budget yet. Apparently, we can rent a couple motor scooters for a song if we book before two." Pattie wrinkled her nose in disapproval. "It'd be just like *Easy Rider*!" Harold implored.

"And with any luck, it would end the same way." Pattie stared out the window at the line of stoic brownstones trailing past.

"I think it's mainly flat from here to San Diego," Harold mused. "If you go through the Southwest."

Pattie shook her head no.

"It might be fun. Didn't you hear what Dr. Rothstein said about you needing to open up your life to creative choices?"

"He was talking about going to that ayahuasca shaman in Williamsburg, not smearing my internal organs across I-80."

"Pattie. Do you remember when Dr. Rothstein gave me a picture of a stapler, and then he asked me to describe the picture to you, so you could redraw it?"

"You described a pair of scissors."

"Yes, but Pattie, the point is, you didn't *go with it*."

"I don't care. I'll sign up for his group cleanse, but I'm not motor-scootering for marriage."

"Pattie, this is why Dr. Rothstein had to grow that beard! You need to allow yourself to be surprised."

Pattie glanced down at the phone in Harold's hand. "It's projecting the flight prices will go down after Labor Day. San Diego will still be there in a month. Or two or three, even."

"Lucky for us, the paradise of San Diego isn't seasonal." The phone suddenly began to vibrate in Harold's palm. He yelped in surprise, dropping the device between his legs. "It's my editor," he said, reading the screen lit up between his feet.

"Pick it up!"

Harold looked down helplessly at the cab's scuffed rubber mat. "It's on the *floor*," he hissed. "Do you have gloves in your purse?"

"Oh, for God's sake." Pattie leaned down and retrieved the phone, handing it to Harold, who accepted it with a grimace.

"Hello? Oh, hi, sir. How's that? You got the—uh huh. Uh huh. Well, sir, it's not improbable that CNN and I were reporting on the same events in language that, constrained by the demands of journalistic objectivity, was not dissimilar."

The taxi pulled to a stop in front of a gray, seven-story building with a blue awning over a door speckled with bird excrement. Pattie pressed a series of buttons on the cab's touch-screen to pay the fare. "Excuse me?" she asked the driver through the plexiglass divider. "It won't let me select 'credit.'" The driver spoke rapidly in a foreign tongue into a hands-free headset. "There's some kind of strange grease on the screen."

"But I've filed quite a few stories since the conventions, sir," Harold protested, cupping his hand over his mouth. "Well, yeah, but Wolf Blitzer has guys he can put on the hunt for a scoop 24/7, whereas I have to eat, and sleep, and get some exercise. Right—no—of course, sir. Yes, a hundred percent, sir. Agreed. No, thank *you* for the constructive criticism. Never too old to learn."

Pattie tapped on the glass. "Excuse me? I don't have cash, and I can't get this screen to work." The driver tilted his head ever so slightly in Pattie's direction, but continued to talk into his headset without acknowledgement.

"What have I been hearing on the campaign trail? Lots, sir. So much, in fact, it would be near-impossible to distill it in a phone call. Well, we're about to go do a story on the coal miners. I mean, I'm going to go speak to the coal miners. By myself. I mean, Trump is going to talk to the coal miners, and I'm going to go with him, and then I'm going to talk to them afterward, after he's done."

The driver leaned back and looked at Pattie skeptically. "Push the buttons," he said irritatedly. Pattie threw up her hands.

"What's that, sir? Breaking story about Anthony Weiner, you say? Don't tell me he was sending pictures of his penis to another woman again, ha ha!" Harold's smile slowly morphed into a grimace. "Ah. Huh. Well, obviously the man needs help."

Pattie tapped on the plexiglass divider. "Hello? The payment options aren't even up now. It's just a video of Jimmy Fallon in Miami with Pitbull."

"Interview him? Well, sure, sir, I'd be happy to, but is he even doing interviews right now? I doubt he'd respond to a request from a prominent paper. Oh? You already set it up? Oh, well, thank you, sir. No, definitely, this is a huge favor. Yes, sir. Slam dunk. No, I'm very grateful. Well, thank you for giving me another chance to prove myself, sir. Only a couple more weeks left to show you? But the election isn't until—oh. Sure. No, understood."

Pattie tapped on the divider again. "Excuse me, are you on Square, by any chance? This isn't working."

"Tomorrow at nine, huh? Not a problem, sir. I'll just head to the airport straight from the coal mine this afternoon. Yup, that's the life we've chosen, ha ha. Absolutely. Have a good one, sir." Harold put his phone back in his pocket.

"Okay, all set," Pattie said triumphantly.

The driver tapped a button on his headset. "Have a nice day," he said hurriedly.

Pattie leaned forward in her seat. "May I ask who you talk to on the phone all day?"

"My wife," the driver answered. "She is my best friend."

*   *   *

Fourteen stories above Union Square, Harold rapped hesitantly on a light maple door. A small dog yipped from within another apartment further down the brightly-lit, austere gray hall.

"I'm coming!" a woman's voice called out.

"Must be one of his lovers," Harold mumbled to himself. He heard a series of clicks and the turning of a heavy door handle.

"Hi," a tall, slender woman with brown hair and puffy, bloodshot brown eyes said tiredly. She had on a tight-fitting HILLARY 2008 T-shirt and a pair of stretchy athleisure pants. Harold noticed that she was wearing no makeup and had dark circles under eyes. "Are you the reporter?" she asked.

Harold made a series of vocalizations that failed to reach the threshold of cognizable words. The woman smelled very good.

"Come in, come in," the woman said. "Anthony isn't here yet. He spent the night at his mother's."

Harold nodded. He noted that the woman's breasts were unusually large for her height.

"Actually, I don't know if he's coming back today or not," she continued, somewhat hoarsely. "I'm sorry," she said, extending her hand. "Huma Abedin."

Harold shook her hand gently, noticing that she wasn't wearing a ring. "Harold Carlyle," he said in his deepest, most masculine voice.

Huma nodded, then her eyes widened slightly. "Harold *Carlyle*?" She looked at him with interest. "You wrote the GOP Bus Exposé piece back in April!" She smiled. "We *loved* that story."

Harold blushed. "I—yes, I did." He attempted to chuckle, but coughed on his own saliva. "Do you want me to come back, or to ask—or just follow up tomorrow, depending on everybody's schedule, or something else?"

"Sorry?" Huma asked. "I didn't understand that."

"Or if you just want to talk," Harold tried again. "Off the record. For background." Huma looked at him skeptically. "You know, so I have your different angles in mind. Of the story."

"This is really a personal matter," Huma apologized. "Honestly, I don't know why Anthony insisted on doing this interview in the first place."

"Maybe he thought I was a teena—obviously, he has a problem," Harold cleared his throat. "Not necessarily one you two can't work through, of course. But, I mean."

"We've been trying to do just that for years now," Huma sighed. "Marriage counselors. Spa weekends upstate. Hillary even bought us a two-week trip to the *Cinque Terre*."

"Oh, really?" Harold's eyes widened. "Is she hiring?"

"She's looking for a new social media ninja," Huma said, wiping her nose with the back of her arm.

"I'm actually very familiar working in real-time across platforms," Harold ventured, smiling to himself. Huma looked at him. He cleared his throat again.

"Sure, if you want to send over your resume, I guess." Huma shrugged. "I obviously have a lot on my plate at the moment, so I can't promise anything." She forced a laugh. "Just trying to make it to November."

"Aren't we all?" Harold muttered. "You know, if you need someone to talk to..."

"I think plenty of people already know too much about my personal matters."

"No, not—I mean, between us, I'm a veteran of couples counseling myself," Harold offered. "My wife and I have weekly hearing sessions with a practitioner on the Upper West Side. He's very good."

"Dr. Schoenberg?"

"Oh, no, he was a little too didactic for us. Dr. Rothstein."

"Dr. Rothstein?" Huma's eyes widened again.

"Yes!" Harold said excitedly. "We've been seeing him for five years."

"The one who puts on the pageant, right?"

"The very same. I was cast as the owl last year."

Huma nodded. "I heard Silda Spitzer played the owl in 2005."

"Ah, yes, that was before our time. Obviously, I'll never be able to jitterbug as well as her."

"There's no beating Silda."

"You know, Dr. Rothstein just did an exercise with us the other day that I thought really helped. We could do it together, if you'd like."

"Oh, Hillary's already showed me how to make a dream journal."

"No, no, this is different. It'll be great. Really reorients your perspective on things. Here, do you have a piece of paper and a pen?"

Huma looked down at the satchel hanging from Harold's shoulder, then turned to retrieve a pen and a pad of paper from a table nearby. She handed them to Harold.

"I loved Hillary's Senate run," Harold said approvingly, glancing at the pen. "This must be a collector's item now." Huma nodded modestly. "Now, I'm going to describe a picture, and I'll need you to draw it."

"Oh, is it a stapler?" Huma asked as Harold handed the paper and pen back to her for the exercise.

"Oh. Yeah." Harold replied, deflated. "How did you know?"

"I do this with Hillary all the time," Huma said nonchalantly. She quickly sketched a nuanced forced-perspective illustration of a stapler, tore the page off of the pad, and handed it to Harold. "It helps her unwind after campaign events."

"This is very good," Harold admired. "When my wife tried it, she drew scissors."

"I always know that it's a stapler," Huma said matter-of-factly. "We did thirteen of these after the Jefferson-Jackson Dinner alone."

Harold nodded. "Can I keep this?"

"Actually, I need to add that to the file," Huma said, snatching the drawing away and quickly folding it into thirds.

"Okay," Harold said glumly. "Want to do a trust fall instead? I make a great bottom."

"I have a conference call with our North Carolina team in three minutes," Huma said, standing up quickly.

"Oh, okay, sure," Harold said, rushing to stand up. "Um, if you ever want to talk, you know, or do an interview, or anything, here's my card." He reached into his pants pocket. "Shoot, I must have left them in the apartment. We're subletting this—well, anyway, Harold Carlyle. My email address is probably in my byline somewhere."

"I'll be able to get in touch with you if I need to."

"Right. Just check the voter rolls!" Harold laughed as Huma began shepherding him toward the front door. Huma didn't smile.

"Oh!" Huma brightened. "I almost forgot to test our new slogan ideas on you. Which do you like better: 'Stronger Americans'? Or 'Americans, Stronger'?"

Harold considered, attempting to parse Huma's tone to determine which slogan she preferred. "I think they're both good," he said, finally. "You know, because Hillary is so strong. And so American."

Huma nodded. "Or 'Hillary Can Fix It?'"

"That one's good, too."

"Great." Huma wrote herself a note on the pad of paper.

"Perhaps you can alternate between the three slogans, you know, on Twitter or something."

"Yep," Huma nodded, opening the front door and nudging Harold out.

"Ooh, or how about this? Put up a poll! Let the voters decide."

"We don't really like to involve the voters on such high-level decisions," Huma explained, slowly pushing the door shut.

"Of course, of course. Disgusting people," Harold agreed. The door closed with an authoritative, bank-vault *thunk*.

Harold lingered in the hall for several moments. He let out a long, contemplative sigh and smiled. Suddenly, his phone began to vibrate. He glanced down, saw Pattie's name, pressed the silencer button, and walked toward the gleaming elevator bank at the end of the hall. He sang softly to himself. *"Cheer up sleepy Jean / Oh, what can it mean / To a daydream believer / And a homecoming queen."*

*   *   *

"Excuse me?" Harold asked a pot-bellied woman with curly black hair who was pushing a plastic cart containing large boxes of individual yogurt containers. "Will you be opening the omelet bar this morning?"

"No," the woman replied without stopping. "Omelet bar's on Tuesdays and Thursdays only."

"Ah," Harold nodded, crestfallen, surveying the short buffet line to his left. A middle-aged man wearing a loose-fitting, faded Swarthmore sweatshirt that vaguely masked a beer-belly jabbed a metal serving spoon into a mountain of pale yellow scrambled eggs. Harold contemptuously studied the gold wedding ring displacing wads of excess flesh fore and aft on the man's left hand.

"Sorry to make you wait," the man said as he slopped a slushy pile of eggs onto his plate and slowly shifted down the buffet line.

"Not in any hurry to get to those," Harold shook his head. "You'd think they could just leave the eggs on for three more minutes, right?"

The man paused mid-ladle, looking quizzically at Harold.

"Kanawha Falls has less liquid than those eggs," Harold smiled. The man looked at him. "That place we drove past yesterday."

The man shook his head. "I can't complain," he shrugged as he nabbed two flaccid strips of bacon out of the tray in front of him with a pair of tongs. "Most days, it's nothing but bran flakes."

"I know, I've stood downwind," Harold muttered under his breath. He took an orange from a bowl of fruit sitting atop a beat-up white microwave and found an empty seat at a long table packed into a bright, windowless conference room. Around the table, harried-looking men and women, their faces still puffy and creased from sleep, stared uniformly down at their phones, typing, scrolling, or simply looking fixedly at their glowing screens. Harold proudly ran his hands up and down his perfectly-pressed pant legs and Brooks-Brothers shirt, smirking inwardly at the baggy, untucked Macy's button-downs most of the men at the table wore. Not wanting to be left out, he pulled his phone out from his right pocket and scrolled through his messages, but seeing nothing from Pattie, he placed it down on the table next to his tray.

"Has Hope sent out his clarification on Hillary's health?" a woman asked, looking up from her phone only to check the flat-screen TV broadcasting CNN from the far corner of the hall.

A man with rumpled hair and a Weezer T-shirt underneath an unbuttoned work shirt shook his head. "She usually doesn't send them until right before their bus leaves."

The woman sighed exasperatedly. "So many plates in the air right now," she muttered. The others around the table groaned in assent.

"Hmm, plates, yeah," Harold murmured.

"Did you ever hear back from her about Trump's tweet?" the man asked. "I still don't have a response from them about whether Trump was serious about Joe Scarborough getting a penis enhancement."

"I think they clarified that he was 'just ribbing,'" the man in the Swarthmore sweatshirt said through a mouthful of eggs.

"*Fuck*," the man moaned. "Well, I gotta call my editor before the bus leaves, in that case."

"Just wait for him to call you," Harold offered, peeling orange rind onto his plate. "Sometimes, they don't even notice."

The man glared at Harold suspiciously, while the woman sitting next to him made a slight choking sound. "You *have* to correct it," she said.

The man stood up, grabbing a tattered blue-cloth messenger bag draped across the back of his chair. "Well, I'm gonna have to do it from the bus. It's almost time to line up."

"Shoot," the woman said, gulping down a half-full cup of coffee and leaping to her feet without taking her eyes off her screen. "I'm getting something about Kellyanne being offline for the next forty-five minutes. Is anyone else seeing this?"

"She just denied my request for a follow-up with Mike Pence about his favorite movies," the Swarthmore man said as he lumbered to his feet, bringing with him a half-eaten scone.

"Dammit," the woman muttered as she headed out the door. "I keep trying to circle back with her about my piece on Ivanka's advocacy for women's rights." Harold watched the doors clank behind the group and looked around the suddenly-empty room. The TV screen displayed video of Donald Trump, proudly wearing a white hard hat perched atop his head, striding across the floor of an industrial plant. Grinning broadly at his side, a small group of white-haired men, noticeably shorter in stature, posed for photos as Trump pointed to a large metal hook hanging from the ceiling.

A perky waitress with platinum-blonde highlights walked over to Harold's table clutching a pot of coffee. "Sir?" she asked. "The press bus is about to leave."

Harold looked at her, then to the double doors, then back up at the television. "Could you turn up the volume?" he asked, nodding in the direction of the screen. "And also, maybe some more fruit?"

The waitress nodded cheerily and walked back in the direction of the kitchen. "Oh," Harold called after her. "And do you have a pen?"

*   *   *

"Left!" a short, wrinkled man with translucent-gray skin yelled as he brushed past Harold and shuffled down the road in black lycra shorts.

"And then my editor calls me a *second* time and says that maybe I should write for the Style section if I'm going to spend four hundred and eighty words on Huma's cheekbones."

"Some people wouldn't know good journalism if it came up and bit them." Pattie squinted up into the morning sunlight beating down through wispy branches of light green leaves and slipped on her sunglasses. Joggers and cyclists cruised past them on either side of the path, snaking deeper into the park. A family of Korean tourists hesitantly crossed the road in front of them and climbed down a small embankment to a hillside of descending boulders tangled in ivy. "You didn't chase down any stories the whole time you were on the road?"

Harold and Pattie turned off of the wide pedestrian boulevard and onto a narrower, root-embedded path, which meandered up a small hill shaded by a dense cluster of trees resplendent in their late-summer finery. "Pattie, I'm telling you, you've never had such a miserable two weeks. You have to be up by six in the morning most days. You spend all day in a bus or a room. The other reporters write down *everything* somebody says. They're like those kids in high school who would start writing whenever the teacher opened her mouth."

"Dorks," Pattie sniffed, wiping sweat from her brow. They paused at the crest of the hill to catch their breaths. The heat was already building, and the air was thick and damp.

"Nobody breaks for lunch. One day, in Philadelphia, they went to the *vending machines*. For 'lunch.' At three p.m., I might add. And then when the day is done, they head to the hotel bar and drink into the small hours of the morning. They swap notes on stuff they heard during the day."

"You didn't get any good leads from them then?"

"When?"

"At the bar. After hours."

Harold snorted. "I don't want to be derivative, honey. My boss told me he wants *me* to break a story."

"Far be it from me to question your process," Pattie muttered.

"And then there was this guy who works for the *Wall Street Journal*. Jay-something. He had a different outfit for morning and evening. I don't know if I mentioned him. He—"

"Jay Solomon. I know. I got the emails you sent me every afternoon," Pattie said exasperatedly. "How did you have time to write those? Weren't you at rallies?"

"There were a lot of things you had to have a press pass to get into, and I couldn't always find mine."

Pattie stopped. "You still haven't replaced that press pass?"

"I tried calling the office, but there's a fifteen-dollar replacement fee that comes out of my paycheck," Harold explained. "*And* I'm in enough hot water with my editor already. All that paperwork would get to his desk at some point."

"Yeah, better not to replace it, in that case."

"No, I'm pretty sure it's in my duffel bag, here at home," Harold assured her. "It just hasn't been in my travel satchel, that's the thing. Anyway, it turns out that CNN still just shows Trump's rallies in their entireties." Harold sat down on a rock shaded by an overhanging elm. "So, what do you want to do about breakfast? We could wait until the ice cream vendor pulls up at the West 72nd Transverse, or we could find a diner."

"Oh, how about we go back to that place off Columbus? You know, where you tried to order a peach, off-menu?"

"Look, there was a peach pie in the display counter. They obviously *had* peaches."

"Allow me to explain how restaurants work."

"So, I have to settle for peach derivatives? That's no way to live."

"We all know you don't settle, Harold," Pattie sighed.

"Pattie, those muffins have probably been in the lobby of the Hotel Wayne since you checked in. I would wonder what the Health Inspector might say about it, but I assume his rotting corpse is in the room next to ours, directly under the air vent."

"At least the Hotel Wayne is closer to the park than the AirBnB was," Pattie offered.

"If proximity to the park is such a high priority, we can steal a piece of fencing from back there and fashion a lean-to by the Jacqueline Kennedy Onassis Reservoir. At least then we would know some effort had been made to get semen off of the walls."

Down the other side of the hill and to their right, a clearing came into view, casually demarcated by a line of rope attached to small metal poles spaced unevenly apart. A group of tanned, athletic-looking men and women in their twenties had staked out a corner of the field and were stretching. Two of them were passing a kickball back and forth.

"I told you I got fired from my first internship because I wouldn't join the kickball team, right?" Harold asked. Pattie shook her head no. "It was at *Time*, the summer after my junior year. They had a kickball team in the park that all the interns were encouraged to play on, on Wednesday nights."

"So what?"

"I had to find a different reason not to go each week. One week, I told them that my family had gone to the circus and my cousin Mitchell had a dangerous encounter with an elephant, but then they saw me going for a jog in the park during the kickball match." Harold breathed in sharply. "Very repressive company." A loud, metallic yawning crescendoed overhead. He looked up to see a jet following a low arc across the skyline and toward Long Island.

"Flying sort of low, isn't it?" Pattie asked. "I guess it's heading to LaGuardia."

"Oh, Christ, today's 9/11!" Harold exclaimed.

"And I thought you didn't use that desk calendar I got you."

"Pattie, this is great!" Harold enthused. Pattie made a face. "No, I'm *supposed* to be in Manhattan today. There's some memorial ceremony downtown. The candidates are going to be there. Well, Hillary and Trump, at least." He pulled out his phone and checked his email. "I completely forgot. I guess that just shows how much we've healed as a nation, right?"

"When does it start?" Pattie asked, pulling out her own phone to look up the details.

"Right now," Harold said, quickening his pace. "I've gotta get downtown. Do you want to come?"

"Eh," Pattie winced. "It's really hot out. I think maybe I'll grab a bagel and walk around the Met. There's a new exhibit on indigenous art from the South Pacific."

"Yeah, that would be better," Harold sighed. He thought. "I could probably file this from the museum cafe. It should be pretty straightforward. Rubble, something about firefighters, 'we will never forget,' et cetera, et cetera." Pattie glared at Harold, who had pulled out his phone. "I bet there's an archive of George Bush's old speeches somewhere."

*   *   *

"One second, one second." Harold held up a palm to the security guard standing before the metal barricades separating the memorial site from the sidewalk. "*She* gets to look at indigenous art," he muttered under his breath. He looked back up at the security guard and laughed affably in an attempt to defuse the tension. The guard remained stone-faced. "It's got to be in this one. Hang on." He reached deeper into his worn leather messenger bag and pulled out a plastic key to the Des Moines Des Luxe hotel, a matchbook from Sardi's, and many empty gum wrappers, placing them on the ground for organizational ease. The security guard, a strong, tanned man with a shaved head and aviator sunglasses, stood impassively before Harold, blocking his way. Beads of sweat glistened at his temples, tracing lines down the side of his face. Behind him, a mass of people crowded around the reflecting pool at the September 11 Memorial. Brass instruments sounded faintly inside, their tones reverberating against the concrete and glass towers encircling the site.

"Surely, you've heard of the paper, at least," Harold implored with exasperation. "Didn't you think it was odd that no one from a major New York journal had arrived to cover the ordeal?"

"Your gum wrappers are blowing into the street."

"Shit," Harold said, thrusting the matchbook into his back pocket and jumping up to retrieve the small metallic papers.

"Unfortunately, sir, even with the proper credentials, we can't let you in. The memorial has already begun, and we aren't admitting late arrivals, out of respect to the memory of the deceased."

"Memories," Harold corrected. The guard tilted his head confrontationally. "You know," Harold continued. "As a writer."

"If you'd like, you can wait with the public across the street."

"The *public*?" Harold exclaimed. "Can't you just make an exception? I'll sneak in undetected. No one will even know I'm there until it's over."

The guard squinted into Harold's eyes. "That's expressly against the rules, Mr. Cropper."

"Carlyle," Harold corrected. "I *showed* you my library card."

"Sir, as we've discussed, there's a fairly strict list of documentation I can accept."

"You know, it pains me to hear talk like that in America, on today, of all days." Harold shook his head and began typing an email to his boss on his phone. "Ceremony very moving," he began. He thought. "Really hot here. Many dignitaries. Themes: America, not forgetting, remembering." He nodded to himself and pressed send.

The guard stepped off to one side to let a horde of men and women in dark suits exit the memorial area. They hustled past Harold, hurrying down the block toward a line of black vans idling curbside.

"See?" Harold exclaimed. "People are coming out. If it's disrespectful to come in late, it's got to be worse to leave early."

"Did *I* let that group out? That's someone else's decision. What I know is, no one's allowed in after the event begins."

"Look, I may not be a lawyer, but I've covered enough public indecency cases to know that a standard is meaningless unless it's consistently appl—"

Harold was interrupted by the wail of a siren as the first van in the line took off from the curb, accelerating into oncoming traffic and running through a red light. Burly men in black suits moved quickly and authoritatively, forming a protective phalanx around the door to another van in the queue. Scattered onlookers holding up their cell phones moved closer to the activity. Another siren squealed, then the remaining vans in the queue took off in a procession, followed by a dark Town Car and two police motorcycles.

"What was that all about?" Harold asked, dumbfounded, looking back toward the ceremony to make sure it was still ongoing.

"Hillary Clinton fainted," the guard said nonchalantly.

"What?"

"You didn't see that? There was a big hullabaloo." Harold looked back and forth from the memorial to the curb, where a local news crew had descended to interview a bystander. The guard wiped his forehead with the back of his hand. "It's really hot."

"Why didn't you tell me?" Harold demanded.

"You're the reporter," the guard shrugged.

"How was I supposed to know that was Hillary's entourage coming out?"

"Hey, look, I think they're actually wrapping up in there if you want to stand near the back."

*   *   *

"And you can put extra tuna on that," Harold advised the waitress as he sat back in an orange vinyl booth, having once again broken a personal rule never to dine in an establishment that featured pictures of the food on its menu. He replayed video of the incident on his phone. "Not much more you can write than 'Hillary fainted,'" he muttered to himself.

"Hey, is that you?" the waitress asked, looking at the video over Harold's shoulder.

"Huh?"

The waitress pointed to a thin blond man in the corner of the screen. "That looks just like you. Same shirt, too." She smacked her chewing gum loudly. "Yeah! Same bald spot, too!"

Harold ran his hand over his crown. "I don't think that's me."

"No, yeah, see? Same shape and everything."

"A lot of men have that," Harold said defensively, reaching for a packet of Splenda.

"Yeah, a lot of men who are balding." The waitress watched as Secret Service agents surrounded the van. "That's pretty cool! You were a part of history!" She pocketed her notebook. "I'll be back with your sandwich in a second, but I don't think we have twelve-grain bread."

Harold rewound the video and watched it again from the beginning, using his fingers to zoom in on the lower right corner of the frame. "A part of history," he whispered to himself. He opened his phone's camera app and raised the device over his head, leaning forward so that his crown would be in the shot. The phone made a synthesized approximation of a camera shutter's click. He examined the photo. "Well, taken from so close up, sure," he said to himself. He repositioned the phone over his head, this time angled a little to the side, when it suddenly began to vibrate excitedly in his hands. Harold dropped the phone in shock, yelping as it bounced off his crown and onto the taut plastic seat.

"Shit," he said to himself as he saw his editor's phone number. Bracing himself, he pressed the "accept" button. "Hello, sir?" Harold gingerly caressed the thin, colorless hairs atop his head where the phone had hit him, making sure everything was still in place. "Sir, I promise you, I'm working on a report right now. I am hunched over my desk, looking at my notes and keeping an eye on the clock, just like you alwa— oh? Yeah, how about that? A part of history, sir!" Harold glowed.

The waitress returned with a sandwich overflowing with tuna salad. She nodded at Harold.

"Miss?" Harold put his hand over the phone. "So this is only regular wheat bread?"

"We only got white, wheat, and rye." The waitress popped her gum.

"Is the rye seedless?"

The waitress sighed. "You wanna come back and look at the bread?"

Harold waved her away. "No sir, no, no, I was just jousting with my wife. We're having a little 9/11 memorial luncheon, here in our apartment, as I put the finishing touches on the story about today. What have I got so far? Well, you know, Hillary left early; she tipped over. Right, fainted. Additional sources? You mean, calling the campaign to make sure she's okay? I'm sure once they get a Gatorade in her—health issues? People have—people have been saying Hillary has health issues? Huh. No, of course I knew that, I just didn't realize how it all fits to—it's really hot, sir." Harold motioned to the waitress, who returned to his table.

"Another iced tea?" she asked.

"Is it free?" Harold asked. The waitress nodded yes. "Sure, then."

"No, no, sir, of course I'm not in a restaurant. You know how wives are, sir. Everything's a negotiation." Harold chuckled with an artificially deep laugh. "How's that? Did Hillary look ill?" Harold smacked his lips. "Hard to say, sir. I mean, she fell over. Right, so obviously, yeah, you could say that she didn't look well. It was really hot out. Yes, definitely, it could have just been the heat. Yeah. Right, or it could have been a health thing. Uh-huh. No, I think you nailed it with those two options, sir. Probably one of those two. No, I mean, I thought about it myself, and those were the two I came up with, too. Yeah, no, I'll be sure to talk about that in the story."

The waitress returned with Harold's iced tea, placing down his bill alongside it. "Whenever you're ready," she said cheerily.

"Sorry? No, that was the missus again. Just discussing the rest of our 9/11 plans. We can never remember, sir. Right, 'forget,' yes. No, no, probably staying inside, after this morning. Oh, you have no idea, sir. Like being in a burning build—no, of course. Not what I meant. Just, it went on and on. Praying. Talking. Singing. Talking. Praying. Standing. Sitting. You have to go already? Sure, if they're showing the Concert in Central Park on PBS, absolutely. Okay, I'll finish up this report and send it off to you. Right, I'll be back on the road tomorrow. Ah, I think we're going to South Carolina, all of us in the gaggle. The corps, as they say. Yeah. Happy 9/11! No, no, I mean—well, *we're* still here, sir. You know, so we can be thankful that we remember. Right."

Harold placed his phone back onto the table. He glanced at the bill and removed a card from his wallet, flagging the waitress's attention.

"All set?" the waitress asked.

"Yes, thank you," Harold said, handing her his card. "Can I get an extra copy of this receipt? My company will be picking this one up. After all, it's not every day you're a part of history."

15
"I Am Deeply Ashamed and Embarrassed"
October 7, 2016

"Hello?" Harold leaned down to speak through the metal grate at the bottom of a smudged bulletproof glass window that read "Hotel Wayne" in chipped orange paint and served as the only opening to the hotel's concierge desk. "Señor Wayne?"

A lanky, older Hispanic man with a crop of jet-black hair looked up from an antenna he was adjusting atop a small, flickering black-and-white television set. The set's painted fake-wood laminate was flaking off. "My name is Natividad, Mr. Carlyle," he said acidly.

"Of course, of course. I'm so sorry. *Lo siento.*" Harold nodded to Pattie, who had walked over to the counter, carrying her opened laptop. "Anyway, Navidad, we've been at the Hotel Wayne for five weeks, and the maid has only refilled the shampoo once in that time," Harold continued.

Natividad shrugged broadly. "You want shampoo. Pay your back rent."

"The bill increases every hour!" Harold protested.

"This is a capitalist country, no? Plenty of people willing to pay for beds each hour." Natividad waved his hand, indicating a group of young women in tight neon dresses and fishnet stockings lounging around a beat-up faux leather sofa at the other end of the dim lobby.

"Wayne, there have been a number of problems besides the shampoo. I even made a list—on toilet paper, I might add, because there's no stationary in the room." Harold reached into his pockets. "Hang on." He patted down his front and back pockets. "Pattie, do you have the list?"

Pattie shook her head no, distracted by a video of Donald Trump speaking to Billy Bush and a tall blonde woman on her computer screen. "We were out of toilet paper yesterday," she explained apologetically. Natividad bent back over the antenna, slowly turning it clockwise as the television's speaker crackled and popped.

"I happen to remember most of the list," Harold warned.

"*Bueno*," Natividad said absently. He slammed his palm against the side of his television set.

"First, this hotel is crawling with spiders. No pun intended. Second," Harold counted off on his fingers, "I have yet to find a wood or wood-like surface that is not chipped. Third, there was a merkin in the Bible instead of a bookmark."

"Mr. Carlyle, what can I say? This is not a private home."

"Fourth, there was blood on the sheets. When the maid brought new sheets, those, too, had blood, as though you have a special arrangement with a laundromat owned by hemophiliacs." Natividad inclined his head with an expression of faux thoughtfulness. "And fifth, but by no means least, on Monday night, when we returned to our room, there were *people in it*."

"He was a trainee. He learn on the job."

"Wayne, that man was stark naked. *Completamente nutado*." He nodded his head authoritatively.

"He is getting better."

"I don't believe you."

"It was David Schwimmer. Rehearsing for mini-series. This is New York. Lots of filming. We have been in many episodes of *Law & Order*."

"Well, that explains the sheets. But there's no way that was David Schwimmer."

"He did have a lot of gel in his hair," Pattie looked up. "And he was pretty whiny. Though, that could've just been the penis cage."

Harold slapped his hand down on the counter. "Wayne, this is inexcusable!"

"You want excusable, you stay at the Plaza!" Natividad shouted, slamming down the antenna. "Oh, it works!"

"Wayne, I'm not sure how familiar you are with other Manhattan hosterlies. I mean—well, obviously you run an upstanding business here." Harold inched out of the way to make room for a bare-chested man, who approached clutching a red-stained shirt around his forearm.

"Restroom?" the man groaned. Natividad pointed toward the other end of the lobby. The bare-chested man nodded perfunctorily and slumped through a makeshift curtain of tan beads.

"As one of the better-traveled reporters in Manhattan, I just want to help you cater to a higher class of clientele."

Natividad turned up the volume on the television. "You owe back rent. Five hundred and six hours."

"Five hundred and *six*?"

"You paid at 3:18 last time." Natividad looked at his watch. "It's 5:32 now."

"Well," Harold started in a huff, placing his hands on his hips. "Does that include last Saturday morning? Because we were at brunch with Pattie's parents until well after noon that day."

"There were things in your room," Natividad shrugged. "Bags, razors, chastity cages. We charge you."

Pattie closed her laptop and leaned down next to Harold to speak through the grate. "Look, Señor Natividad, if we pay the back rent we owe, plus an advance on another week, will you clean the room of all spiders, blood, and fetish paraphernalia? Maybe throw some shampoo in there for good measure?"

Natividad considered the proposal. "*Sí*. I even have one of the girls bring you a bath mat."

"We don't *have* the rent," Harold whispered to Pattie.

"I know. I keep some extra cash stowed away for a rainy day," Pattie shrugged.

"From your bat mitzvah?" Harold asked. "Those sure go a long way."

Pattie rolled her eyes and pulled out her checkbook. "Here, let me just write you a check."

Natividad tapped on the bulletproof glass above a sign reading, "Cash only. Dispose of all needles in proper receptacle."

"Okay. I'll have to stop at the bank. Five hundred six hours, you said?" she asked Natividad.

"*Sí*," Natividad nodded gruffly.

"Excellent," Harold assured. "Don't you worry, Señor Wayne. We'll get this all taken care of."

"*Sí, sí*," Natividad said dismissively, waving his hand. His attention had returned to the television set in front of him, which was airing the video Pattie had been watching on what seemed to be an endless loop, occasionally cutting to some very concerned-looking people sitting in a news studio. "You see this?" he asked Pattie. "He say when you are a star, they let you do anything."

Pattie shook her head mournfully. "Yeah, I've seen it."

"He is a cocksucker, *sí*?" Natividad asked.

*　　　*　　　*

The elevator's blue metal door creaked open, and Harold and Pattie stepped in.

"Hold the door!" An African-American woman in a baby blue dress and ruby slippers ran toward the doors, which were wheezing shut. A slender woman with dyed blonde hair and Slavic-looking brown eyes, a thin, angular nose, and singularly poised breasts reached out her arm to keep them open.

"Thanks, baby," the African-American woman smiled sweetly at the blonde woman, who nodded back. Harold and Pattie pressed up against the back wall of the tiny elevator as the two women filed on, and the car lurched disconcertingly downwards before beginning its uphill climb with a loud *thunk*.

"Just got back from O'Reilly's. He wanted to wear the gorilla suit again," the African-American woman said, pulling out a compact and checking her eye makeup in its small mirror. She shook her head. "I guess I shouldn't complain. If not for that pre-show ritual of his five nights a week, I'd be back at Port Authority. And I didn't get out of Minneapolis just to sell MegaBus tickets."

"Yes, very lucky we are," the blonde woman sneered. She spoke with a thick Eastern European accent. "In Russia, I was treated like Czarina. Most beautiful girl in all of Moscow. I was a nine. The gentleman told me so."

"Honey, look at you. You're a knockout any country you're in." The African-American woman put her arm around the blonde woman's shoulders and pulled her in closer to her. "If I pulled even one of the Johns you did, I'd be able to retire." She shook her head. "Fuckin' cheapskates. You'd think being held on retainer, I'd be okay on cash flow. Singing 'Shortenin' Bread' to Tucker Carlson over and over would cost them a fortune if I charged my usual rates," she grumbled. "But you've seen how Rupert runs his ship."

"I was the only one Donny actually pay. He always say I remind him of his daughter."

"These assholes will do anything to get out of paying a bill. Sean Hannity once insisted for forty-five minutes that I hadn't finished him off. Oh, really? I guess he just shouts '*sic semper tyrannis*' all the time?"

"All of the glasses in the Ritz were always clean," the blonde woman mumbled. "They send us here. Someone named Steele want to ask too many questions." She shook her head. "So what? I see Carter Page every day for a month. He only want to talk, too. I am, how you say, used to it." She sighed. "They say the Steele man know about videos. Say I have two choices." She tossed her head, flipping back a lock of platinum-blonde hair. "At least I am here."

"Carter Page, Carter Page." The African-American woman smacked her lips. "That's the guy who looks like a frog with a bowel problem, right?"

Harold leaned forward from the wall. "Actually, a lot of people think Carter Page has rather handsome features."

The blonde woman turned and studied Harold's face. Quickly, she grabbed a pendant hanging from around her neck, pressing down on an emerald embedded within the gold setting. "This summons Dimitriov," she warned him.

*   *   *

Harold sat awkwardly perched atop the nightstand in their hotel room, one leg crossed tightly over the other for balance, peeling a tangerine. The low ceiling creaked overhead, on which a large, yellow-brown stain had formed from some prior or current leak. A bare light bulb hung directly over the bed, swaying precipitously in reaction to otherwise imperceptible airflow. Its light cast an ominous shadow from an austere Virgin Mary figurine mounted on the wall above the worn wooden headboard. In the corner, a small, curtainless window looked through a set of steel bars into the cardio room of a women's gym across the alley. Harold looked up occasionally from his tangerine, watching a heavy middle-aged woman with a frizzy ponytail swing her legs vigorously back and forth on an elliptical machine.

"Oh my god!" Pattie exclaimed from the bathroom.

"Oh no," Harold said, swallowing the last wedge of the tangerine. "Did the maid menstruate all over the linens?"

"Josh at the *Today* Show just got me an interview with Billy Bush!" Pattie rushed into the bedroom clutching her phone and ran to her laptop, which was perched on an upturned milkcrate.

"Josh?" Harold asked. "Billy Bush?"

"Just, wait for it to hit the newsstands." Pattie typed excitedly. "Also, the toilet handle came off."

Harold shook his head. "It's like we're staying in the Third World."

"At least there's that good chicken place downstairs."

"Miss Lily's Jerk Shack is a *restaurant*?" Harold's eyes widened. "I should probably go down and apologize."

Pattie made a noncommittal noise, staring at her screen and continuing to type hurriedly. "I wonder if there's any old *Access Hollywood* footage on YouTube I can study up with," she mumbled to herself.

"Are you auditioning for something?" Harold raised his eyebrows inquisitively. "I thought you didn't like being on that side of the camera. You didn't even like playing the horse last year."

"I'm *interviewing*. I scored one of the first interviews of what will be a long week for the latest Bush to fall short of America's already-adjusted expectations."

"Did Billy Bush call Al Roker the N-word?"

"Really got your finger on the pulse there, Harold."

"You know, he's thin now."

"Haven't you been checking your phone?"

"I turned off all of my alerts. They were making me nervous."

Pattie rapidly typed something on her computer, then turned the screen around to face him. Harold hopped off the nightstand and crossed the room to get a closer look. He read aloud the headline that was splashed across Pattie's monitor. "'Trump recorded having extremely lewd conversation about women in 2005.' What's the follow up? 'Opens Tacky Hotel?'"

"Harold, this is a real 'get.' This story is everywhere. It could seal the election for Hillary."

"What happened?"

"Watch the video." Pattie clicked her spacebar, and the video that Harold had noticed her watching in the lobby began to play.

"You know, bitches aren't particularly known for the way they move on people."

"Right."

"Oh! That guy! I thought that was Ryan Lochte."

Pattie watched Harold watch the video's conclusion. "*Everybody* wants to talk to Billy Bush now."

"Well, that's great," Harold said quietly. "When's the interview?"

Pattie looked at her watch. "At my office in about two hours."

"At nine o'clock?"

"Billy's people want to get out in front of this thing. That's why I pounced on it," Pattie said, smiling with pride.

"So, should I bring extra pens, or do you have a box at the office?"

"Why would *you* bring anything?"

"It's just, it'd be a shame to get all the way down there and not have a pen."

"This is my interview, Harold," she said matter-of-factly.

"Pattie, my career! My boss said I only had a few more weeks to prove I could do this, and he just rejected my fourth follow-up to the 9/11 Memorial story."

"All the more reason at least one of us should be successful."

"It's different for you," Harold snapped. "You can always have kids if you get tired of this. Well, I mean, probably only for another couple years, but..."

Pattie slowly and deliberately put down her laptop and walked over to her suitcase, staring straight down at the floor. "I'm going to need you to go to the fundraiser tonight, now," she said coldly after several seconds, not looking up. "I promised Natalie I'd go, and if one of us doesn't make an appearance, she won't invite either of us back to the Yacht Club next summer."

"Which one was that, exactly?"

"What *do* you pay attention to?"

"You go to a lot of fundraisers."

"This one's the Ruth Spellman Legacy Scholarship." Pattie moved quickly, searching through the zippered pockets for her earrings

"I thought Ruth was still alive."

"She is," Pattie said levelly. "They started planning for the scholarship last winter, and I think they were just playing the odds."

"Okay, I can do that," Harold agreed quietly. "I didn't have anything planned tonight, anyway."

"Good," Pattie said tensely, rushing into the bathroom. "You need to cash that check for Natividad on your way there, too."

"For who?" Harold called.

"Señor Wayne."

"Oh, right. Alright, just write me the check, and I'll cash it and then head over to the dinner. Where is it, exactly?"

"It's in the old McGraw-Hill building on 42nd. In the Penthouse."

"The Penthouse? Wow." Harold rummaged through his bag for a dinner jacket. "Imagine where it'd be if she were dead."

Pattie reentered the room, adjusting one of her earrings. "There was talk of renting out Bemelmans, but Dorothy Fitzsimmons was just diagnosed with renal failure, so I think they're going to hold out for that."

*   *   *

"Is this it?" a slender, tanned man with gleaming white teeth, impressively thick, feathered hair, and the gray eyes of privilege asked, glancing around a sparsely-decorated vacant office overlooking Lower Manhattan's twinkling lights. The darkness and Friday night stillness of the building's corridors made the room seem even more brightly lit in contrast.

"Yep," Pattie said, setting up her laptop and pulling a fresh yellow legal pad and ballpoint pen from the top drawer of her desk."

"So make-up will come in here?"

"There's no make-up guy," Pattie explained politely.

"Cool. I always carry a travel case in my bag."

"No," Pattie corrected. "This is a magazine."

"So, it's just a video for the website?"

"No, I'm going to write down what you say."

The man nodded with comprehension. "Like, for subtitles on the video."

Pattie sighed. "Let's just get started."

"Okay." The man moved a white imitation leather swivel chair from the corner of the room and sat down in it across from Pattie's desk. He inhaled and exhaled slowly. He had dark circles under his eyes and looked as though he had lived through several years in the past few hours. "Looking back on what was said on that bus, I wish I had changed the top—"

"Hold on," Pattie smiled. "I'm going to *interview* you. You don't just have to talk."

"Oh, okay." The man looked relieved.

"So, describe to me what today was like. You wake up, you're Billy Bush. You have a gig at the *Today* Show. Things are going pretty well. Then this video drops."

"Yeah." Billy Bush exhaled again. "Looking back on what was said on that bus, I wish I had changed the topic. Trump liked TV and competition. I could have said, 'Can you believe the ratings on whatever?' But I didn't have the strength of character to do it."

Pattie nodded. "It sounds like you've already done a lot of reflection about this."

"Well, Katie, it's been a wake-up call. A time to become a man. I was kind of bopping along, and I don't know if it was God or what that said, 'OK, you've developed. You're a pretty good guy. Let's see how you handle this.' And ka-boom!" Billy Bush put his face in his hands. "It all comes apart."

Pattie scribbled a note down on her legal pad. "Do you recall what was running through your mind at the time? I know it was a number of years ago."

Billy Bush furrowed his brow. "Um, regret. Remorse. You know, I'm a father. I have three daughters. So, you know, deep shame, and thinking, the universe is challenging me."

"Right, but—2005 Billy Bush. What's he thinking? He's on the bus. He's speaking with then-reality-TV host Donald Trump. What's his reaction?"

"When I was talking to Ryan Lochte on the beach this summer, he told me, if he could go back in time, and see that God was challenging him not to pee on that forecourt, he would have done a lot of things differently. That's how I see it. If I could, I would not have gotten on that bus."

"Definitely, in retrospect. But, at the time? You thought, 'I should not have gotten on this bus'?"

"If a moment like that arose again, I would shut it down quickly. I have three daughters. The youngest one is twelve years old. She will never watch this tape."

"Absolutely. Is that what you were thinking of at the time?" Pattie offered.

"You know, you live, you learn. You aren't born a man. You have to become a man. Those were the sorts of—that's the kind of experience that—you go through the fire, and you come out of it a man. If I could, I would not have gotten on that bus."

*　　*　　*

Harold strolled down the length of a rococo wooden table covered in what looked like pieces from a Smithsonian exhibit about the nineteenth century's monied class. His eyes caught a cardboard picture display of a brown hillside tumbling into an expanse of sparkling deep blue water. Leaning in closer, he noticed that Ernest and Diana Van Der Kampt's winter condominium on the La Jolla coast was being auctioned off on a week-by-week basis from November 15 through January 15, exclusive of the week between Christmas and New Year's. Harold read through the description excitedly. "Mere steps away from the beach. We love to spend winter nights out on the terrace, listening to the seals bark."

"*Seals*," Harold whispered to himself, whistling with pleasure. He looked at the suggested opening bids at the bottom of the placard and reached into his back pocket, clutching an envelope stuffed with twenty dollar bills that he had obtained from the bank. Perhaps if he wrote some freelance articles, he thought, he could make up the cost by the end of the month. He scribbled down his bid on the form and stepped away a couple feet, feigning interest in other nearby items, all the while keeping an eye on anyone coming too close to the display.

"Harold!" a woman's voice called out from behind him. Harold turned around to see Natalie Apfelbaum approaching. "You don't have to jump, it's only me," Natalie said. "How *are* you? It's been entirely too long. Pattie texted saying you'd be here."

"Oh, Natalie!" Harold smiled politely as Natalie pecked him on either cheek. "I'm fine. How are you?"

"I mean, shocked and disgusted tonight," Natalie winced, "but otherwise, pretty well."

"I know, this chicken. It's like someone dumped a jar of paprika on each kebab."

"I meant the Donald Trump video." Natalie looked at him. "The food was catered by refugees."

Harold cleared his throat. "Right, right, the video. No, the food is very inspiring."

"Anything here to your liking?" Natalie asked, gesturing to the auction items next to them.

"Oh, yeah." Harold eyed the Van Der Kampts' display cautiously. "I was just about to put a bid in for this item right here, actually," Harold said, indicating a collection of black and white wooden masks with long, grotesque noses.

"Ah, the Venetian plague masks! I'm sure you've seen the set in our study." Harold nodded warily. "Well, you've got a keen eye there, Harold. I had no idea you were such a collector."

"Oh, we have a couple shelves going," Harold said, bending down to write a bid on the form. "Pattie and I love the plague."

"You don't say? Wait until I tell Anthony. He's an absolute nut for artifacts from the Republic of Venice. I'm sure he'd love to come over and see your collection."

"Fantastic," Harold said evasively. "Once this election wraps up, we'll figure something out." He shook his head slowly as he closed his eyes to indicate that he could not believe the stress under which he labored. "It's been a monster year."

*　　　*　　　*

Billy Bush sighed deeply and ran his hands through his feathered hair, which fell perfectly back into place. "I want to make that clear," he enunciated solemnly. "I deeply regret it, and I regret the Americans who I—who I let down, tonight."

A janitor entered Pattie's office, pulling behind him a large trash cart, and crossed the room wordlessly.

"You mean, eleven years ago." The janitor reached over Pattie to grab the waste paper basket next to her feet. Pattie ducked down in her seat to maintain eye contact with Billy. "Were you thinking, at the time, 'I'm letting down America?'"

"I am deeply ashamed and embarrassed," Billy replied. "The people of America"—the janitor banged his hand against the bottom of the waste paper basket, trying to dislodge a soiled sandwich wrapper into his trash cart— "The people of America deserve better than this behavior," Billy spoke louder. "Going forward, you can be sure that I will not participate in anything like that. And I will keep my eyes out and do what I can to stop it from happening."

Pattie sighed and clicked her pen closed. "Right."

The janitor grabbed ahold of the swivel chair in which Billy sat and began to drag it across the room. Billy looked up at the janitor, then back at Pattie. "Are we done now?"

*　　　*　　　*

"No, *sí, sí*," Harold spoke loudly into the phone's receiver. Pattie pushed open the door, which squealed as she forced the hinges to move.

"I got all of the air fresheners they had," she whispered to Harold, motioning to a plastic bag. "I had to get a bag."

Harold nodded appreciatively at her. "No, the bed has been made," he continued into the phone. "Yes. *Gracias.* No, well, the problem is, there now appears to be vomit in the bed. Yes, the bed is made. Yes, thank you."

"These are for cars, but they were cheapest," Pattie whispered, opening a package of tiny black Christmas trees. Harold mouthed the word "anything."

"Right," he said loudly and clearly into the mouthpiece, "but it seems that, either before or during her making of the bed, the maid vomited in it. *Justo.* Indeed. That's what's so baffling about it, Wayne."

Pattie began hanging tiny black Christmas trees from available perches, cursing as a doorknob fell into her hand upon contact.

"Well, for starters, we need someone to come up and change out the sheets," Harold said sternly. "And I'd like this hour deducted from our rent." Harold tapped his fingers impatiently on the dresser, causing the room to shake. "And some complementary shampoo would be great. Okay. *Gracias*, Wayne." Harold hung up the phone, looking back over at Pattie. "He says the soonest the maid can come is next Tuesday."

"Why is he still giving us the runaround?" Pattie asked, spraying an aerosol can back and forth above her head. "We paid the back-rent we owed."

"Yeah, the back-rent," Harold said evasively. "You know, I decided to take my boss up on his offer to fly me to the debate in St. Louis on Sunday."

"His *offer?*"

"Does everything have to be a cross-examination with you? Fine, his *assignment*. But I decided, since there aren't a lot of leads in New York, and it's so hard to snag a decent interview around here, I may as well cover it in person."

Pattie hung up her blouse and slipped on a T-Shirt from the 2012 New York Marathon. "I'd like to watch it in person too, if you have a hotel there. I'll just dip into the rainy day fund again, I guess." She sat down on the edge of the bed, and one of the thin metal legs collapsed underneath her. "You gave Natividad the money, right?"

Harold leaned against the window's steel bars and contemplated for a moment. "I haven't told you about the banquet yet!" he said, standing back up.

"Was the bank still open?"

"Oh, yeah, no, the bank was open. But it was very confusing, at the silent auction—no one tells you that the 'silent' part also extends to a lack of instructions—and I think we own a pair of Venetian plague masks now."

"You *think* we own?"

"Oh, no, I mean, we definitely own. But we have another few days before the rent is really due here."

"Oh, for God's sake. That was from my rainy-day fund!"

"Yes, but—bright side! Since we're decamped here for a bit longer, we can at least get some use out of the plague masks."

16
"The Language Merits Further Development"
October 8, 2016

The following transcript was found within a classified dossier covertly obtained from the Kremlin.

TRUMP: So, I told the guy, "Look, if you want your money, you can find it on your sister's dresser. Okay?" Some people. So ungrateful. So disloyal.

PETROV: Yes, Mr. Trump.

TRUMP: I didn't pay him, see.

PETROV: Right.

TRUMP: I'll invite you down to Mar-a-Lago for a weekend, once all this election baloney is over and done with. Fabulous resort, Petrov. High, high ceilings. People come, they say, "Look at these high ceilings."

PETROV: I'm looking forward to it, Mr. Trump. Now, if we may move onto more pertinent matters.

TRUMP: Absolutely. Did you see what David Brooks tweeted about me? Do we have anything on him?

PETROV: Mr. Trump, we are very pleased to inform you of the Main Directorate's progress in infiltrating your American voting systems. We have covertly acquired the voter rolls for a number of states, focusing on those that typically prove more crucial under your electoral college system. We are learning a great deal about voters at the local and even individual level.

TRUMP: Terrific, terrific. Did your guys get any information on Iowa? They love me there.

PETROV: Iowa is not considered to be a decisive state in this election, Mr. Trump.

TRUMP: Are you sure? They love me there, Petrov. Love me. I took my helicopter there. Gave people rides in it. They loved it. This one girl in particular. She was a real knockout. A farmer's daughter, you know what I mean? Do they have that term in Russia?

PETROV: Not since Stalin. We now have sufficient data to begin the weaponization process. Fake news articles will be targeted at individual voters on Twitter and Facebook, designed either to discourage them from voting for your opponent, or voting altogether. Just as we discussed in June.

TRUMP: Big, beautiful, juicy jugs. Had never been in a helicopter before. I said, "I'll take you in a helicopter."

PETROV: While we are on the subject of meetings, Mr. Trump, I must ask that your associates stop trying to arrange meetings with Ambassador Kislyak. He is a most busy man. He has many engagements. It is, as you say, *enough already.*

TRUMP: Oh, okay. Sure, sure.

PETROV: Last week, for example, he met with Jefferson Sessions, Mikhail Flynn, Jared Kushner, Jared Kushner again, and then Eric.

TRUMP: Oh, no, he definitely wasn't supposed to meet with Eric.

PETROV: He has his own life, you see.

TRUMP: Oh, you don't have to tell me about that. I have a very, very busy life. Everybody wants a piece of me. Just now, Maggie Haberman called asking whether I'll give an interview if she prints Ivanka's prom photos.

PETROV: Mr. Trump, as you know, you have another debate with Mrs. Clinton scheduled for tomorrow night. The Kremlin is eager to know the status of your preparations.

TRUMP: I am so, so prepared. I got a couple tricks up my sleeve. Get this. I've invited all the women Bill's banged.

PETROV: Mr. Trump—

TRUMP: Well, not the fat one with the dark hair. But most of them. The good ones.

PETROV: Unfortunately, Mr. Trump, it is unlikely that this will dissuade the media from raising the subject of the videotape that, how you say, *dropped* yesterday.

TRUMP: American media is sick, Petrov. Sick. Do you know I even apologized for that? I made a video last night, a video for CNN, all the cable news networks. I apologized. The most sincere apology you've ever seen, believe me. Sick.

PETROV: Yes. Be that as it may, it would be good for you to rehearse a statement to deliver tomorrow.

TRUMP: Bill screwed so many women, Petrov, and nobody ever talks about it. Nobody brings it up. Women I didn't even screw. Fat ones. Ones with small racks. Grown women, with tiny racks, he did them.

PETROV: If you would humor me for several moments, Mr. Trump, I would very much like to practice some questions with you, which you may hear at tomorrow's debate.

TRUMP: Absolutely. I love the debates. I do so well at them. Did you watch the Republican primary debates? The best ratings there have ever been for debates. Everyone says it. Even the New York *Times* had to say it.

PETROV: Our sources indicate that Mrs. Clinton's campaign is vaguely aware of some relationship between your campaign and Russia. It is possible, Mr. Trump, that she will bring this up.

TRUMP: What relationship?

PETROV: Mr. Trump.

TRUMP: Look, I'm not doing anything that anyone else isn't doing. You think Hillary wouldn't take your call?

PETROV: Regardless—

TRUMP: You didn't call her first, did you?

PETROV: Mr. Trump, what would your response be if Hillary Clinton were to insinuate that you were a puppet of the Russian government?

TRUMP: Puppet? No, no puppet. No puppet!

PETROV: That is the essence, but the language merits further development.

TRUMP: No, trust me, that's great. People remember the catchphrases. "You're fired!" "Make America great again!" "Michael, tell that guy with the billy club to wait for her in the parking garage!" People have short attention spans. They like simple things.

PETROV: Your daughter, Ivanka, has prepared a response to the question, which she will rehearse with you.

TRUMP: Oh, wonderful. You've seen Ivanka, right? Amazing. Three children, but she still looks like she's seventeen.

PETROV: She is a lovely woman, Mr. Trump.

TRUMP: Listen, if you looked anything like her, these meetings of ours would probably go a lot different, let me tell you.

PETROV: We would also warn you that Mrs. Clinton may attempt to play what you call a head game tomorrow night. To distract you, make you angry. You understand?

TRUMP: Already thought of that, Petrov. Already thought of that. I have a plan. An old business tactic. I'm gonna follow her around.

PETROV: You will do what?

TRUMP: I'm gonna hover around her through the whole show. Anytime she answers a question, I'll be right behind her like Eric on the nanny. She'll turn to address the crowd and—boom—there I am out of the corner of her eye. Pretty great, right?

PETROV: In light of the recent videotape, we must advise against this strategy.

TRUMP: No, no, leave it to me, Petrov. Trust me. I know business tactics. Did you read *The Art of the Deal* yet?

PETROV: Perhaps whenever Mrs. Clinton is speaking, you can try picturing someplace that makes you happy. I am told the men we keep for interrogation often try this tactic to remain calm.

TRUMP: Petrov, look, I know what I'm doing here, okay? I have the best ideas. The best ideas. A few years back, I pitched this idea to NBC, but they didn't like it. So, so dumb. It was a spinoff of the *Apprentice*, but instead of business, I judge women based on their legs.

PETROV: Yes.

TRUMP: We could have had Wayne Newton do the music. I've met him. A terrific entertainer. A friend of mine, a very good guy. So, we would have had Wayne Newton on the music.

PETROV: Finally, the issue of your ta—

TRUMP: So many ideas for shows. They come to me like that. Like snapping your fingers. My fingers are so strong, it's hard to snap.

PETROV: —your tax returns.

TRUMP: Maybe a show on Ivanka. You know, such a great, great body. I haven't worked out all the details on that one yet. Maybe, I don't know, we show it at night.

PETROV: Mr. Trump, for obvious reasons, you cannot disclose most of your tax returns, but it would be beneficial to develop a longer answer to this question, as well. We have prepared an explanation that is getting circulation on Twitter, which we would like you to amplify at the debate. If you look on this notecard—

TRUMP: I don't need a notecard. It's very simple. I'm not releasing those, Petrov. I am not releasing those. They already made me do the debates. I did not want to do them. So unfair. I was so good, I thought, this is a waste of time, right? Because everyone knows Hillary will cheat. But the media is so corrupt, they would not cancel.

PETROV: Mr. Trump, this concludes the time we have this evening. Please listen closely to Ivanka and practice your apology with her. Everything is proceeding according to plan, so we simply need to avoid any unnecessary errors.

TRUMP: Of course, of course.

PETROV: Take, for example, Mike Pence. He studied very well for his debate and remembered all of the responses that had been prepared for him.

TRUMP: Such a loser. Are you wiretapping him? We have to make sure he doesn't go rogue. Thinks he's such a big shot. Indiana.

PETROV: Governor Pence knows that we are in possession of the plastic straw *and* the statue of St. Francis with the lubricated stigmata holes.

TRUMP: Great, great. We have to make sure he stays in his place. Usually, I'd move on his wife, but, I mean, have you seen her? I have a reputation to protect. I'm running for President of the United States.

PETROV: Mr. Trump, this, of all things, should not concern you.

TRUMP: Terrific. Did Putin like the ties I sent? I saw a photo of him in the paper the other day, and he wasn't wearing any of them.

PETROV: Yes. They are his favorites. He wears them when he is relaxing.

TRUMP: Oh, fantastic. Fantastic. Remind me, and I'll have Hope send him some socks to match.

17
"Looks Like a Meme Forming"
October 9, 2016

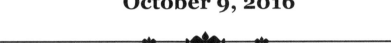

"It's a tad modern, don't you think?" Harold sniffed, gazing up at a squat, rectangular brick-and-glass edifice as he and Pattie pressed toward a back entrance to Washington University's athletics complex. "One thing I really like about Columbia is the consistent neo-classical architectural ethos."

Pattie maintained her focus on her cell phone, her face lit blue in the dark evening.

"And Columbia has these beautiful, stately open spaces," Harold continued. "It was a nice break from the claustrophobia of Manhattan. Not like here. The open spaces here seem more like cow pastures than public squares."

Pattie continued to scroll through her phone.

"Yep, Columbia sure knows how to construct a quad. That's for certain. That Grecian influence. It's like if Thomas Jefferson designed a university." He inhaled deeply, breathing the crisp fallen leaves and faint chill of early autumn. "I mean, sure, UVA. But we don't count that."

They made their way through a small, gray foyer to a second set of doors, roped off and guarded by a shriveled, elderly man, and queued up behind a line of weary-looking men and women, all of them ill-attired in clothes that either tightly accentuated rolls of neglected flesh or loosely draped the few slim, lively bodies that had escaped the degenerative effects of days spent slouched before computer monitors. Harold spied a middle-aged man wearing a faded Swarthmore sweatshirt and shielded his face with a program as he made his way to the rear of the line. Pattie glanced at Harold quizzically.

"Press?" the elderly man wheezed at Pattie from his high stool as they approached the velvet rope.

She looked up from her phone. "Oh, no, I'm with him," she explained, pointing her thumb at Harold. "I'm just here for the show."

"She's my girl Friday," Harold said proudly. Pattie glowered at him.

"I'll need to see your credentials," the man croaked.

Harold sighed. "I don't have my press pass. It's in Nantucket. If you call the front desk at the—"

"Unreal," Pattie muttered.

"What?"

Pattie sighed. "I'm not even going to comment on it."

"Well, you started to do just that, so let's hear what zinger you have cooked up. You know what they say about critics. Frustrated artists."

Pattie turned to the elderly man. "Do you happen to know if there's a bar close to campus that might be showing the debate? My husband has a crippling fear of success and self-sufficiency."

"Self-sufficiency? Who has a 'rainy day fund'?"

"Harold, that's my personal savings. See, some of us are actually responsible with our finances."

"Oh, come on, Pattie. That money's from your parents. I know it. We *all* know it!" Harold waved his hand, gesturing to the elderly man next to him.

"Leave him out of it!"

The elderly man cleared his throat. "It seems to me that you two are talking circles around what's really the matter," the man spoke matter-of-factly. "Resentment doesn't go away if you don't talk about it." He looked from Harold to Pattie and back. "You two need to talk when you're both calm. Not about press passes and rainy day funds, and not when you're all boiled up. Now, if you'll excuse me, you're in the wrong line."

Pattie turned on her heel and stormed off down the corridor. Harold turned to go after her, stopped, and looked back. "Do you have a business card?" he asked the man.

*   *   *

"Inconsiderate, incompetent—after everything I've done for him!" Pattie muttered. "That's the last Dr. Rothstein session I'm paying for. The last one," she promised herself. She weaved her way through an inadequately-lit hall lined on both sides with cases of glistening athletic trophies and overflowing with men wheeling cameras, women firing directives into cell phones and walkie-talkies, teenagers carefully carrying trays of catered food and glasses of wine, and wealthy-looking elderly couples who seemed to be present simply by a homing instinct that drew them toward nexuses of power and consequence. She spotted a line of impressively attractive men and women, all of whom seemed to have recently arrived from a hairdressing salon, filing behind another roped-off open doorway. Inside, Pattie could see blue-curtained booths set up in rows on a basketball court covered by a morass of thick cables. Potbellied technicians were setting up cameras and light rigs, while polished men and women stood patiently, smiles frozen on their faces as they stared dead-eyed into the camera lenses.

"Pattie? Pattie Stechler?" a man about Pattie's age asked. He had large brown eyes set behind wood-rimmed glasses, a strong chin, dark hair brushed boyishly to the side, and wore a handsome, European-cut suit.

Pattie turned around. Her eyes widened. "Chris Hayes?"

"What are the odds? I had no idea you would be here. I thought you did TV reviews now. I heard about the Pulitzer," Chris Hayes smiled nervously. A coterie of handlers made a half-circle behind him as he stopped to talk to Pattie, who had turned a dull shade of red.

Pattie faked a breezy laugh. "Oh, thanks, yeah. No, I'm—"

"Pattie! Pattie!" Harold called, running at full speed down the corridor and swerving to avoid two burly men wheeling a camera toward him. "I met a cleaning woman named Rosa who said she can get us in through the service entrance if we—oh, hello," he said, catching his breath as he drew to a halt near Pattie. He looked around at the protective enclosure of handlers flanking them on either side, then glanced quickly at Chris Hayes, his eyes flashing with skeptical recognition, before turning back to Pattie. "You found a line," he observed lamely. "Do they not check for press passes here?" he asked, looking intently at the line Pattie had half-joined and feigning not to notice Chris Hayes or his assistants.

"Harold, have you met Chris before?"

"Campus Dance, right?" Chris Hayes asked politely, extending his hand. Harold shook it quickly.

"I think we met at your ten-year reunion," Harold said curtly.

"We dated at Brown," Pattie reminded Harold.

"I almost didn't recognize you," Chris Hayes continued, addressing Harold. "In Pattie's profile picture on Facebook, you have, um...." he trailed off, waving his hand back and forth over his head, "you're a lot less tan." Harold quickly patted down the stray hairs that marked his old hairline.

"So you guys were having trouble getting in? Do you not have a press pass?"

Harold sighed. "It's in Germany. Long story."

"Well, I can get you into the TV area. Come on."

"That's so nice of you!" Pattie said brightly.

"No problem. Just fall in line behind me here, with the team."

"Thanks," Pattie said, shuffling in line behind a man holding a bag overflowing with electrical wires. Harold edged in next to Chris Hayes, skeptically looking at his shoulders to see which of them was taller.

"How's the sewage game?" Chris Hayes asked Harold.

"I cover politics now," Harold said testily. "So, your wife didn't come?"

*   *   *

Harold hastily led Pattie into one of the booths lining the interior of the gymnasium and pulled the blue curtain shut. Hot incandescent lights glared down on them as they stepped carefully over an unattended video camera. The din of reporters and crew shouting orders and setting up heavy equipment rumbled beyond. "Very nice, flaunting Chris Hayes around," Harold hissed.

Pattie laughed. "It's not like I sought him out. I told you, he spotted me."

"Sure, and then he tried to bring you backstage."

Pattie smirked. "To a room filled with teamsters and the Stepford Wives they put on Fox News?"

"I know how these things work, Pattie! *TV reporters. I* know what they get up to back here. I heard a couple women at the Hotel Wayne say that Geraldo Rivera won't go on screen until he's had 'a couple of bitches over the fucking table.'" Harold snorted. "Chris Hayes—you know, he's basically Rachel Maddow for men who are uncomfortable with their sexuality."

Pattie shook her head. "What on earth does that even mean, Harold?"

"You *know* he started on MSNBC as a substitute for her when she was away, right?"

"Well, he has his own show now. *All in with Chris Hayes*?"

"Pattie, that's disgusting."

"No, Harold—"

"They didn't even *want* him. Is that the kind of man you want to throw your lot in with? The second string?"

"So spoke Columbia's finest alternate coxswain," Pattie muttered.

Harold paced back and forth. "I can't deal with this right now. You're out flirting with some playboy TV reporter while I'm fighting tooth and nail to keep my job."

"And we're all very impressed."

"Do you want to me to go back on the sewage beat? Is that what you want? Me coming home late every night, smelling like the Hotel Wayne after a thunderstorm? Because that's what's at stake here."

"You know what they say about the Peter Principle."

"I don't have time to hear about any more of your ex-lovers, Pattie." Pattie turned to go, but Harold took her hand. "Pattie, listen. I *belong* here. I went to Columbia. I used to speak French. I can't go back to reporting on waste treatment commissioner runoff elections. Do you know how few 'runoff' puns there are?"

"Harold," Pattie shook her hand free. "I get it, but why the hell didn't you put more energy into breaking some stories the last ten months? It's not just about acting the part."

"That's what these people notice! *You* know who works at these legacy journals. Remember Philip Boutin, the guy you met at the Christmas party? He went to Dalton. He went to prom with Emma Bloomberg. They starred together in a performance of *Damn Yankees*. And *his* cubicle has a view of the park. Why put Philip on the sewage beat when he's *real* Manhattan?"

"Harold, if you put in the work and write well, you'll move up. It's like what Tom Lehrer told me one year at Bubbe's Thanksgiving—"

"Hey, guys," Chris Hayes poked his head in from the other side of the blue curtain, jovially waving his hand. "Am I interrupting something?"

Pattie forced a smile onto her face. "Just chatting."

"Did I hear one of you mention Philip Boutin? We bunked together at Camp Treetops three summers in a row."

"Ah, small world!" Pattie enthused. "Isn't that something, Harold?"

Harold grimaced. "Yes, we're colleagues."

"Tell him I say hi, would you?" Chris Hayes asked Harold. "I was thinking I could show you around the room, if you'd like, introduce you to some of the other talent."

"That'd be great," Pattie nodded.

"Can't," Harold said brusquely. "I'm waiting for a call from Huma about this Bus Tape."

"Huh," Chris Hayes said, mildly surprised. "I didn't realize she did a lot of press contact."

"It's select contact," Harold answered quickly. "There's an angle to this that hasn't come out yet, but she's reaching out to a few trusted journalists."

"I see. Well, bravo." Chris Hayes clapped him on the back. "Pattie, are you game?"

"Sure," Pattie smiled.

"If you get off quickly with Huma, come find us," Chris Hayes called over his shoulder as he led Pattie away. "Now, you were at Camp Seneca, right?" he asked Pattie.

*　　*　　*

Pattie graciously shook hands down the line of crewmen, makeup artists, and interns who had been diligently shadowing Chris Hayes. "You have an impressive staff," Pattie observed.

"Well, it takes quite the production to make this old mug look presentable," Chris Hayes laughed with false modesty. "Oh, and here comes my segment producer, Bruce. Bruce, this is Pattie, an old friend of mine." He pointed a beefy man with a salt-and-pepper goatee and rectangular glasses in Pattie's direction.

"Hiya. Bruce." The man shook Pattie's hand affirmatively.

"Pattie Carlyle," Pattie said.

Bruce nodded.

"So, you produce Chris' segments?" Pattie asked helpfully.

"Yeah. I do the remotes," Bruce said in a gravelly, cigar-strained voice.

"This guy's a dynamo," Chris chimed in. "I don't know what I'd do without him."

"I do what I can," Bruce shrugged.

"Is it exciting being out in the field?" Pattie asked. "I'm just a TV critic, myself. The furthest my work takes me is the Paley Center research library."

"These remote segments are only good for a few days a month," Bruce explained. "I'm also an executive producer on *Kids Baking Championship*. You know, on the Food Network."

"Oh wow," Pattie feigned excitement. "I think I've seen that. With Valerie Bertinelli, right? To be honest, those shows are a little hard for me to watch because I'm always so nervous that the kids are going to screw up."

"Yeah, it's a real pain finding kids who can cook. About three-quarters of the audition tapes we get, we have to turn over directly to the FBI. That doesn't exactly leave you with the pick of the litter." Pattie opened her mouth to speak, then nodded, turning back to the group.

"And this is Haley," Chris said, approaching with a plain-looking woman a few years younger than Pattie. "She's one of my writers."

"Oh!" Pattie said, turning around to shake the woman's hand. "So you what? Write the one-liners and the editorials?"

Haley nodded. "And the questions to the guests." She considered. "And the recap of the breaking news. And any breaking news. And the introductions of the guests. And the cues to commercials." She paused. "And the handoff to Rachel Maddow. And his signature sign off at the end of the night."

"Right," Pattie nodded thoughtfully. "What's your sign off again?" she asked Chris.

"'Thank you,'" he said proudly.

"And the explanations of what the different government agencies do. And the pronunciation guides for foreign names. And—oh, you mentioned jokes. Well, jokes. And, if someone is substituting for Rachel, the handoff to whoever is substituting. And the holiday greetings, if there's a holiday. Those are fun."

*   *   *

Harold approached the outer edges of a dense circle of men and women huddled around a small TV screen. Standing on his tiptoes, he craned over their hunched heads, hoping to get a glimpse of the candidates. He could see the top half of a middle-aged person's yellow hair but, unable to hear, could not make out who was talking or what had occurred.

"Who do you think is winning?" a woman with dyed black hair asked the collective.

"Well, Trump had a poor performance last time, so he should come back," a reedy, pale man in his early thirties with a thin, slightly creased face and deliberately rumpled clothes answered determinatively.

Harold searched his pockets for his notepad. He leaned toward a man with a shaved head and stubble standing next to him. "Do you have a pen?" he whispered. The man shook his head no. "Trump should come back, Trump should come back," Harold murmured to himself, hoping to memorize the information.

A broad-shouldered man with dark-rimmed circular glasses and slicked-down silver hair leaned closer to the screen from his place in the huddle. "You can see where Trump's answers are direct and forceful," he commented. "He's drawing a clear distinction in leadership styles."

"Mmm," concurred a slim African-American man in a charcoal suit and cobalt blue tie. "Yeah, that should play well. I think we're in the second act of the debate now? Hillary'll start to fall short of the audience's expectations. She's getting too nuanced, and this election is about clear change."

"You think that makes sense for the character?" a bouffanted woman with glistening gold bracelets asked skeptically. "Hillary's well-defined as haughty and morally dubious, but not nuanced, necessarily."

"Good point," the African-American man agreed. He thought for a moment. "Well, she hasn't talked about her paid speeches."

"There we go. Although she was typically competent, she conspicuously avoided addressing any of the scandals that have plagued her candidacy."

Harold shook his head in wonder. "Where do they get these scoops?" he whispered to himself. "It's like watching Brian Wilson record *Pet Sounds*." He studied the faces of the people standing around him, searching their eyes and pensive expressions for stories unwritten. He took a step closer to the man with the shaved head. "What network are you from?" Harold asked.

"You're not with CNN?" the man asked skeptically.

"Oh, um," Harold began.

"Oh, wait, you're with CNN-Netherlands, right?" A look of recognition swept across the man's face. "You guys speak English better than we do," he complimented gruffly.

"You speak very well, yourself!" Harold smiled, affecting what he felt was a Dutch accent. "Harold van der Kampt."

"Brandon Christopher." They shook hands.

"So, how's it going?" Harold asked. "There are so many leads here, it is crazy!"

Brandon nodded knowingly. "Absolutely electric. Unbelievable, some of the shit I've heard."

Harold leaned in conspiratorially. "What have you heard?"

Brandon looked around. "You know Trump Model Management?" he whispered.

Harold contemplated whether to nod yes or no. "Brandon!" the African-American man called, clapping him on the back. "You're missing this! He's stalking her!"

"Ah, damn!" Brandon exclaimed, turning his attention back to the TV. "He's like a hunter on the prowl."

"Definitely," the man with slicked gray hair said. "He's appealing to voters' preternatural instincts. In prehistoric times, the leader of a tribe would have been the best hunter. And the most sexually virile."

"America is seeing the presidential pivot," Brandon commented, rubbing his chin. "It took Bannon and Kellyanne a little while to find that balance and shape his tone, but I think tonight we're seeing a more refined version of the elemental qualities that attracted Americans to him."

"Did you see how deftly he handled that 'puppet' question? He reframed the entire exchange. That's a new discipline we didn't see in the primaries."

Harold followed the exchange, mouth half-agape, as the journalists bounced analysis from one to another like a volleyball match. "New discipline," he whispered to himself. "Trump should...*damn it.*" He had forgotten what Trump should do, his thoughts clouded by vague images of primates and dominance rituals.

"Tell me, are elections in Holland as crazy as they are here?" Brandon asked Harold, his eyes still fixed on the TV screen.

"No, *non*," Harold said, drifting in and out of accents. "They are more...respectful? But we have many political parties. It is not like here."

"I've heard that," Brandon nodded. "You have, like, Nazis and Socialists running for parliament over there, right?"

"Uh, *ouais*. Yes."

"That's nuts. Like seeing World War II play out every couple years. Must be a blast to cover those elections."

"Yes, yes. Very stimulating." Harold paused. "Also, we have many beautiful cathedrals." Brandon looked at him. "It is not related to the elections, but it is a very nice part of living there."

*   *   *

"Did you go back for the fifteenth this year?" Chris Hayes asked, leading Pattie toward a rickety brown folding-table in the corner of the gymnasium.

Pattie shook her head regretfully. "I wanted to, but this year has been crazy with the election. Lots of travelling."

Chris Hayes nodded knowingly. "Did you go with him?"

"Sometimes," Pattie said vaguely.

"I guess he can expense a lot of that," Chris Hayes thought out loud. He chuckled. "You should go with him if he covers anything in LA. It's gorgeous in Southern California this time of year."

"So I've heard," Pattie replied evasively. They continued silently for a few seconds.

"Hey, do you remember that class we had together on Antebellum America?"

Pattie nodded. "That was a really chaotic time in our nation's history."

"Really puts things in perspective."

Pattie and Chris Hayes reached the brown folding-table, where a group of men and women caked in makeup and wearing paper doilies tucked into their collars sat around in metal chairs, sipping coffee out of small styrofoam cups.

"Well, I have a California King," a petite blonde woman in a cinched-waist dress boasted. "I slept horizontally across it last night."

"My mattress is so plush, when I rolled over, I couldn't even see Kayleigh on the other half of the bed," an indistinguishably scruffy man in a trim suit challenged.

"Are you on the Club Level?"

"There's a Club Level?"

The petite woman sniffed superiorly. "Yes. Floors eight and nine."

"I'm going to have to talk to Wolf."

"Everyone, this is Pattie Stech—Pattie Carlyle," Chris Hayes called, gesturing toward Pattie. "I can't get used to that name!"

"Takes a while," Pattie smiled.

"Jenna Posner," the petite blonde woman offered. Pattie shook her small, dry hand. "What network are you with?"

"Oh, I write for *The New Yorker*, actually," Pattie answered. "Chris is an old friend, just showing me around."

"Beau Reinhardt," the scruffy man interjected, looking at Pattie's left hand and relaxing his aggressive grin as he noticed her thin gold band.

"So how's the debate been going?" Chris asked. "I've been pulled in a million different directions. Thank god for the writers, right? I live and die by that highlight reel."

"Sounds like Trump is taking this one," Beau said dismissively. "I'm sure they'll send out the surrogates soon, and we can get some soundbites to run at the top."

"Makes sense, makes sense," Chris agreed. "So we go into the finale with a tied series, winner take all."

"I heard Hillary's performance is typically competent, but she isn't connecting emotionally," Jenna said, checking her phone. "It sounds like she's been dodging questions about the scandals that have plagued her with voters."

"Oof," Beau winced. "That's going to hurt her with the undecideds."

"Do you have hypo-allergenic pillows in your suite?" Jenna turned back to Beau.

"Those are standard in every room," Beau shrugged dismissively. "But you want to talk about bad pillows, could you believe the ones at the Long Island Sound Sleeper? Talk about a dive."

"I *know*!" Jenna grabbed Beau's wrist, mock-aghast. "It's like, we're journalists! At least find us a Hilton. There are standards."

Beau shook his head. "I knew it was bad news when I heard the pun in the name. That's *always* bad news." He adjusted his belt. "Always."

Pattie looked from Beau to Jenna. She opened her mouth to speak, but stopped, and pursed her lips in consternation.

"I like covering the Grammys," Beau continued. "Not really the news, but you get to stay at the Fairmont."

Jenna murmured in agreement. "No one really asks if you need to get there a day or two early, either." She glanced at her nails. "Last year, Blake Shelton gave me the Galaxy Note7 that came in his gift bag. I think he was flirting with me."

Chris shook his head. "Lucky dogs. The most I can hope for is a hurricane hitting Fort Lauderdale. But even then, Chris Matthews gets first dibs."

"I was down there last spring for a remote. Upgraded my rental to a BMW and no one in accounting was the wiser."

"Oh, shit, are you seeing this?" Beau interrupted excitedly. "Some fat lard just asked a question, and it's blowing up on Twitter."

"What did he ask?" Jenna demanded, grabbing her phone.

"Something about coal, I think. That's not why, though."

"Looks like a meme forming," Chris announced. "He looks like if Mister Rogers were younger, heavy, and moonlighting in porn." He passed his phone around. "I think that's the joke."

"Dana!" Jenna called to a thin Asian-American woman holding an iPad. "Do we have people on this guy who just asked the question?"

"Ken Bone?" Dana asked.

"Is that his name?"

"The guy in the sweater with glasses? Yeah. We've got a listicle going and Mark's working on a couple of one-liners."

Jenna digested this. "Great. And if someone can stay on top of why it's significant."

"Absolutely."

Jenna turned to Pattie. "People love these stories."

Pattie nodded.

Jenna looked at her phone. "God, he's really fat."

*   *   *

The pack of people surrounding the television suddenly dispersed, the assembled running frantically to the tables and booths dotting the gymnasium. Harold darted into the path of a man in a blue cardigan and grabbed him by the arms. "What's happened?" Harold asked. "Did Hillary cry?"

"Some fat guy's going viral! Let the hell go of me!" The man in the blue cardigan wrenched himself free of Harold and raced away to his work station.

Harold looked around forlornly. He spotted a brown-skinned man in a navy blue suit standing to the side of the nearest booth and moved toward him.

"A fat guy's gone viral?"

The man sighed. "One of the voters asked a question. He's sort of strange looking."

"Ah," Harold said, not completely understanding the importance. "Does he have boils?"

"No, but he has a bright red sweater on. And he has a mustache. And he's fat."

"I see," Harold nodded. "So, just, kind of a weird loser?"

"Exactly."

Harold thought. "Do you know where I could get a list of the audience members? Maybe like a kind of Facebook?"

The man looked at Harold blankly. "No."

"Like, passport photos and their names and addresses," Harold pressed. "For the news."

"Are you a journalist?"

"Yes."

"You should talk to one of the other journalists."

"I see. And who are you?"

"Governor Bill Richardson."

"Oh." Harold looked around. "I think I saw one of the people I was watching with go that way. Nice to meet you."

"Okay," Governor Bill Richardson said, staring straight ahead. "I'll be here later if you want to talk about Hillary's minimum wage plan."

"Great. Absolutely," Harold promised, quickly walking backwards and looking for Brandon Christopher before he disappeared into the morass of excited journalists. He turned right and walked with ever-greater speed, breaking into a gallop as he searched for Brandon's dome of pink flesh. *"That's* a bald man," he said to himself. He continued forward, scanning the room wildly, when he abruptly collided into the middle section of a larger woman walking with her head buried in an open manilla folder.

"I'm sorry, I'm sorry," Harold apologized, holding her arm to steady himself. "I'm with CNN-Netherlands," he explained.

The woman brushed herself off. "We're all busy. Be more careful, though."

"What are you looking at there?" Harold asked, peering into the open file.

"Oh, just getting some background information on Ken Bone. He's exploding."

Harold's pulse quickened. "Is that information on the audience members?"

"Well—yeah. But I—"

"Could I just borrow that for a second?" Harold tentatively placed his thumb and forefinger on the file's corner. The woman firmly pulled it back.

She glared at him. "Get your own."

"I have a lead. A real hot lead. I'll trade you. How well do you know that list?"

The woman eyed Harold with distaste. "Why?"

"I just need another fat loser on that list I can do a story on. Just one name," Harold said urgently.

"Ken Bone," the woman said disdainfully.

"No, everyone's already doing him. I have to get out ahead of the next one. They packed that hall full of American voters. It's got to be lousy with tub-o's."

"I don't know. Watch the debate and choose one." The woman tucked the folder under her arm. "Now, what's your trade?"

Harold leaned in. "Do you know about Trump Model Management?" he whispered.

The woman listened intently. "Sort of," she replied. "What about it?"

"Well—oh, shoot!," Harold said hastily, pretending to check his phone. "I'm getting some breaking news from the Netherlands. Um, a Nazi and a Socialist are running for our Parliament. Very nice to meet you!" Harold ran deep into the crowd.

*　　*　　*

"Okay," the elderly man said, shifting on his stool and emitting a wheezy cough. "Pattie, your turn. Tell Harold what you're afraid will happen if you get mad."

Pattie opened her mouth to speak to Harold, then turned back to the elderly man. "Do I have to sing it?"

The man shrugged. "No."

Pattie looked back to Harold. "Huh."

"You should really hear her when she sings about her childhood," Harold told the elderly man.

The man smiled faintly. "Good. Just talk."

Pattie inhaled. "I'm afraid he'll get mad."

The man nodded deeply. "Harold, even if you got mad, you would still love Pattie, right?"

"Sure."

"No singing," the man reminded him.

"Sorry," Harold apologized. "I've been working on my melismas."

18
"Wait Till You Get to the Stuff About Marcus"
October 28, 2016

The bus lurched to a sudden stop. Harold looked over the top of the seats to see a long line of idling cars four lanes wide on the highway in front of them. He threw himself back in his chair with a scowl on his face. "Terrific."

Pattie looked over at Harold with a look of mild pity. "Do you want to watch with me?" she asked, offering her iPad. "It's a *Masterpiece Theatre*."

Harold glanced down at Pattie's screen disconsolately. "That's alright," he said glumly. "I think I'll just sit here and stare at the seatback in front of me."

Pattie took out her earbuds and placed her iPad in her lap. "Buck up, Harold. We're on vacation! Sandy beaches. Ice cream cones on the boardwalk. Remember...San Diego!" She drummed her hands on Harold's legs.

"Norfolk-Virginia Beach," Harold corrected forlornly.

"Both Roamify and Wanderlust said Norfolk-Virginia Beach is the San Diego of the Mid-Atlantic," Pattie reminded him. "Here, let's make a list of all the things you can expense."

Harold shook his head. "I'm finished. I guess the paper's not above putting mustachioed fat tubs above the fold, but albinos with lazy eyes are where they draw the line."

"That's no way to think when we're going to California!"

"Pattie, we're going to Vir*gin*ia."

"Harold, California is ninety percent a state of mind. I don't know about you, but I'm thinking 'San Diego.'"

Harold sighed mightily. "Pattie, I'm a lot better at this than you."

"Come on. Let's celebrate wrapping up one heck of an assignment this year. Where's that old Carlyle spirit?"

"In the gutter, along with my career," Harold moaned. "There's nothing to celebrate, except that I have, probably, three more days to milk this job for all it's worth before I'm back on a trash barge on the Long Island Sound."

"At least no one will expect you to travel with the press gaggle anymore," Pattie reasoned. "You can be your own man again. Making your own rules. Taking your life in your own two hands."

"Pattie, the only thing anybody ever took into their own two hands was on the D Train."

"This is fucking ridiculous!" a woman yelled from several rows behind them. Harold peered down the length of the aisle and saw a young woman speaking animatedly into her phone. She wore a zip-up fleece sweater, black athleisure pants, and brown suede Ugg boots. Her blonde hair sat in a ponytail atop her head. "This driver has no idea where he's going. First we were on the highway, then we went off the highway, and now, like, we're back on the highway again, but there's a ton of traffic?"

Harold turned to Pattie and raised his eyebrows, motioning with his thumb to the woman behind him.

"I don't understand why I'm the only one on the bus upset about this. It's crazy. Everyone else is just sitting staring out the window, like sheep." The woman paused, apparently listening to the person on the other end of the line. "No, I can't just enjoy it! We're in fucking *traffic*. Ugh!" Harold and Pattie heard a dull *thud* as the woman threw her phone down on the empty seat next to her. "What an asshole!" she called out.

"Harold, that woman is your *id*," Pattie whispered.

"How does she have someone in her life to call in the first place?" Harold asked.

"I always assume those people are calling their mothers," Pattie shrugged.

Harold fidgeted in his seat. "Where *are* we, incidentally?"

Pattie pulled up the map again on her iPad. "About an hour outside of D.C., it looks like."

"I need a skyline for a point of reference. I'm like a sailor on a starless night out here," Harold complained.

Pattie looked out the window. Just beyond the highway's concrete barrier, she could see a row of ramshackle homes, their paint speckled and chipped, lawns browned and abandoned. Further back, a rust-colored smokestack passed wisps of dark air into the light gray sky. A smattering of half-heartedly modern glass towers stood in the distance. Pattie noticed two boys who appeared to be in their pre-teens standing at one of the chain-link fences bordering the highway, throwing rocks at the cars stopped in traffic. "I guess I can see what these people are so upset about," she murmured.

"Gram and Gran lived in a house like that," Harold pointed. "It was a different era. Middle-class, upper-middle class people lived in houses like that then."

"I wonder if they offer wifi just to frustrate people who try to use it," Pattie scowled, tapping on her iPad. "The MSNBC app loads *everywhere* else."

"Oh, it's Art Garfunkel." Harold gestured vacantly toward Pattie's screen.

"Do you want to listen?"

Harold shrugged. "I interviewed him two times, for all the good it did me."

"Let's just see what he has to say." Pattie handed Harold an earbud, which he reluctantly accepted.

"Mika, this letter is much ado about nothing," Garfunkel explained amiably over simulcast. "It's a procedural formality. Director Comey has to check out these emails for procedural reasons, and he'll find that there's nothing there, and then he'll send another letter to Congress saying, hey, there's nothing there."

"Who's Director Comey?" Harold asked.

"The FBI Director."

"Oh." Harold thought. "I didn't realize Garfunkel knew so much about FBI procedure."

"He had to do something while Paul was writing the songs."

"It's similar to when I announced I was parting ways with Paul to pursue my acting career," Garfunkel continued. "Right, Mika, an actor, too. Well, listen, the press were going crazy, after that announcement, saying that there was bad blood between us. And I told the press, that's hooey. That's a lot of nothing. And Mika, this is a lot of nothing."

"Do you think *Catch-22* is on Netflix?" Pattie asked.

"Right, the press called me. But, Mika, look. What the American people should be focusing on now is Donald Trump's horrendous, disgusting history with women. Twenty women have come forward to accuse Donald of sexual assault. The American people should be asking themselves, is this person really worthy of serving in the highest office in the land?"

"The audio and the video aren't matching," Harold complained.

"It's the wifi. It's buffering," Pattie explained distractedly.

"Can you try lowering the video resolution or something? I feel like I'm watching *Godzilla*."

"I don't need to tell you, as a pop icon, I was no stranger to the attentions of the fairer sex. A woman is, to me, like a porcelain vase, Mika. To be treated with awe and respect, and as a source of beauty, like in the Keats poem. There's a song I like very much, which I sang—singer as interpreter, as the channel—'Only You,' by The Platters, and—oh, sure. No, right, if David Alexrod's linkup is ready from D.C. Absolutely. A pleasure for me, too, Mika. Right, and if I see Paul."

Harold took out his earbud. "What letter? What was he talking about?"

Pattie had pulled out her phone and was reading an article on her news aggregator. "The FBI found emails from Hillary's server on Anthony Weiner's laptop." She scrolled down. "They had the laptop from investigating his texts to that underage girl. You know, the thing you tried to interview him about."

"Oh, man," Harold said distantly.

"So James Comey had to write a letter to Congress saying he was reopening the investigation into her server."

"Well, sure," Harold nodded, scratching his chin.

"Hillary's still ahead by 5.2 percent on the *RealClearPolitics* aggregator," Pattie said nervously. "Maybe that's enough of a buffer. She just has to get through eleven more days."

"Oh, don't worry about that," Harold smirked. "Are you kidding? Even if Hillary had shown up drunk to the last debate, she'd still win. Trump *can't* win. It's mathematically impossible."

Pattie grunted skeptically, continuing to examine charts and heavily annotated maps of the United States.

"I wonder if anyone's talked to Huma about this," Harold mused.

"Probably the FBI." Pattie gritted her teeth. "Hillary's already ropey in Pennsylvania."

"No, no. Pattie, think about it. What an angle for a story. The presumptive next president's chief of staff is married to the man whose priapistic use of technology created a last-minute campaign scare. I *know* her. I'm covering the campaign. I have the in to put all the pieces together!" Harold's eyes had lit up, and his head bobbed up and down unconsciously as he rolled the idea over in his head. "I think we should get off in D.C."

"Thank God. I promised myself I wouldn't use the bus bathroom."

"No, to *stay* there. Someone's going to cover Huma, and I'm just the man to do it."

"So, no beach, then."

"Are you kidding? This is going to save my career!" Harold spoke quicker and louder, a smile breaking across his face. "I'll score with Huma, get a big, juicy byline, and then after the election, my editor will be so pleased, he'll probably send us to San Diego himself! The real one!"

"You know, after all this time, I think I'd be sort of disappointed if we actually ended up in San Diego. It'd be like when Gatsby actually meets Daisy again."

*   *   *

"No, that's *Carlyle*, with a *y*," Harold corrected. "Joshua Martin did have this beat, but he, um, ended up with a pretty heavy load on his shoulders."

A receptionist with mousy brown hair and a pale, tired face quickly typed a few words and clicked her mouse, turning her screen to the left as Harold peered across the desk. Bright fluorescent lights glared against her outdated computer monitor. Behind her, trim, well-dressed young men and women, most of whom appeared to have been imported directly from Ivy League campuses, bustled about, never acknowledging each other's presence as they stared directly into their phone screens.

"Oh, *Harold* Carlyle," the receptionist said with a tone of dawning comprehension. "You should really carry your press pass." She clicked her mouse again. "It doesn't look like you've ever been to any of the press events?"

Harold shifted in place. "Well, I'm on a number of beats."

"I think someone took your name off our list after you no-showed at the last meet-and-greet on the Scooby Plane. Hence the confusion."

"The what?"

"Hillary's plane. She talks to the gaggle most nights."

"The press flies on the plane?" Harold asked intently. "Is this an ongoing thing?"

"Uh huh!" the receptionist said cheerily. "I'll make a note that you weren't fired."

"Thanks, I appreciate that." Harold drummed his fingers on the desk. "Is there anything in particular I have to do to get plane access?"

"Just come to the events. You're in the system again." The receptionist typed a few keys with a flourish and a printer behind her began to whir. "And you should really carry your press pass."

"So," Harold said, opening a jar atop the desk and taking an orange Tootsie-Pop, "is Huma in?"

The receptionist's smile evaporated. "And what is this regarding?"

Harold sucked on the lollipop and pulled it out of his mouth with a loud *smack*. "I was assuming that she had some press availability, given today's events, and I was hoping to get right in there."

"I see." The receptionist pulled out a desk calendar. "Huma's hard to pin down."

Harold sighed. "You don't have to tell me. I've already tried to get access, but she was all closed up." Harold tried to gnaw on his lollipop to dig down to the bubblegum center, but his efforts proved premature. "I figured if she were in today, I could grab her for a quick quote."

The receptionist looked at Harold quizzically. "I see. So you want to know if Huma's in the office?"

"Yes. Is she available?"

"She's online, yes."

"Right, but is she present?"

"Well," the receptionist tilted her head, "she's present in the sense that she's engaged with the voters and the issues, yes."

"Rig—okay, sure. So, is she in her office?"

The receptionist typed rapidly into her computer and leaned forward, squinting at the screen. "Yes, I can confirm that she is in her office."

"Great, so in the back, then?"

The receptionist's eyes widened with a look of alarm. "I think she's busy, though."

"But you said—"

"I think she's watching an infomercial," she said hurriedly.

Harold looked at the receptionist disbelievingly.

"She's very interested in the *Crank Chop*," the receptionist nodded. "Each crank is like twenty-seven knives chopping your food."

"Is it?"

"It's been a hard year for Huma," the receptionist explained.

"Can I wait?"

The receptionist considered. "There's a chair behind you, against the wall."

"Right." Harold glanced at a wood-frame chair with navy blue cushions and a pillow with an "H" embroidered on it. "Do you have any idea how long she'll be?"

"It's a long infomercial," the receptionist said reflexively. "The more you crank, the finer it chops."

*   *   *

"Can I help you?" a blonde woman in her late twenties wearing a tight-fitting tweed jacket and pencil skirt asked Harold. She was carrying two oversized accordion folders in one arm and holding her phone in her free hand, which she gazed at as she spoke. He looked up from a leather-bound copy of Hillary Clinton's 1969 Wellesley commencement address.

"Yes, I was here to speak to Huma," Harold said politely, rising out of his chair. "If she's finished with her infomercial by now."

"Huma?" the woman asked, not looking up from her phone.

"I mean, after forty-seven minutes, I'd think they'd have chopped up everything in the studio."

"Trump is up one today," the woman said absently, still staring at her phone screen. "Tess, tell Duncan we need to roll the second wave of Tweets ahead of schedule," she told the receptionist. She placed her phone in her jacket pocket and looked directly at Harold for the first time.

"If you could just let her know Harold Carlyle is waiting to speak with her. She should remember me from our last tête-à-tête."

"She's not here, Mr. Carlyle."

"But the receptionist said she was in her office."

"She is. Her office in Brooklyn."

Harold looked menacingly at the receptionist, who ducked her head under the desk. He sighed. "Well, is there a good number for me to reach her? I'd like to reconnect—for a story."

"Sure, Mr. Carlyle, let me just—wait, Carlyle?" the woman asked. "*You're* Mr. Carlyle? Harold Carlyle? From New York?"

"You followed the Long Island Waste Treatment Runoff Election," Harold beamed proudly.

"You wrote the GOP Bus Exposé!" The woman placed her two folders on an empty chair and reached down to shake Harold's hand.

Harold nodded. "A part of history," he said softly.

"I'm Abigail Charles Macaulay, Hillary's Senior Assistant to the Field Director," the woman introduced herself, her eyes glowing with excitement. "Why don't you follow me back to my office?"

"I'm married," Harold apologized lamely, standing up and following the woman down a fluorescent hall.

"Great," she said dismissively. They rounded a bank of noisy photocopiers, a clearing of burgundy-colored cloth sofas, and proceeded past a large, open room filled with long tables lined with more young, well-dressed men and women quietly typing on laptops or talking into desk phones in hushed tones. Finally, they arrived at a gray door in a deserted back corner of the floor. Abigail Charles Macaulay unlocked the door and ushered Harold into her office. He stepped over a banker's box filled with blue metal buttons that read "Together, Stronger" into a small space that barely fit a white Ikea desk.

"So, are we pulling up Huma on WebEx or...?" Harold asked, sitting down in the seat opposite Abigail's desk.

Abigail put her phone to her ear. "Declan, can you meet me in my office? Right away, yes. No, it's related to, um," she lowered her voice, "*Project Transcript*. Exactly. Okay." She slipped her phone back in her pocket. "It'll just be a moment," she said cheerily to Harold.

"Terrific!" Harold drummed out a beat on his thighs. "Could I trouble you for a seltzer, perhaps, as long as we're waiting?"

Abigail cocked her head. "We have filtered water or Perrier."

Harold beamed. "Perrier is great."

Abigail typed something on her phone. "Declan will bring you a Perrier."

Harold nodded thanks. He searched for a clue to the Senior Assistant to the Field Director's life that could offer fodder for conversation while waiting for Declan, only to realize that the room lacked any personal items or decoration. He tapped his foot nervously. "Have you been with the campaign for long?"

"Just since I graduated from law school in May."

"Oh, cool. Where did you go to law school?"

"Massachusetts."

"Oh, where in Massachusetts?"

"Boston."

"Ah." Harold shifted impatiently, wondering when Declan would arrive.

"Harvard," she added anxiously.

"Very nice," Harold nodded. "You know, at Columbia—" He exhaled with relief as he was interrupted by a knock at the door. A tall, portly man with a bushy beard and a prematurely-graying moptop stepped over the banker's box, carrying a small green bottle of Perrier in one hand and tightly clutching something in the other. He placed both on Abigail Charles Macaulay's desk and wiped his brow, apparently having worked up a sweat.

"Declan, this is Harold Carlyle," Abigail said brightly. "Declan's our Deputy Assistant to the Field Director."

"A pleasure," Declan said gruffly, shaking Harold's hand. "Hillary's new to yoga, so we're really just looking for some basic exercises that'll make her look more relaxed when she's up at the podium."

"No," Abigail corrected, "Harold *Carlyle*, the reporter who wrote the GOP Bus Exposé. The one we discussed?"

"Oh!" Declan exclaimed, a look of comprehension spreading across his face. "I see, hence the..." he trailed off as he pointed to the mysterious item he had placed on the desk. Harold noticed that it was a small, sky-blue flash drive.

"We *loved* the GOP Bus Exposé," Abigail interjected. "No one else had the guts to infiltrate the Republican inner sanctum and show Americans what their true agenda is. Hillary even read it. That's real journalism!"

Harold blushed. "Every day, you have to wake up thinking that you're the best damn reporter in the world," he explained. "Believing it is what gives you the nerve to get out and swing for the fences like that."

"Wonderful. Just wonderful," Declan said, nodding his head.

"So, should we ring up Hum—"

MICHAEL BLEICHER & ANDY NEWTON

"We have some highly sensitive material we've obtained from a British source," Abigail said, lowering her voice to a whisper. "We've been hearing rumors about this for months, but we finally got our hands on it two days ago." Abigail picked up the flash drive from the desk and handed it to Harold.

"Uh huh," Harold said. "So did Huma mention that we had a chat, or did she—"

"*Shh!*" Abigail hushed. "We were going to contact you, but our Communications team told us you had been let go."

"Oh, that," Harold winced. "Well, I was going to leave to start work on a book, but I figured, you know, with the election, I may as well wait another few days."

"And now here you are. It's like the universe is ready for the first woman president, and it's putting everything into place."

"Right," Harold said solemnly. "Everything."

"We're going with you because you've proven yourself to be a crack reporter," Declan whispered conspiratorially. "Aces."

"Well, sure," Harold agreed. "So, do you want me to just hang onto this, or what?"

"I think you'll know what to do once you open up the files," Abigail nodded. "The transcripts have been dated and time-stamped. A cursory Google search will show that the locations match up to his campaign calendar."

"Got it," Harold agreed, placing the drive in his rear pants pocket. "His campaign calendar?" he prompted.

Abigail nodded vigorously. "Are you sure that's a safe place?" she asked.

"Oh, don't worry. I'm never back there," Harold assured her. "I mean, I'm not just walking around with my hands in my back pockets."

"You'll love what we've got here," Declan chuckled. "Wait till you get to the stuff about Marcus."

"*Shh!*" Abigail snickered. "We have a private intelligence agency looking for the cat o'nine tails and Scold's Bridle, just on the off-chance," she confided.

"Good thinking," Harold said blankly.

"Now, it goes without saying, no one on the campaign can go on the record about this," Declan cautioned.

"Of course, of course."

"Are you sure, Mr. Carlyle?" Abigail urged. "We can't stress too strongly the sensitivity of this material. Our source's life could be endangered if it were revealed how you got this. They could trace this from us to him."

"I'm not worried," Harold assured her. "I was on the bus, remember?"

Abigail smiled. "There just may be a Director of Communications appointment around the corner for you, Mr. Carlyle. We're still waiting to hear back from Chris Hayes, confidentially, but it doesn't sound like he's a 'yes.'" She handed Harold his Perrier and smiled as she shook his hand.

"So, Huma's not calling in?" Harold asked, dejected.

"No," Abigail answered. Her smile quickly disappeared as her attention moved back to her phone. "Declan will show you out."

Harold sighed. "Okay."

"Oh, I almost forgot to ask you!" Abigail called, as Declan stepped over the box and motioned to Harold. "Which slogan do you like better, 'She's Got It,' or 'She's Got This'?"

*   *   *

"So, I go all that way, and Huma's not even *there*," Harold groused as he and Pattie sank into the frayed black leather seats of an Uber SUV that seemed entirely too big for the narrow side streets its driver was choosing. "I missed the scoop. Yet again."

"Did you see anything while you were there? Maybe you could do a story about the campaign headquarters," Pattie offered sympathetically.

"Nope," Harold sighed, leaning back in his seat. "I met a couple of glorified interns who gave me some kind of a Hillary freebie."

"A T-shirt?" Pattie asked. "What size is it?"

"Not even," Harold rolled his eyes. "Some thumb drive. They tried to hype it up so that I'd look at it. Classic PR move to get a journalist's attention." He rubbed his eyes tiredly. "You should've seen the commotion they were making. It's probably filled with a bunch of press releases about Hillary's jobs plan, but you'd think it had the Manhattan Project on it."

"Well, if we're sticking around D.C. for the next couple days, maybe you can pound the pavement a little."

"I'm not a prostitute, Pattie."

"My mistake." Pattie gazed out the window.

"Speaking of prostitutes, you know what that is over there?" the Uber driver interjected. He pointed with a stocky arm to a sprawling, cylindrical concrete building. "That's Watergate. All the D.C. scandals have happened there. Monica Lewinsky. White-watergate." The man thought. "Watergate." Short and heavy-set, he had pencil-thin sideburns that sketched out his otherwise imperceptible jawline, joining together at his chin. A Washington Redskins jersey strained to contain his midsection.

"Mon-i-ca Lew-in-sky," the driver sounded out, savoring each syllable. "Bill likes the ladies chunky. No doubt about that." He gave a hoarse laugh. "But who can blame him, right?" He swerved to avoid a parked VW Beetle's side mirror. "Me? I'm *only* with big females, you know what I mean?" the man asked, evidently expecting a combination of surprise and newly-earned deference from his passengers. "I was with a big, large female. Six foot tall, two hundred and seventy pounds. Could barely hold her. I had to use all of my strength, you know? All of my physical strength."

"Mm," Harold voiced noncommittally.

"And I'm a strong guy. But this female was so big," the man continued. "So big, it took all of my physical strength. I got this six foot two, two hundred and eighty-five pound female. And I'm sayin', *'unh, come on, honey!'* Using all of my strength." He flicked the turn signal. "Nearly broke it off."

"Right," Harold said. "This is us, here."

"A six foot five, three hundred and twenty pound female. I could barely hold her down. She's loving it, and I'm using all of my physical— oh, this is you?"

"Yes," Harold said. "Thanks."

"You two have a good night!" the driver called as they climbed out of the car.

19
"What About Tanks?"
November 7, 2016

The following conversation was transcribed from a recording made covertly by a foreign intelligence agency.

PETROV: Thank you for having me once again, Mr. Trump. How are you feeling? Do you have, as they say, the butterflies?

TRUMP: No, no, this is high-quality stuff. The best, a prescription.

PETROV: Oh, I—of course.

TRUMP: I have the most incredible focus, Petrov. Incredible. Did Putin get the gift I sent him?

PETROV: Yes, Mr. Trump. He did.

TRUMP: Well? Did he like them?

PETROV: Mr. Trump, they were young girls.

TRUMP: Yeah, right? Beautiful. Handpicked, personally by me.

PETROV: Mr. Trump, the president—

TRUMP: They were originally from Estonia, so really, we're sending them back. But they know how to grill steak now.

PETROV: The president is enjoying the consorts, although he notes that he has repeatedly expressed to you his preference for an *eromenos*. A boy.

TRUMP: Well, did he see the ass on the blonde one? You get her on a Peloton bike, *whoosh*.

PETROV: We are working on your speech for the final rally tonight. A final draft will be with Kellyanne by five pm.

TRUMP: Oh, I don't need a speech. I'll just wing it. People love that. Love it. I was thinking of reminding people about the bags under Hillary's eyes. So ugly. No one has mentioned that. The press isn't reporting on it. CNN, NBC, not even jewcancer.blogspot.com. So unfair.

PETROV: Nevertheless, the speech will be loaded in your teleprompter.

TRUMP: Do you guys own *JewCancer*? Someone told me you were getting into news. Such a good property. So many things that CNN doesn't talk about. I might buy *JewCancer* for the new Trump Media. Bright future ahead. Bright, bright future.

PETROV: Mr. Trump, speaking of the future, I would like for us to discuss how we will make contact once the election has concluded. This meeting, unfortunately, will be our last face to face conference.

TRUMP: Right, right. Of course. Don, Jr., can you get me that pen? Good. No, don't come over here. Just hand it to me. Good. No, just sit back over there by the window. Yeah. Sit down.

PETROV: After election day, we will—

TRUMP: You do everything but take off your pants and shit on them, and they still don't learn, Petrov. But he's a good boy.

PETROV: Mr. Trump, after election day, the Kremlin will go dark for several weeks to avoid detection by hostile intelligence services while a secure back channel is coordinated.

TRUMP: Right. Don't worry about that, Petrov. You just send the seed money for Trump TV through Cyprus to the Caymans, and we'll get it out of the Taj Mahal before the accounts close. Did you see the Taj Mahal? Tremendous, tremendous property.

PETROV: Yes. It was abandoned. But—

TRUMP: People ask me, how did you manage to build a casino that was so, so beautiful, and so incredibly successful? And I tell them, I'm a winner. I win.

PETROV: Exactly, Mr. Trump. By this time tomorrow, we will be watching as the American media reports the most stunning upset since Truman defeated Dewey.

TRUMP: Right, right. Wait till those faggots at NBC get a load of the network I'm gonna launch. We're gonna blow them right out of the water.

PETROV: Certainly, Mr. Murdoch has a network already in place, Mr. Trump, but you will soon be in command of far more than media channels.

TRUMP: I like your vision, Petrov. We're gonna have a whole media empire. TV. Internet. Bannon's gonna make movies. Wait and see. Fantastic, fantastic movies. Isn't that right, Steve? Don't talk. You can just nod. Good.

PETROV: Mr. Trump, by the end of tomorrow night, you will be elected as the next President of the United States.

TRUMP: What exactly are you getting at, Petrov?

PETROV: Everything has gone according to plan. You will win the electoral vote tomorrow night.

TRUMP: Why?

PETROV: Jared, here, can review how our strategy has borne fruit after the general meeting has concluded.

TRUMP: Are you trying to screw me, Petrov? What kind of a bum deal is this?

PETROV: Mr. Trump, do you recall what we discussed in Balmedie? This is the deal we made.

TRUMP: Petrov, I only make good deals. This is a horrible, horrible deal.

PETROV: Mr. Trump, the girl in the tape is still alive.

TRUMP: Did she ask about me?

PETROV: The president is more than willing to give her over to your American media. His patience has already grown quite thin. Thirty years of generous...investment in your *businesses*, yet this race is, shall we say, hanging by the thinnest of wires.

TRUMP: You know I took that girl back to the Ritz? You know how many orphans get to visit the Ritz?

PETROV: Her statement has been filmed, and the FSB will release the corroborating evidence at the first sign of your disobedience.

TRUMP: So, so unfair. You help somebody get their start in the modeling industry—a very, very competitive industry, let me tell you, very competitive.

PETROV: You are free to test Russia at your leisure. Now, the first item for our mutual benefit, once you are elected, will be the lifting of sanctions imposed by the current administration.

TRUMP: Right, sure. Flynn, you talk to him about that afterward.

PETROV: We will expect to see positive action within the first sixty days, in accordance with the plan we developed at the Republican Convention.

TRUMP: Not a problem. I'll work that one so fast, it'll make your head spin.

PETROV: Of course. Mr. Giuliani, would you mind taking a step back? Your boa is tickling my neck. Thank you. Mr. Trump, have you put any thought into what the future First Lady will take on as her primary agenda? We have a short list of suggestions.

TRUMP: Oh, Ivanka'll take care of all of that herself. Such an incredible, incredible girl, Petrov. She'll make the best first lady.

PETROV: Yes. Of course, *Melania* will be the first lady.

TRUMP: What?

PETROV: The president's wife is the first lady, Mr. Trump. By definition.

TRUMP: You are fucking me up the ass today, Petrov.

PETROV: We have that tape, as well.

TRUMP: Christ, fine. Kellyanne, this sounds like a woman problem. Deal with it, okay?

PETROV: I believe she may be comatose.

TRUMP: That's just the way she is after lunch. Hey, any chance that bootlicker Pence can take this job, instead? Is it too late to do that?

PETROV: Much too late, Mr. Trump.

TRUMP: You could just tell everyone I'm giving him the job. Pence is a nerd. He'd love this.

PETROV: Mr. Trump, the American people want you.

TRUMP: Very true, Petrov. Very, very true.

PETROV: Mr. Trump, this thing of the cold feet is quite normal. Before I got married—

TRUMP: Did I tell you what I did the night before I married Marla Maples?

PETROV: —I was—

TRUMP: I screwed her younger cousin. Younger cousin, true story.

PETROV: Mr. Trump, this is a way to expand your empire beyond your wildest dreams.

TRUMP: Huh.

PETROV: You will be the leader of the United States of America. You will live in the White House. You will possess control of the world's *second* most powerful military. Kings and paupers alike will hang on your every word. You will have a nuclear arsenal at your disposal.

TRUMP: Uh huh. What about tanks?

PETROV: Yes, you will have tanks.

TRUMP: We could have them just rolling down Pennsylvania Avenue, every day.

PETROV: Absolutely.

TRUMP: It would be a good tie-in at the hotel. You know, I opened the most beautiful hotel in Washington. Maybe, you pay a thousand dollars, you get to ride in a tank.

PETROV: You will be president, Mr. Trump. You can do whatever you want. The people will adore you all the more for it.

TRUMP: Did I tell you about the time I stuck a spoon up a waitress' skirt at—

PETROV: Yes, Mr. Trump.

TRUMP: Great, okay. It's like I've always said, Petrov. I'm going to make the best president. The best.

PETROV: We will make sure of that. There will be much to discuss after the election. But for today, I believe this concludes our business.

TRUMP: Great. I look forward to hearing from you, Petrov. Don, whyn't you show Petrov out, would you? Kellyanne, Steve, hang outside the door. I wanna talk to you for a few minutes after. Flynn, Rudy, I'll see you at the rally tonight. Okay. Jeff, a pleasure. Not getting any taller, are you? Hope, can you reach that dry spot on my back? Yeah, terrific, thanks. Yeah, see you, Paul. Watch those sweets. Corey, Avi, Brad, Mike, keep up the fight. Robert and Rebekah—the Mercers! Mercy Killer! Jared, yeah, sure, okay. Erik, how are the guns doing? *War Dogs*! Wilbur and Alex, don't worry, I've got something for you. Jeffrey, see you after the rally. Eric—who let Eric in here? Oleg, Sergey, Felix, my very, very best to you all. Emil, loved the new song. Terrific stuff. Natalia, thank you again. Yeah, and a pleasure to meet the rest of you, as well; Dmitri, Alexei, Nikolai, Fyodor, Pyotr, Grigory, Ivan (I must break you. You guys get *Rocky* over there?), Nikita, Borya, Lyosha, Matvey, Sergey—two Sergeys!—Yuri, Josef, Anastasiya, Stiva, Keith—stay behind, Keith, I got a project for you—Kid Rock, stand-up guy. Terrific hat—Hannity! Hit any birdies lately? Oh, and how's your golf game? Great. Great. Where's Ivanka? Can anyone get me Ivanka on the phone? Have you seen my daughter, Ivanka, Emil? One of the great, great beauties. When she was twelve—

The recording ceased at this point in the meeting when the surveillance device reached its storage capacity.

20
"Yes, Sir, in America"
November 7, 2016

"Yes, Carlyle. Right, with a 'y'. How many ti—okay." Harold uncrossed and recrossed his legs impatiently, holding his cell phone to his ear. He glanced out his hotel room window across a chilly gray street from his position behind a traditional black wooden writing table. "Is Huma available? Okay. Sure. And later this afternoon? An appointment with her chiropractor. Right. Well, no, I'm just a little surprised she'd schedule an appointment today, since she just saw her chiropractor three days ago." Harold thought. "Also, what with it being the day before the election. Okay, well, just, tell her I called." Harold glumly placed his phone on the desk, opened a thick, black leather binder, and absently began to study the Willard's room service menu.

"Still no luck?" Pattie asked distractedly from the bed, her eyes fixated on the television screen.

"You know, I don't think she's really at the chiropractor."

"There's your scoop." Pattie changed the channel. "Let's get out of the room."

"I want to be close to my laptop in case Huma calls."

"Harold, Huma's not asking you to prom. It's time to go in on a limo with your friends." Pattie turned off the TV and tossed the remote next to her onto the plush comforter. "Why do you still want to talk to her, anyway? Comey already sent that letter saying there was nothing on Anthony Weiner's laptop."

"Yeah, but," Harold began, then paused to think. "Huma is still married to Anthony Weiner. It's still a story," he concluded defensively. He looked down at the menu. "Do you want some crab cakes?"

"Why don't we go back to New York? Both Trump and Hillary are having their victory rallies in Midtown. That's where all the action is going to be."

"*Everyone* is going to cover those. 'Hillary Wins in Landslide,' 'America Elects First Woman President,' 'Steve Bannon Re-Frozen.' I'm the one guy who can publish a conversation with the woman who was married to the pervert who almost brought down the whole show."

"Well, we've done all there is to do in D.C. already. Twice. If I have to listen to that recording of Neil DeGrasse Tyson talking about the moon landing one more time, I'm gonna blow my brains out."

"We could walk around the Tidal Basin again. Last time, we accidentally went through the FDR memorial backwards, so—"

"No," Pattie refused stoutly.

"Come on, that couple just thought you were cute."

"There's a train that leaves at noon. If we pack our bags right now, we can be back in New York by four."

"Maybe if we just stop by the Hillary office on the way to the—" Harold began, when he was interrupted by a tinny recording of "Stars and Stripes Forever." Pattie looked at his phone, then at him. "I changed my ringtone in honor of electing the first woman president," he explained. "It's a big deal, Pattie." Harold put the phone to his ear. "Hello?" he answered.

"I'm going to get us two tickets for the noon train," Pattie whispered. "I can't stand in line for a sandwich behind another flock of UVA grads." Harold waved her quiet.

"Hello? Oh, hi, Abigail Charles Macaulay. How's it—the what? Oh, right, the souven—the flash drive. Yeah. Oh, no, I've been looking at it. No, yeah, my jaw definitely dropped. Yeah, all the way to the floor. I got fuzz in my mouth. From the carpet, because my jaw drop—right. No, yeah, of course we're going to break the story." Harold quickly searched his back pockets with this free hand. "No, um, we were actually thinking of running the story tonight, as a matter of fact. Ah, it's actually on my editor's desk right now. Yeah, well, you know how editors are. I'll touch base with him as soon as we get off the phone and see where he is with his edits." Harold jumped up and began rummaging furiously through identical pairs of khaki pants in the top drawer of the hotel room's stately wooden dresser.

"Oh, you know, if we take the Acela at 12:25, we'll actually get into New York earlier," Pattie nudged. "Interested? My treat!"

"Do you know what happened to that souvenir I got from the Hillary office last week?" Harold whispered, cupping the receiver.

"You were using it as a bookmark."

Harold's eyes lit up as he snapped his fingers. He leaped over to the dresser on his side of the bed and pulled out the Book of Mormon. A small, sky-blue device fell to the floor. "Did I tell you about this thing with the plates?" he whispered to Pattie, pointing to the book's open pages. "How's that, Abigail?" he asked into the phone. "Oh, you don't need to tell me the timing is crucial. Remember, I'm the bus guy? You can count on it. Yeah—oh, really? That would be fantastic, Communications Director. Absolutely. If I what? No, I don't play ball, though I was the alternate coxswain—Yes, and thank *you* for the job offer—oh, okay, well, yeah, but *when* it hits the papers! Definitely!" Harold hung up his phone, his face flushed and eyes beaming. "Oh my God!" he exclaimed to Pattie. He leaped up onto the bed and began to jump up and down in his socks, jostling Pattie unexpectedly off the side.

"Harold, what the hell?" Pattie yelled from the floor.

"It's all happening!" Harold exulted.

"What?"

"Pattie!" Harold jumped off the bed and pulled Pattie to her feet. "They gave me this flash drive, and apparently there's all sorts of juicy, incriminating stuff on Trump on there. She said 'explosive' five times. No one's reported any of it yet! They want *me* to write an article about it! And then Abigail offered me Communications Director! If I—something about a ball, playing ball with them—some kind of intramural government softball league, I guess. I wasn't paying attention by then—*Pattie!*" Harold said breathlessly.

Pattie shook her head and blinked as if waking up from a dream. "You?" she asked.

"*Me!*" Harold grabbed Pattie's hands and tried to twirl her around, but she remained confusedly in place. "Pattie, this is going to change everything. I'm going to be working in the West Wing. I can probably expense my *clothes* from now on. They'll put us up in a row house somewhere—remember that Italian restaurant we went to on Saturday? Right by there, if we want! Travel, food. We'll get invited to all sorts of state functions. Maybe we'll have a chance to meet Ted Kennedy!"

"Ted Kennedy is dead."

"Oh, right." Harold paused. "Well, Alec Baldwin. Pattie, we'll get to meet Alec Baldwin! And I can—Pattie, I can write a *book* about whatever explosive things are on this flash drive, like Carl Bernstein— Pattie, we can get you your own TV show! You don't have to write the little blurbs any more! You can be the *creator*! Pattie, Pattie, Pattie!"

"Harold, I...wow." Pattie collected herself. "This person offered you a job just now?"

"Yeah. I mean, you know how they talk."

"And you've met her before, right? You know for sure that she works for Hillary Clinton? You didn't meet her in line at a Starbucks, did you?"

"Pattie, that man *was* a magician."

"I mean, it sounds great, but it just seems very out of the blue. The election hasn't even happened yet, and she offered you a position over the phone."

"Oh, you know how fast government works. *Zip! Zap!* Just like that. These are decision-makers."

"I'm just—*why*?"

"Because she gave me this flash drive! And it's full of—oh, right." Harold skipped over to the nightstand and retrieved the small blue device. "I need to look at this," he said, waving it before Pattie's face. "This is going to buy us matching BMWs."

"Okay, you'll be working for the United States, not Saudi Arabia."

"Sure, they'll have a limo to take me to work, but what about weekends?" Harold sat down in a crushed-velvet red armchair, placed his laptop in his lap, and plugged in the small blue drive. "I could get license plates that say 'TRTHTLR.' Truth-teller."

"Oh, but then what will mine say?"

Harold didn't respond. He leaned forward, his face inches from his laptop screen as he furiously clicked on his computer's trackpad. "Shit," he said under his breath, his mouth agape in shock. "Pattie! Pattie!"

"What's on there?" Pattie asked. She walked over behind Harold's chair and leaned forward.

"Look at this! Look at these transcripts!"

"What is this?" Pattie squinted at the screen. "'The Russian government will work to secure your electoral victory, with the understanding that, once elected, you will approve a change in policy toward Russia and help the Kremlin to erode the American government from within through mismanagement and corruption.'" Pattie gazed at the screen, then repeated the sentence more loudly, as if searching for a second meaning. "Jesus. He's working with them."

"It's real! They—he—look at this!" Harold opened another file. "This, this Russian guy, Petrov, whoever that is—they have transcripts of every conversation he had since last January! Look at this one!" Harold pointed excitedly to the screen.

"'Mr. Trump, we are very pleased to inform you of the Main Directorate's progress in infiltrating your American voting systems,'" Pattie read quickly in a hushed voice. "'We have covertly acquired the voter rolls for a number of states...' Jesus Christ! They—"

"This is unreal! Let's see what this one says." Harold clicked open another file. "Oh, this one's just a picture of Ivanka in a bikini."

"Is she peeling a potato?"

"Who do you think knows about this?" Harold asked, looking up at Pattie.

"Yeah, it's a potato." Pattie squinted, then looked at Harold. "Well, it sounds like the Hillary campaign knows all about it. Thank God. And this guy whose name is on all the files. Christopher Steele."

"I have to call my editor," Harold said urgently, retrieving his phone from his pocket. He moved his computer off of his lap, standing up as he put his phone to his ear. Pattie immediately took his place in the chair, continuing to peruse the documents on Harold's laptop.

"Sir, hello!" Harold called into his phone. "Sir, have I got a scoop for you! No, about the election. No, I'm still covering the election. No, I would have remembered that, sir."

Pattie chuckled from her spot in the chair. "Trump goes on for five pages here trying to sell a warehouse full of steaks to the Russian government."

"Well, the Willard had an available room on short notice, and I— to catch up with the Hillary campaign, sir. And sir, you are not going to *believe* what I found out. They entrusted me with a flash drive filled with transcripts of—yes, *they* entrusted *me*." Harold shifted his weight from foot to foot. "Well, because of the quality of my reporting, sir. Yes, I gave them my name. Well, a lot of people in the Hillary camp *do* click on them, apparently."

"On July 14th, Trump called Petrov eight times between midnight and one. Looks like the transcriptionist had a tough time with his voicemails. I've never seen so many 'unintelligibles.' Something about trying to schedule a river cruise with Putin? It doesn't say whether Petrov returned any of his calls."

"But, sir, these transcripts. They're of Trump plotting with someone from Russia. No, someone in particular. Someone from the KGB. Right, GRU. Whatever. Sir, the point is, it's a massive conspiracy to try to swing the election! They've been meeting for months! No, Russia is helping Trump, with hacking, and disinformation, and targeted—Trump and Russia, yes. Yes, sir, in America."

"Oh, my," Pattie put her hand over her mouth. "Make sure you're not in public when you click on the 'Mike Pence' folder."

"We have to get an article out about it right away, sir! I'm reading through them, and I'm going to write up a rough draft for you this afternoon. What time do you need it by to make it to pr—no, sir. I have the documents to prove—with all due respect, sir, I do *not* make up stories. Well, an interview that Garfunkel gave to Mika Brzezinski is not 'made up,' inasmuch as he did, in fact, give it. I don't want to split hairs, but I promise you, this is one hundred percent real. No, it *could* happen—sir, it *is* happening! Think about our paper's motto! 'The Guardian of Democracy!' Really? Are you sure? I always thought that was our motto. Regardless, sir—"

"And then on August 23rd, Trump called Petrov eleven times from a green room in Austin, Texas, to try to arrange a game of catch with Putin." Pattie snorted.

"Sir, you're making a big mistake here! N—no, sir. Well, if that's really what you think—Sir—Well, you know what, sir? In that case, you may consider this my resignation. Effective immediately. You know, this paper used to be a crusader for truth, freedom, and justice, casting the bright light of day on the darkest corners of corruption. And sir—sir, you can just wait for Barbra Streisand to call you back—it is with this paper's reputation in mind that I am stepping down. For I cannot in good conscience—hello? Sir?" Harold looked down at his phone. "Well, fuck him."

Pattie shot up from the chair. "So you quit? Just like that?"

"That paper is being run by cowards and political stooges," Harold declared. "I don't need them. I have the transcripts, don't I? I'll write a book. Think of how giant this is, Pattie. They could give me the Nobel." He leaned over the chair and scrolled through the transcript Pattie had left open. "Huh, Ivanka is a 40D."

"Harold, you can't just qui—"

"Do you have any idea how much digging I had to do to get this story?" Harold interrupted indignantly. "I never gave up. I finally have my reward. And I have the Communications job with the Hillary administration, too."

"I think they were offering that job as a carrot."

Harold looked up from the screen. "A carrot for what?"

"If you got the transcripts to press, *then* you could get the Communications job."

Harold considered for a moment. "Maybe that's how things work for TV reviewers. This is government. They can't just openly bribe people."

Pattie checked her phone. "We have to get out of here if we're going to catch the train."

Harold quickly shut his laptop. "Excellent. I have some publishers' houses to visit."

"Just make sure you don't take their first offer." Pattie placed her suitcase on the floor and began removing her clothes from the closet.

Harold nodded, dashing about the room to gather his belongings. He jumped over Pattie's open suitcase and picked up his laptop, removing the small blue flash drive. "I have to make sure I keep this on my person," he declared, placing it atop the writing desk next to his room key and two stray pens. He thought for a moment. "Do you have any room in your suitcase?"

"Why?"

"I really liked the towels."

Pattie shook her head. "For God's sake." She zipped up her suitcase. "I'm ready. Let's go."

"Okay," Harold agreed reluctantly. He scooped two glasses off of the writing desk, wrapped them in a monogrammed bathrobe, and stuffed them into his duffel. "Do you want to stop at the deli, or see if we can get some crab cakes to go from the restaurant downstairs?" He zipped his duffel and slipped into his jacket.

"Let's just go."

"Okay, okay," Harold said, switching off the light and following Pattie out the door. "Or, hey, you're a TV person—what about a miniseries? After the book comes out, I could see this as a miniseries, right?"

21
"It Is a New Day in America!"
November 8, 2016

"Raise your arms," a hunched, elderly man told Harold gruffly, flicking Harold's wrists with his tape measure. Harold raised his arms dutifully, admiring the elderly man's work as he watched their reflection in the three-paneled mirror positioned in front of him.

"This is the kind of suit Obama's press guy wears, right?" Harold asked. "It looks the same." He eyed himself in the mirror. "Slender, European cut."

"Sure," the elderly man muttered curtly. He was a small, stoop-backed man with wild tufts of gray hair wrapped around the sides of his otherwise shiny, bald head. An unbuttoned black vest hung loosely from his shoulders, and the cuffs of his wrinkled corduroy trousers dragged under his shoes as he shuffled about the chalk-stained carpet. "You want cuffs?"

"Does Obama's fellow have cuffs?"

The man grunted.

"No, no cuffs," Harold decided. "Or, could you roll up the legs for a second so I can see what they look like?"

The man grunted again.

"Yeah, you're right. No cuffs. I don't want to seem ostentatious." Harold waited for the man to reply. "I'm representing the people now." The man hacked a thick, phlegmy cough. "Okay, okay, not representing, but I'm speaking to them. I'm going to be the face of the Clinton administration."

The man stuck a pin into Harold's ankle. "Sorry," he mumbled. "Don't move."

"Now, I remember Obama wore a tan suit. Could I see your selection of tans, as well?"

"In a minute." He stuck his fingers inside Harold's waistline and jerked his pants up and down quickly.

"I think Hillary will want me to project that image of youth and vigor. Something Obamaesque, or Kennedyesque." The tailor ran a measuring tape along the arch of Harold's groin, saying nothing. "Do you have a seersucker ensemble? Maybe for outdoor events, like an Easter egg roll?"

"Raise your arms again."

"Are you from Germany? My wife's Bubba used to say 'arms' the same way."

The man shook his head no. Sticking a safety pin between his teeth, he rose with great effort, his joints creaking as he did so. He slowly ran the tape measure along Harold's wingspan. "Normal arms," he said to himself.

Harold noticed a framed picture hanging on the wall above the mirror, featuring the man, a bright smile on his face, standing with his arm around a younger man in a smart blue suit with slicked-back dark hair. "Who is that with you in the photo?" Harold asked, gesturing with his head. "Do you carry that suit in the store?"

The man glanced over at the photo, and his face became suddenly animated. "That is my son, Jacob," he answered proudly. "He is Chief of Staff for Gary Johnson."

"Huh," Harold said, visibly deflated at this pulling of rank. "I like the lapel on his suit."

"Very well-connected, Jacob."

"I'm sure, I'm sure. I'm no stranger to political insider-circles, myself," Harold said quickly. "I'm not sure how it is in the Libertarian campaign, but I learned some things that never even made it to press." He shook his head. "The media got complacent this election."

"Between you and me," the elderly man said confidentially, leaning in close to Harold, "my Jacob tells me this Mr. Trump fellow is in bed with the Russians."

Harold put down his arms suddenly, giving the man a sidelong glance.

"The Russians made a deal with Mr. Trump," the man whispered. "They hacked the election, with computers, in exchange for Mr. Trump doing Russia's bidding. They have the business, you see, on him. He has been in debt to them for years."

Harold's face drained of color. "I doubt that's true. You know, Gary Johnson likes his..." he inhaled sharply through his front teeth.

The elderly man shook his head. "The whole thing is fucked," he whispered.

*   *   *

Pattie crossed the five lanes of Eleventh Avenue, approaching the Javits Center's cheerless, sprawling glass boxes rising up above a line of television vans topped by a morass of small satellite dishes. The clear, chill late autumn evening made her face tingle, and she turned up the collar of her dark green hunting jacket. Bright yellow windows from the skyscrapers behind her lit up the early dusk with mysterious promises, and Pattie felt the strange, unnameable excitement in her stomach she remembered, strangely, from the morning before her Pulitzer lunch and the afternoon before senior prom. Every inch of sidewalk not cordoned off by plastic white cones and television crew members was occupied by people standing, jostling, waving signs, and leaning toward the nearest news camera. She spotted a woman dressed entirely in black talking to a salt-and-pepper haired man adjusting his glasses. "Natalie!" she called, raising her arm to signal to her friend among the rapidly growing crowd milling about outside. "Hi!" Natalie and Anthony's eyes clicked into focus as they recognized Pattie amongst the throng, and she wove her way up the sidewalk to join them at the rear of a thick line clogging the entrances to the Javits Center's impassive translucent doors.

"Hi!" Natalie gave Pattie a quick hug.

"Are you ready to witness some history?" Anthony bubbled.

"I've been on pins and needles all day! I could barely eat!" Pattie exclaimed. She glanced at the people gathered around them. The crowd chittered with exultant anticipation. A large group of fresh-faced young men and women wearing HILLARY tees over layers of long-sleeved shirts danced in place, taking selfies of each other in different groupings and ritualistically checking their phones. "One percent reporting from Florida," a young man who was trying to cultivate a beard announced. "Looks like it's for Hillary. She's got this locked up." The group cheered. "Miami-Dade is the most important county."

Behind them, an elderly couple stood silently grimacing arm-in-arm, their gray skin speckled with unidentified crust in the folds of their wrinkles and around their mouths. They wore matching faded tan wool coats, which were adorned with an array of buttons pledging support for George McGovern, Geraldine Ferraro, and "Ban the Bomb." The woman held an unused megaphone limply at her side.

"Harold's not coming?" Natalie asked Pattie.

"No," Pattie sighed, "he won't be joining us."

Natalie widened her eyes and leaned forward sympathetically, patting Pattie's arm. "I'm sure it's for the best," she said gently.

"We've known since you couldn't come out after we fixed the jetty," Anthony confided.

"No, I wish," Pattie laughed. "He's out shopping for suits."

"Oh!" Natalie reddened. "So you're still...?" She moved her index and middle fingers back and forth quickly.

Pattie nodded and pulled out her phone. "I wonder if Hillary can flip Texas."

*   *   *

"This is probably what the convention was like," she mumbled to herself, gazing up at the high glass ceilings as she made her way out of the security line and into the main hall. American flags had been attached to every available piece of scaffolding, and bright white lights shot through the hall, divorcing it from the evening sky the glass walls let in. The open floor buzzed with a crowd of people sporting T-shirts, buttons, and pennants bearing slogans, their nervous energy shrinking the room. Pattie said the slogans to herself quietly, searching for one that stuck: "Together, Stronger," "Americans, Together," "Stronger Americans," "Hillary: From Us to You," "Hill Yeah," "Nasty Woman," "Take an American Dream and Make It Together," and "Grab This." The throngs stretched in eternities to the base of the raised stage, an ocean expanding below the largest flag of the bunch, suspended triumphantly from the ceiling, and the microphone and teleprompter waiting patiently several feet before it. Pattie gazed around herself in a daze, straining to take in as much of the expectant rumble as she could, feeling slightly apart from her own body.

"Oh, there's Carrie," Natalie said, jolting Pattie back to earth as she pointed through the dense crowd to a short, rotund older woman standing to the side of a set of bleachers and speaking animatedly with with a pair of blonde girls wearing matching blue and red face paint and large buttons reading "Madame President." "Carrie!" Natalie called, waving her hand high in the air.

Carrie turned, squinting through her square, transition-lens glasses. "Natalie!" she cried. She waved in return, clutching a hat topped with blue flowers to her head so that it didn't fall off. Natalie embraced her when she approached, and Anthony primly shook her hand. "What a day!" Carrie exclaimed. "It reminds me of the day I was nominated to be the Room Rep for Ben's first grade class. 'We need an advanced reading group!' was my motto."

"It's truly amazing," Pattie agreed. "Do we know when the first states will start to call?"

"Probably not for another hour or so," Anthony answered promptly. "It's gonna be an early night, though." He waited for the group's assent. "I was reading in the *Atlantic* that the Democrats have about 250 electoral votes banked by Election Day, so Ohio, Virginia, Michigan, Wisconsin, Pennsylvania and Iowa are pretty much the only states where Trump even has a chance." He shrugged confidently. "Demography is destiny."

Carrie nodded. "Carl and I study the maps every year, and if I had run for South Jamaica Fire Drill Instructor just two cycles later, I would have swept the district." She adjusted her hat. "Of course, we moved to Westport in 1991, so what can you do?"

A giant screen on the far side of the hall flickered to life, and above CNN's familiar logo, the enormous visage of an elderly man with a rim of curly hair framing the rear side of his crown appeared above the masses of Hillary supporters below.

"Oh, look!" Natalie pointed. "It's the tall one."

"Art Garfunkel," Anthony said quickly.

They watched Garfunkel's lips move silently for several moments before the Javits Center's sound system crackled on amid a brief howl of feedback. "Yes, that's right, an actor, too," Garfunkel explained.

"Really?" Natalie asked. "An actor, too?"

"He was in *Catch-22* and *Carnal Knowledge*," Anthony interjected hurriedly.

"I, for one, am very optimistic about Hillary's chances tonight," Garfunkel said. "You can feel it in the air—in every town and city across America—there's a real electricity. It reminds me of the night when I learned that my album, *Breakaway*, made number nine on the U.S. charts—right, my album. Uh huh, just me on it. No, number nine in the U.S. No, Paul wasn't on it. Anyway, the atmosphere tonight—well, let's see. Iowa, I think she'll win Iowa."

Natalie turned to her husband. "Wasn't Shirley MacLaine in *Carnal Knowledge*?"

"Ann-Margret," Anthony answered without taking his eyes off the screen.

"Ohio," Garfunkel continued thoughtfully. "You know, I once played a show in Cincinnati that—no, a solo show. Well, I had a guitarist accompaniment, but I was the only name on the bill, see. No, someone besides Paul. No, people knew it wouldn't be Paul."

*   *   *

Harold lifted a brown leather loafer off of the display mount and rotated it in his hands, inspecting the quality of the stitching around the sole. "Do you have this in black?" he asked.

The sales clerk, an African-American man in his sixties with graying hair shaved close to his scalp and a bushy mustache that he stroked absentmindedly, sat on a shoe-fitting stool further down the aisle, an earbud in one ear, his attention focused on his iPhone.

Harold watched the man for a moment, waiting for a response, or a vague acknowledgement of his presence, before placing the loafer back on its pedestal and continuing to browse the selection of dress shoes. He picked up a tan, suede loafer and ran his fingers against the grain. "Is this formal enough to wear with a suit if no one actually sees your feet?" he asked the salesman.

The man stared, motionlessly, at the phone he held in his right hand.

Harold smacked his lips twice and placed the shoe back on the shelf. "Thanks," he said politely. "It's hard to know what people are wearing in the corporate world these days. Well, I shouldn't say 'corporate,' but, you know." He picked up a blindingly white running shoe and used both hands to push the heel into the toe. "A job at the intersection of media and politics, I guess you would say." He placed the shoe back on the shelf and kneeled to inspect a moccasin. "Do people still keep coins in their penny loafers?" he asked. "I remember Gran used to scold me for taking the dimes out of my shoes and spending them at the arcade."

The man sighed very slowly.

"I tried to fit quarters in there once, but Gram told me I'd get mugged." Harold shook his head. "Not—" he paused, glancing at the man's face nervously. "—It was—I had—what's your most expensive shoe?" Harold picked up a shiny, black leather shoe and walked over to the salesman. He stood uncomfortably beside the man for several seconds before clearing his throat.

"Sorry. I was just wondering if you would—if you're not busy—if you could measure this for me. I mean, measure my foot. For the shoe." Harold held up the shoe. "This one."

The man looked slowly from Harold to the shoe and back to Harold. "That's the one you want?" he asked.

"Oh, I mean, no, if you can think of a better one," Harold apologized. "That's not a challenge, I mean. You obviously know a great deal about shoes, whereas this was just one that..." he trailed off, helplessly holding the shoe limply in his right hand.

The man nodded. "Sit down," he said, inclining his head toward a row of dark green vinyl chairs. He unplugged his earbuds from the iPhone and set it down on the carpet next to his stool. The dulcet sounds of a defensive, Queens-accented tenor emanated from the tiny speaker. Harold looked down at the screen.

"The tall one's arguing with Newt," the man said.

"Who?" Harold asked, pleased that they were communicating more and sensing a step forward in the relationship.

"Newt Gingrich," the man explained. "Former Speaker of the House."

"No, the—" Harold glanced down at the screen again. "Oh! It's Art. I should've known by the voice. You know, he sang the high harmonies."

"These early wins for Trump mean nothing," Garfunkel explained. "Indiana, Kentucky, West Virginia? There was never any question Trump would carry these states. It's like when Paul and I were on tour in the *Sounds of Silence* days. We never expected to sell big with the teeny-bopper crowd. We weren't the Monkees or Herman's Hermits. With our lyrics, we were a part of the counterculture. Uh huh, our lyrics. Well, we both sang them."

"He came in here once," the man said disinterestedly. "Asked a bunch of questions about walking shoes and didn't buy a damn thing."

"Well, don't forget, Newt, Vermont was just called for Hillary. And, you know, we can expect the rest of New England to come in, in the next hour or so. Pretending to know the election from Indiana, Kentucky, and West Virginia would be like—here's a story. A parable, if you will. A memory, culled from my eclectic past, that flits across my mind in this madcap hour. Huh? Oh, right, the story."

Harold had removed his right shoe and began shifting his foot impatiently.

"Paul and I originally thought, to be famous, you gotta have a stage name. So we went by 'Tom and Jerry.' Now, just think, what if we had stuck with those names? We would—no, Tom and Jerry. We would never have—look, just, trust me."

"'Bridge Over Troubled Water,'" Harold commented. "Beautiful song."

The man slipped a metal Brannock device around Harold's socked foot. "Listen to Aretha's version," he grumbled. "You gotta have some guts to sing a song like that."

Harold nodded thoughtfully. "The leather is really soft."

"This is all to say, we would be jumping the gun by trying to infer anything from these early returns. See, if we hadn't changed those stage names, Paul and I never would have hit on our iconic folk duo image, and neither of us would ever have embarked on this journey. Right, neither him nor me. Well, no one paid just to see Stan Laurel."

"Excuse me," Harold said politely, pointing down at his left foot, which was still in the Brannock. "Would you say my feet are narrow?"

*   *   *

"Sorry," Pattie said, attempting to wedge her way between a pale, fair-haired, heavily pregnant young woman and her skinny, tousle-haired, stubbly-faced husband. They wore identical long-sleeved T-shirts with stylized images of Hillary Clinton's face superimposed on the Statue of Liberty. "I'm just trying to get to the bathroom."

"No worries!" the woman said cheerfully, gently tracing concentric circles along the top of her rounded, distended abdomen with her hands.

Pattie glanced around the couple at what appeared to be a long, amorphous line snaking toward the wall on the far side of the convention floor. "Do you know, is this the line for the bathroom?" she asked the pair.

The couple looked at each other. "We haven't really been asking," the woman said.

"We're too caught up in the moment," the man added.

"I can't leave *this spot* until they call Pennsylvania. It's been sort of an odd start, but that's because the heavy hitters haven't come in yet." She inhaled sharply. "Fingers crossed."

"Yeah, definitely," Pattie nodded. "So, are you two not in line at all, then?"

"Nope, just taking pictures for Hillary's scrapbook!"

Pattie cocked her head, her interest piqued. "Do you work for the campaign?"

The woman pointed to her stomach. "This little critter!"

"Ah," Pattie nodded. "When is she due?"

"Oh, we don't know the sex yet," the woman corrected.

"By the time our child is old enough for kindergarten, gender distinctions won't matter the way they do now," the man explained helpfully.

"Smart planning," Pattie smirked. The couple beamed.

"We conceived the child after Hillary won South Carolina," the woman added. "That was really a turning point."

"But we would have named the baby Hillary anyway," the man added. "We wanted our child to be one of the first."

Pattie nodded. "You don't want it to become derivative."

The woman looked up at the screen and shrieked in surprise. "Michigan counties are going for *Trump*?" she exclaimed, studying the giant screen mounted on the far wall. "And they still haven't called Pennsylvania!"

"Those are just the first precincts reporting," Pattie reminded. "And, I guess Pennsylvania was always going to be close..."

"Don't worry." The woman patted her stomach. "Hillary's kicking. Ze knows."

*   *   *

Harold strolled leisurely up a darkened Madison Avenue, whistling "Bridge Over Troubled Water" and stopping occasionally to admire the store window displays lining the block. He pressed his face against the cool glass of the window to an antique store, admiring its meticulously arranged displays of solid oak writing desks, globes in brass stands, and wooden telescopes.

"If anyone's earned a new ship in a bottle, it's me," he muttered to himself.

"Emily!" Harold heard a man's voice yell from up the block in a thick, slurred speech. "Emily, wouldja stop for a sec, and just turn around?"

Harold looked to his right to see a young woman in her early twenties with long black hair wearing a short blue dress stretched taut around her hips, walking briskly in his direction, her arms crossed over her chest. She looked straight ahead with a determined scowl, her eyes and cheeks puffy and red.

"Emily, you wanted to go home, so we're going home!" the man called, emerging from an unlit crosswalk. He wore a glossy black button-up shirt, open wide at the collar. A pompadour of brown hair was combed back and to the side and held aloft with whisks of mousse, while the sides were closely buzzed in. He hurried in pursuit of Emily, though Harold noticed he was careful never to catch up to her. "We're doing what you wanted to do, okay? I left."

Emily shook her head ruefully and quickened her step, choking back a sniffle. "You can go back," she said tremulously, stifling a sob.

"Emily!" the man called as he finally caught up with her. "I didn't say I wanted to go back, okay? That's all in your head."

"You're *mad* at me," Emily said, turning to face him. Harold pretended to inspect an astrolabe in the store window.

"No!" the man checked his voice. "No," he continued, more quietly, "I'm mad, too, okay? You think I'm for Trump? I was just saying it's not such a big deal that we have to leave early."

"You're mad at *me*, with everything that's happening tonight?" Emily began to cry. "Hillary needed Ohio."

"I *told* you, Emily, you can't run a campaign and ignore the Rust Belt. Everyone knows that!" The man sighed. "Pennsylvania isn't in yet. And even if it goes to Trump, the Republicans'll rein him in. Paul Ryan's not a Nazi. He's a fiscal conservative."

"This isn't *about that*, Josh," Emily burbled. An cacophony of police sirens wailed as a line of cruisers rounded the nearest corner and raced uptown, their blue and red lights flashing across the dark street.

Josh studied her. "Is this a woman thing?"

"Just, fuck off," Emily sobbed. "You don't know what a rejection this feels like for everyone who's tried to be *perfect*. And *still*."

Josh suppressed an involuntary laugh. "It's not a rejection of *you*, baby!" he chuckled reassuringly. "It's a rejection of what a shitty candidate Hillary is. It's like Newt was saying: who ignores the Rust Belt in a presidential campaign?"

"I can't believe you're taking *his* side in all of this!"

"Emily, Hillary made virtually no trips to any of the Rust Belt states. It's not my fault Newt Gingrich is right that Hillary's campaign was too arrogant!"

"*Stop it!*" Emily screamed. "Hillary had a plan! She was going to have jobs retraining for all of those people! Trump just yelled the word 'coal'!"

"Yeah, true, but jobs retraining was a totally impractical—Emily, shhhh, it's not that big a deal," Josh strained to modulate his voice to a soothing tone as Emily sobbed loudly. "It's not even over yet." He hesitantly put his hand on her shoulder. "Maybe we just need to go back and cuddle."

Emily shook his hand off. "You need to go home tonight."

"But I'm already walking in this direction!"

Emily shook her head. She turned on her heel and took off again, brushing past Harold.

"Emily!" Josh began to chase after her, then paused under a broken streetlamp. "What about the two hundred and sixty-nine days Hillary went without a press conference?" he called. She didn't look back, and after waiting a few moments, he trudged back in the opposite direction. "Fucking frigid bitch," he muttered.

*   *   *

Pattie pushed through the crowd, glancing up at the gigantic screen mounted above them as a hush suddenly swept over the convention floor. "Chriiiiiiiiiiist," she moaned miserably. "North Carolina, too?" An earth-moving groan drifted across the hall as another state on the television screen turned red. She jumped as she heard a primordial scream behind her and turned around to see an extremely well-dressed man rip open his button-down shirt, revealing the words "FUCK TRUMP" painted in blue letters across his chest.

"Pattie, thank God!" Natalie exclaimed, emerging from behind the dense wall of people, Anthony and Carrie a step behind her. She threw her arms around Pattie. "What's going on?"

"I have no idea," Pattie replied. "This is insane."

"Where have you been?" Natalie asked. "Did you find the bathroom?"

"No, but I did get to meet Alec Baldwin," Pattie shrugged. "He asked me to buy him a gin and tonic, and then he called me his 'little piglet.'"

Carrie looked up at the screen, ignoring Natalie and Anthony's shock at Pattie's story. "It's like I always say," she said proudly as she shook her head. "When they're out to get you, they're out to get you."

"If Hillary wins the rest of the toss-ups plus all of the solid Democratic states, we may still squeak by," Anthony reasoned.

"Anthony's right." Natalie agreed. "There's still plenty of fight left."

Pattie bit her lip and breathed heavily through her nose, looking back up at the giant screen looming over them. "Trump has had the momentum all night. She hasn't gotten a single break."

"I mean, if you ran the election a hundred times, thirty times, Trump would win. It's possible we're just seeing a night when a lot of those balls aren't leaving the park," Anthony explained. He sighed slowly. "It would be the end of an era for us," he said solemnly.

"So much promise, wasted," Carrie said bitterly. "Just like when I ran for Junior Class Treasurer in 1966." She tilted her head back and blinked rapidly. "The prom theme was *What's New Pussycat*. I said it needed to be Vietnam. It's like I was predicting all year, history repeats itself until we learn."

"I can't even begin to think about what a Trump win would mean." Natalie shook her head, her eyes beginning to brim with tears. "I showed you those plates my grandmother took with her out of Germany in the Thirties, remember? It gives me chills to think we're two states away from…" she trailed off, looking up at the screen. "I hate these ads where they show the group of people a Chevrolet and don't tell them it's a Chevrolet."

Pattie felt a vibration in her front pocket and pulled out her phone. "Where *are* you?" she demanded.

"I'm at a diner on 58th and Sixth," Harold said. "Hillary isn't winning," he added in confusion.

"I know," Pattie said gravely. "Things are feeling really dark here."

"Did you have dinner there?"

"Did you hear what I just said?"

"I'm just curious. I'm having a grilled cheese."

"I feel scared."

"Don't worry. Nothing will change. The pendulum swings left, it swings right. It's the way of society. Look at the nineteenth century. Romanticism. Empiricism. Romanticism. Empiricism. The sun still shines, the grass is still green. I got a great suit for my job, by the way."

"Your jo—" Pattie pinched the bridge of her nose in vexation. "Harold, do you think Hillary will need a Director of Communications if she's not president?"

Harold was quiet. "Wouldn't she still communicate?"

"You better hope that suit works for weddings and funerals."

"I mean, sure, maybe she doesn't keep the whole team, but Pattie, the *director*." Harold chewed. "Honey, we have to come back here. This grilled cheese is really good."

"Harold—"

"Well, look," Harold began, a tremor in his voice. "She hasn't lost yet. So it's a nailbiter. These networks are probably building suspense intentionally for the ratings. I used to do that with the Long Island—."

"Harold, are you watching TV?"

"Yeah, they have one on in the diner here. Art Garfunkel is singing 'Angel Clare.'"

*   *   *

Harold bit off a corner of his grilled cheese sandwich and chewed it distractedly as the electoral map once again splashed across the screen of the bulky, flickering TV set mounted above the counter. The line cook, a middle aged man with an unshaven, pockmarked face and thick oval glasses leaned back against the lip of the stove, his head tilted back sharply to watch the television as a watery mound of eggs bubbled and sputtered behind him.

"There goes Florida," the line cook muttered.

"Looks like Hillary's just about sunk," replied an old, pot-bellied man with a bulbous red nose and a white mustache. From his seat further down the bar, Harold could smell the pungent stench of stale cigars wafting off of him. Immediately to the man's left, a woman with unwashed, stringy gray hair sat hunched over in a soiled, oversized orange coat. Silently, she removed a wadded ball of newspaper from her coat pocket, smoothed it out methodically on the countertop, wetted one side with drops of water from the glass on the counter in front of her, and pasted it to a blank page of a notebook she kept clutched in her other hand.

"Seems so," the line cook replied evenly, refilling the man's mug of coffee.

"I think it'll be good," the man said decisively, cradling the warm cup of coffee between his calloused hands.

The line cook pursed his lips, not looking away from the TV screen. "Americans," he muttered cantankerously. "This guy rides in trying to sell the whole country a boys' band."

"Of course, I don't agree with all of the stuff he's said this election. All that stuff on the bus—there's no place for that kinda talk in politics—but he says what's on his mind, that's for sure. You gotta respect that. You know where the guy stands."

"I suppose so," the line cook grunted. He turned, swirled around the mass of eggs on the griddle with a long flat metal spatula, then turned back around to face the TV.

"Not like these other double-talking politicians. He doesn't apologize, you know what I mean? So he likes women. That's who he is. You know what you're getting."

"You *do* know what you're getting," the line cook nodded. "You got me there."

"You keep hearing Russia, Russia. So he wants to have a better relationship with Russia, right? That's how I see it. He sees things, and he says, we don't have a good relationship with them, and he's going to make a better one. He's a negotiator. So he looks at this and sees a place to negotiate." The man took a long sip of coffee. "He wants to run the country like a business. I don't see any problem with that. You can't run a country like this, that's for sure. You gotta be responsible, rational. Level-headed."

"Sure describes the Donald," the line cook grimaced, still gazing at the animations of states turning red and blue on the flickering screen.

"That's for sure," the man emptied the rest of his coffee and set the mug down on the counter with a pronounced *clink*. He turned to the woman sitting next to him, who was unwadding another ball of newspaper. "You about ready to go?" The woman slowly looked up from her work and nodded, her blank eyes blinking with confusion. "Alright, good," the man said, rising from his stool. He fished a few bills out of his pocket and tossed them onto the counter. "Have a good one, Sid," he said to the line cook, nodding in salutation.

"Yeah, you too, Pete." The line cook waved his fingers in a halfhearted, mock salute as the man and woman shuffled past Harold and out of the diner.

Harold glanced toward the door as the bell chimed with the couple's departure, then turned his attention back to the television. The map of the United States appeared to be swallowed up in a red tide sweeping toward the West Coast. He pensively bit the inside of this cheek, feeling as though his stomach were sinking several inches deep. Harold considered the last bite of grilled cheese on his plate before finally discarding it and reaching into his pocket to retrieve his phone. He scrolled through his recent calls and picked the one number that wasn't Pattie's. Listening to the phone ring on the other end, he rocked back and forth on his stool, crossing his toes.

"Abigail Charles Macaulay?" he asked, when a businesslike woman's voice finally answered. "Yes, this is Harold. Um, Carlyle. Right." He swallowed. "So, how's it going? Uh-huh, no, yeah, I saw that. Well, maybe it's like in 2000, with the chads." He held up his empty mug of coffee to the line cook, who dutifully refilled it. "Anyway, I'd been meaning to call to find out what day you want me to start. I realize my residence probably won't be ready on such short notice, but I'm more than happy to find a room somewhere in the meantime."

He held the phone away from his ear, and the line cook broke his gaze from the television screen, distracted by the sound of a tiny voice screaming from the receiver.

"Okay, sure. So, that's a solid 'no,' then. Well, I thought she might still need someone to run communications. Not a whole team, obviously, but someone in journalism who—no, no, point taken. No, I did write the article!" Harold raised his voice to make himself heard over Abigail's harangue on the other end. "But my editor wouldn't run it.

Well, you can call Dean Baquet if you want to—" Harold glanced down at his phone, which had suddenly gone silent. He stared at the empty plate sitting in front of him for several moments, unmoving. Finally, he looked up at the TV screen. "Shit," he said. The line cook nodded in grim affirmation. Harold pushed his plate forward a half inch, stood up, pulled a twenty-dollar bill out of his wallet, tucked it under the plate, and walked out onto the dark sidewalk, hearing the door rattle definitively behind him. "Shit," he said again into the cold night.

*   *   *

"Sean! Leave that flag alone and come on, wouldja?" a young woman called across the convention floor, now nearly deserted. She kicked a discarded Hillary Clinton bobblehead and sent it skittering across the ground as she shuffled past Pattie, shaking her head.

"It's like I've been saying all along," Carrie was explaining triumphantly. "The most qualified candidate never wins. You can have the best ideas, the best education, even some sex appeal—none of it matters."

"What are we going to do?" Natalie asked. She sat on the hard concrete floor, her knees clutched to her chest, absently rocking back and forth. "We should leave, right? I feel like we need to leave the country."

Anthony crouched down beside her and gently rubbed her back. "You know, that's not a terrible idea. We could spend a few months in France, maybe Belgium. My old college pal Lucas, he has a beautiful little flat in Bruges. Sits empty most of the spring." Natalie shivered. "Bruges is beautiful in the spring."

Carrie turned to Pattie. "True visionaries have the hardest time. American politics is a reality show at every level."

Pattie nodded absently.

Carrie tutted to herself. "I've seen it over and over again. When I volunteered to organize the ice cream social in fifth grade—"

"Did none of this matter at all?" Pattie interrupted. "The race-baiting? Talking about penis size during the debates? The Access Hollywood tape? The twenty sexual assault victims who came forward? The Khans? Miss Universe? The jokes about Hillary's butt? Did none of that make one shred of a difference?" She ripped a Planned Parenthood flyer someone had given her in half. "What the ever-loving *fuck* was the point of the past goddamn mother-fucking year and a half?" She turned to Carrie. "Huh? What was the point of any of it?"

Carrie looked at Pattie helplessly, her mouth agape. She breathed in and out nervously. "I...I don't know."

Pattie looked Carrie square in the eyes with a fierce intensity, as if Carrie's dumbfoundedness was somehow responsible for the last fifteen months. "We were supposed to have a woman president," Pattie said quietly. She looked down, where Anthony was still comforting Natalie, then back up at Carrie, and finally to the empty stage, where two men in white T-shirts and jeans were removing the American flags from their stands. "I'm going home," she murmured. She slowly put on her coat and trod forward past Carrie, who was still looking at her emptily, toward the main doors.

Stepping out onto the curb, Pattie closed her eyes and slowly took in the chilly, damp late-night air. She heard a boat's horn bleat wearily from the Hudson churning behind her. She glanced back at the Javits Center. The streetlamps' gauzy yellow glow reflected off of it into the river beyond. "Stupid fucking glass ceiling."

Exhausted, she looked around, contemplating whether or not to take a cab back to the pair's most recent sublet, when a string of twinkling lights attached to a red-and-white pretzel cart caught her eye, and she trudged over.

"Do you have any pretzels left?" she asked a stocky man with translucent blue eyes who stood behind the cart.

"Yes," he said, nodding affirmatively. "Pretzel with syrniki. Five dollars."

"Syrniki?" Pattie asked, confused. "I don't want syrniki. Just a pretzel."

"It is good," the man said encouragingly, his voice marked with a thick Eastern European accent. "Fried curd patty. Just like back home."

Pattie studied the man's face. "Have you ever lived in Cleveland?"

The man stroked his chin playfully. "Cleveland? No. But I hear is a exciting city. Many things to see and do."

Pattie looked from the man, to his cart, to the empty avenue beside them.

"Rock and Roll Hall of Fame," he added impishly.

"Never mind," she said finally. "I'm not hungry." She turned and started to walk sullenly down the block, flipping her jacket collar up against the early-morning cold.

"Cheer up!" the man called after her. "It is a new day in America!"

*   *   *

"I know how disappointed you feel because I feel it too," Hillary Clinton said from the television screen. Pattie laid in bed, her head propped up by a sloping mound of pillows, and listlessly watched the TV monitor mounted on the wall in front of her. She loosely cradled a half-eaten bowl of cereal in her hand, which she periodically brought to her mouth for another spoonful, the woven wheat squares long turned soggy and rapidly disentangling into long mushy strands. "And so do tens of millions of Americans who invested their hopes and dreams in this effort," Hillary continued from the TV. "This is painful, and it will be for a long time. But I want you to remember this: our campaign was never about one person or even one election. It was about the country we love and about building an America that's hopeful, inclusive and big-hearted."

"So much for all that," Pattie muttered while chewing.

"Pattie, you haven't seen my light brown jacket, have you?" Harold asked, manically rifling through the contents of a closet next to the bed. "The corduroy one?"

"Nope," Pattie replied, her eyes not leaving the screen.

"I know I had that jacket with me in D.C.," Harold thought aloud.

"You did," Pattie confirmed. "You wore it incessantly. You were hoping someone would mistake you for a Georgetown professor."

"And it worked, didn't it? Remember, those Hungarian co-eds asked me what street the Urban Outfitters was on?" Harold stopped to take a gray, long-sleeved T-shirt with "Columbia Lacrosse" printed across it in blue letters, which he draped admiringly over his front.

Pattie looked up. "Did that come with a free bottle of rohypnol?"

"I found it at the gym," Harold said defensively. "But I know today is hard for you as a woman."

"Harold, shut up."

"We spent a year and a half bringing together millions of people from every corner of our country to say with one voice that we believe that the American dream is big enough for everyone," Hillary declared, "for people of all races and religions, for men and women, for immigrants, for LGBT people and people with disabilities—for everyone." Pattie nodded solemnly.

"Pattie, I'm on your side here, okay? If I can find that thumb drive, I can write that book, win a bunch of awards, maybe get invited on *Fresh Air with Terry Gross*, and we can sink Donald Trump ourselves." He turned a pair of navy blue slacks upside-down and shook them vigorously, grimacing when only a tiny plastic turtle emblazoned with a picture of Jeb Bush fell to the floor.

"Did you call the hotel in D.C.?"

"Yeah." Harold opened a wicker box filled with ascots and began pawing through the brightly colored silk patterns. "They just kept asking about some missing linens." He dejectedly placed the lid back on the box and returned it to the closet. "Totally unhelpful."

"Well, it's your own fault for not saving the files locally," Pattie sniped.

"Remember what that old man at the debate said about keeping our criticism *constructive*?" Harold crawled under the bed.

"I don't know what to tell you, Harold." Pattie scooped the last bite of cereal into her mouth and set the bowl down on the carpet next to the bed. "Your evidence is gone. Donald Trump is our next president. Maybe if you hadn't burned every single scrap of your credibility, you could've published that article when it would've counted."

"Pattie!" Harold emerged from under the bed. "I didn't even get that flash drive until, like, a week ago!"

"And to the young people in particular, I hope you will hear this," Hillary said from the television. "I have, as Tim said, spent my entire adult life fighting for what I believe in. I've had successes and I've had setbacks—sometimes really painful ones. Many of you are at the beginning of your professional, public, and political careers. You will have successes and setbacks too. This loss hurts. But please, never stop believing that fighting for what's right is worth it."

Pattie bit her lip. Harold looked up and noticed her eyes watering. She met his gaze and quickly looked away. "These fucking Americans," she muttered.

"What about the Russians?" Harold asked.

Pattie laughed acidly. "Yeah, Vladimir Putin spent the last forty years recasting Jim Crow as law and order."

Harold pulled open the top drawer of Pattie's dresser and began inspecting her undergarments. "You saw the transcripts. We couldn't have stopped this. They even had the banks!" He yanked out a black strapless bra.

"Harold, I assure you, it's not in there."

"Pattie, this is Russia we're talking about."

"You know, scripture tells us, 'Let us not grow weary in doing good for in due season, we shall reap if we do not lose heart.' So my friends, let us have faith in each other. Let us not grow weary, let us not lose heart. For there are more seasons to come and there is more work to do," Hillary concluded. "I am incredibly honored and grateful to have had this chance to represent all of you in this consequential election."

Pattie switched off the screen and sighed slowly and heavily. She stared silently at the dark screen for close to a minute while Harold removed a handful of panties from the drawer and laid them out methodically across his side of the bed. "You know, I could actually stand to hear Art Garfunkel sing right about now," Pattie said to herself with a half-smile.

"Did you hear him sing 'American Tune' to Joy-Ann Reid last night?" Harold asked as he pressed down on each pair in turn, searching for any flash drive-shaped lumps.

"Which song is that again?"

"Oh Pattie, it's beautiful." Harold rummaged through the folds of a pair of gray bikini-briefs. *"And I don't know a soul who's not been battered / I don't have a friend who feels at ease."* He collected the underwear and shoved the pairs back into the top drawer. *"I don't know a dream that's not been shattered or driven to its knees,"* he continued in a light tenor.

"That's really pretty," Pattie said softly. Harold nodded. "Garfunkel sang that?"

"Yeah, last night," Harold replied, pulling open Pattie's makeup kit. "Paul wrote it, though."

Epilogue
"I Think If You Just Bop Them on the Nose, They Leave You Alone"
December 20, 2016

"I don't think this is even a real pizza," Harold sniffed. "I think this is a frozen pizza, heated up. 'Wood-fired,' my rear—" he coughed on a shard of burnt crust.

Pattie rolled her eyes. "It's not Little Italy."

"But it's supposed to be a tourist paradise," Harold pouted, dropping his slice of pizza back onto the faux-wood table, where it rattled like a piece of plastic as it settled on his plate. An evening breeze wafted sea air across the beach and up onto the raised patio, where Harold and Pattie sat huddled under a space heater and a string of Christmas tree lights in the shapes of candy canes and pineapples. Dim outlines of palm trees swayed in the dusk.

Pattie speared a piece of halibut. "Let's try to be positive! It's not every day that you find yourself in...San Diego!"

Harold sighed. "Yeah, you're right." He looked from the partially eaten personal pizza sitting in front of him to the ocean, which crashed and yawned across the road in the soft blues of twilight. He reached for a piece of bread from a wicker basket in the center of the table. "Remember the bread at the Italian restaurant in Boston?" he asked wistfully. "That was really good bread."

"Harold."

"I'm not saying anything! I'm just remembering some good bread." He shook his head sadly. "We really ate well on that beat."

"I like traveling this way, on our paid vacation time. All the hustling and the lies, it's exhausting."

"Exhausting, or thrilling?" Harold sipped his water. "I mean, the most interesting thing that happened to me last week was when a seagull grazed my head and almost made me fall off the side of the evening trash barge to Matawan."

"Your editor gave you your old job back. Be grateful."

"If I have to sit through another online ethics course, I'll shoot myself in the head," Harold muttered. "How many different ways am I supposed to say I'm sorry?"

"If not for this job, you'd be freelancing for *Slate*. Is that what you really want?"

"I could've written a book," Harold said petulantly. "I had everything right there at my fingertips." He stretched his hands out in front of him, miming a fruitless attempt to grasp some invisible object that eluded him.

A chorus of ebullient barks drifted on the breeze across the patio from further up the beach. Pattie turned around in her chair and squinted into the obscurity of the descending nighttime. "Oh, Harold, look! Seals!" She grabbed his arm and pointed toward a herd of seals vaguely visible in the blue-gray evening.

Harold raised out of his chair and peered over Pattie's shoulder. He could just make out the creatures' outlines across the road near the bend in the coast. Several seals were splayed out on their bellies on the wet sand, the waves crashing in behind them and lapping at their tails. A particularly large one clapped his flippers together and leaped into the tangle, starting a dogpile on top of a confused pup. "Look at that!" Harold said gleefully. "A rookery of seals, cooling off in the evening air after a taxing afternoon of swimming and hunting. They're truly majestic creatures, don't you think? Why—" Harold suddenly gagged on his own words. "What the hell is that?" he retched.

"I don't know," Pattie said, scrunching her nose in disgust. "Maybe a pipe burst inside."

"Too salty for sewage," Harold said authoritatively. The breeze picked up, bringing a fresh wave of the putrid stench across the patio. "It smells like leftover clams," he groaned, pinching his nose.

"I think it's the seals," Pattie whispered.

"The seals?"

Pattie raised her eyebrows. "Think about it."

"But they live in the ocean," Harold protested. "They basically spend their entire day in the bath."

"I think they roll around in their own urine."

"That's absurd. Even pigs don't do that."

"Well, I heard that seals do."

"Pigs copulate in the muck, and *they* don't smell like that."

Pattie attempted another bite of halibut, then put down her fork. "That is pretty strong."

"I can't believe anyone would want to swim with these filthy beasts," Harold said incredulously. "Excuse me!" He signaled to a lanky, greasy teenager wearing black pants, a black shirt, and red tie, who dutifully slouched toward the couple's table.

"Do you want some more water?" the teen asked.

"Do you smell this?"

The teen looked at Harold. "What?"

Harold huffed. "The unspeakable odor that's enveloping us like some kind of medieval plague."

The waiter looked momentarily confused, then his face lit up with understanding. "Oh, the seals," the waiter nodded. "Give it time. You get used to it."

"That's what Pol Pot told the Cambodians, too." Harold took a sip of water. "This is unacceptable."

"I can't imagine we're the first people to complain about this," Pattie said apologetically.

"Oh, no, definitely not," the waiter laughed. "The manager's called the city a dozen times, but they say the seals are protected or something."

"It's just really strong."

The waiter nodded. "That's what I thought at first, too, but there are a ton of laws." He looked toward the seals. "The animal groups," he explained.

Harold shook his head disdainfully. "That's the last time we think about adopting a cat from the ASPCA," he told Pattie.

"Can't the city just relocate the seals?" Pattie asked helpfully.

The waiter snorted. "They're not Muslims."

*   *   *

"In the waiter's defense, he did say he was just being sarcastic," reasoned Harold as he swerved in a fruitless attempt to avoid a pothole.

The rental car made a loud *thunk* as it crashed over the crater. "Jesus, you feel like you're riding around in a tin can in this thing."

"Yeah, I admit the PT Cruiser leaves something to be desired," Pattie conceded. "It's killing my back."

"Whoever would have thought that an entire nation's auto industry devoting itself exclusively to making cars that a person would only rent or drive at gunpoint could one day go bankrupt?" Harold impatiently jabbed three different buttons on the center console. "I thought I ordered satellite radio," he groused. "I guess satellite radio is the rental car companies' version of Trump's wall."

"Hey, look, there's parking in front." Pattie motioned from her window to a dirty white two-story motel. A chlorinated green light emanated from beside the complex, reflecting off a quartet of sickly-looking palm trees, and an overgrown hedge separated it from an abandoned cinema.

"Really?" Harold asked. "I can just drop you off in front and drive across to the Rite-Aid again."

"No, look. Right under the big 'Padre Trail Inn' sign."

"'Where the freeways meet,'" Harold read the hotel's tagline, emblazoned in neon orange lights along the bottom of the sign.

"Good thing we couldn't afford to stay near the beach," Pattie offered. "The only thing you can smell from our hotel is the enticing aroma of...San Diego!"

*   *   *

"Let's stop in the lobby," Harold motioned as Pattie began to walk up the dilapidated wooden stairs to their second-floor room. "I want to take a shower."

"You know, a funny thing about our room..." Pattie began, but dutifully followed Harold through a single metal door with a drawing of a seal sunning itself beneath a palm tree etched into the glass above the words "Where the Freeways Meet." The lobby, covered in tired Spanish tile, was haphazardly draped in red tinsel. A small pink and green plastic Christmas tree stood at the base of the front desk. As they stepped across the tiny room, their feet swished against a thin layer of sand that had been tracked in by countless prior guests.

"Excuse me!" Harold called to the man behind the front desk, who was wearing an ill-fitting brown suit and a shiny plastic name tag reading "THAD."

"Yeah!" Thad said. "Mr. Carlyle? Checking out?"

Harold looked puzzled. "No, no," he said. "I just wanted to ask if you have a shower cap."

"For...you?"

"Yes," Harold said very precisely. "I intend to take a shower."

Thad bent down below the desk to look.

"Also, if you have any shampoo," Harold added. "Or bathrobes."

Thad stood back up. "No shower caps," he reported. "You sure you're not checking out tonight?"

"Our reservation is for the entire week," Harold said. "We just got here yesterday."

Thad paused. "Do you think you'd like to check out early?"

"Why?" Harold asked, audibly concerned.

"Oh, no reason," Thad said. He absently sucked on his front teeth. "Just wanted to make sure. We have a real liberal policy about early checkouts."

"Okay." Harold studied Thad. "For now, we'll just keep the reservation as is."

"Sure, if you want to," Thad said indifferently. "We'll have someone here till eleven if you change your mind."

"Okay," Harold nodded. He inched closer to the door, motioning with his head to Pattie to follow suit. "So, no shampoo?"

Thad shook his head. "There's a Rite-Aid across the street," he offered.

"You know, most hotels offer shampoo as a courtesy," Harold added as he turned toward the door, extending his hand for Pattie to join him.

"If you go to Rite-Aid, would you mind picking up a string of Christmas lights?" Thad called. "We'll reimburse you."

Harold and Pattie walked back across the parking lot to the stairs leading up to the second story of the motel. Harold was silent, his mouth pursed with thought. "Why do you suppose he wanted us to check out early?" he asked finally.

"I think he was just being helpful," Pattie replied, looking down at a pamphlet she had picked up in the lobby. "Do you want to go parasailing tomorrow?"

"What do you think happens at eleven?"

"Thad goes home, smokes a joint, and watches *The Office* for three hours before passing out?"

"No," Harold grabbed Pattie's arm, pausing halfway up the stairs. "Think about it. He wants us to leave *tonight*."

"Harold, he was probably just mixing us up with some other guests who *are* checking out tonight. Thad doesn't really strike me as being on the ball."

Harold exhaled heavily. "I *told* you we shouldn't have stayed where the highways meet. You know what's true about highways, Pattie? Anyone can go on them! And when you have two highways *meeting*— well, I don't have to spell it out. That's an awful lot of people."

"Let's just go up to the room. You'll feel better after you shower."

"Wait." Harold grabbed Pattie's arm again. "Did you see those black spots in the tub?"

"Spots?" Pattie asked, her patience waning. She pushed past Harold and continued to the top of the wooden stairs.

"Pattie, I think our room has black mold. That must be why Thad wants us out so bad. He probably can't come right out and say it because his manager will fire him."

"If Thad could put all those ideas together, he'd be working somewhere closer to the beach." Pattie turned a corroded key in the lock to their room and forced open the door. "Also, I'm pretty sure they only get black mold in states like Florida."

"Hello? The beach?" Harold yanked off his jacket and tossed it on a sagging king bed that occupied most of their pale yellow room. "Water? Dampness? A criminally negligent hotel owner? All the ingredients for a mold renaissance."

Pattie switched on the television, which flickered to life with a loud *pop*. "You think *I Love Lucy*'s on channel six still?"

"Thad's conscience must be eating away at him," Harold conjectured. "Keeping a secret like this. He's got no dog in this fight." He rushed into the bathroom. Pattie heard a variety of water sounds and the stamping of feet as she clicked through the channels and settled into the creaking mattress to watch Desi Arnaz cook a Spanish omelette. Harold emerged from the bathroom, his meager crop of hair dripping wet. "The black mold wasn't there."

"You washed it off?"

"No, Pattie, it was *gone!*" Harold sat down on the edge of the bed. "What does asbestos look like?"

"I think you just know it when you see it." Pattie kicked off her shoes, wiggling her toes with glee.

"Okay, I've never known what that means." Harold jumped up and began examining cracks in the walls. "Pattie, really," he moaned, bent over the baseboards. "This was the best place you could find?"

"*You* have a prohibition on staying in 'Lodges' that aren't in the woods," Pattie reminded him.

"Is asbestos like dust?" Harold asked, knelt over a space heater that had been set up in the corner of the room.

"Harold, if you don't know what asbestos is, you can rest assured that Thad doesn't, either."

"I know it's bad!" Harold jumped up again and rushed to the nightstand on his side of the bed. He removed a copy of the New Testament and began to rifle through it.

"What on *earth*?" Pattie demanded. "I'm trying to watch!"

"Checking for clues. You remember the Hotel Wayne."

"Just, calm down. Sit down and watch. Nothing's going to happen."

Harold sat down petulantly on the edge of the bed and continued leafing through the Bible. "We're not going to bed until after eleven," he warned her.

"Fine. The episode after this is a good one, anyway." Pattie turned up the volume again.

"I hate San Diego," Harold muttered.

*   *   *

"Have you ever felt so lucky to wake up alive?" Harold asked. "After all that drama with Thad last night, I don't think I fell asleep until two."

"Yeah, it really makes you appreciate the little things." Pattie expertly tapped the side of a bottle of ketchup, dispensing it onto a crispy slab of hash browns on her plate.

"I didn't notice him at the front desk when we walked past the lobby this morning. I wonder if he got fired."

"Harold, he has the night shift."

"Oh." Harold's face fell. "Right. Well, still." He speared a hunk of French toast with his fork and pushed it across his plate, sopping up a puddle of maple syrup. Chomping down on the hunk of dough, he gazed out of the large front window next to their table, squinting into the morning sunlight's glare, which reflected off the cars in the parking lot encircling the restaurant. Beyond the parking lot, trucks on their morning runs lumbered up and down the flat, four-lane boulevard, beyond which was a small Rite-Aid and another parking lot. He looked back at Pattie. "It's odd that people here just live with palm trees."

Pattie nodded distractedly, her attention captured by a small sign propped up against the cash register. The words "Immigrants Are Welcome Here" were scrawled across it, each letter written in a different color marker. She pointed to the sign with her fork. "That's good."

Harold turned in his chair to see the sign. "Oh, yeah," he said approvingly. He turned back around. "Did you see the Porsche in the parking lot?"

"No," Pattie said, still admiring the sign.

"Why do you suppose a man driving a Porsche is eating here? Which one do you think he is?" Harold scanned the restaurant. "Maybe he's that really confident-looking black guy."

Pattie put her finger to her lips.

"With everything awful happening in this country, let's just pretend it's his."

"It's a plan." A television set mounted above the cash register caught Pattie's eye as three-dimensional gold letters flashed across the screen. The intertitle dissolved into live film of a bloated, orange-colored man stuffed into a black suit, white shirt, and red tie stretching well past his groin, gesticulating wildly at a bank of microphones.

"We have a disaster in our urban centers, right now. It's a war zone. I mean, have you seen Chicago? Total, total chaos. I will fix it so fast, it's going to make your head spin," the man promised. "I have my own system for solving crime. Revolutionary system. The think system. I think about law and order, and we have law and order. The think system."

Pattie shook her head. "It's how all dictatorships start. Picking a minority and scapegoating them for society's ills."

"We have crime, we have drugs, we have ISIS. I have such a plan for dealing with ISIS. Tremendous plan. We are going to have a ban. A great, big, beautiful ban, until we can get everything straightened out in this country."

Pattie shook her head again. "I don't feel safe here anymore."

"It's disgusting," Harold agreed. "Good thing they have that sign. We have to make ourselves known. Like the safe houses on the Underground Railroad."

Pattie turned to look at Harold. "The what?"

"I'm assembling the best cabinet. Some of the best, best minds this country has," the man continued. "Rex Tillerson. The ExxonMobil guy? He's just terrific. World-class player."

"I was seeing some people online wearing those safety pins," Pattie said. "You know, that's not a bad idea. Show people we're allies."

"Yes, definitely," Harold nodded vigorously. "These racists don't realize they're outnumbered."

"Yes, but Trump is only making them more emboldened. Just look at that waiter last night. It's more important than ever for people like us to stand up."

"Absolutely," Harold nodded again. "Have you seen some of these videos online of racists harassing women in headscarves on the subway? Those women could very well be Abbäs' wives."

"We should take one of those seminars. So we're not just another bystander when something like that happens."

"Yes! I was reading online that if you encounter a racist, you should try to make yourself as big and imposing as possible. You know, raise your arms up and make a lot of loud noises."

Pattie glanced sidelong at Harold. "I think if you just bop them on the nose, they leave you alone."

Harold put down his fork. "Let's buy the sign."

"Which?"

Harold tilted his head toward the handmade sign in front of the cash register. "We need one of these."

"Harold, we can just make one."

Harold waved her quiet. "Excuse me! Excuse me!"

A small, bronzed woman wearing a blue dress and a white apron lumbered over to their table. "Coffee?" she asked.

"Well, sure, but, we were admiring this sign you've made. We're allies, too, you understand," Harold explained. "Part of the resistance," he whispered. "We live in a tiny apartment in New York without room for crafts projects, and we were wondering how much it would be to purchase the sign."

"What sign?" the woman asked.

Harold got out of his chair and retrieved the sign, holding it toward the waitress. "It's really important to us to let everyone in this country know that they're loved."

"I didn't even know that was there. People're supposed to talk to Doug before they put anything up on the cash register."

Harold nodded and pulled out his wallet. "I can give you five, no, six dollars for it," he offered. "Or ten, if you're on Square."

The woman shrugged. "You can just take it. You let someone put up one goddamn sign, next thing you know, you got missing cats and lance-a-boil ads all over your restaurant."

Harold balled his hand into a fist and pounded his chest solemnly. "I hear you."

*   *   *

"Come on, Harold, put your thighs into it," Pattie urged as she pushed down on the pedals   of a red surrey bike with a bright yellow and green striped, fringed canvas roof.

"I'm steering," Harold explained next to her on the bench, its black nylon baking in the California noonday sun. He kept his hands gripped around the surrey bike's translucent red steering wheel, occasionally glancing at the sand and surf to his right or the rambling lawn lined with palm trees to his left. In the distance, he could hear trains ricketing up and down the banks of a white wooden roller coaster and the hurdygurdy of carnival noises. A slender, chiseled man whizzed past the stalled bike on a pair of rollerblades, glancing amusedly at them.

"I wonder if the inventor of this bicycle intended it to be a metaphor for dysfunctional marriages," Pattie muttered.

"Look, Pattie, parasailing! You don't still have that brochure from the hotel, do you?" A vibration suddenly started in Harold's pocket. He fished out his phone and looked at his caller ID. "My editor," Harold said sullenly. "Good thing I wasn't pedaling."

"Aren't you going to answer it?"

He looked from his phone to the beach. A row of kites glided high on the breeze, their tails fluttering behind them, and the ocean's waves tumbled gently into shore, the foamy surf climbing up the sandbank as little children darted into the shallow water, shrieked, and ran back. "I guess so," he grumbled. "Fat chance they'll reimburse me the vacation time I'm using on this phone call, though."

"I think you're still going to see a net gain there."

Harold put the phone to his ear. "Hello? Yes, sir, I am enjoying my week off. No, it's pretty different from one of my work weeks. Sir, if you're calling about that string of recycle bin thefts in Long Island City, I can have a draft on your desk first thing when I get back. I'm just waiting on a source to—Russia, sir?"

"Do you mind getting out and walking alongside the bike?" Pattie panted.

"Pattie, this is about Russia," Harold hissed, placing his hand over the receiver. "I have to think."

"Good thing you're not trying to chew gum, too."

"How's that, sir? The Russia story's a go? Well, I told you, that tugboat operator is only allowed to take a one-hour lunch break, but—oh. No, sure, the *Trump*-Russia story. Yes, well, I could have told you that six weeks ago, sir. Absolutely. Well, apology accepted, sir. Yes. It takes a big man, sir. Have you heard the TED talk about non-traditional working styles? Well, might be good to keep in mind going forward, sir."

Pattie took her feet off the pedals, and the bike coasted quickly to a halt on the path. "I see a soft serve place over there. Do you want a chocolate-vanilla swirl?" she asked, dismounting from her seat.

Harold waved Pattie away. "Really? Above the fold? No, of course, I could have a new draft for you by the end of the week. Well, patriotism doesn't take a vacation, sir. Yes. Th—the thumb drive, sir? Right, with the evidence, sure. No, no, I was just playing dumb, sir, in case any Russians were listening on the line. Of course I still have it in my possession, sir. How else do you think I was planning to write the article?"

Pattie came back to the bike, a plastic cup of ice cream in each hand. "They were out of cones," she said apologetically.

"Is this low-fat?" Harold whispered. "The consistency is weird."

"I think the machine was overheating."

"So, I'll just drop by your office with the flash drive when I get back to work then, huh? No, sir, of course I know how to access our secure server. Absolutely. Where do you think I save all of my reports, my Gmail outbox?" Harold bit his lip.

"I regret getting this," Pattie sighed through a mouthful of ice cream. "All this dairy won't sit well with the pedaling."

"No, definitely. I'll have those files to you as soon as possible. Well, sir, it is three hours behind here. Yeah, and we were planning to go to the zoo. No, of course I understand that it's a priority. Right. America first." Harold carefully balanced his uneaten ice cream cup on his right knee. "Sure, talk to you soon. Happy Hanukkah, sir. Really? I always thought you were—huh. Well, Merry Christmas. Yeah, no hard feelings. No, my wife is a quarter—oh, no, you gotta do Secret Santa. Sure. Yeah. Bye, now." Harold jammed his phone back into his pocket. "Pattie, put those feet to the pedals. We gotta book it!"

*   *   *

"Abigail Charles Macaulay, hello," Harold spoke into his phone, pacing the room. Pattie laid on the bed, absorbed by a dog-eared paperback. "I just wanted to leave another voicemail about that item you gave me a couple months ago. If I could get my hands on another copy of that for journalistic purposes, well, that'd just be dynamite. Obviously, there's nothing I can do at this point for your, um...your gal, but there's a chance we can take down the—*dethrone the King of Spades*." Harold looked at Pattie and shrugged. She looked up from her book and gave him a thumbs up. "I can't say any more here, but, um, give me a call back at this number. This is Harold Carlyle, incidentally." He hung up the phone. "She's probably in a meeting."

"Harold, it's been three hours."

"Hillary's probably hungry for Chinese, if I know anything about that office." Harold looked down at his phone, considering.

Pattie put her book down beside her on the bed. "Alright, let's hit the zoo?"

"Hit the zoo? Pattie, I'm on the cusp of something big here. This is my Watergate!" Harold yanked open a dresser drawer, which fell out of the bureau and into his arms. He frantically threw a series of swimsuits and T-shirts behind him, turned the drawer upside down, shook it violently, and placed it on the bed.

"Were you planning to do a photoshoot on the beach?" Pattie asked, gingerly removing a pair of tropical-patterned swim trunks that had landed on her head.

FROM THE CAMPAIGN TRAIL OR THEREABOUTS

"Do you know all the red tape we'd have to cut through? No time for that now," Harold said, gathering the trunks and cramming them into his suitcase. "We've got to get on the next plane to D.C."

"Oh, for Christ's sake, Harold." Pattie snapped. "I hate to say it, but that flash drive is as good as gone."

"That's why we're going to go see Abigail Charles Macaulay in person." Harold zipped up his suitcase. "It's going to be much harder for her to ignore me face-to-face."

"That's certainly what I've found."

"Maybe I'll even offer her twenty percent of the royalties from the book," Harold mused, running into the bathroom and returning in seconds clutching a shower cap and his shaving kit. "Maybe not twenty. Maybe five. Where's my laptop?"

"Harold, Jesus, would you slow down for a minute? Just...breathe!"

"Pattie, I gotta find my laptop!" Harold wheeled around, knocking his duffel bag to the floor and scattering stray bric-a-brac across the room's matted brown carpet. "Shit." He knelt down to gather his belongings, hurriedly returning the items to his duffel bag, when suddenly his hands stopped. "Shit!" he gasped, holding a small, sky-blue device between his forefingers.

Pattie looked up. "What?"

"Pattie, it's the flash drive!" Harold exclaimed! "It's—" he lowered his voice, "—the flash drive. *William of Orange is on the boat.*"

"Wait, really?" Pattie jumped up from the bed and bounded over to Harold. "Where was it?"

"It fell out of my bag," Harold explained. He knelt back down. "I must've stowed it in this little inside pocket here—oh, and my press pass!" Harold proudly clasped a laminated white badge with a blurry photo of his much younger self. "I *told* you I packed it." He gazed proudly at the two objects. "I *told* you!" He shook his head back and forth with sheer joy.

"You win, Harold."

"You're darn tootin'!" Harold's pocket began to vibrate, and he pulled out his phone. "Maybe it's Abigail Charl—oh! Even better!" He answered the call. "Hello, sir? You'll never guess what I found! I mean, what I still have. And am putting on the server as we speak. It's a banner day for us, sir. Well, because we fou—because we still have the flash drive. No, well, you know the Russians." Harold stood up. "So, did you just call to congrat—oh, okay. Shoot."

Pattie sat back down on the bed. "I guess that's a 'no' on the zoo, then?"

Harold waved her quiet. "Backlog expense reports, huh? Well, like I told you, I have that problem, where I order two entrees at each meal. How's that? A purchase of Plan B medication in Tallahassee? Well, sir, the Hillary staffers were notoriously tight-lipped. A reporter's got to do some digging."

Pattie shook her head disgustedly, motioning for Harold to finish the call.

"Ah, yeah, I had to take the LIRR quite a bit the past month, what with the waste-sorters strike and all," Harold grimaced. "And, the LIRR is down so often, you're gonna take a few cabs. We'll just have to chalk that up to crumbling American infrastructure. Yes, sir. You wonder how we ever managed to get to the moon."

ACKNOWLEDGMENTS

We'd like to thank our significant others, Kate and Leah, who had to suffer watching *The Office* by themselves while we worked on this book in the other room.

We owe a debt of gratitude to Marty Dundics, comedy impresario, Editor-in-Chief of the *Weekly Humorist*, and the publisher of this book, who has been a great champion of ours and published the short pieces that in part formed the inspiration for this novel. We also appreciate the tireless work performed by Marty's interns, Delaney Murphy, Rachel Keller, Elsa Nierenberg, and Chloe Schneider, in proofreading our manuscript and convincing Marty to read this novel before publishing it.

Michael Gerber, humorist and publisher of the *American Bystander*, generously offered advice and feedback that was crucial in developing the characters we created and approach we took. Thanks to Michael, for example, you did not just read three-hundred odd pages of two young writers from the San Francisco Bay Area attempting to approximate the speech of a middle-aged British man.

Author and cartoonist Bob Eckstein, as well, gave us lots of encouragement and guidance about navigating the publishing industry, his soundest advice being that it would be nearly impossible to sell our novel to a mainstream publisher.

Many thanks to those who read portions of working drafts and provided invaluable criticism and feedback: Professor Philip Gould of Brown University and Eric Johnson, your thoughts helped us focus our revisions and gave us confidence that other people might eventually enjoy reading what we came up with. No need to let us know if that confidence was misplaced.

Although we wrote this novel all by ourselves, we are both quite grateful that we were not raised by wolves, and for that, we would like to thank our families.

Finally, we would like to express our appreciation for Paul Simon. You forget how many great songs Paul wrote.

ABOUT THE AUTHORS

Michael Bleicher and Andy Newton have been writing together since their senior year at Brown University. Since then, their humor and short fiction has appeared in such publications as the *Weekly Humorist*, *National Lampoon*, *McSweeney's Internet Tendency*, *Vulture*, *Points in Case*, *Public House*, and *Crack the Spine*. Michael is a graduate of Harvard Law School, and Andy holds a Master's degree in Italian literature from UCLA. They are above average in height and know the harmony parts to most Simon and Garfunkel songs.

CPSIA information can be obtained
at www.ICGtesting.com
Printed in the USA
BVHW081431300819
557242BV00001B/58/P